About the Author

John Maxwell was born and raised in New York City and attended NYU Film School as an undergraduate. His first job was working as a production assistant on rock videos, where, as well as surviving twenty-eight-hour days of deep boredom mixed with hard, often dangerous physical labor, he also got a firsthand look at the reality of the music industry. He currently works as a sound recordist for film and television and lives in New York City. *Point Fury* is John Maxwell's first novel.

Point Fury

·/·

JOHN MAXWELL

SCRIBNER

NEW YORK LONDON TORONTO SYDNEY SINGAPORE

♨

SCRIBNER
1230 Avenue of the Americas
New York, NY 10020

SCRIBNER and design are trademarks of Macmillan Library Reference USA, Inc., used under license by Simon & Schuster, the publisher of this work.

For information regarding special discounts for bulk purchases, please contact Simon & Schuster Special Sales at 1-800-456-6798 or business@simonandschuster.com

Designed by Colin Joh
Text set in Galliard

Manufactured in the United States of America

1   3   5   7   9   10   8   6   4   2

Library of Congress Cataloging-in-Publication Data

Maxwell, John, 1965–
Point fury/John Maxwell.
p. cm.
1. Musicians—Fiction. 2. Maryland—Fiction. I. Title.

PS3613.A9 P65 2002
813'.6—dc21
2001049054

ISBN 0-7432-2207-5

For all the old crew

"Is that how you learn what you are? Marrying and
    having a family?"
"Why not?"
"A steady job and a house in the suburbs?"
"It is how most people live."
"I'd rather die."
He gave a shrug of regret, but as if he didn't really care
    any longer who I was or what I felt.
                                    —JOHN FOWLES *The Magus*

Living in the limelight,
The universal dream
                    —RUSH

PART ONE

·/·

Some Time Off

1

"Well, hello there, and I guess you must be Chris," Ted Harper said at the door in a booming, deep voice, and speaking with the same jovial, disarming Southern twang that Chris had first noticed at a gas and coffee pit stop somewhere in or near the state of Delaware.

"Hi, Mr. Harper, it's nice to meet you," Chris managed to answer, while returning an almost painfully strong handshake from his new landlord—or employer.

Standing face-to-face, Chris thought that Ted Harper looked almost exactly the way he'd imagined: a big, heavyset man with sturdy features, pink skin, and white hair, dressed for a late-fall weekend at the beach in a stiff, yellow, button-down shirt, gray cardigan, and khaki pants with a bright green belt. Chris even thought he had pictured the gold Rolex and class ring; the man looked like all of Chris's father's old friends from college: successful, conservative, Ivy League businessmen. Ted Harper was merely the Dixie version.

"Well, come in, come in. How was the drive, okay?" At last he released Chris's hand, and then he opened the door to his stunning summer place.

Chris hadn't thought about the house very much, but even if he had, he wouldn't have come up with anything like the modern, austere, beachfront mansion he'd driven up to. It was the kind of thing you would see flipping through the pages of *Modern Architecture* or the real estate section of the Sunday *Times,* never quite believing anyone actually lived there. Ted Harper had apparently started out in business as an investment banker, but had then gone on to create his own shipping company, underwriting other companies' importing and exporting ventures . . . or something like that. Chris's father had explained it to him, presenting it as something he should be impressed with. Now Chris could understand why.

The house was on an island sandbar that jutted off the mainland with the ocean on one side and a small bay on the other. To get there, he'd had to drive over a little one-lane bridge after turning onto an unnamed road—following directions he'd taken by phone and scrawled onto the back of an envelope and then only just barely remembered to bring when he left. It was a good thing he had, since neither the road nor the place itself seemed to exist on the road map he'd bought. Beyond the bridge there was nothing except for three other houses he could see off in the distance; aside from that, only bulrushes, beach grass, some stunted-looking pines, maybe two or three other types of plants and bushes he couldn't identify; and, of course, beach: lots and lots of it, pristine, unblemished, white, and sandy. The whole setup gave him a twinge of something that was either disgust or jealousy.

Inside, the house was all open spaces, dark woods, and bright white surfaces. The enormous main room, a combined living room and kitchen and dining room, had a wall of almost continuous glass looking out over green dunes to the ocean, and ceilings that Chris estimated to be fourteen feet easily at their highest point. Crossing over it upstairs, also facing the view, was a balcony with a silver metal railing, lending the whole place the feel of something between a fine yacht and a space station.

Mr. Harper led him to a carpeted, sunken living room area next to the great expanse of windows, where he held out his hand to a white canvas and chrome couch.

"Have a seat, Chris," he said.

But Chris came to a stop well before he reached the sleek, expensive-looking piece of furniture; even though his only communication with Mr. Harper had been two brief phone conversations, he'd never stopped to think that his arrival here would also be his job interview.

And now he was in no shape for it. After he'd stayed up all last night packing, stuffing every single item he owned in the world into the five-by-eight U-Haul trailer he'd rented, the drive had been a grueling ten hours: taking I-95 down to New York; crossing over the top of Manhattan and the George Washington Bridge; then all the way down the New Jersey Turnpike to the Delaware Memorial Bridge; then finding Route 13 and continuing south on that—by which point he was already so wasted he felt as if he might be hallucinating, and when once he'd looked around and noticed the transformed scenery, of quaint old farmhouses and open farmland and churches, the sensation wasn't so much like having traveled but of having gone back in time. (It was right around here where he'd noticed the accent, too, which at the time had actually shocked him because it was the first thing to cut through his delirium and really seem real. It wasn't particularly surprising that he didn't remember it from his calls with Ted.) And still he'd had farther to go, hours farther down his new, already badly tangled road map; deep into a territory that, although he'd maybe flown over it once or twice as a child on his family's Caribbean vacations, he had never before actually been to. It wasn't until the sun was dipping below the tree line, well into Maryland and close to the shoreline, with billboards for all-you-can-eat crab houses and amusement-park water slides, that he'd exited off the main highway and followed the twisting back road to the small bridge and the exclusive island. By the time he finally discovered Ted Harper's wooden castle by the beach, he was almost, not quite but almost, too utterly gone to care what it looked like.

Of course, added to all that was everything from before: his approximately two months of some very unhealthy living, a period during which he'd probably not once gone to bed either sober or without still coming down off something, and usually neither of the two, and that was when he'd gone to bed at all. In a way it was pretty ironic: an all-day drive after an all-nighter should have been nothing to an experienced pill fiend such as himself. But in what he later considered a very foolish, very rash move, he'd flushed the last of his supplies down the toilet *before* he left, not even saving himself one little tab of amp for the road. The gallons of coffee he'd consumed along the way were a poor substitute, which had seemed to run right through him but other than that have no effect at all.

There hadn't been a set time for him to arrive, so at least he hadn't been late. Only now he remembered that he hadn't thought to turn his music down when he'd driven up, either; he'd had an old Helmet tape cranked on the stereo to help keep him awake, which must have been heard in the perfect silence here. Nor did he exactly look the part he was supposed to be playing. The flannel shirt and jeans he was wearing had been ready for the laundry even before he'd left, and his hair . . . But that was a somewhat longer story. He'd been shaving his head and dyeing the stubble blond while playing with X Bomb, the band he'd parted ways with, also some two months ago. Since that time it had been left untended, and currently the dark roots against the lighter tips looked nasty, like something out of the early days of British punk. It hadn't even occurred to Chris to do something about it, and only now did he stop to realize what Businessman Ted must think of him.

But now was obviously too late. Ted Harper had already settled himself into a matching chair on the other side of a glass coffee table, leaning back and steepling his fingers in front of him, the hotshot negotiator about to enter battle. Still cursing himself, feeling resentful as hell, Chris took his appointed place, too.

"You know, I think the last time I saw you, you were wearing diapers, Chris," Ted commented, chuckling heartily, as soon as they were facing each other.

Chris tried not to think about that and wondered instead if he should say something about his hair. He decided not to and just smiled weakly.

"Well, so, anyway, what do you think of it?" Ted said, leaning forward, opening his hands in a deceptively friendly gesture; an invitation to hang himself, Chris thought.

He took a deep breath before answering. "Oh, the house is fantastic. It's incredible," he said as enthusiastically as he could manage.

"Yep, I think so, too. And my aim, Chris, is to keep it that way. Which, as you already know, is why you're here. Now, I don't know how much your father already told you about this, but last winter this place really took some damage. People came—locals is how I figure it, but of course no one knows for sure—and they didn't just rob the place—we've had *that* kind of thing for years here; all these houses on the shore are sitting ducks for burglars in the winter. But I mean these people came, and it looked like they stayed and had themselves a three-day party. I'm telling you, you wouldn't have believed what they did. They turned all the furniture upside down. They wrote on the walls, they used the bathrooms even though the water was turned off. Now, only two summers ago I'd gone and installed what I was told was a very good security system, but do you know what they did about that? They just went and snipped the darned phone line. So the thing went off, sure enough, but all that stupid, asinine box really did was make a phone call to the police or whoever, and in the end it did no good at all."

Ted Harper shook his head and smiled, like a man admitting he'd been taken by an easy swindle. Chris nodded respectfully.

"Anyhow," Ted went on, "clearly something had to be done, because there's no way I'm going through that one again, not if I can help it. This house has given me and my family great pleasure and great memories through the years, and that kind of desecration, well, it hurts more than you'd think. Now at first, you know, I came up with all kinds of crazy schemes. I wanted to get a full-time guard for the entire island, build him his own house with a tower, maybe put up a gate on the other side of the bridge so he can keep track of who's coming and going. But this summer, I go up and down talking to my neighbors, trying to get something worked out, and, guess what? Their houses weren't bothered, and nobody wants to pay for it. Big surprise. So, finally, I settle for plan B: get my own place winterized and have some-one stay here, let everyone else find out for themselves what can hap-pen. At that point I was actually thinking of trying to find someone to rent it from me, until I stopped to think what kind of a hassle that would be. But also, if I rented, who's to say whoever-it-is would be here all the time. They might take off for a week or two and the same thing could happen again. So, now I realize I'm going to have to hire some-one, just for the months when the place is really deserted, you know, from now, late October, through the beginning of March. I don't quite know why that is, by the way, that more people don't stay put or visit in the fall and winter; it's a beautiful time to be here. But everyone just treats this like a summer place, and so out of season it pretty much sits here like a ghost town."

As he sat on the luxurious couch, a fresh wave of exhaustion had washed over Chris. In order to hide and stifle a yawn, he leaned over and rubbed his burning eyes.

"But now, I have to tell you right here, Chris," Ted droned on, "when I made that decision, you were not at all what I had in mind.

What I was thinking of was maybe some older couple, or, I have a woman who cooks for us over in Charlotte, and I thought she might have an aunt or an uncle or something. Around that time, though, I just happened to speak to your father, who I haven't seen in years. And, as you already know, he suggested you. He said you were taking some time off from . . . you're a musician, is that right?"

Chris had to clear his throat. "Yes. Sometimes. Most of the time."

Ted looked mildly confused by the answer. "But you're getting out of that now, is that correct?"

"Well, no, not really. But the band I was playing in sort of dissolved, and so I'm kind of between jobs that way."

"Well now, Chris, you know I really need someone who's going to stick it through for the entire winter. So if you're planning on taking off the moment you hear of something better . . ."

"No, no, I'm not. Not at all."

"And what are you planning on doing all the time that you'd be here alone?"

"Well, I won't really be all alone. I've got Charlie, my dog I told you about, who's still out in the car. And I'll get a job somewhere. I've worked at a lot of restaurants, and if I can get even two or three shifts a week, that should keep me from going too stir-crazy."

"Well, that all sounds okay, Chris, but I don't know how much luck you're going to have with the job part. Both in the town here and in Ocean City, across the water there, they pretty much shut their doors and close down for winter, as I already said. So I doubt there'll be an opening for you."

"I'm sure I can find something, and if I can't, then I can't."

"And don't forget, Chris, I'm already paying out good money. I realize it's not a fortune you'd be making, but I do expect something in return for that wage. I don't want someone who's going to take an all-night bartender gig somewhere. I want someone living in this house, coming in at night, every night, and turning the lights on."

"Oh no, yeah, of course I wouldn't—"

"I mean a day or two here and there, I obviously can't object to that. But the whole point of this thing is that I don't want those hoodlums coming back. This isn't just some windfall position you've happened onto."

"No, no, I understand that completely, Mr.—"

"And I mean there are still other options that I have. There are apparently security services—"

"Mr. Harper," Chris interrupted, speaking as assertively as he dared, putting up both hands palms out in a gesture of appeal and capitulation. Ted Harper seemed right on the verge of sending him packing, and Chris couldn't let that happen, couldn't even imagine what he'd do if that happened. Through his fatigue and humiliation, he tried to think clearly.

"Mr. Harper," he started again, "let me just assure you that I wouldn't take any job that would interfere with my being here and taking care of this place. What my father told you was true: I am taking some time off from music, and I'm not looking for anything else right now. I'm sorry if I seem a little laid-back or indifferent, it's just that I was up all last night packing, and I'm very tired. But I do, I would take this very seriously. I would fully plan to be here, and to take care of the place for you all winter."

Chris looked up to a spot somewhere between Mr. Harper's shaven pink chin and his sagging but penetrating blue eyes, hoping, praying that this rambling pledge would be good enough.

The older man seemed to ponder over the words for a long time. At last, though, he nodded and stood up.

"Well, okay then," he said, switching back to the jovial tone he'd first greeted Chris with. "If you're going to be living here, I guess I better show you the rest of my house."

Chris felt little jubilation as he forced himself back to his feet, however. Mostly he felt humiliated—that and the exhaustion.

2

The band I was in sort of dissolved, Chris heard himself say again, following Mr. Harper up the circular stairway.

Already he'd been taken around the downstairs, hearing various and elaborate lessons and instructions on the trash compactor, the trash disposal, the communal garbage cans on the other side of the bridge, the range, the microwave, the washer-dryer, the electric heaters. At the phone in the kitchen, Ted had him copy down what seemed like about fifty numbers he might need, as well as directions to the town and the post office where he would be picking up his small, bimonthly off-the-books paycheck. It should all have been simple, but Chris was so spent and it seemed like so much to remember. And for some reason he kept coming back to—

The band . . . dissolved.

Which wasn't quite true, he knew. Because just a few states to the north, a band with the same name still existed, still played gigs in Boston and Providence and wherever else on that puny college-nightclub circuit they could find an empty stage. That band, X Bomb, merely had a different guitarist now, a guy Chris knew, in fact, a guy named Danny Hersh, who was technically a good player. And when Chris thought about Danny as the new fourth member of that band, working night after night through those same songs that Chris knew so well (he'd written a good portion of many of them), he had mixed feelings. On the one hand, he was glad, because he'd been wasting his time, and if what had happened hadn't happened, he would still have left anyway. On the other hand, he had to admit that it hurt, that he missed it: being up there, getting that energy from the crowd, getting into that live groove. Only right now he had to concentrate because—

"—of these two rooms," Mr. Harper finished.

"Umm, I'm sorry?"

Ted Harper looked momentarily irritated. "If it's all right, I'd prefer it if you stayed in one of these two bedrooms. I don't want anyone staying in any of the other rooms."

"Oh, okay, that'll be great, sure."

Both of the bedrooms they had looked in on were roughly the size of the subletted apartment Chris had left behind in Boston. Or, no, that wasn't quite right. Not if you counted bathroom and closet space in his old apartment. They continued along the open balcony to the next door.

"And this is my daughter Elise's room," Ted announced.

Inside this one, the color scheme was pastel pinks and oranges, with a big pink bureau and a dressing-room mirror complete with the little lightbulbs around the frame. There weren't any rock-idol or super-model posters on the walls, however; those had been replaced by the same boring, mostly nautical paintings and watercolors as in the rest of the house. On the bedside table there was an incongruous stack of hardcover books as well. The little girl had grown up in spite of her room, it seemed.

"And this one here is my son David's room," Mr. Harper said, pointing to the last door. "We don't really need to go in there."

But he opened this one as well, to a light-blue boy's version of the same thing.

Chris only glanced in. His attention was taken instead by the pictures on the hallway wall just beyond. There were three of them, in expensive-looking silver frames hung in a corny staircase pattern: at the top, what had to be Ted's wife, thin and in good shape, possibly having had a face-lift or two; in the middle his blonde, cute-but-probably-serious-and-hardworking daughter, Elise; and on the bottom his all-American jock son, David. David and Elise looked to be in their late teens or early twenties in the shots, all three of which were posed, outdoor portraits, the subjects dressed in colorful, preppy clothes. Ted Harper was not a man who went in for snapshots, apparently. Or pictures of himself, for that matter.

"Ahh yes, there's my brood there," Ted said, noticing Chris looking, closing the door, and coming to stand behind him. "Maybe you'll get a chance to meet them sometime, although it seems like we never even see each other anymore. My young ones have growed up and moved on, I'm afraid. My son's in New York, hustling on Wall Street, and my daughter's out in Atlanta with her new husband. Real happy couple. Now I'm just waiting for them to deliver me up some grandchildren."

Chris tried to smile, but for a split second he caught himself wishing Ted and his happy family the absolute worst—daughter raped at knifepoint, son hit by a drunken driver, wife with cancer. He immediately felt ashamed and forswore all of it, but there really was something a little too self-satisfied with Ted Harper's attitude, he thought.

If Ted sensed any of the ill will, he didn't show it. He ushered Chris forward, to the end of the balcony and up another four or five stairs to another door.

"Anyway, this one here, this is *my* room," he said leading Chris in.

It was easily twice as big as the ones they had already seen. The stairs put it on a level of its own, a third floor almost, separating it off from the rest of the house. Unlike the other bedrooms, which faced the bay side, this one had its own wall of glass facing the ocean, as well.

"Thankfully, when we had our break-in, there wasn't any damage done to the upstairs," Ted said. "This room is sort of my sanctuary. I come in here sometimes to do my serious thinking. When my wife sees me at that desk, she knows to just leave me be awhile."

Chris couldn't help wondering what kind of thinking a man like Ted Harper would consider serious. Mulling over the latest turn of the Dow Jones index, perhaps? But the room *was* stunning, and Chris took a few steps toward the big desk. It was made of some dark, lush wood, the burled surface reflecting the orange, late-day light of the sky behind it. There was nothing on top but a green-visored desk lamp, a black phone, a closed laptop computer, also black, and a silver pen in a holder.

Ted Harper seemed introspective suddenly. He clasped his hands behind him and walked around to the windows, where he stood with his back to Chris, looking out on the vast, placid blue ocean.

"Chris, let me just ask you a couple of questions," he said from there. "How old are you?"

"Twenty-nine."

"You go to college?"

Immediately Chris's guard went up. He hadn't attended the hallowed institution of Yale University, as both his father and, he knew,

Ted Harper had. In fact, his own college career had been famously inglorious, having been pulled over and arrested for DWI and possession of cocaine while in his senior year at Boston University. He had been put on probation and had just barely avoided expulsion, and he wondered if that was where this was going now.

"Yeah," he answered tentatively.

"And you graduated?"

"Yeah."

Ted twisted back to face him. "Then, would you please tell me, why does a young man like yourself, college graduate, want to spend a whole winter living out here in the middle of nowhere, doing next to nothing?"

Which wasn't exactly what Chris had been expecting, but was close enough. "Well," he said, swallowing, "actually, I wanted to try and write some music. I always play other people's material, and so I wanted to take some time off and try writing my own for once."

Ted Harper nodded solemnly, still craning his head around, looking like an actor in a movie—some old lawman, Chris thought, telling it like it was.

"Now, don't get me wrong here, Chris," Sheriff Harper drawled. "You have this job if you want it. Your father says you're a responsible man, and his word is as good as greenbacks as far as I'm concerned. *And,* maybe some time off in life is a good thing, although personally I wouldn't know about that because I never had much of it. I started out *my* life on a farm, you see. My father grew soybeans and had dairy cows over in Knoxville, Tennessee, yes, sir. Now farming, that's work, I'll tell you. School was the easy part of my day. Then, later, to pay for college, I had a job as a night bookkeeper at a hardware store. And soon after college, I got married and had kids, which was when my real work started. We didn't have any money in those days, and it seemed like between trying to get my business going and helping out at home, well, if I wasn't trying to build something, fix something, buy something, cook something, or wash someone, my eyes were closed and I was too tired to snore. But this now . . . to me what this sounds like is just a whole lot of time you're going to be wasting."

That part about his family had to have been rehearsed, Chris thought; and a lot of what Ted Harper said had the familiar patter of some righteous backwoods preacher. Still, he had heard it all before. The job interview did seem to be over, which was good, but the conversation had really only evolved into a more familiar form of punishment. After he'd reached a certain point in his life—somewhere near the end of high school—it seemed to Chris that almost no one had been encouraging of his chosen career, and from that point on he'd endured countless lectures like this one, delivered mostly by well-meaning relatives or friends of the family like Ted. There were a few notable exceptions: Chris's father had himself flirted with acting right through college, before reluctantly leaving it behind to pursue his law degree, and had always been understanding and supportive (even if he hadn't always been around to provide that support); and there were others, teachers and professors mostly. But, for the most part, since he'd become a young man, the world of his elders had met Chris with these long-winded exhortations, and he'd had to become expert at ducking innuendo and ignoring blatant gibes, while standing up for himself however he could.

Right now, however, seething with exhaustion, in a plainly supplicant position and standing inside this incredible house that itself somehow counted as evidence against him, he didn't even feel up to an internal self-defense, much less trying to explain to Ted Harper how he didn't consider spending a few months getting material together for a demo tape a waste of time (while also cleaning himself up and drying out, of course, although he would leave that part out).

"Well, we'll see how I like it," was all Chris said, softly, in a vaguely repentant tone.

"Yes, I suppose that we will." Ted made a shrugging, dismissive gesture with his hands, as if he had tried and failed. "Oh, and tell me, do you have some girlfriend or someone who's going to come and stay here with you? It's fine by me if you do."

Chris noticed the *or someone*. "Nope, you might say I'm taking some time off from women as well," he answered—wondering why he bothered, why he should care if this guy thought he was gay or not.

The way his hair was, he looked like a freak to Ted Harper anyway. For just an instant after that he thought of Cassie, of calling her up. But he knew he couldn't, wouldn't do that.

Ted had turned back to the window. "Well, anyway, I guess you'll have plenty of time to think things out," he summed it all up in his ominous preacher's voice, which Chris was coming to hate.

3

He was finally dismissed from the bedroom while Mr. Harper packed his things to leave. Chris was told to take a walk around the place on his own and see if he had any other questions. So he went downstairs, looked around once, and then fell right back onto the same couch he'd been sitting on before. He knew he shouldn't sleep; it would be disrespectful to Ted; and Charlie, his yellow Labrador retriever, was still out in the car. The dog had had walks and water from a paper cup on the drive down, but still, he'd been in there a long time now. Chris decided to close his searing eyes for just a second, though, or maybe two . . .

He was shocked awake some unknown amount of time later by a knock on the front door.

"Get that, please, and tell them I'll be there in a minute," came shouted down from upstairs immediately following.

For an instant, Chris's bleary, crabby mind contemplated some form of rebellion; living here was one thing, but he wasn't going to be somebody's houseboy. He reminded himself that his new landlord/employer would be vacating the premises shortly, however, and forced himself to his feet.

He opened the door to a woman in her late thirties probably, dressed in a purple, cable-knit sweater and denim skirt, with carefully done, short black hair and an ample amount of makeup.

"Oh, hi, is Ted still around?" she asked, taking a step backward as if she were startled to see Chris there.

"Yeah, sure, he's upstairs. Do you want to come in?"

He held the door open for her, and she started to come forward, then hesitated and stopped, looking awkward.

"I just . . . I'm Donna Laney, from the art gallery in town."

She offered her hand, which he took.

"Chris Nielson. I'm going to be staying here for a while, looking after the place this winter."

"Oh, well, I just needed to speak to Ted for a second. It's about a purchase he made from us."

"Yeah, he should be down in a second." Once again he motioned to invite her in.

"That's okay. I'll wait out here."

Chris nodded, but afterward didn't know what to do. Going back inside and leaving her out felt rude, but it was absurd to stand there and try to make small talk through the door with a total stranger. Thankfully, he heard Ted on the stairs.

"Who's there?" he called out in his resounding orator's voice.

"Oh, it's, umm—"

"Hi, Ted, it's Donna," she jumped in. "I was just driving by, and I knew you were leaving, but I wanted to tell you that we got in another Kimble, that local artist you liked."

"Which one was he again?" Ted said.

"The one you were looking at last week, and I knew you were interested in something larger if we got one . . ."

Chris left them and headed back toward the couch. His vision had started to swim and he felt as if he was getting ill. He thought that, as soon as Ted Harper finally left, he wasn't even going to change or unpack or anything, but just go get his dog out of the car and then come back and sit here and let himself drift off into sweet, deep sleep again. He forced his eyes open. No, not yet. Not quite yet, he told himself.

He felt a cool breeze against his face, and when he looked up, he saw the front door standing open with neither of them in sight. They had probably gone out to her car to further review the fine points of cheesy paintings of seagulls and docks and fishing boats that Ted seemed to like so much. Maybe Ted would even want him to pick up some new masterpiece and bring it back to the house—which would be fine, Chris thought, just fine and dandy; as long as it wasn't right now; as long as it didn't have to be today.

Even in his wasted, nearly catatonic condition, however, he couldn't help stopping to think that it was strange for a woman from an art gallery to come over and visit unannounced like that. Couldn't she have called on the phone, or was that some Southern hospitality thing? Although she hadn't sounded particularly Southern. But other things didn't add up, too. When she'd first come to the door, she'd said it was about a purchase Ted had made—Chris was sure of it. And yet when Ted had come down, it was about a painting he'd *liked*, not *bought*. A big difference. And then there was how nervous she had been . . .

A tired smile spread across Chris's face as the lightbulb finally turned on in his head: the two of them were having some kind of affair. He thought again about her being so nervous—Donna. She wasn't the most attractive woman in the world, with sort of lopsided features and a nose a size too big for the rest of her face. But she was tall and looked like she had a good, if generous, body, and Chris could see how an older guy might find her attractive. If only Donna Laney knew how little he himself would care if she and Ted were about to elope and had seven illegitimate children hidden away somewhere. In fact, the whole thing cheered him up quite a bit; Ted Harper's family-values, Republican world wasn't quite so perfect as he'd made it out to be. But mostly, Chris just didn't care. He had never been more tired in his life. It occurred to him that he might spend the entire coming winter as a bear does, hibernating straight through.

Mr. Harper was a lot smoother than she had been. He came back inside all business, immediately pulling a set of keys out of his front pocket.

"Okay, here you go, Chris," he said. "This one is the front door, this one is the garage, and this one is for the alarm box, although I stopped paying the bills for that damn thing after the break-in, so I don't suppose it's connected up anymore. Anyway, just don't bother with it."

Chris stood up on wobbly legs to accept the keys and, after that, followed as Ted went first to retrieve a canvas bag he'd left by the table, then through a door beside the stairs that led to the two-car garage and a sapphire-blue Mercedes sedan sitting in the nearer bay. Chris stood and watched as Ted tossed his bag in on the seat beside him, got into the car, and then triggered the garage door with the remote on the sun visor.

Once Ted started the engine, he rolled down his window. "I guess you're going to need this, too," he said over the noise of the garage door still rolling up, and tossed over the little, white remote box, which Chris caught.

When the big door clanked to a stop on its track, Ted Harper looked him over one last time—the image of an old Deep South plantation owner regarding a slave he didn't much care for but was stuck with came to Chris.

"I want you to stay in touch and let me know what's happening, all right?" Mr. Harper said.

"Okay. You got it."

Ted sat there for a few moments longer, then finally put the car in reverse and began to pull out. "You take care now," he said, raising his left hand off the wheel.

Chris watched the elegant Mercedes back out, turn around, and drive off. He was left looking at his own car sitting outside on the driveway, a previously restored, just-starting-to-rust-again, white '72 Mustang, currently hitched to the bright orange U-Haul trailer that would have to be returned. He walked over to the passenger door and opened it for Charlie, sitting up on the seat with his snout halfway out the cracked window. The big dog jumped to the ground and looked around the empty, silent place.

Chris went back inside and got out a china serving bowl from one of the kitchen cabinets and filled it with cold water. He set it down on the tiles, where Charlie lapped up a little of the liquid, but soon wandered off to explore their new home.

Chris found himself in the garage again, staring out at the view: of sprawling, undeveloped sand and beach grass leading down to a bay as smooth as a reflecting pool; on the other side of it a thin stripe of sand, trees, and then amber sky. He should unpack, he thought. But instead, he hit the button on the remote he'd stuck in his shirt pocket, and the garage door clunked to noisy, churning life again.

By the time it came to a stop, he was back in the main room, sitting on the couch once more. The silence afterward was shocking, unnerving, and for a moment Chris felt something like panic rising up in his chest. Then he squelched that feeling off, the way an adult convinces himself he's not afraid of the dark. Soon he closed his eyes, lay down on his side, and was fast asleep anyway.

4

For the next week and a half, Chris did little besides sit on that very same couch, either sleeping under a thick wool blanket he'd taken from the upstairs linen closet, or just staring out the window, trying not to think about how ill he felt, or how a certain combination of chemicals he knew of would very probably snap him out of his deep depression.

In that one department of his life he was now doing good, though, he told himself. He hadn't had anything more than a couple of cigarettes since he'd gotten here, on his late-night walks with Charlie, either along the perfectly smooth beach or up the road, where he walked right on the dotted line since there were never any cars. (He hadn't actually been told not to smoke in the house, but there were no ashtrays out, and it was just as well he try to quit that, too, since it mostly reminded him of other things.)

His night routine was to either cook himself a simple meal in the massive kitchen or go out for a burger at the one diner in town, where he did his best to avoid small talk with the older waitresses. And after that he would usually just turn in early, even if it meant lying awake for an hour or two. He longed for the escape of sleep, which had so far always been deep and dreamless. He invariably came awake feeling groggy and like shit, but it was still better than the usual double hangover: one from the pills or the blow, one from whatever he'd drunk to help him come down off it. Or was it a triple hangover, when he'd also played until two or three or four in the morning, sucking down beers and cigarettes on top of everything else, not even noticing how fucked-up he'd gotten because the lights were so hot and the music was so loud, and the crowd gave you that crazy energy that made you think you were invincible, only you came down like dying on the inevitable long drive either home or to some slimy motel. God, he was glad to be out of that, he told himself.

He hadn't got around to looking for a job yet, but he'd tentatively decided to skip it, or at least put it on hold for a while. On the short main drag of the inland town here known as Whistler's Cove, he had quickly located any and all important spots: the tiny post office, the supermarket, the bank, the cheap-gas station, the diner. But a lot of other places were already closed for the winter, and he thought he might just spare himself the humiliation of walking in somewhere and asking if they were hiring. Just ten or so miles up the road was Ocean City, a major summer beach resort complete with a boardwalk, an amusement park with a Ferris wheel, and beachfront hotels as big as the ones in Atlantic City. But he hadn't done more than drive halfway through it yet, on his trip to return the U-Haul trailer. The place made him nervous, maybe because he could just picture himself getting lost in whatever scene was there: the locals who all knew each other and went to the same few bars and clubs; the bleak, off-season boredom. And on some street corner or in some dark hallway, someone selling something: meth or dex or black beauties, or maybe even straight coke. For some reason, it was the cocaine he fantasized about the most; he could do it right off the glass coffee table, he thought.

Mostly just out of a need to put the stuff somewhere, he had set up his makeshift studio—consisting of his four electric guitars and his one acoustic in their stands, plus his amp and his effects rack, plus all his other recording stuff—on a clear space of floor behind the couch. And on what he was pretty sure was Wednesday morning of his second week there, in a fleeting, coffee-induced spurt of energy, he walked over and for the first time picked up the acoustic with the intention of making music with it. Unfortunately, after sitting down with the instrument, the very first chords his hands chose to play were the opening changes of "Sickle Run," an old X Bomb tune, which immediately brought back the anger, the hurt, and threw him right back into the same depression.

He had actually first started playing for X Bomb, all those years ago now, just as a lark, just as a favor to the lead singer, really. He had first heard of him from Mark, his old drummer from his college band, No Kill I (a dumb name, Chris thought now, but at least they'd been trying to do some interesting and different stuff). It was the year after Chris had graduated, when he'd gone back to Boston just because he couldn't think of anything else to do, waiting tables and practicing like crazy and looking in local papers for openings in bands.

Hey, Chris, you want some free food? Mark had told him over the phone. *There's some rich kid named Kyle Recio, all hot to start a band, and he like has dinner brought in every night for these running auditions. You should go check it out, just for kicks. It's a total scene.*

So Chris had taken his guitar and his amp and a single effects box and driven there, to Kyle's huge, street-level loft, where, sure enough, there was enough Chinese food set out to feed a small army. And it *was* a scene. There were maybe ten or fifteen guys there when he first arrived, all standing around eating, their equipment scattered in piles around the big open room. A few of them Chris recognized, guys who'd played, or still played, with various college bands. But most of them he had never seen before, and it turned out they'd come from all over, one drummer having flown in all the way from Ohio.

It had been going on for almost a week, Chris learned, and it was always about the same: hang out and eat first, and then at some point Kyle would show up and thank everyone for coming. Then after that they would play, mixing and matching in no particular order to form different bands, everyone working on the same song, which Kyle would lay out for them beforehand on an acoustic. The song Chris heard that first night was simplistic, puerile crap, he thought right off. But it was nice to be playing with other people again, and Kyle could actually sing reasonably well. And at the end of the night, when Chris finally got to play lead, he took an almost sadistic pleasure in blowing the doors off the four other guitarists, who'd shown up with their Les Pauls and their Marshalls and barely any real chops to speak of.

At the time he hadn't really thought about where it was going. He'd just been having fun, participating in this weird farce because it was something to do. But when Kyle stopped him at the door as he was leaving to tell him he had the slot if he wanted it, and to ask him to come back and help choose the rest of the band, Chris couldn't help feeling flattered and getting ludicrously excited about the whole thing.

Although, for a few years there, X Bomb, the band they became, had seemed like something worth getting excited about. They all worked like madmen that first winter, Chris practically moving into Kyle's loft with him. They had their first live show that spring, and in the summer, in a studio Kyle rented for them, they started work on what would be their first album, *Xplicit*. That next year, when all the students returned, they developed a kind of regular following in Boston—not groupies exactly, but people who would reliably turn up at their shows. And then one rainy day in spring Kyle called for a meeting at his place, where that night they all met a man named Darren Snyder, who worked for Messiah Records in Seattle. Darren, a balding, old chain-smoker who wore all black like a minister, offered them what had at the time seemed like a fortune for what amounted to a two-album deal, which they all happily, immediately signed.

Chris could still remember perfectly the celebration following that. They all went out to a bar, where the drinks and the beer had never tasted so sweet. They took a booth in the back and made more noise than anyone, for once really not caring what people thought of them, really feeling like who they were supposed to be. In just a few hours time, they'd all gone from being the pariahs of society to its princes, or at least that was the way it seemed. Chris was already seeing Cassie by then, and she had joined them, and the two of them ended up taking the party back to his apartment, staying awake together until the light of morning, when, bleary-eyed and still drunk, they'd both had to get up and go to work.

Those were good times, and for a while they got even better. Their album came out a few months later, and whether Darren had actually done something to promote it, or Kyle's tireless efforts at pushing their stuff finally paid off, "Sickle Run," which everyone agreed was the best song they had, started to get airplay on progressive-rock stations, and the CD started to sell. Unfortunately, when it did, they quickly realized what a bad deal it was they'd signed onto. However it was worded, or whatever the numbers were, they got almost no additional money for their success, even at the top of their popularity, when the single hit 32 on the *Billboard* Modern Rock Tracks and the album touched 140 on the Top 200 (soon afterward, as Darren had put it, they both foundered). Then, even worse, one of the clauses in their contract that they somehow hadn't noticed was that the "advance" that they had already been paid was supposed to cover certain promotional projects, including two rock videos that would be "overseen" by Messiah Records, which meant, basically, that Darren could come and spend all of their money for two weekends of shooting some stupid, glitzy video for MTV.

That was the first parting of the ways for Chris and Kyle; because, after a little bitching, Kyle had no problem with them laying out their cash for the videos (which would feature mostly him, of course). Kyle's attitude was that he had paid for most of the album, so the rest of the band could certainly pony up for the video. But Kyle had a trust fund or whatever to live on. For Chris, the money meant freedom from waiting tables, and he didn't want to give away more than half of it for something they shouldn't have been paying for anyway. Eventually they reached a compromise, where—so, in Darren's words, it wouldn't get messy—Messiah would cover half of one video, but it still rankled Chris. It was all a waste anyway, it turned out. By the time the video (which sucked) was shot and edited, radio had moved on and MTV wasn't interested. That was the way it went sometimes, said Darren.

The real problem came later, though, long after *Xplicit* had stopped selling, and "Sickle Run" had mostly been dropped from the playlists, and a tour with the Stone Temple Pilots had also vanished out from under them like the finale of some cruel magic trick. It all started when, maybe a little over a year after the album's release, Chris received a single royalty check for "Threw Me Away," one of the two tracks that he had taken credit for. The check was a few thousand dollars for a song that, as far as he knew, had barely ever gotten played—which in itself was fine with him. It was when he stopped to think about the kind of numbers Kyle must have been getting for "Sickle Run" that his blood began to boil, especially when he recalled how Kyle had negotiated with them about the video. Even worse than that, though, Chris could remember clear as day that when they'd recorded the song, Kyle had brought into the studio only bare bones and lyrics, and that it was he himself who, in a moment of inspiration or luck or whatever, had come up with the main hook—what you would hum if you were trying to describe the song to somebody. Kyle had ended up with all the royalties just because, when *he* did the credits for the album, he had put himself down as the sole writer.

When Chris approached him about it, before a show one day, Kyle merely shrugged it off, saying, *You didn't seem to have a problem with it before,* which infuriated Chris all over again because they both knew, and knew they knew, exactly what had happened: that at the time neither of them had had any idea how important those credits were. No amount of arguing made a difference, however, and when Chris went to Franklin and Tom about it, their bassist and drummer, he received only resigned shrugs. They had stopped caring long ago, Chris realized, and only right at that moment did he see how bad things had really become among all of them.

Things were to get far worse, however, when they finally started to work on a new album. Because, in retaliation for Chris's accusations, Kyle now began to do his best to leave Chris out of the process altogether, reducing his role in the band to basically playing rhythm—which was bullshit, and probably part of the reason all of their music sucked after that. When Chris confronted him about that, Kyle just denied it, and Chris supposed he should really have quit right then.

But even though he had definitely built up some poor feelings toward Kyle by the end there, what finally happened, that whole trauma, had *not* been a result of those feelings, no matter what anyone thought. What it was, Chris had finally decided, was just one of those bizarre instances in life where circumstances line up in a certain, specific way, almost as if there really were some mystical hand of fate at work, pushing dormant conflicts to the surface and then stepping back to let someone else take the blame for it.

That last weird scene had played itself out at a little college-town club called The Cat's Paw, in Boston, which had over the years become a regular gig for them. The place was a hangout for rowdy jocks, mostly, who came to drink beer and listen to what they thought was punk hard core but was most of the time more like top-forty pop. It was a Thursday, Chris remembered, an iffy weeknight, and they'd had some horrible all-girl warm-up band going by the name of The Motor Moms, who despite all the booing hadn't wanted to give up the stage, so they ended up starting late, too. Yet for whatever reason the house was pretty full when they finally did go on, and X Bomb was actually sounding decent for once—probably by chance Reinhold, the Cleveland houseman, had got the mix almost right. And so maybe that was why Chris did something he hardly ever did anymore: he pulled out his earplugs. He wanted to hear it full on that night. That high-decibel, power-chord thrash, even if it was total garbage, could still sometimes affect him the way it used to, igniting whatever it was that boiled deep inside him. (Probably it was one of the reasons he'd first got into coke and speed: it was just like what everyone said, he was forever chasing that original high.)

Then about halfway through the set, they went into "Suicide Net," a blatant Nirvana rip-off with a slow rapping part thrown in to confuse people. The crowd knew the song, though, and they went wild as usual, starting a pit up close to the stage. And it was all going beautifully for what it was, until Kyle started doing this thing he'd never done before, running from one side of the stage to the other, jumping over stage monitors like some eighties hair band asshole. It was embarrassing, and not only that, he starts screwing up the lyrics, like it's more important to be jumping around and acting like an idiot than to actually sing the song.

After that, no one really knew what happened. They were in the chorus, the fast part, which is almost like a guitar solo of power chords, and Chris turned to the side of the stage to face the PA wall and get a little feedback working. Just as he did, though, he saw Kyle running toward him again—and not even singing anymore, just running back and forth, dragging the mike by its cord like a retarded Roger Daltrey with a buzz cut. So just to stop it, just out of embarrassment mostly, Chris took a step sideways, meaning to cut him off and send him back the other way.

Only in the heat of the moment, it didn't quite work out that way. Kyle must have been coming a little faster than Chris thought, or been a little closer, because they collided. No one, least of all Chris, seemed to have noticed what happened after that. He barely even felt the impact, and they kept right on tearing through the song. After a while, though, they realized no one was singing anymore. Kyle was nowhere to be found, and so there was nothing to do but wrap up the song, and the gig, without him.

It was only later, outside the back door, with an ambulance idling by the curb with its lights going and a mob of dumb jocks looking on, that

Chris finally found out what had happened. There, in a scene right out of *Spinal Tap,* Kyle had stood yelling at him, telling him he was a jealous fuck who'd tried to murder him and make it look like slam dancing. Because it turned out he had gone right off the stage; only, instead of being caught by the crowd or anything hip and cool like that, he'd apparently connected with the corner edge of a chair, chipping a tooth, cutting up his mouth pretty badly, and possibly breaking his wrist.

Chris had just stood there listening, taking it, trying to make sense of Kyle's insane ranting, trying to calm him down. Until at some point Kyle had interjected: *And your playing sucks anyway.*

The next thing he knew, the two of them were down on the ground, slugging it out (Chris had been on something that night, probably meth, and it did make him edgy). Chris won the fight handily, but hadn't even noticed until Franklin pulled him off how Kyle's arm was in a sling, his hand fastened with Velcro to a shiny piece of aluminum.

Okay, okay, you fucked yourself, dude, you're gone! Kyle kept yelling after that, blood and spittle flying from his mouth in a pink mist while one of the EMT guys herded him into the ambulance.

You fucked yourself, dude, you're gone!

Which, looking back on it now, was sort of true, Chris supposed. After that, he *had been* gone. He had stayed in Boston for another two months, but, after more than five years of playing with X Bomb, he didn't seem to know what to do with himself. He stopped showing up at his day job (he'd long since blown his contract money on guitars and studio electronics and clothes and a new car—and some of it, he supposed, on drugs) and just sank slowly into depression and self-pity—and, of course, more drugs, of the kinds he could still afford. And what happened after that with Cassie was really just part of the same thing, as if once that big toilet had flushed, there was no stopping it until every part of his old life had swirled away from him.

And so maybe he hadn't made it out of that toilet until now, Chris told himself: today, sitting here in this huge, empty beach house hundreds of miles away. Probably it wasn't all over yet. Probably he would still be kept up a few more nights thinking about Kyle—acting all self-righteous with his chiseled features and his bloody, swollen mouth (and how much Chris would have liked to have taken that splint on his hand and bent it into a doughnut just to hear him scream). But maybe he could finally deal with it, finally accept it. And get on with his life.

Chris put his hands on the strings again, but changed his mind and set the guitar down beside him. But he would play again, he thought. And little by little, he would get stronger, and better, and he would make that demo tape.

5

The next morning when Chris came out of his room, the house was in near darkness, and he looked up to discover an ominous sky through the big windows, with black-edged clouds rolling in off the ocean so thick and low they looked as if they might crash into the sea at any moment, either that or their bottom edges would knock over houses and drag down telephone poles if they reached land. He stood there gazing out at the cheerless spectacle for a minute or two, but didn't give it much thought beyond that, turning and wandering into the bathroom, starting his day in his usual leisurely manner.

While he was outside with Charlie, however, walking the dog along the path through the dunes that led to the beach, the wind suddenly picked up to a shriek, flattening dune grass and bending over the short trees, whipping sand painfully against his bare hands and face so that he was practically blinded. He covered up as well as he could and ran for the house—quickly overtaken by Charlie, who didn't seem to like it any better than he did—and the two of them made it back inside only moments before the rain started, which didn't build up either but came down all at once in big, thick drops that banged against the windows like little rocks.

Badly winded from his run, Chris went over and collapsed on the couch, expecting to watch the rest of this display of nature's fury with a weary, jaded detachment. The first thunderclap made him jump at least an inch into the air, however, and when Charlie let out a long, sighing whimper and came over, Chris broke a rule and let the dog come up, too, happy for the moment to have another living being beside him, even if it meant carefully brushing off the cushions later. The lightning show that followed was awesome even while it was terrifying, one bolt of electricity hitting so close the entire sky was momentarily transformed into the arc of a giant klieg light, and in the aftermath of the deafening crack Chris swore he could hear the sizzle of boiling water and melting sand.

When eventually he got up to make himself a late brunch, he realized from the dark refrigerator that the power had gone off and, after that, forgot about eating and began searching around for a flashlight or candles. He became almost frantic when he couldn't find either, thinking of choosing between going outside and trying to drive to the store or spending the coming evening and night in the pitch black with that storm raging outside. Finally, he located both items in the same place: the very bottom drawer beside the sink. There were fancy crystal candleholders in one of the high cabinets, and Chris got these out as well, to have them ready.

Sure enough, the maelstrom lasted all day, the ocean, when he could see it, having metamorphosed into a white, angry froth, the rain pelting down so hard sometimes he began to wonder if the windows could actually break. For dinner that night he ate by candlelight a cold ham sandwich (the stove was electric and also out of commission), and since it was still pouring, he walked Charlie by merely pushing him out the front door, then waiting with a towel in his hands for the dog's bark to let him in again.

Later on, trying to wash his plate in the dark, shadowy kitchen, the water also gurgled to a stop, which gave him the idea to check if the phone was still on. When it was, he decided on the spur of the moment to make a call he'd been putting off anyway and dialed a number he knew by heart.

"Hello," a voice answered almost before the second ring. It was a bright and chipper voice—a *determinedly* bright and chipper voice, it always seemed to Chris now.

"Hey, Mom," he said.

"Chris! How *are* you? Where are you, hon? Are you okay? Is everything all right?"

Almost in reflex, Chris started to feel in his pockets for cigarettes. He didn't have any on him. "I'm fine, Mom."

"So, Chris, you never told me what happened. Did you take that job you were talking about, with Ted Harper?"

At one of his lowest points in Boston, Chris had for some reason decided it was in his best interests to fill his mother in on the basics of the calamitous state of his life, a thing he now regretted doing very much.

"Yeah, I took it. That's where I am now."

"How is it? Is it all right?"

"It's fine, Mom."

"Give me your number there."

So Chris gave her his number, straining in the nonexistent light to read the numbers off the plastic strip below the buttons.

"And you're taking care of his house? What's that like?"

"It's not really a big deal. It's a place to stay for a while, basically."

There was a boom of distant thunder.

"What was that?"

"Nothing, Mom. We're having a little storm here, that's all."

"How long will you be there?"

"Awhile. All winter."

"And what about Cassie? How will you see her?"

"Mom, we broke up. I told you that."

There was silence on the other end. Confusion or disapproval—or both. Chris cut it off.

"Listen, Mom, I'm calling because I can't make it to Thanksgiving." He said it all at once, the way you would pull off a Band-Aid.

There was another dreadful pause, accompanied by more thunder. "Chris, you're not coming?" she said finally.

"No, Mom, I can't. I have to be here," he lied. "And anyway, I really can't afford it right now," he added, which was truer.

More disappointed silence. "Chris, why don't you come? It'll be good for you to see your brother. He says you two never talk."

"Mom, I'm sorry. I'll try to make it up there soon."

"Chris, come on. Maybe Greg could pay for a plane ticket."

"Mom, I don't *want* Greg to pay for a plane ticket! I can't make it, and I'm sorry. Why can't we leave it at that?"

"Oh, Chris, come on. It's not going to kill you. And you can invite Cassie anyway, for old times' sake tell her—or tell her *I* want to see her."

"Mom, you know if Seth said *he* had to work, you wouldn't get all over his case about it. And I'm not *seeing* Cassie anymore! We're broken up, and it's really none of your business, okay?"

There was yet another long silence, and then when she spoke again, it was in her troubled voice, the one that always made him want to step in front of a speeding bus.

"Oh, Chris . . . can't you see . . . I just want you to know that . . . that you don't have to live like this. And I know, believe me I know, what it's like to be outside things all the time. But I also know that things can be different."

And here we go again, Chris thought. *Right back to the same place we always end up at.*

"Mom, I'm doing *fine!*" he said, right on the edge of control. "I know you don't want to believe that, but it's true!"

Silence again. That was the worst. *They always know what's worst,* Chris thought. "Look, I'll give you guys a call, okay?"

He stood there for a full minute after hanging up, fuming, going over the conversation in his mind again and again. It was just her whole act on the world now that he couldn't swallow, he told himself—his mother as the perfect aging country-homemaker matriarch; her and Greg Malloy, the man she had married after Chris had gone away to school, who was just such a blowhard phony, wearing tweed jackets and driving his Jaguar like a lord of the manor on his little Connecticut estate. But it wasn't even him who was the problem. It was her, her trying so hard to render void a whole segment of her life and pretend that things had always been just peachy. When they hadn't. When for a while there, in fact, at the time he was around fourteen and his father had just moved out, things had been so far from peachy that it often seemed doubtful whether she was going to be able to stay out of the nut hatch.

But was *that* even what was bothering him? he wondered suddenly. All at once he wasn't so sure, and even worse, he found himself missing all of it terribly: his family, Boston, playing in the band, Cassie—especially Cassie. For a moment he got a perfectly clear image of her standing there in a floral sundress in the hallway of his old apartment, with her blonde hair pulled back and her old, torn-up, pink Converse All Stars on her feet.

But he was just tormenting himself. He had been through it a million times before, and his old life had been leading him down a road to precisely nowhere. As painful as it might be for him, he thought, right here was where he *needed* to be.

Outside, the rain continued relentlessly.

6

The storm continued all through that night and most of the next day as well, the power only coming back late the following afternoon. Chris went outside again for the first time just as it was getting dark, walking Charlie along the road in the leftover misty drizzle, stepping around the lakes of puddles that had formed, kicking aside branches and seeing in places how the sand itself was now covering the pavement, like the earth swallowing up civilization in some postapocalyptic landscape. And the place *felt* different somehow, he thought, as if an indefinable barrier had been crossed.

The next morning, Saturday, walking Charlie along the beach, Chris thought he knew what that was: a major front must have passed by and put them into a whole new weather system. Today the sky was mostly clear, and the wind was blowing from a new direction, off the bay, the air already much colder.

As if to prove him right, the temperature kept on plummeting, dipping possibly into the thirties that night, according to the clock radio in the bedroom he had chosen for himself. On Sunday morning, after waking up shivering cold, he went and got one of the big electric heaters out of the garage and plugged it in pointed directly at his favorite couch, backing it off only just enough so that it wouldn't be a fire hazard. Later that afternoon, however, he made an alarming discovery: even after running the heater constantly on its highest setting, he could feel no effect whatsoever on the rest of the big house; it was warm sitting right in front of the thing, but after that the heat obviously went right up and out through the big windows, leaving the rest of the place seeming even colder. It was bad enough now, which made him not a little uneasy thinking about how it would be in January or February.

He finally dealt with the problem the only way he could, by going up to his room and putting on one of his two pairs of long underwear, resolving to start wearing them, along with the sweaters and thick wool socks he'd brought down from Boston, as a matter of course, whether inside or out. He tried to tell himself it was rustic and romantic and imagined all the funny stories he would someday have to tell.

In reality, though, little was amusing about the situation, and that night he got a glimpse of just how bad it was going to get, sitting there cuddled up to the glowing heater, staring at his reflection in the pitch-black wall of glass like a convict in some futuristic prison. One thing he hadn't even noticed when he'd first walked through this place was that it didn't have a television—a lack that, even if he had caught it, he wouldn't have thought would bother him so much, or that he might not even mind a clean break from CNN and the nightly news lately, which had certainly been doing nothing to help him with his depression. But almost from the first day on, he'd found himself yearning for his ancient, left-behind Sharp color TV like some lost lover (although in reality that particular set had been broken by the time he'd left, and when he remembered how, he always quickly put both it, and the specific incident, out of his mind). And now, being stuck in one place like this, it was much, much worse; so much worse that he began to honestly doubt whether he would be able to make it through until spring. There was a stereo here, a sleek stack of Bang & Olufsen components sitting flush to the wall in a custom-made well; that, along with a whole shelf of classical CDs. But he hadn't turned it on yet, and he still didn't. He didn't want to listen to music now. And he was too preoccupied to read. He didn't even try.

Absentmindedly, in a kind of low-level desperation, Chris threw off his blanket and stood up. He walked over and reached for his acoustic again. But he set it back down only a moment later. It was still too soon for that, he told himself.

After all, he had a whole winter.

PART TWO

·/·

Visitors

7

Early the next morning the phone rang, the sound shocking Chris awake, sending him almost to the floor scrambling out of bed. He had never once gotten a call in this house before, and he jogged halfway down the balcony toward the stairs before he thought to change direction, remembering the closer extension in the master bedroom.

"Hello," he said, snatching up the sleek black handset, standing there bent over in his underwear, already freezing cold in the unused room. He was all set to give his mother hell for waking him up then, when he heard:

"Hey there, Chris! How's things going out there?"

"Oh, umm, good, good. Everything's good," he replied after a pause—adjusting on the fly to speaking to perhaps the only person in the world he had to be pleasant to right now. "Everything's fine."

"Well, good, good, I'm glad to hear it," the voice on the phone drawled. "Listen, though, I'm actually calling you up for a reason. I saw on the TV about that storm coming through. It looked like it hit you pretty bad, and I was wondering if there was any damage to the place?"

"Damage? No. None that I noticed. It rained pretty hard, but I don't think there was any damage."

"Yeah, those nor'easters, they'll give the windows a good rattling, huh? Listen, though, I want you to do something for me. I want you to go and check the other houses farther out on the point. There are three of 'em, and I want you to look them over, see if they're all still there. If they are, see if any of 'em have lost shingles off the roof or anything like that. Would you do that for me?"

"Uhh, okay, yeah, sure."

"Great. And get back to me sometime this morning, would you? Listen, though, don't call the office number. I'm at a different number, let me give it to you."

"Hold on a second." Chris grabbed the cold, heavy, expensive-feeling pen from its holder on the desk, then slid open the wide middle drawer and pulled out something that looked like an old receipt. "Okay, go ahead."

Ted read him off the number, then said, "And everything else is good?"

"Yeah." *This place is freezing, and it gets lonely as hell at night—the worst rehab I've ever been to.*

"Well, okay then. So you give me a call back this morning, all right?"

"Sure."

Chris hung up and immediately wrapped his arms around his bare, chilled torso, falling back into the big, opulent desk chair and wincing as the cold leather hit the skin of his legs and back. For a moment he gazed out the window. It was another overcast day; you could barely see the ocean, and the glass was covered with a salty rime that didn't help matters any. He wasn't wearing his watch, but it felt to be way early—leave it to a go-get-'em guy like Ted Harper to call Monday morning at the crack of dawn. There was no way he was going outside to look at the other houses right now, he decided, and planned to just hop back into his warm blanket-laden bed and catch a few more hours' sleep.

As he leaned forward, however, something caught his eye, and he slid the desk drawer the rest of the way open. Lying flat on its back was a simple black picture frame. When he picked it up, he saw mounted behind the glass an old business letter, the fold creases visible in the yellowing paper. The letter was dated May 13, 1976, and the letterhead said Mr. Jeffrey Bauer and gave an address in Washington, D.C.

Ted,

I'm writing to you personally today, before lawyers and accountants get involved, to ask for an explanation as to how my investment capital ended up entirely in I.C.L. stock, when this was clearly not what we talked about or agreed upon. If this was simply an oversight on your or one of your traders' part, I am hereby demanding that the situation be rectified immediately, with any resulting interim losses reimbursed in their entirety. Since we have known each other for a long time, and I have always considered you a personal friend, I am giving you this chance to right your error or oversight with no penalty. If, however, the situation is not immediately corrected, my next communication will come to you through my lawyers.

Sincerely,

And then it was signed, with a flourish, *Jeffrey Bauer*.

Chris supposed it was a trophy, of sorts. I.C.L., he remembered, was Intercontinental Leasing, Ted's own company. So this was probably from some guy who'd got cold feet at the last minute and decided he didn't want to be invested with Ted after all, only to lose out on millions when the stock hit it big. Chris wondered who Jeffrey Bauer was; that he had "lawyers" made him sound like a big shot, so maybe that was why the letter was worth framing. Somewhat grudgingly, Chris acknowledged Ted Harper's achievements in business, whatever those were, and put the picture back and shut the drawer.

Just on a whim, he leaned over and pulled on one of the two big side drawers to the right. It made a solid, chunking-thud sound and hardly budged. A single keyhole was mounted above them, and Chris supposed that Ted, thinking of his previous burglars, must have locked it. There were no drawers to the left on this stylish desk.

Chris stood up, taking with him the number he'd jotted down. He'd probably already caught pneumonia, he thought, and was definitely heading back to bed. But when he got to the door, there was Charlie, standing in the hallway, wagging his tail and looking at him expectantly.

"Oh, fuckin' hell," Chris said. On his way past he gave the dog's snout a playful shake, though, and went to put on some clothes to take him for a quick walk.

It was while he was outside, shivering miserably at the head of the driveway while Charlie snuffled around in the bushes, that the anger hit. Now, apparently, it wasn't enough that Ted Harper's house didn't get robbed this winter; now the guy wanted a chance to show off to his neighbors that he had a boy in his place by calling them up and telling them a deck board had pulled loose on their patio or something. Well, maybe he wouldn't do it, Chris thought; maybe he would just give good old Ted a call back and tell him he'd done it and hadn't seen anything. Or, not finding any real satisfaction in that, maybe he wouldn't call back at all.

Chris was still so angry when he came inside that, instead of going upstairs to finally return to bed, he stepped behind the couch and strapped on his main guitar, a dark green '68 Stratocaster. He hadn't played it once since that night in Boston, but he didn't even think about that this time. He set his Mesa/Boogie for a blistering overdrive with the volume cranked almost to full, clicked a fuzzbox effect on, then tried to do some property damage of his own. *(Hey, Mr. Harper, I guess I found a broken window after all.)*

He started out tearing into a deranged Hendrix medley of "Purple Haze," "Foxy Lady," and "Hey Joe," mixing and matching parts, changing keys and tempo at will. When he got tired of that, he for no reason at all took up the old Spin Doctors hit "Two Princes," liking the way that happy riff sounded with the amp set on Pure Evil. Taking the joke a step further, he played "Ticket to Ride" next, excruciatingly slowly, picking out the simple, staid progression as if it were some heavy metal anthem. Laughing at that, in a reasonably good mood again, he looked up to see Charlie lying stretched out on the floor with his nose pressed up against the front door, as if the house were on fire and he were trying to breathe the air coming under the crack.

Out of deference to the dog, Chris lowered the master volume a little. But he left all the other settings the same. This was an idea for a song right here, he thought: a sort of a novelty tune; a simple, happy guitar part with matching saccharine lyrics, only the whole thing mixed as if it were devil-worship stuff. It wouldn't really be completely original to do that, of course, but who cared? And maybe the real joke would be that the song itself, through all the fuzz and distortion, would be good and catchy in its own right, like the Nirvana concept, only taken a step further.

With this in mind, Chris began fishing around, picking out barre chords trying to find a suitably simple structure. It came to him almost immediately, a little C-into-G thing that sounded just right for this. Soon a melody was shaping up, and within an hour Chris had recorded the whole thing onto his digital multitrack. It still needed lyrics, of course, but since they were to be tongue-in-cheek, he thought they would be easy to come up with.

Finally, after listening to the piece on headphones four or five times, feeling triumphant and good, he sat back on the couch and closed his eyes.

8

Almost immediately, he stood up again. In his new, elated mood, Mr. Harper's request seemed like an insanely trifling thing to have gotten so worked up over.

He looked outside. While he'd played, the sky had gone from gray to grayer, and it now looked as though it was going to rain again at any moment. *Shit,* he said to himself. But if he went right away and did it quickly, he thought he could still miss the downpour.

Moving to the dining table, he grabbed his leather jacket off a chair on his way to the garage and the car. The instant Charlie saw this, he leaped up and got there first, but Chris shuffled around the animal, caging him out, and shut the door on his hurt, perplexed expression.

He backed out while the garage door was still going up. And then, for the first time ever, he turned his car right instead of left leaving the driveway, heading roughly east toward the tip of the sand point. He would start from there and work his way back, he decided. Since no one was around and the road was straight as an arrow, he gunned it and got up to an even seventy before it was time to hit the brakes.

The house at the end turned out to be a simple, one-story gray box, a far more modest structure than Mr. Harper's place, though clearly with a superior view. The beach was at least twice as wide out here, and the sand and the ocean wrapped all the way around, the surf extending for miles out into the sea breaking over a shallow bar, while it was smooth and calm on the other side like a bay.

He made a quick loop of the house, walking over deck, sand, and beach grass, glancing into a few dark windows on the way. As far as Chris could tell, the house was fine. All of them were going to be, he felt reasonably certain, and it was a stupid chore. But just to be sure, he got back in his car and headed on to the next place.

This one, at the end of a long driveway, was a monster, a big blond-wood compound that looked to have three stories and a whole system of decks and walkways surrounding and connecting its various wings. If it was missing any shingles from its roof, Chris wouldn't be able to tell without a helicopter, and he merely walked up the long ramp to the main entrance, touched the doorknob, and turned around and went back to his car.

The last, closest house was styled to look old-fashioned and traditional, with wooden-shake shingling and white-trim windows. It wasn't actually old; the window frames were made of aluminum and plastic, and the design was a kind of hybrid, with a gaudy central spire sprouting right up through the middle of the saltbox shape. He walked around on the deck to the beach side, where long, wide steps went down to the dunes like the front of a Greek temple. He turned around to leave and call the job done, but instead stopped right where he was.

One of the sliding doors was standing open a good three inches.

He stood looking at it for a long time, telling himself that he wasn't seeing it right; that what he was seeing was the screen door, and the glass one behind it was shut just as it should be. But when he walked closer, it wasn't merely an illusion of glass and light; both doors were ajar, and the house had been sitting there exposed to the elements. He was about to reach out and slide the door the rest of the way open, when he stopped and thought better of it. Instead, he leaned forward and put his mouth to the gap.

"Hello? Anyone home?" he called out in his best friendly-neighbor voice.

His words echoed back from inside, but aside from that there was nothing.

"Hello!?" he tried again, louder.

Still nothing, and he pulled the door open in a smooth whoosh. He was looking at a cozy living room, with a wicker couch and chairs, the kitchen off to the left down a short hallway. The floors were wooden planking, but they seemed fine, dry as a bone, even after all the rain they'd had. Chris was about to shut the door and just forget about it when he saw something else. It was a suitcase, a yellowing, old Samsonite or some type of hard luggage sitting flat on the seat of one of the chairs. The suitcase, like the door, was cracked open an inch or two, and a few swatches of clothing were visible inside.

For an even longer time he stood there staring at the overstuffed case and eventually found himself vacillating between two possible explanations: the first, that someone had just arrived, was here now, and had taken a quick walk on the beach or a drive to the store to do some shopping and that was why he or she wasn't around; or, the second, that no one was here, the case had been left behind by whoever had closed up the house for winter, the same absentminded person who had left the back door open—which would also explain why, other than the case and the door, the place looked totally abandoned, with no lights on and nothing else out of place. The fact that the wooden floors were dry and unharmed, though, always brought him back around to the first idea again.

He almost stepped inside at least three times before changing his mind once and for all and closing the door. Instead, he walked down the steps and around to the garage, which was a separate structure from this house. The day had become so dark by now that he could barely see in through the row of windows there, but it was enough to tell that no car was there. Which still didn't answer the question one way or the other, he knew.

He looked over at the house again. Obviously, if he wanted to, he could go inside and probably find out pretty quickly what was going on, but he still didn't quite dare to do that.

And then, while he was standing there, one of the first big, cold drops of rain splatted right down on the crown of his head, and he decided it was time to leave.

When he got back, he used the phone in the kitchen, retrieving Ted Harper's new number out of the back pocket of his jeans.

"Yeah, hello!" Ted's voice saluted in his ear.

"Hi, Mr. Harper, Chris Nielson calling back."

"So, what did you find out?"

"Well, I went and looked at the houses, and they all looked fine. At least I couldn't see any damage."

"Was the point eroded down at all, could you tell?"

"The point?"

"Yeah, you know, beyond the McCloskey Monstrosity, as I like to call it—at the gray house at the end there, did it seem like the water had come up?"

"Oh, I couldn't tell. If it did, it didn't flood the house or anything like that."

"But did they lose any beach?"

"You know, I hadn't ever been up there before, so I really couldn't tell you."

"You never took a walk around the point?"

"No, I just hadn't ever thought of it."

"Huh. Well, do me a favor, will you, Chris? Start keeping an eye on the beach up there. Just take a drive by every now and then if you don't want to walk it. I like to know what it's doing because, I'll tell you something, none of them other houses are even supposed to be out there. When I built where I am, I got a special dispensation from the state, and I had an expert on seashore erosion come out and determine that where my house is, is about the only safe place on that entire island. Then, after that, everyone else came in and just plunked down houses wherever they felt like it. All those other places are basically illegal, and it's just a matter of time before the storms start taking them away. So, anyway, I just like to stay . . . apprised of the situation."

Chris felt something between exasperation and amazement. He hadn't taken his little tour for Ted Harper's bragging rights; he had taken it because Ted actually wished the worst for his neighbors. The man was pissed off that, however it had happened, he didn't have this stretch of perfect beach *all* to himself.

"Okay, yeah, sure," Chris answered.

"And you're positive you didn't find anything else? Nobody lost any windows or anything?"

"No," Chris said, trying to sound definitive about it.

"Okay, Chris. Thanks for doing that. I appreciate it. You take care, and I'll speak to you sometime in the next few weeks."

Before Chris could think of a polite way of asking why they had to speak in the next few weeks, Ted Harper had hung up. Chris just shook his head, put the phone in its cradle, and told himself to forget the whole thing.

Or, almost the whole thing.

9

At a little after six that night, Chris opened the front door for Charlie and stepped out behind him. The rain seemed as though it had finally let up for good; the air was crisp and clear, and a few stars could already be seen in the dimming sky over the ocean. It wasn't really a typical time for the dog's walk, but Charlie was always glad to be outside, and Chris wanted him around for the implicit excuse if he needed one. When he got to the road, for the second time that day he turned right.

It was farther than he'd thought walking, and this time when he reached the head of the other house's driveway, he stopped and considered just turning around. In the late day's gloom there were still no lights on in any of the windows, which meant no one was home; which meant he really shouldn't be here. But Chris started down regardless, remembering what he had seen: the open door, the suitcase on the chair. And something else, too. Inside of that suitcase, peeking out from one corner of the opening, there had been a piece of white, frilly lace cloth that could only have been a woman's undergarment.

He'd gone only about fifty or sixty feet when he noticed it then—in one of the bottom-story windows, not so much a light as just a dim glow, as if a night-light were on somewhere, or some piece of electronic equipment . . . like a motion detector for a burglar alarm.

He stopped again. Here was something else to consider: Somebody *had* come by for a few days but Chris had simply never noticed them and happened to stop by when they weren't around. Now they were gone, though, the place was locked up, and he was about to trigger an alarm that would get him in all sorts of trouble.

Grimly, he resumed walking. He didn't know that much about burglar alarms, but didn't think you could set one off just by being outside a house. And, if worse came to worst, he was just doing his job as the island's watchman. Instead of following the driveway around to the right this time, he walked to the left, stepping into wet sand and brush. He went up to the pane of the glowing window and put his face to it.

He almost gasped out loud. It wasn't a night-light or a burglar-alarm sensor. The light was bright white, coming from a crack under a closed door. A light was on inside somewhere, but whether on purpose or by accident, you couldn't see it at all from the road.

Feeling like some hybrid between a policeman and a psychokiller, Chris walked back to the driveway and up the steps to the deck. As he had last time, he went around to the sliding door he'd closed that morning. It was still closed, and he leaned his forehead against the glass and peered inside. All was the same as it had been, except that in the dim light he could just make out that the suitcase on the chair had vanished. And looking off to the right, Chris could see it again: a thin line of light under a door that led to a hallway or bedrooms probably. He rapped on the glass smartly.

A moment later, the light went out, and the house inside was in total darkness.

For a full ten seconds Chris stood there not knowing what to do. At last, more out of simple frustration than anything else, he reached for the handle. He didn't know if it was going to, but the glass door slid open easily.

"Hello," he called into the house again, this time more brusque and businesslike than polite. "Hey, I saw your light on, and I just wanted to speak to you." He slid the door open a little more and took a step inside.

There was still nothing but silence, and for a few frightened moments Chris wondered if he'd made a mistake; wondered if these weren't the same visitors that Mr. Harper had had before, and whether he'd been too bold coming up here like this.

Then, from somewhere on the other side of the house, there was the sound of footsteps. And an instant later, like some half-dreamt ghostly manifestation in the dark, a woman stepped into the room.

"Oh, sorry, I was sleeping and I didn't hear you," she said.

She turned to her side and switched on an overhead light, and for a few moments after that Chris wondered if he actually could be imagining all this. She was a full-on knockout, with perfect, delicate features and china-doll skin. Her thick, black hair was hanging loose, cut straight across just above her shoulders, and she was wearing clean, perfectly faded jeans with a thick, furry, black V-neck sweater over what looked like a man's pin-striped shirt. On her feet, she had red socks, like hunting socks.

Aside from that, Chris saw two inconsistencies at once: she didn't look as if she'd been sleeping, and she sounded apologetic and timid, even though, if you thought about it, he was the one who should have been doing the apologizing.

"Oh, I'm sorry if I woke you," he said anyway. "I just thought I'd come by and introduce myself. I'm Chris Nielson, I'm staying in Mr. Harper's place just next door. So I guess I'm your neighbor."

Charlie came bounding up onto the deck right then, and Chris had to shut the door behind him a little to keep the dog from entering, which he thought might seem threatening. After that, more than halfway in already, he left one leg in the gap to hold off Charlie while he leaned forward to offer his hand.

She had to step forward to take it, which she did only after a quick recoil—as if he'd meant to reach out and strike her, Chris thought. Her hand felt thin and cold in his, and she quickly pulled it away.

"Nice to meet you," she said. "I'm Caroline." And that was all.

"Oh, well, nice to meet you Caroline."

Not knowing what to do then, Chris stepped back outside and grabbed Charlie by his collar, brushing a little goo out of one of his eyes so he looked more presentable. "And this, this is Charlie," he said.

She gave a tiny shrug and nod of her head, once again as if she were terrified of something and all she could think of was getting rid of him.

"I, umm, I came by this morning and saw that someone was here, and so I just wanted to make sure, you know, everything was all right."

"Thanks. Everything's fine."

"I'm, umm, actually pretty much brand-new to this place," he went on, trying to make conversation. "I mean I've been here for a couple of weeks now, but before then I'd never been out here. Mr. Harper"—Chris motioned back toward the other house—"he's actually hired me to stay here this winter, just to keep an eye on things. Is this . . . your house?"

"It's a friend of mine parents' place," she said in that same too quick manner. "The Coopers? I don't know if you've heard of them. Anyway, I'm only staying for a few days."

Chris nodded slowly, not sure what to make of it all. Maybe it was a lie—why else would she have turned her light out that way? Then again, she certainly didn't look like anyone who would be breaking into houses because she didn't have a place to stay. So maybe she'd turned her light out and kept the house dark just because she'd wanted to be alone; didn't want anyone to know she was here because she didn't want some creep like him pestering her . . . like he was doing right now.

"Oh," Chris said, nodding, feeling all of a sudden like a naughty little boy. "Well, great. It's nice to have you here. If you need anything"— once again he made what felt like a pathetic gesture toward the other house—"just come by and knock," he finished equally lamely.

"Okay, thanks," she said hollowly.

He waved once quickly and turned to go, closing the door and then goosing Charlie's thick neck out of nervousness on his way down the steps.

10

He was so rattled by his awkward visit that he made it all the way home before he stopped to think of what else was strange about his beautiful new neighbor, something he had already noted but then completely forgotten the moment he saw her. It was her car, or, as far as Chris could tell, her lack thereof. Because, even if she hadn't been there that first time he'd come by and found the door open—and hadn't just been sitting in some other room waiting for him to go away—why had he *never* heard a car go by? Yes, he supposed it was possible that a car might have slipped past unnoticed sometime between when he'd first been there and when he'd returned, but he didn't believe it. Somehow, he knew that that garage was still just as empty as it had been that morning.

The thought obsessed him for the rest of the night, because how was she coping out here without a vehicle? Where was her food coming from? And how had she first arrived—by taxi? On foot? Someone else was with her, he decided eventually, her boyfriend, or whoever, who was the one with the car, and who had dropped her off and left her here for whatever reason but would return shortly. Yet even the chance that that might be wrong, that she really was stranded, and that she really *had* been lying and didn't know the owners of the house but was just squatting there, gnawed at Chris constantly. For a while he racked his brains trying to think of ways to verify the name of the owners she had given him, but finally he gave up on that. Obviously, he couldn't call Mr. Harper or the police. And even if it was the right name, it still wouldn't prove anything; these weird houses had no mailboxes, but that information would likely be written down somewhere, on a bill or a letter or something.

Early in the afternoon of the next day, after a distracted lunch of a ham and cheese sandwich heated up in the microwave, he decided what to do. This time, he took Charlie with him in the Mustang.

Pulling up to her house again, he glanced longingly at the little garage off to the side, wishing he could stop and take another quick look inside. If there *was* a car in there now, he was about to seriously embarrass himself. But it would be for one time only, he vowed; if she gave him the deep-freeze treatment again, he would leave her alone for good.

He went up to the front door, leaving the dog in the car, and then just waited a moment, girding himself for what could possibly be a very harsh blow off, perhaps even a yelling at, either of which would hurt immensely coming from her—Caroline. And how old was she? he wondered. Twenty-five? Older? Younger? It was actually hard to tell. Another thing he hadn't thought of before was to check for a wedding band on her finger, something that he would be very disappointed to see, although it wouldn't necessarily change anything as far as he was concerned.

Finally he went to knock, but before he had a chance to, the door snapped open in front of him, shocking him, as if she'd gone to the window to see who it was and now she *was* going to yell at him.

Only she didn't. She just stood there staring at him, and once again he found himself at a loss for words in front of her, even though he'd been rehearsing what he was going to say for at least the past hour.

"Oh, hi, listen, I'm sorry to bother you again," he stammered out at last, "but I was driving into town to go to the store, and I thought I could either offer you a lift, or, if you needed anything, I could pick it up for you."

She glanced behind him once quickly looking at his car, and Chris could tell that he'd been right about her at least in one respect, about her not having a vehicle. She immediately looked down at the floor after that, though, and then to her hands clasped in front of her—as if she *was* afraid, he thought again, afraid of something.

She barely raised her eyes before answering. "Okay, umm, thanks," she said. "Can you wait a minute for me?"

"Yeah, sure, take your time."

She closed the door when she went inside again, and he dashed to the Mustang to push Charlie into the back. The dog had pretty much claimed the passenger seat as his own lately, and Chris tried to clean up the vinyl as well as he could with the flat of his hand. After that, he considered opening the door for her, but that seemed too much like a come-on and so he left it closed.

She came out a few minutes later, having put on hiking boots and a tan lambskin coat, the kind with the fur curling around the outside of the lapels and collar. She walked to the car with her head held low, an expression on her face that said she was doing this, subjecting herself to the humiliation of getting into a car with a total stranger, only because she had to. She got in and closed the door softly, then immediately looked down at her hands again.

While turning the car around, Chris managed a glance at them as well. One small silver band was on her left pinkie, but her thin, white ring finger was unadorned.

They rode together in perfect silence until well after the bridge, when Chris could stand it no longer.

"So, have you been out here for a while?" he asked her.

"No, I just arrived yesterday."

"And, umm, you don't have a car? I just . . . I'd never heard a car go by, that's why I came by to offer you a ride."

"No, my car's back at home. I didn't know how long I would be here so I didn't want to rent one. It just didn't seem worth it, you know?"

"Where's home?"

"I live in Los Angeles now, but I grew up around here, in Charlotte, where I know Jennifer from—that's the girl whose house it is."

Chris nodded to all this, thinking it sounded reasonable enough. Now that she'd said it, he could hear a soft, almost unnoticeable Southern lilt to her voice, probably diluted by years of mass media and living elsewhere.

"So, you just took a cab here or something?" he asked.

"Yeah, I took a cab from Norfolk. It wasn't a big deal. I've done a lot of traveling, in Europe and other places, so I'm used to getting around without a car." She gave him a bland, fake smile.

"Right, but so what were you going to do about shopping and all that?"

"Oh, there's a few places in town that deliver. And I can always call a cab. They think you're a little crazy, asking them to take you shopping, but I don't care. I really needed this vacation."

"So you're just . . . taking some time off?" he said, fishing again, putting it as casually as he could.

"Yeah, just for a week or two. I really like it out here."

What it was she was taking a week or two off *from,* and what had compelled her to come all the way from California, was left a glaring mystery, but she didn't volunteer to fill in that blank, and Chris thought he'd been pushy enough, for now.

Without talking about it at all, he drove them to the same supermarket he always went to and rolled down his window an inch to leave Charlie. They walked across the parking lot side by side, where he realized that with her boots on she was just as tall as he was. His relative shortness was somehow appropriate, he thought; he felt immature and awkward with her. In fact, it had all begun to feel like a bad date.

Inside, they separated, and she went over and casually took a shopping cart from where they were accordioned together beside the cash registers.

He ended up picking out orange juice, some cereal, a loaf of bread, some assorted cold cuts in shrink-wrap, and dog food, which he didn't need but which he thought would make his bags look convincingly filled out. He found these items quickly so that he would be sure to make it to the registers well before she did and managed to do it without once catching a glimpse of her in the vast aisles.

On the way back, things were even worse. Leaving the parking lot, Chris asked her if she needed to go anywhere else, assuring her it would be no problem. But she just said, "No, that's okay." And that was about the only conversation they had on the entire trip, the silence between them building into something almost palpable, so that breaking it seemed unthinkable, a punishable crime. All the time she just sat there with her gaze locked straight ahead, as if they'd been married for years and were in the middle of some terrible spat.

By the time they pulled into her driveway, Chris had pretty much given up hope. The girl simply didn't want company, he'd decided, or not his company, at least. He brought the car to a stop by the front door and just sat there (also at some point having decided against the gallant gesture of offering to carry her stuff inside for her). She got out without a word, pushed her seat forward, and reached in back to get her two grocery bags—inside of one, Chris had glimpsed such grown-up items as scallions and a box of Uncle Ben's rice. As she was picking up the farther one, Charlie twisted around to smell her hand.

"Hey there, Charlie," she said, and patted him on the head once. But she managed to do this the way she did just about everything else: cautiously, almost wistfully; as if such meaningless pastimes as petting dogs were for other people, or happier times.

When she had her bags under her arms, she left the door open and took a step back to speak through it. "Listen, thanks a lot. You really helped me out."

Chris was morose now, and disgusted with himself for being morose. "Oh, sure, no problem. Listen, just knock on my door if you need anything else."

"Well, I do actually need to ask you one small favor."

"Okay."

"I don't actually know if Jenny, that's the girl whose house this is, has told her parents that I'm staying here. So if you talk to anybody, you know, in town or whatever, I'd really appreciate it if you could just not mention me. That is, if you haven't already."

"No, I haven't," he said, shrugging, going back to wondering if she wasn't lying about everything. "And also no problem."

"Thanks. It would probably be cool, but I'd just rather not find out, you know?"

"Yeah, sure."

"Hey, I've got an idea," she said suddenly, perking up as if she'd just come awake, as if she'd spent the entire trip to the store sleepwalking. "I've got all this food now. Why don't I make you dinner tonight, pay you back that way?"

Chris thought he couldn't have been any more shocked if she'd flashed him her tits. "Great, that would be great," he managed to reply.

"Is around seven okay?"

"Sure, perfect." And he cursed himself for it, but fuck all if his heart hadn't started to pound in his chest. With about ten words, this girl had taken his zero mood and shot it through the stratosphere.

"Okay, I'll see you later." Before she turned away then, she showed him the closest thing she had so far to a real smile.

He drove home in a daze. He thought he hadn't felt this way since high school, having a crush of this magnitude.

11

Chris decided to be fashionably late and left at five after seven, taking the car on the chance that she might want to drive around later, maybe try to find a bar somewhere. In the intervening hours he hadn't done much except walk from room to room, play-fighting with Charlie sometimes, who had such a soft mouth you could put your whole face in there if you wanted to. Once he picked up his acoustic, but he put it down again about five seconds later.

This time when he drove up, all the lights were on, even the outdoor bulbs illuminating the driveway and the deck. Which meant what? he wondered. Whatever it was, he was still missing it.

As he was getting out, he caught sight of her through a fogged window. True to her word, she was in the kitchen cooking, leaning over a frying pan and peering into its contents with great concentration. He suddenly felt dumb for not having brought a bottle of wine, or at least something. But even more than that he was astounded all over again by her looks; she was really almost fashion-model beautiful, he decided. And then he realized something else: she had put on makeup for him; her eyes looked darker and sleeker, her lips redder, fuller. Quickly, he stepped around the corner of the house, from where he could be seen staring in at her. *Don't get all bent out of shape about it,* he told himself. But by the time he knocked he could feel his heart working in his chest again.

"Hey, you made it," she said, opening the door. "Come in, come in."

"Hey, somebody cooking for me, I wouldn't miss that."

She was dressed the same, in the same jeans, black sweater, and striped button-down. He noticed a thin gold chain around her neck, hanging outside of her white T-shirt, with a tiny, delicate cross as a pendant.

She didn't shake hands or kiss him or offer to take his coat or anything, but immediately went back inside. They turned right and ended up in the modern kitchen he had seen through the window.

Where something else became clear to him. It looked like she was cooking them pasta, making some kind of sauce in a frying pan with a big Crock-Pot of water going on the back burner. The water was just barely boiling, but already the place was filled with steam, the air thick and damp with it. Because it was cold in here, even colder than in his place, Chris thought. He decided it was okay to mention it.

"Boy, it's cold in here, huh?" he said, coming up beside her at the stove.

"I know, that's the drawback of these houses in the off-season. They look big and solid and real, but they were built to just be summer places. I've been wearing two pairs of long underwear ever since I got here."

Chris tried not to think about her long underwear. "Is there any heat in here at all?"

"There's actually a wood-burning stove in the living room, but I don't know if there's any wood. And anyway, I'd rather not start a fire, you know, and risk burning the place down, when I'm not even supposed to be here."

Which wasn't quite the way she'd presented the matter to him at first, Chris thought again. He went and leaned against the far counter across from her. He noticed the cold again—it was really freezing in here. At least he knew why she hadn't offered to take his jacket.

"Oh, you know what, I was going to get some wine or something, but it just never happened. Sorry," he apologized, not able to think of anything better to say, mentally kicking himself for it again.

"Well, guess what, Chris," she said, turning to face him. "You're actually off the hook, because . . . look what I found!" And she pulled open an otherwise empty cabinet near where he was standing and took out a single bottle of unopened red wine, presenting it to him as if she were modeling a game-show prize.

It was Robert Mondavi, Chris saw by the label, a pretty decent wine as far as he was concerned, and as she handed it to him, he suddenly began to feel a little light-headed. Because, after all, what were the chances? Here he was, out in some rich man's summer hideaway in the middle of nowhere almost at the start of winter, and a mysterious, drop-dead gorgeous girl appears out of nowhere and moves into the closed-up house next door all alone. Then she invites him to dinner, starts to act quite friendly, and left behind in that closed-up house there just happens to be this nice bottle of red that goes perfectly with the meal the drop-dead gorgeous girl is cooking for you.

"Pretty good luck, huh?" she said, summing up his thoughts exactly, or maybe putting a tag line onto whatever spoof TV commercial he'd fallen into.

"Yeah," he mumbled, almost to himself.

"Well, don't just stand there, Chris. Find something to open it with."

After he'd opened the wine and poured them both glasses, he set the kitchen table, hunting around through cabinets looking for suitable plates, finding place mats and silverware in the drawers underneath the counter near the sink—he didn't want to ask her where anything was for fear that it might come off sounding like an accusation. He also didn't want to risk spoiling her nearly flirtatious manner by asking her things like why the hell was she here, or why had she turned out the lights like some convict on the lam last night when, theoretically, the most she should be afraid of is getting her friend yelled at by her friend's parents. Unfortunately, with all of the obvious questions off-limits, and her saying next to nothing, they were soon slipping into that fatal silence again.

Which, also once again, didn't seem to bother her at all. Or didn't seem to bother her any more than whatever else was bothering her. He watched her as she killed the heat under the water and poured off ravioli into a colander in the sink, working with that same patient, sad expression she had shown in the car.

"This wine is really good," he said for maybe the third time.

She just nodded.

She finished cooking by dumping the drained ravioli into the sauce, then carried the frying pan to the table and set it down directly onto the varnished wood. That sort of surprised Chris; if it was too hot, he knew, it would scar the finish. But he didn't object, and of his own accord, he found two large serving spoons and brought them with him when he sat down.

"Well, cheers," he said, raising his glass to her. "Thanks again for inviting me, and here's to . . . seclusion."

"Seclusion," she echoed, and they clinked glasses and drank—and in that instant Chris thought that this was almost certainly the first time he'd ever eaten dinner alone with a woman in a house that wasn't a small inn or a bed-and-breakfast; and that if this was what marriage was like, he could maybe see the attraction after all.

"I hope it's good," she said. "This is a dish I used to cook all the time, although I haven't made it for a while now."

"Well, you're not exactly talking to a food connoisseur here," he said, putting his napkin in his lap, picking up his fork.

Yet on his very first bite he could tell the ravioli was badly over-cooked, and the sauce was incongruously peppery, a taste that didn't go at all with the mild cheese inside the pasta. Still, he ate gratefully and picked up his wineglass again when he said, "Oh, it's really good."

"Thanks. And thanks again for driving me today. I'm sorry if I seemed a little . . . preoccupied."

Chris shrugged. *Preoccupied,* he thought. But again she just left that hanging, and he got the feeling he wasn't supposed to ask about it. So, once more he began racking his brain, trying to think up questions that wouldn't be too interrogative. This time, however, she spoke up first.

"So tell me, Chris, what brings you here? What brings a young man like yourself to want to spend a winter all alone—except for Charlie, of course, can't forget Charlie—but what brings you out to the middle of nowhere?"

Yet again, Chris was almost astonished. In the course of this one day, beautiful Caroline had gone from treating him like a bill collector to sitting across an intimate dinner for two and asking personal ques-tions as if she actually cared about his life and his well-being. He was helplessly flattered and found that he was more than happy to talk about himself.

"Well, a couple of things, actually," he answered. "Part of it was just that I was burned out and needed some time off from the rest of the world. I'm actually a musician, I play the guitar. I was in this band called X Bomb, up in Boston?"

She gave him a blank look.

"We had this one semi–hit song. It went like: 'He's gonna get you, you, you, and you!'"

Still nothing, and Chris dropped it. "Well, it was a lousy song anyway. But that's why my hair is like this. It was sort of a dress code, and I know I have to get it cut. Anyway, in the course of things, I had a little falling out with the lead singer, and then with my girlfriend. So it seemed like a good time to move on. Then I heard about this job: watch someone's house all winter, all you have to do is stay there. So, I took it. And, I know it's kind of weird in a way—I'm like Norman Bates or something out here all by myself—but I had actually wanted to take some time off for a while now, because I've always wanted to try writing music on my own. I'm at the point now, you know, where I'm sick of playing other people's stuff, and I want to try doing my own thing for a while, eventually see if I can get my own band together."

When Chris finished, he felt a little giddy. He had just confessed to this gorgeous total stranger his most personal hopes and dreams. But it was just because he didn't know her that he could be so open about his life, he told himself. It wasn't like he was falling in love or anything.

"Well, I actually already knew that you played the guitar," she said.

"Really? How?"

"How? Well, let's see. The very first morning I was here, at about eight o'clock or so, I was woken up by what I thought at first was the end of the world. Then I recognized Jimi Hendrix."

"Oh my god, you heard that?"

"Heard it? Chris, it shook the whole house."

"Oh my god, I'm so sorry."

"And was that the Beatles after that?"

"Yeah. I was sort of . . . sending them up."

"Well, no offense, but I think John turned over in his grave."

Chris was so embarrassed that he laughed. What else could he do?

"And then like an hour after that, you drove by here doing about nine hundred miles an hour. I swear, I thought I was staying next to some lunatic metalhead or something. Anyway, I heard you come by that first time, but I had no idea what you wanted, and so I just stayed in my room. Sorry about that."

"No, that's okay. I really don't blame you," he said, shaking his head. And here was the reason why she'd been so strange to him at first, he thought: because he'd acted like a psychopath on that first morning. It still didn't quite add up, he knew vaguely, but he was too preoccupied to think about that right now.

"Listen, my playing isn't like that at all," he said almost frantically. "I was just angry about . . . something, and taking it out on the old ax, you know? I would never have done it if I'd known anyone was going to hear, although I think Charlie lost a few dBs of hearing. But listen, you have to give me a chance to redeem myself. Come over after dinner and I'll play you something for real. It won't take long, I promise. And then I'll walk you home. I just, I won't be able to sleep tonight knowing you think that's what my music is like, okay?"

But when Chris looked at her again, he knew he'd said something wrong. The black expression was back on her face—really, she seemed right on the verge of tears suddenly. She said nothing for a long time, reached for her wineglass, but ended up merely spinning it around by its stem.

"I don't know, maybe tomorrow," she said finally.

"Yeah, sure, whatever." Chris was utterly bewildered and was about to assure her that he hadn't been making a pass at her, when he thought that that would sound even more like a pass. "Or maybe I'll just play really loud again, and you can listen from here," he added extemporaneously instead.

A moment or two later, he recorded a major victory for his side when a smile broke through her mask of doom. "You do, and I'm going to come over there and break that thing over your head, young man," she said, laughing.

He decided to press his advantage. "Well, okay then, so you have to come over. Just for a little while."

"Okay, okay." She smiled again and looked away and took a sip of her wine.

12

By the time they left, having cleared the table and loaded up the dish-washer, leaving the pots and pans in the sink, Chris thought that he was probably too drunk to be driving on normal roads. Already he'd had more than his share of the wine at dinner when, in yet another unex-pected move, Caroline had reached over and refilled his glass for him. And she'd done it two more times during the meal, each time topping off her own glass as well, but having drunk hardly anything herself.

As they pulled away, Chris noticed that she'd left all the lights burn-ing, and his heart sank a little. That meant she really did intend on com-ing right back, he figured. Still, the night wasn't over yet, and the last remnants of the storm had finally blown away, leaving the air crisp and cold and the sky clear with a million stars out over the road as they made the quick drive together.

"Ah, what I've come to call my humble abode," he said, pulling into the Harper residence, where a just few lights were on downstairs for Charlie. In his present condition, Chris didn't trust himself to navigate into the garage and parked right there in the driveway.

"Not so humble, if you ask me," Caroline said, looking the place over on the way to the front door.

Which, Chris stopped to think, was yet another strange thing, since the Harper house was right on the road, and if she'd been out here before, she must have seen it many times already. But it was probably just her way of giving him a compliment, he decided.

"Don't forget, I'm really just the janitor here," he said, opening the door, unlocked as always.

Charlie was there to greet them, and after attempting to push his nose into Chris's crotch, he turned on Caroline.

"Charlie, she's holding me hostage, trying to rob the house, attack her!" Chris joked, patting the big dog on the backside.

"Ha ha, very funny," she said, fending off Charlie with one hand, pat-ting him on the side with the other.

Chris flipped on the overhead track lights, but only brought them halfway up on the dimmer. It gave the place a spooky, unreal feeling at night when you could see out through all those windows.

"Hey, do you want a drink, or do you want some water or something?" he called to her on his way to the kitchen.

"No, thanks, I'm fine," she said—which he somehow knew she was going to. He was already drunk, but he opened the refrigerator, found a bottle of Budweiser in the door, and twisted off the cap and threw it in the sink. *What the fuck,* he thought.

When he came out, Caroline was admiring the huge open space, walking slowly toward the sunken living room and all that black glass looking out on ocean and night sky.

"This place is amazing," she said without turning to face him.

"You've never been in here before?" he asked, coming up beside her. They were both still wearing their coats, but Chris didn't quite have the nerve to offer to take hers.

"No. Actually, I seem to remember that the Coopers don't get along with whoever it is who lives here."

"The Harpers; Mr. Harper. Yeah, well, I can understand that. You see, according to Mr. Ted Harper, the owner of this fine establishment, none of the other houses on this island have a right to be here. By his figuring, he alone has the rights to this entire stretch of seashore. And do you know what? The guy actually calls me up sometimes and wants me to go and check and see if the ocean is eroding the point away, just praying that one of the other houses will get taken away."

"No, you're kidding," she said, turning to him, placing a soft, infuriatingly light hand on his forearm.

"No, I'm serious. The guy is like some kind of psycho. I mean, can you imagine having this place, on this land, and not being satisfied with that? It blows my mind."

"God, rich people," she agreed, shaking her head.

"Yeah, I know, it's like, crazy."

Only he wasn't even thinking about that anymore. She had taken her hand away, but the brief contact had broken through some barrier in his mind, so that now this incredible specimen of female right in front of him actually seemed havable. He was drunk, he knew, and he very badly didn't want to blow it because he was deluding himself into thinking there was something when there wasn't. But, on the other hand, she *had* invited him to dinner. And maybe, just maybe, the real mistake was in not making the move, not reaching out and grabbing what was right in front of him, so close it was like some kind of exotic torture.

Whether she'd sensed the impending pass or not, the window of possibility vanished when she turned away from him. "So, come on, you were going to play me something."

"Oh yeah, right," Chris said, although he hadn't forgotten by any means. And even though it seemed ridiculous, he had the idea that playing for this girl would be almost as good as necking with her anyway.

He walked over to his amp and flicked it on standby. His Strat was in its stage stand, still plugged in from yesterday, and he picked it up by its neck and tossed the strap over his shoulder the way he'd done a million times before. The amp warmed up and came to life with its beautiful low buzz, which faded away again once the tubes got a little hotter. He pulled a pick out of his back pocket, ran a few scales just to get his hands warmed up, turned to the amp and set the controls for clean, switched it and his effects rack on, but clicked off the fuzzbox—if she had heard him before, he wanted to do something completely different now. Or maybe not completely different.

"Okay, this is something I've been working on for a long time," he said. "My cover of Stevie Ray Vaughan's cover of a song called 'Little Wing,' which is by Hendrix, although you may have never heard it, or may have only heard it by Clapton. Obviously, all of those guys are great, beyond great, and I wouldn't even play the song if I didn't do it a little differently . . . anyway." And he knew it was time to just shut up and play.

He turned up the volume on the guitar and hit the first minor chord of that achingly beautiful song. As he played, he thought that he was glad he'd gotten a little buzzed first. It somewhat canceled out the nervousness of performing like this—which was so different from being up onstage with a band, where hardly anyone noticed or cared if you made a single mistake.

He did slip up once or twice in the beginning, but by the end of the song, once he'd got into it a little and told himself to forget she was there, he thought he played it about as well as he ever had.

When he finished, she clapped enthusiastically and called out "Bravo" a few times. He bowed deeply and thought he felt better than he had in possibly about five years. It didn't even matter to him that she wouldn't know how he had changed the song, which parts were from his own hand, his own composition. He had played, and she had liked it, and he just felt like thanking whatever God there was that such things as music and six-string electric guitars existed in this world.

"Let me just play you one more thing?" he said, his head and his whole body throbbing in excitement.

"Sure."

"Okay, this is a song that I managed to write on my own while I was still in my old band, about a year ago. And I don't really know how this is going to go, and I obviously don't have a mike set up to sing into here, which is probably lucky for you, but . . . here goes." He thought about taking the guitar down a little to sing over, but then figured it might sound better with him belting it out a little louder anyway. He reached out to tap an octave effect with his foot, but thought better of that, too. If it sucked, it sucked, and all the guitar effects in the world wouldn't make any difference.

"It's called 'Hold Me Down,'" he told her, and then he started, strumming the first chord, A7.

The opening chorus went:

> *You hold me down*
> *If you can hold me down*
> *But if you ever let me up*
> *You've only held me back*
> *And I'll be back*
> *I'll be back again*

At one point while he was playing he looked over at her, and at that moment her expression seemed pained to him, as if she were holding a smile frozen on her face. But he told himself it meant nothing, that he was just nervous and trying to trip himself up by imagining she hated it.

She clapped again when he had finished and said, "Wow, that was great."

But he thought she didn't seem quite as impressed as she had been by the instrumental—which anyway was to be expected; the first piece was polished and showy, while the second was just a roughed-out shell of a song. And he didn't even have a mike or any kind of rhythm section.

"Well, anyway, thanks for listening," he said. "I guess I probably still have a ways to go with that one."

"No, it's good. It's a good song, Chris. It's really tight."

"Yeah," Chris said, putting his guitar back, switching off the amp, "you really think it's okay?"

"Yeah, the song seems *good* to me. I mean, you know, it's simple and it's catchy. Anyway, what do I know?"

But Chris still got the feeling there was something she wasn't telling him. While he was thinking of the precise question he wanted to ask her, however, she suddenly stood up.

"Well, I should really get going," she said.

The words left him heartbroken, devastated. The idea that she should leave right now seemed outrageous to him, madness. He began to think of any possible grounds for objecting.

Only a moment later he let it go. He was even more drunk than he'd realized and was actually glad he wouldn't have a chance to stand here and fish for compliments about his playing—as if the future of his career hung on her words of approval.

"All right, sure," Chris said, and followed behind her with his hands in his pockets, vowing once more not to let her see how upset he was.

13

When she reached the front door, she opened it, but then stopped and turned to him again. "Aren't you going to walk me home?" she asked.

"Oh yeah, right, sure." Chris felt an ember of hope blooming in his chest once more. And it was funny the way that kept happening with her, he thought clearly for a moment, as if she were playing with him, keeping him on a string almost diabolically. He threw that thought in the trash, too, though. It came from the same cesspool as the others.

"C'mon, Charlie, let's go," he said, clapping his hands.

"Wait, let's just . . ." she started to say, but stopped when Charlie darted out ahead of them into the crystal-clear night.

"What, I've got to walk him anyway," Chris said, confused all over again. Did she want him to sleep over now? If that was the case, he thought, then Charlie could just sit outside on the deck all night.

Whatever she'd been thinking of, though, she seemed to forget all about it, and he followed her outside and shut the door behind them.

There was still no moon out, every star appearing to shine with twice its normal intensity as they walked side by side in the pitch black along the empty road. Once more they fell silent, but this time Chris decided it might be okay. Maybe this was just the way she liked it, her being the silent, loner type, who only happened to look like a five-ten, china-doll knockout. He found himself thinking of the great story it would make if they *were* to eventually get together and fall in love and someday get married: how they'd met on a deserted island. Every now and then, to break the tension, he called out to Charlie, who mostly ignored him and stayed out of sight.

When they turned the corner onto her driveway, the burning lights from the other house illuminated everything to a range of about a hundred feet, but blinded you once you'd looked into them. Which was probably the reason neither of them saw the car pulled off into the bushes until they were standing right next to it.

It was an old American muscle car, dark red in the glinting light—a Camaro or Firebird from the seventies or early eighties with the back jacked up and shining mag wheels. When Chris saw it, his first witless thought was that it was abandoned, that it had been stolen. Then he glanced over at Caroline, saw her frozen, terrified expression, saw her take one stumbling half-step backward away from it.

"Oh, shit," she said, and the words had a pleading, spent helplessness about them that he couldn't have imagined issuing from her a moment ago.

Not a second after that, the door clunked and creaked open, and the figure that emerged, backlit by the deck bulbs, seemed enormous, tall but neither thin nor fat, just as if his whole frame had been built on a slightly larger scale. Chris couldn't see him clearly, but his silhouette was captivating. He had blond, curly hair that caught the light and shone like a halo, and the high shoulders of what looked like a motorcycle jacket gave his clothes a military, almost imperial trim.

Neither Chris nor Caroline moved, and no one said anything as he walked up to her.

"Hi," he said finally with a slow, calculated malevolence. "Remember me?"

Through what was still more confusion than fear, Chris noticed that this guy's accent was about the same as hers—Southern, but not too much. And he found himself thinking, and hoping, that this all had to be a joke, that this was her boyfriend and they were about to laugh and throw their arms around each other, even if that would mean the worst as far as his own chances with her.

But if it was a joke, there didn't seem to be a punch line. Caroline and whoever this guy was continued to stand there, him leering, her cowering, and as the reality of what he was seeing and what was going on sank in, Chris began to feel frozen to the spot, like a scarecrow nailed to a post.

"I *think* I'm the guy you used to live with. Do you remember that, Caro*line*?" the guy went on, still speaking in that slow, taunting voice, giving her name the full Southern spin. "Or is that going too far back for you? You've already moved on? But I know you must have missed me."

"Duncan, look, I just had to—"

"SHUT UP!" he screamed suddenly, shockingly, agonizingly loud, cutting her off like a bomb exploding in her face. Chris's whole body jumped as if on a string. His hands were trembling and his heart felt as though it might pull loose inside his chest from the pounding that had started up.

"I'm going to do the talking here, you got that!" the guy said, only a little more in control of himself.

"Hey, listen," Chris said, speaking up before he could think better of it, "let's just—"

"Little buddy, if you had any idea what was good for you right now, you'd turn your ass around and run away."

Now this specter of pure violence and hatred turned his attention to Chris, stepping right in front of him like a bully in a schoolyard. Chris's nose came to about the guy's chin. "This doesn't concern you, little buddy, okay?" he said softly, going back to the taunt. "Only you better just hope that all you've been is her little buddy, because if you've even touched her . . ."

"Duncan, please, leave him alone. I barely know him," Chris heard from some world outside the one he currently occupied alone with this madman.

"Oh, is that right," the madman continued, speaking only to Chris. "Well, in that case, you're free to go. But don't even think about coming back, okay? Because this thing goes back a long way between Caroline and me here, and we've got a few things to work out tonight, okay?"

Amazingly, shockingly, Chris found himself wanting to believe this man's words, telling himself that they were reasonable, and that, since it wasn't like Caroline didn't know the guy, and since she wasn't asking Chris to stay, the only reasonable thing for him to do *was* go away. He felt himself walking backward, glanced over at Caroline once, who was still standing there cowering, but then found he didn't want to look at her anymore. He even found himself angry at her, for putting him through all this with her old boyfriend, or whoever the guy was. Almost without his willing it, he felt his feet turning him around on the loose gravel of the driveway, taking the first steps back toward the road and the darkness.

Her scream brought him back. There was a scuffling sound, and then the guy grunted something, and that was when she screamed, and it turned Chris around and sent him running back toward her. He was absolutely positive that he was going to get beaten up, badly, maybe even to the point of dying, but he also knew that there was absolutely no way he could keep going after that scream. And maybe it was only because he was drunk, but he was still sure that it was the right decision.

The guy, Duncan, had grabbed Caroline's forearm while she was pulling away, and their backlit outline looked like some logo for spousal abuse. Chris had no real plan beyond separating them and just ran blindly, straight at the guy. He achieved his one goal even before he got there, however, because when Duncan saw him coming, he forgot about Caroline and turned to face him. So now, Chris realized quite clearly in some part of his brain unaffected by time and circumstance, he was about to either get killed or at least wind up in a hospital.

Yet before he even got halfway there, something else happened. He heard a breathy yelp from behind him, then felt a far swifter body brushing past, going right by his hip.

After that Charlie leapt, white teeth flashing up to head height in the backlight, a piercing, growling bark emerging from somewhere way deep down in his throat. Duncan hadn't seen him coming and screamed as he fell back, pushing the snapping animal away from his throat as he tumbled, perhaps saving his life at the last second. By the time Chris reached him, Duncan was on his side, trying to get up, and Chris just pushed him on the shoulder, sending him scrambling away a little farther.

But Charlie was still barking up a storm, turning from his first attack, and a moment later the guy howled in pain and spun around again, having been bitten from behind. Charlie stood his ground after that, barking like crazy, seemingly ready to kill, white foam flying from his mouth in big dollops.

"Fucking dog!" the guy hollered in outrage and surprise, one hand covering his ass, limping now, almost falling toward his car.

Chris would later think that the only truly brave and smart thing he did that night was what he did next, going up to Charlie from behind and grabbing him by his collar before he could make another lunge at the retreating man. The dog whipped his head around when he felt the restraint, but was smart enough not to turn and attack his owner—although it was definitely a close call. Then, still holding on to Charlie, Chris was running at Caroline, scooping an arm around her waist to get all of them moving toward the house. By the time the engine of the car roared to life, all three of them had reached the wooden stairs to the front door.

Caroline ran inside immediately, crying hysterically. Chris stayed outside on the deck, pulling Charlie around the corner where he could see up the driveway.

"Good boy, it's okay," he kept saying over and over, although he still didn't quite dare to pet the animal, and in truth, he wasn't sure it *was* okay yet or if the guy didn't have a gun in the car, or if he wasn't going to attempt to drive right through the house or something.

In a few moments the hot rod pulled onto the driveway, crashing and tearing through the brush it had been hidden in. After that it just sat there, spluttering out in the dark where Chris could barely see the outline of the hood and the grill. Then all at once the headlights came flaring on, but only to diminish in size and brightness as the car reversed, whining and spitting gravel under its tires. It hit the road skidding and turning at the same time, then peeled out with an unnerving shriek, the engine sound building and building. Until finally, at last, it began to fade away in the distance.

14

When Chris came inside, Caroline was nowhere to be seen or heard. He went into the brightly lit kitchen, still leading Charlie by the collar, and knelt down to take a look at him. There was drying white froth on his snout and between his eyes, and a drop of dark red blood hanging from one of his jowls. Chris went over to the counter and picked up one of the paper napkins they'd used for the meal, ran it under cold water, and used it to clean up the dog's face and mouth as well as he could. The blood probably wasn't human blood, Chris figured, but was only coming from Charlie's mouth, where he'd bitten his own jowls during the attack. The last thing Chris did was to find a bowl and fill it with cold water.

"Okay, Charlie boy, I guess you earned your keep for the winter," he said, putting the bowl down, ashamed at how frightened and unsteady his voice sounded in the silence. Charlie only sniffed at the water.

Chris walked from the kitchen into the living room, the room where he'd first met Caroline. She wasn't in here either, but his eyes went to a black phone in the corner, on a low end table. He went over and sat down on the couch and picked it up. Surprisingly, there was a dial tone—he supposed it didn't matter to whoever owned this house that they paid their phone bill right through winter.

He thought about it for a moment. On the one hand, nothing much had really happened, or nothing that the police would find significant and be able to use as evidence. On the other hand, though, Chris believed the mystery of Caroline had just solved itself, that tonight he'd met the real reason why she was here, living in a house with no heat, leaving all the lights off at night and walking around looking half the time like a hunted animal. It had to be done, he decided, and dialed 911.

"Chris, what are you *doing*?" Caroline said from the doorway. He glanced up and saw her standing there, still in her long coat, blinking through swollen, red eyes, looking at him pleadingly—yet she'd said it more as if he were about to cut off a hank of her hair.

Keeping the receiver in his hand, he pressed down the little discon-nect button on the phone's cradle. "Caroline, I'm calling the police," he told her. "If this guy's harassing you, that's what we need to do."

"No, Chris, don't. Don't put us through that tonight, too."

"Caroline, that's the only way this is going to stop." He tried to sound more sure of himself than he actually was, and once again let up the disconnect and laid his thumb over the redial button of the mod-ern phone.

"Chris, don't you think I've already done that!" she cried out sud-denly, choking back fresh tears. "I did it in L.A, and so they put out some kind of restraining order on him. So what? It just made him twice as crazy!"

Chris looked down at the phone again, still didn't press the redial. And in another moment he knew she was right. The police would come, and they would listen, and they might even make out some kind of report. But after that they would leave, and the next time Duncan showed up it would just be Caroline and her madman again. Or him. With the fear and realization of all that had happened and was happen-ing still catching up, still sinking in, Chris hung up.

"Okay, so what do we do?" he said, aware that it wasn't the manly thing to ask her, but needing to ask anyway.

Caroline left the doorway and walked into the room, running her hand through her hair, taking a swipe at her tearing eyes. "Well, I'll tell you one thing, he's not coming back here tonight. At least not with you and your dog around. And tomorrow I'm just going to do what I was trying to do in the first place, which is get lost for a while. It was stupid to come here, he knows about this place as well as I do."

Chris was too freaked out to take any pride in the compliment, even for Charlie. And he didn't believe it anyway; he could easily see Duncan coming back here, at any moment. "But, Caroline, you can't keep running your whole life," he heard himself say—although, hav-ing met that guy, it actually sounded like a pretty good plan to him right now.

"Oh, this won't last forever, Chris. Duncan's just . . . he's just a little insane right now. He'll get it together one way or another. He's just got to get himself cleaned up and off drugs and then . . . come to terms with a few things. He just needs some time, that's all."

As Chris watched her pacing the room, running her hands through her hair again and again, taking deep breaths to calm herself down, he felt a kind of awe. All this time she'd been living with this threat looming over her, and still functioning, still carrying on. Chris, having entered her nightmare even briefly—he prayed—didn't think he would be able to stand up nearly so well.

"So this guy, Duncan, he's been doing this, chasing you around for a while now?" he asked her gently.

"I guess. It's a little over a month since it started."

"He's not your husband or anything like that, is he?"

"No, he's not my husband. He's this guy I used to . . . I used to live with, out in L.A."

"And he followed you all the way here? *Driving?*"

"It would appear that way."

Chris shook his head. His pulse rate had slowed somewhat, but he was starting to feel sick. There was even the possibility he might still upchuck all he'd eaten and drunk tonight. "What happened?" he said.

"Oh, it's a long story, Chris. I don't even know if I could stand telling it right now."

But she came and sat down beside him on the couch, turning toward him and putting one hand on the wicker back as if she needed to brace herself before delving into her past.

"We used to live together in L.A.," she told him again. "We shared an apartment first, and then the bottom story of this house. It wasn't anything, really, we were just like roommates. Although it was sort of more than that. It seems complicated now, looking back on it, and I'm sure he thinks it was. But it wasn't. We were really just friends, by his doing as much as mine. We both grew up around here, that's how he knew where I'd be—he knew Jennifer, too—and that's how we first met. I'd seen him around a few times in high school, at parties and stuff, but it wasn't until the summer after I graduated that we really started hanging out together.

"I was supposed to go to college that fall—I won't tell you where but it wasn't any great school—and I had this job waitressing over in Ocean City. But mostly I was just bored, frustrated, and angry then. And I wasn't even excited about going away; college just seemed like a dead end to me, you know? Like have you ever felt like time was going so fast and you're only going to be young for another second? That's how I was, and after four years college was just going to spit me out into the world along with everybody else, and all that precious time would have been wasted without really getting me anywhere. Or so it seemed to me at the time. But what did I know? I was young, and dumb. I was a dreamer. I thought that I was beautiful, and I was sure if I could just get a chance at it, just get someone who knew about these things to look at me and meet me, that I could be a world-famous actress, film star, whatever."

She shook her head in disgust and breathed some more, taking a break from her nonstop talking.

"Anyway," she went on, "into this immature, self-delusional fantasy walks Duncan, who wasn't anything like what you just saw. And who, believe it or not, thought, or still thinks, that he's a musician. He was playing the guitar with some local band at the time—and, Chris, I can't even tell you how strange and horrible that was, on that first morning, to hear rock guitar music like that. It was like Duncan was out there, playing me one last song before breaking in to slit my throat or something.

"Well, anyway, I basically just totally fell for his act, like a lot of people used to. And I guess he liked me well enough, and so he told me he was planning on moving to California and invited me to go along with him. I practically pissed in my pants I got so excited about it. My parents raised hell, but I barely even heard it. I just packed up a bag, told them I would write, and ran across the front lawn and jumped into his car without looking back. Cliché, right?

"Anyway, we got there—after breaking down in the middle of Arizona and almost dying—but we got there, and, believe it or not, at first things seemed really good. After staying with a friend of his for a while, we managed to get this crappy little apartment near Venice

Beach. He started working at this club as a barback, even though he was underage, and I got another job as a waitress. But he was also starting to play around and meet people, and I showed up at enough auditions to get some commercial jobs and get my SAG card. And it all seemed really good and healthy at first. We were both young and in great shape, you know, and we could stay out all night and work all day, no problem. We used to have this rule that, no matter what we'd done the night before, we had to go for a run on the beach every morning—and some of those mornings, I swear to God, I thought I was going to drop dead. But we did it. We always went running. And it seemed like we were meeting so many cool people, and everyone was behind us all the way.

"And then it wasn't like things went bad all at once, either. We lived in that apartment together for almost two years, and we were pretty happy. I guess it was when we left and moved into this house with these two other guys that things started to get weird. We got a really good deal and had the whole lower floor to ourselves, and we were a lot closer to the beach and with a lot more room. But these two guys were real druggies. Duncan and I, we both did some drugs, but it was for fun, you know? Get a little fucked-up to help you party, you know? These guys were hard-core—young guys, too, I don't know where their money came from, probably their parents. But anyway, more and more it seemed like Duncan would be hanging out upstairs with them. And then he started to get weird and paranoid about little things. Like he always used to think someone had been messing with his guitar or his amp. He'd accuse me of changing the settings or detuning the strings or whatever. But even all that wasn't so bad, and things were still about the same for us. Or they weren't, but they weren't bad enough yet, so that they seemed about the same.

"That lasted up until I got my first real job. The only thing I'd ever landed before were commercials, print stuff, or extra parts, which I hated doing. But anyway, I got called back for this movie, and then they actually chose me for it. Like the lead role. Which still wasn't really such a big deal; it was for like no money, and the director was paying for the thing out of his own pocket—which also meant it was almost definitely going nowhere. But anyway, it was still sort of a big break for me, it was exposure, and I decided to do it.

"And at first, you know, Duncan is so proud of me. He throws this big surprise party like the night before we start shooting—which is really kind of stupid, because I have to be there at like seven in the morning. But so I stay up all night, and sleepwalk through that first day. And I still think things are okay, or I'm not really even thinking about it anymore because I'm working like fourteen hours a day now, and when I come home, all I can think about is getting some sleep. Only suddenly Duncan has a million plans for us every single night, and he won't take no for an answer, and after a while it's like I'm not getting any sleep at all. And so one day this director comes up to me, and he tells me that when he cast me, he didn't know that I was a heroin addict. At first I think he's joking, until I see that he's really serious about it. And he's really furious at me, because here he is pouring his last dollar into this film of his, and his leading lady, who's supposed to be a happy, healthy, world-famous marine biologist, is slowly but surely turning into a vampire.

"So anyway, the long and short of it is that I move out. For the first week or so I just start sleeping at this lighting guy's house—nothing sexual, you know, he lives with his girlfriend. And I guess after that I start staying with this wardrobe woman. But all my stuff is still there in the house, and somehow I'm still kidding myself that things are okay there—although I guess I also sort of know they're not, since it's not like I'm ever calling. And I probably could have handled the whole thing better, only I swear I was so tired all the time and it was like it was all I could do to get through the day. It was later on when I found out that I was pregnant, by Duncan, of course, but that's a side of the story I'm not going to go into right now, thank you."

Caroline put up a hand when she said this, as if to ward off that specific memory.

"But so, you know, eventually I have to go and get my stuff out of there. And I decide to do it on a Sunday morning, which I figure is safest, since he's probably dead to the world. But of course he's not. He's wide-awake, most likely from two nights before, strung out on something. He looks like death has already claimed him and he's just waiting to get picked up on the return trip or something. Immediately when I walk in, he slams the door behind me, and then he starts ranting at me, all the craziest stuff you've ever heard. According to him, now we were engaged to get married, only his star wasn't rising fast enough or something and that's why I dumped him. He starts saying how since he was the one who brought me here, he's my manager, and I owe him at least half of everything I'm making. He keeps talking about calling a lawyer, as if that's a realistic threat.

"Anyway, eventually I became really terrified, and I realized that if I tried to leave again, he was going to kill me. This was it: there was no one else in the house—those guys always took off for somewhere on the weekends—and if I even made a move for the door, he would go into a rage and kill me. And so I just sat down and stayed. I stayed there for the whole day, trying to calm him down, trying to soothe him, praying that whatever he was on would wear off so that he'd finally pass out. At one point he tried to rape me, which he couldn't do for obvious reasons, and so he just starts hitting me, banging my head against the wall until I thought I would go unconscious.

"Finally, at almost three in the morning, he did pass out, and I just ran out of there—I didn't even get any of the stuff I had come for. I went straight to that director's house and told him what had happened. He was the one who called the police that first time, and they went over to the house that night to arrest him. But when they got there, he was gone. He must have woken up, realized what he'd done, and hit the road.

"Anyway, for the next three weeks, man, I *lived* with that film crew. Thinking it might confuse him or something, I would sleep at a different crew person's house every night—the big joke on set was about how true it was that L.A. actresses slept around. Then one day he showed up while we were filming, and it was horrible. It took like ten people to restrain him, and he hit this one woman over the head so that she had to go to the hospital—although I think she was really okay, and she just went so there would be some kind of charge out on him. But again he got away before the police could show up. After that I always kept at least three people around me. He showed up twice more before we were done filming, and each time it was about the same. He looked like death—God knows where he was living—and each time he vowed to beat me up, or kill me, or something, but then ended up running away before the police could get there.

"And so, once the movie wrapped, I figured it was a good time to take a vacation. Only I guess I didn't go far enough away. Which brings us up to right about now, Chris.

"Oh, and thank God he doesn't know where my parents live anymore," she added in one final spurt of words, as if she had just thought of that.

Afterward, she put her face down in her hands and cried in short, gasping bursts, her shoulders hitching up and down like broken bird's wings.

"Wow, I'm really sorry," Chris said eventually. It was about all he could think of. He raised an uncertain hand to place on her back to comfort her, but before he could, she stood up again.

"God, what am I doing?" she said, heading for the kitchen. "I have to get this place cleaned up."

Chris just stayed behind. Listening to Caroline's long, disconnected narrative, his emotions had passed from jealously to rage, then moved on to something like pity. Strangely, by the end he couldn't help seeing Duncan's side of it, too. To have had a woman like Caroline, taken her for granted, and then lost her that way must have been a terrible blow.

And then there was her being pregnant, which somehow seemed like the biggest tragedy of all. And was she still? Probably not, but he decided he couldn't ask.

15

"Chris, would you mind just staying here with me tonight?" she said in a purely businesslike, unflirtatious tone. After the sound of running water and opening and closing cabinets had stopped, he had heard her go and lock the front door. She'd flicked off a few lights on the way, but had left the ones in the kitchen on when she came back into the living room.

"Yeah, of course—I mean, no, not at all," Chris said, watching her lock the sliding door to the back deck. He tried to think of some joke about how she really only liked him for his attack dog, but let it go, thinking it neither very funny nor appropriate. Charlie had already settled down on the rug under the coffee table at Chris's feet, put his head on his paws, and fallen into a twitchy, disturbed sleep.

"I'll just stay here on the couch," he said instead. "That way, if there's any noise outside, I'll hear it." And since he didn't plan on actually sleeping, he thought that he would most definitely hear it.

It was a little after eleven, about an hour since they'd come upon that dark muscle car in the bushes beside the driveway, and with his fear from the actual incident somewhat abated, Chris was beginning to dare to hope that Duncan might not be coming back tonight after all. For a long time, sitting there, he'd been convinced that what they needed to do was flee this house, get away to anywhere else besides this deserted, dead end of land where *he* already knew where they were. Now, though, however illogically, it was beginning to seem safer just to stay put and not go out into the dark again, where God knew where that psycho might be hiding. There was still tomorrow to worry about, of course, and all the days after, but Chris wasn't even thinking about that. The future seemed wide-open in a way that it hadn't for years, and he'd decided to take one thing at a time and try not to let his fear paralyze him.

Caroline had stopped there, facing him, and for a moment it seemed that she was going to say something else. Then she turned and left the room, going out through the door she'd come through that first time yesterday evening, which now seemed like eons ago. She returned a few moments later with a pillow and a thick quilt.

"Here," she said, handing the big bundle to him.

"Thanks."

"Well, good night." She turned and went back to the door. "Thanks again for everything today. I'm really sorry to put you through all this."

"No, that's okay, really."

"Do you want me to turn this light off?"

"No, I'll get it."

And then she walked out again and was gone, and Chris told himself that he had done the right thing after all not making a play for her earlier. Soon he was thinking about the guy again anyway: Duncan, and how likely it really was that he was going to come crashing through a window or glass door at any second, probably brandishing a bat or an ax this time.

For the longest time Chris lay there in the dark, listening to the steady, low roar of the ocean, hearing every sigh the wind made outside. He made contingency plans: he would go into the kitchen and pull out a steak knife; he would take the poker from the fireplace in the corner and use that like a sword against him. Yet soon it all began to seem remote and unreal, even the blood he'd cleaned off Charlie's mouth, which had only really been a little worse than the dog got after a tug-of-war with a stick sometimes. The concept of someone stalking around outside became too weighty to maintain, and so Chris began to cheat it, telling himself vaguely that the guy must have calmed down by now, composing an image of his car on a highway heading west, away from this place forever.

It was while he was in this half-dreaming state that she came to him, opening the door with a quiet creak that somehow didn't scare him at all, crossing the room with footsteps so light they sounded angelic. By the dimmest glow coming in from the kitchen he could see that she was wrapped in a dark blanket, but the white skin of her face seemed to shine on its own, from some internal source of light.

"Chris, are you asleep?" she whispered in the darkness, breaking the silence and then re-creating it, changing the whole structure of the universe with those few breathed words.

"No."

"Do you mind if I just lie here with you?"

"No."

As she climbed onto the couch beside him, lifting up the quilt and coming underneath, Chris told himself he was grateful just to have her here, just to cuddle a little in the cold night, which was all she had in mind, he was sure. Yet the touch of her body against his own was instantly something else, the shared pressure not just friendly, but more urgent than that. In a moment they were kissing, and then she was rolling over on top of him, his hands groping, going up her back, under her T-shirt, coming up against the tight strap of her bra and the unbelievably smooth skin underneath.

"Oh, Chris," she said, moving softly against his jeans. She was wearing her previously mentioned long underwear, and soon Chris's hands were finding their way beneath those, slipping under the elastic waistband to her bare body beneath. Actual sex was impossible, of course, out of the question—until after maybe a minute it seemed inevitable, all but unavoidable.

"It's okay, I want you to. I want you to," she kept saying, guiding him forward in a process he wanted to change somehow, take control of, but which he found himself all but helpless in nevertheless. It ended well before he would have wanted it to as well, with her shirt and bra still on, his own pants and underwear down around his knees. And yet it was also more exquisite than he could have imagined.

"Oh, God, I'm sorry," he said when he had finally stopped shuddering against her, inside her.

She kissed him on his nose and then his forehead. "Don't be sorry. It's okay, really."

"You're sure?" Chris said, not really knowing exactly what they were talking about, but unable to see any other way that this could have ended up and forgiving himself for now, telling himself he would accept any and all consequences tomorrow.

"Of course I'm sure. Just relax, go to sleep."

16

In the morning, the rising sun came slanting in through the sliding glass doors to hit the couch like a spotlight, waking Chris to a pounding hangover. At least it was warm, though; he thought he felt truly warm for the first time in weeks, all over, right down to the tips of his toes.

Aside from that, however, the illuminated scene was a little depressing. There in a big heap on the floor were his jeans, his sweater, his underwear, his socks, her pink panties, the blanket she had brought in. He was still wearing his shirt, but below that he was completely naked, his ass bare against the rough canvas cushion of the couch. He had a guilty notion they might need to flip that particular cushion over, too.

Yet Caroline was nowhere to be found. Until a moment later he heard and then saw her. To his grave disappointment she was already dressed, wearing the same black sweater today but no makeup, her face the way it was when he had first seen her, different shades of white like fine porcelain. She came right up to the couch, picking up the blanket and then her underwear with quick efficiency. Their eyes met a moment later.

"Good morning," he said sheepishly.

"Oh, sorry to wake you." She tossed her panties down on a chair so that she could fold the blanket. Chris's eyes followed the delicate undergarment; it seemed like the sole keepsake of last night's passion. "But we should get going anyway. I really have to leave." And then she walked out again, taking the folded blanket and keepsake with her.

Chris slowly sat up and began to dress. Charlie came over to him, wagging his tail, and Chris looked at his mouth again. This morning there was no trace of the heroic wound on the animal, but when Charlie, taking Chris's holding of his snout for playing, suddenly whipped his head around to take a mock bite at his owner's wrist, Chris was so startled that he jumped. Afterward his fear and dread from the night before came swimming back to him. Duncan was probably outside right now, Chris reasoned, waiting there with a gun in his hand, or in his car again ready to try running them down. Chris wondered what that guy would do if he found out what had happened here last night—although he honestly couldn't imagine anyone in a more wrathful state than Duncan had already been in.

Leaving the quilt where it was, Chris went and looked out the kitchen windows. From here he could see almost halfway up the driveway to where the gravel roadbed bent away out of sight. There was nothing out there as far as he could tell, but somehow that made it even more ominous.

"Oh, don't worry about Duncan," Caroline said from behind him, making him jump again. "I'm sure he's just now drunk himself to sleep somewhere. He has no idea where you live, either, and he probably won't even remember you were here anyway."

Chris turned around to see her folding his quilt. Multiple objections to her optimistic outlook sprang to mind—*the guy wouldn't come all the way from California just to let you get away again so easily; he saw us walking here together and all the lights had been on at the other house, the only other house lit up for miles; if this guy's so obsessed with you, I should be about all he's thinking about right now*—but it seemed cowardly to contradict her, and so he didn't. He told himself that she had been through this before and knew what to expect better than he did.

"So what now?" he asked instead, as he had once before.

"Look, I just have to walk through the house a few more times and make sure I've put everything away and everything. Why don't you go get the car, and by the time you come back I'll be done."

"Okay," Chris said, just slowly enough to convey his fear of doing that.

"If you're scared of Duncan, take your dog."

"No, Charlie should stay here with you," Chris heard himself say, feeling the spit drying up in his mouth, suddenly desperate for a drink of water.

Once he was outside, though, it was better. Chris left through the sliding doors and walked on the beach, where there was nothing for anyone to hide behind, and in the salty wind and bright sun it was hard to imagine that dark, menacing hooligan from the night before.

He took the sand path leading around the side of the Harper house, the way he always came back from walking Charlie, and stopped before poking his head around the front. But no one was there, just his trusty old Mustang, sitting where he'd left it with the keys still in it, which he must have done in last night's drunken abandon. He got in and started the engine.

The scariest moment of all was turning back into the driveway of the other house, but this morning there was nothing, only a few branches and scraps of brush torn up by that other vehicle.

When he drove up, Caroline was standing on the deck in her coat, with her suitcase in one hand and two repacked bags of groceries and probably garbage hanging from the other. Charlie was already down on the driveway, and Chris felt fleetingly like the father figure in a happy family as they converged on the car. That faded fast, though, once they got in and Chris turned around. Somehow only then did it sink in that she was leaving.

Without saying anything about it, without hardly even knowing that he was going to, he stepped on the brake as they were passing his own place and pulled into the driveway. He put the car in park, killed the engine, and got out and walked around and sat on the hood—well aware that they were in plain sight if Duncan decided to drop by again, but for the moment not caring.

"Chris, what are you doing?" Caroline said anxiously, opening her door and coming over to him.

"Look, I've been thinking. Don't go. You can just stay here. You said yourself that he's not going to come looking here. And there's plenty of room—I'm even authorized to have one guest, and Charlie doesn't count."

"Oh, Chris, that's nice of you, but I can't."

"Why not? It's perfect. Look, we'll just lay low for a couple of days. Duncan will come by and see that that house is empty and locked up, and then go looking someplace else. He'll probably go back to California and probably end up dead or in jail after trying to kill some highway patrol cop on the way."

"Chris, look, that's just not going to work. I still couldn't."

"Why not?"

Caroline let out a breath, looked up at the sky for a moment. "Chris, no offense, but you're not what I need right now. I just . . . I just *came* from living like that—with an artist, you know, someone trying to take on the whole world. It just doesn't . . . I can't live that way anymore."

"Caroline, I hope you're not comparing me to *him*. I mean, just because we both play the guitar. I mean, *I'm* not some out-of-control drug addict. These days I live more like a monk than a rock star." Which was all true, Chris thought. Not the whole story, but true.

"No, Chris, but listen to me. Just listen to me for a second. I don't think you're the same. I don't think so at all, not in that way. But the situation would be the same for *me*—you know, that totally unstructured, free-floating life. It would just be that same . . . unrealness again. And what I need now is to be with people with both feet on the ground, planted in reality. I need to work again, anywhere, doing anything, getting up in the morning and getting out of the house to go somewhere and do something. Can you understand that?"

"So you're saying you think my life is pretty unreal?"

"No, Chris, don't get me wrong. It's great that you're doing what you want to do. And you're incredibly talented, you are. You're incredible on the guitar, really. But I need something else right now. I just can't do the dreaming thing anymore."

Chris was looking away, at the house, at his boots on the gravel. "So what I am, then, basically, is out here just dreaming my life away. And you don't ever see it as more than that, do you? You just see it turning more and more into a hobby for me, while I grow old taking care of people's summer places, becoming the local weirdo. That's really what it comes down to, and why you don't want to have anything to do with me."

"Oh, Chris, come on, I didn't say that. Please, try and understand. It's just, I feel like what I've finally learned is that *making it* is too much to ask for, for you or for me, or for anyone. It's just too much of a long shot. And I can't live my life *chasing* that anymore, or being around someone who's chasing it. Because it just drives you crazy in the end. I need a normal life now, whatever that is."

"Caroline, you know, it's not necessarily this all-or-nothing thing. I mean, you could still be successful without becoming Meryl Streep or something. And I mean, I could be successful without being the next Pete Townshend—"

"No, Chris, no. It doesn't work that way. Believe me, because I've been there and I've seen it. In California, you know, there are so many great, brilliant bands, and they're all out there, all playing around, living on nothing, hoping for their big break. And you can't sing, Chris, and there are so many other guys out there who can."

That stopped everything, and Chris just stood there, feeling suction in his ears as his world collapsed around him.

"Oh, I'm sorry. I'm so sorry I said that. I shouldn't have said that."

"No, that's okay. You should have said that. You should have said that," he repeated dumbly.

"Look, please, please just forget about me, Chris. And forget I ever said that. You're a great guy, Chris. You are."

She reached over to stroke his arm, but had barely touched him when she pulled her hand away again, as if it wasn't what she wanted to do after all.

Feeling like a zombie, dead but still moving, Chris stood up and walked around and got back in the car. When Caroline got in, he started it up again, then put it in gear and pulled out. Dimly, remotely, he registered that Caroline had her head down and her hand on her forehead, the pose of someone who had said too much and was sorry for it now; and that Charlie, sensing all the heavy emotions in the car, had his head down as well, resting warmly on Chris's leg. But these things seemed unimportant, far away. Chris lowered the window so the cold air was blowing over him and breathed deeply and wished for nothing more in the world at that moment than a single line of coke.

By her mumbled request, he drove her to the center of town, where in a building he'd never bothered to notice before there was a small taxi company with two of its dark blue cars idling outside. They, she explained, would take her to the airport in Norfolk, and Chris didn't argue.

"Chris, please, please believe me that I'm sorry, and that I never meant to hurt you," she said the moment they pulled over and stopped.

"I believe you."

She waited a moment, but then opened the door and got out, going into the backseat to pull out her stuff.

"Do you want these groceries, I was—"

"No."

"Right," she said softly, and took them with her. She had her hand on the door and was about to swing it closed when Chris spoke again.

"Caroline, just tell me one thing, okay?" he said. "And I need you to be honest with me. If I . . . changed my life around completely, got a real job somewhere, or maybe went back to school, would a guy like me have a shot at you? I mean, if I came and found you again someday and was more like a real person, with real prospects and all that?"

"Oh, Chris, I—"

"Just tell me. Yes or no."

"Chris, I mean, no, I couldn't. I mean maybe . . . but not like that I couldn't. It would just be too much pressure, and I mean, we barely even know each other."

Chris nodded, looking straight ahead. "Yeah, you're right. You're right." And then he forced himself to turn and look at her one last time. "Good-bye, Caroline."

She didn't say anything, but just nodded and pulled her head back and shut the door. And then he took off into the nonexistent traffic of whatever early hour it was and didn't look back as he drove away.

17

He came awake with no idea where he was. He knew only that he was freezing cold, and that his leg had gone to sleep from being curled up practically in a ball. It was all a nightmare, he thought for an instant— Mr. Harper, that lonely house on the beach, his wrecked life—and now he was waking up into some soon-to-be-remembered normal existence. But the nightmare turned out to be the reality; he was on the white couch in the sunken living room. It was early afternoon, and he had just dozed off thinking about . . . Caroline, right.

The morning had passed in slow torture. He had spent most of it lying in bed with his arm clamped over his eyes, trying desperately to fall asleep. Only he couldn't for the most embarrassing of reasons. Almost dormant since he'd left Boston, probably from all the pills, his libido had reawakened with a vengeance, prowling the cage of his body like a hungry tiger. At one point, he'd actually found himself moaning out loud over their not having had sex at least one more time—so unfair, he thought, when that first time he was half-asleep and it had all happened in the dark and too quickly for him to even appreciate. He figured he had already lost any semblance of pride, and so he tried shamelessly to satisfy himself in the upstairs bathroom. But once, while he was masturbating, looking at himself in the mirror, tears began to pour out of his eyes, and it terrified him because for that moment, standing there with his dick in his hand, bawling like a little kid, he thought he might actually be going mad. Finally he went downstairs, where he eventually wound up on the couch and some-how managed to drift off, a frustrated, half-limp, wet, and cold hard-on still in his jeans.

All of him was cold now, and he swiveled his legs to the floor and leaned over to flip on the heater, which for some masochistic reason he'd left off—but right then froze where he was. Something had woken him, he realized: he'd heard a car start up, a car with a big engine that rumbled like a drag racer.

Immediately, he got to his feet and ran for the stairway, terrified in a way he wouldn't have thought himself capable of anymore, almost tripping and falling on his face since his body wasn't fully functioning yet. Charlie saw this and scrambled over, and Chris grabbed his collar and took him along up to his room. He shut the door behind them and thanked God that all the lights were out, and that he'd bothered to put his car in the garage this time coming back from taking Caroline to her taxi. Now, he reasoned, his life just depended on whether that insane predator had forgotten seeing that this was the only other house occupied for miles around last night. Which, however, the more Chris thought about it, the more unlikely that seemed; and the more certain the other possibility became: that now, after having his life dreams shattered by the girl, Duncan was going to come and find him and snuff out his miserable, pathetic existence in a way more horrible than he could even imagine.

As the engine sound swelled, coming closer, Chris slowly approached the window, hanging back and staying low so he could just see over the sill to the road outside. But the vehicle that came into view a moment later wasn't a car at all. It was a pickup truck, gray and rusted with big balloon tires, making its way back from one of the other houses and moving toward the bridge.

As soon as Chris saw it, he ducked out of view. He didn't even feel relieved. He just felt a little more stupid than he had before.

18

And Duncan never did show up. In fact, nothing happened, nothing at all. The days continued to pass, empty and unused since Chris had given up on music and therefore didn't need to play anymore. He drank a lot of beer but was still clean—although the reason for that had changed, he thought. Now it was because he'd hit a new, never-before-reached low, where he couldn't even take the trouble of going out and finding drugs to buy. More and more, he began to feel like a character in a science fiction movie, someone who'd slipped out of time and into another dimension entirely; into the land of Life Having Passed You By, he thought bitterly.

Without even realizing it, he ate a Thanksgiving dinner of spaghetti with cold sauce sitting alone at the dining table looking out on a gray, roiled Atlantic. Then, later, when he finally remembered what day it was, it was too late to call home as he'd promised, and so he had that to feel like shit about as well.

That night, sitting where he always sat, staring into the glowing coils of the heater, he started to cry again. He'd stopped to wonder what Caroline was doing right at that moment, then that thought led him to contemplate her future, where she would probably meet some guy, some lawyer or investment banker or someone, and they would get married and live happily ever after. He knew he shouldn't be thinking about that; that, if anything, he should be working on a way to get his own life back on some kind of track.

Only suddenly he knew he was really kidding himself, and he would never be able to turn his life around. After all, what would he do? Become a lawyer, a doctor? How could he, when even just the thought of going back to school—or even *applying* to school again—made him feel physically sick?

So this was it, he thought. This was what he'd ended up as; this was as far as he would get. For an instant then he saw a single image of himself, upstairs in his room when he was maybe fifteen or sixteen, standing there in front of his mirror practicing on his old Yamaha in the middle of the night, with his homework untouched, the school morning looming like a bright nightmare in front of him. That was when all this had really started, way back when he was too young to have had a clue about what he was doing—and Christ, he thought, why hadn't someone stopped him? Knocked some sense into him when there was still time? Although he supposed that his mother, as well as about a thousand other people, had tried.

Yet never his father, Chris thought with a sudden rush of anger. His father, even before he'd moved out, had always seemed more interested in being a hip and cool *friend* to his sons than in providing real guidance the way a father was supposed to. Right then Chris got another memory, from even earlier, back when he was maybe twelve or thirteen. It was a hot, bright, sunny afternoon, and he and his brother, after coming home from doing whatever it was they'd been doing, probably from somebody's pool, had found the cellar door standing wide open and climbed down the steep stairs into the moist coolness. Contractors had been putting a new back porch on their house that summer, and the large downstairs room had been turned into a makeshift woodshop, with sawhorses and stacks of long planks and plywood. The two of them were enchanted and, assuming the situation to be permanent, went about making what changes they could to improve upon it. The sawhorses, capped and then walled by sheets of plywood, soon became their clubhouse and stronghold, the planks utilized to create a myriad system of catwalks over an imagined moat, either connecting up with various pieces of furniture or ramping down to the concrete floor.

Chris couldn't recall ever thinking of what they'd been doing as wrong. Yet somehow the moment he'd seen his father on the stairs, he *had* known, and both he and Seth had frozen there in the act of pilfering yet another plank from the endless stack.

He could remember his father's expression exactly then. It had started out as blank curiosity as he was coming down the stairs, his eyes still squinty and tired, the way they always were when he first came home from work. From there, once he'd seen and taken in all that the two of them had done, his anger had cycled up and up, until, by the time he reached the bottom step, it had bloomed into a rage that on his face looked like a close relative of panic. Chris had braced himself for the storm, perhaps even shutting his eyes as his father crossed the room to them.

Yet that storm never came. Instead, his father merely stood there, pretending to be admiring their work while really waiting for whatever cauldron was boiling over inside of him to cool down. Finally all he'd said was something like *What are the two of you up to down here?* followed by an earnest, friendly talk about getting older and responsibility and always asking permission before moving other people's things.

And as far as Chris knew or remembered, his father never had blown his top with either of them—as if at some point he'd made a conscious decision and had always managed to stick with it. Then on those rare occasions when he did give advice, it was always straight out of some self-help book: *Just do whatever you want to do, Chris. Don't let other people make your decisions for you, Chris. After it's all said and done, you'll only have yourself to answer to, Chris.*

Which had all been and sounded great at the time, he supposed, but just look where it had gotten him . . . here, to this freezing-cold, dead-end, no-man's-land hell, where all that was left for him in life was to sit and contemplate everything he'd given away chasing his ludicrous, impossible dream.

Right at that moment, however, he came to a certain decision.

He found himself eventually leaning over the sink in the downstairs bathroom, letting hot water run over his hands, looking at his unkempt, unshaven face in the mirror. An old razor was in the medicine cabinet, the double-edged kind that screwed into a holder—old and rusty, if it mattered—and he had already taken it apart and laid the raw blade at the edge of the counter. He had also taken a kitchen barstool and propped open the front door for Charlie, figuring that the dog could wander off and find a new home for himself somewhere.

He picked up the blade in his right hand and brought it to his left wrist. It was this simple, he thought; it didn't have to be bold or dramatic; it didn't have to hurt; it didn't even have to matter. He needed only to make one small adjustment, and he reached up to turn off the hot-water knob so that it would run full cold.

Before his hand got there, he paused. Right now the water was steaming up into his face, reminding him for some reason of the pasta water when Caroline had cooked dinner for him, like the perfect couple they would never be.

He set the razor blade down, turned off both taps, and stood up, his hands dripping on the floor like two out-of-sync metronomes.

Why *was* the water on in that other house in the first place? he wondered. You couldn't leave a house like that all winter with water in the pipes; when it went below freezing, the water would turn to ice and expand and all the pipes would burst, everyone knew that; when Mr. Harper had said that he'd had this house "winterized," all he'd probably meant, Chris had found out the hard way, was that he'd had the pipes covered or whatever so that wouldn't happen. So had that been done to the other house, too? But, even so, without anybody staying there, and without any kind of heater going, could they— would they—just leave the water on?

Chris tried to work it out, but found that he couldn't.

And later, sitting on the couch again, all the other inconsistencies he'd noticed but chosen not to think about began to recur to him as well: such as Caroline's pale white skin, when she should have been at least a little bit tanned from all her running on the beach in L.A.; or her lousy cooking, as if she'd never once made that dish before in her life; or the way she'd set that hot frying pan directly down on the table, the way no one who'd grown up being invited to fancy summerhouses should ever have done; or perhaps most significantly, the way she'd been so positive about what her deranged ex-boyfriend would and would not do.

Until the whole thing began to unravel in Chris's barely tethered mind, twisting and twining into one enormous, bizarre, burning riddle.

19

It was the morning after Thanksgiving, Friday, November 23, when Chris stood in front of the house with the pointed roof again. The place looked little changed from the last time he'd seen it—a little over a week ago now, although it seemed like much, much longer. He could still remember that last scene perfectly, however: Caroline standing there waiting for him on the deck with her case and her groceries, a sense of danger still lurking in the air, adding urgency and gravity to everything that had happened and was yet to happen.

He went up the steps and tried the door. It was locked, so he continued around the deck, pulling up on every window sash he passed. He was basically trying to break in, in broad daylight, but he barely gave that a thought this time. Every single window on the ground floor, and the sliding doors, were locked tight, however, and with a groan of bitter frustration, he ended up back where he'd started.

There had to be some way in without breaking a window, he thought. And then, as if his mind could have conjured the object out of thin air, he found the key in the first place he looked: up on top of the molding of the window to the immediate right of the entrance. He slipped it into the keyhole in the center of the doorknob, turned it, and went inside.

The place seemed unnaturally silent and dead, the noise of the opening and closing door shattering the tranquillity like thunder. The kitchen looked exactly the same as how they'd left it, with everything put away and neat, the dishwasher door still cracked open an inch. When he went to the sink and turned on the taps, however, there was nothing, not even a gurgling in the pipes. He opened the cabinet beneath and found the plug for the drain trap removed and sitting on top of the pipe. The kitchen phone, when he picked it up, still had a dial tone, which for a long time he stood listening to; this phone was the same as the one in the living room, and it, too, had a redial button. But when the sound of the tone clicked off, Chris hung up.

He walked into the living room. Everything was as if nothing had ever happened. Well, almost everything. He went over to the center cushion of the couch and looked down at it. He never had flipped it over, and there, roughly in the middle, a little to one side, was a chalky white stain on the light green fabric. It was hardly noticeable, almost round with one spike pointing off toward a corner, like the universal symbol for man. Without even thinking about it, Chris kneeled down and put his nose to the spot. The whole cushion smelled musty, probably from years of damp bathing suits, and he wasn't sure he could smell anything. He ended up putting his tongue to it, and the taste was salty and pungent, alive somehow. He closed his eyes, tried to remember.

He was shocked out of it by a piercing, high-pitched yelp, the muscles in his back and neck cramping up in agonizing surprise. But it was only Charlie, who'd been left outside and wanted in.

20

Chris drove slowly down Route 611 outside Ocean City—clearly the bad part of town, where the houses were like shacks that had been plunked down at random distances from the road, many of them with decaying vehicles sinking into their lawns. He'd found out who owned the pickup he'd seen from the first person he'd asked: the old woman behind the cash register at the diner he ate in. It was just as he'd thought. The man's name was Sam Burnett, and he was the local handyman and caretaker. Chris found Sam's address in the phone book they had, then got directions from a gas station on the highway. And now he was studying the numbers on the widely spaced mailboxes out in this weird little patch of nowhere, wondering at the people who lived here and already had their Christmas ornaments up.

When Chris finally got there, he found he didn't need the number anyway. The big, primer-gray pickup was outside, backed up on the driveway. The house wasn't small, but it didn't look to be in good shape, with peeling white paint and a sagging porch in front. It was the kind of place that he would normally associate with college and college towns, like some old frat house. Only here, obviously, the disrepair represented genuine poverty, not the temporary, funky lodging of rich kids.

He pulled up in front and saw a man making a trip out of the garage with an armful of two-by-fours, carrying the long boards out to the open bed of the pickup where the lumber stuck out an ominous five feet beyond the gate.

Chris got out and watched him make another circuit, watched his labored breath come out in clouds in the cold air. With his long, thick beard, he looked like an Amish farmer—wearing the unusual costume of a black baseball cap and Carhartt overalls. Chris was finally noticed on the return trip.

"Well, hello there," the man said, then came up and clapped his leather work gloves together right in front of Chris's face. "And what can I do for you today?"

Chris took a step backward, not sure what to make of it—whether this was actual hostility or just unknowing rudeness. The man sounded angry, though, which with his thick accent was scary, like something out of *Deliverance*.

"Hey, how's it going?" Chris said as soothingly as he could. "Listen, I'm sorry to bother you, I'm looking for a Mr. Burnett."

"Yeah, that's my name."

"Oh, well, hi. I'm Chris Nielson, I'm staying in—"

"Yeah, I know where you're staying," Sam cut him off.

"You do?"

"Yes, I do, because you're kind of hard to miss." Sam motioned to his own head to point out Chris's hair. "You're the kid Mr. Harper's hired to live in his house, now that he's gone and fired everyone who's ever done anything for him, because he blames me and everyone else for what happened to him last winter, which is ridiculous 'cause I got me almost twenty-five houses to look after. I have to, since it's the only way I can make a living. And things are hard for me right now, 'cause I got a wife and three kids, see? Now, I know you probably wouldn't know what that's like, either, but it's hard, and so I need the work."

Chris nodded for a while, trying to seem appropriately gloomy about all this while really just figuring out if the new information affected him at all. He decided it didn't. "Well, the reason I came was, I happened to see you drive by a few days ago, and there was someone staying in the house next to Mr. Harper's, the one with the pointed roof. I was wondering if you were the one who opened and closed that place up, you know, with the water and all?"

"And why do you want to know that?"

"Because I was actually wondering if there was any way you could help me get in touch with this person who was staying there. What happened was, I met them on the road one day, you know, and we actually had a long conversation. And anyway, this woman, she said she might have this job for me out in California. Anyway, I was supposed to go by and get her number, but by the time I did she was gone."

Sam continued to fume in his boundless animosity. Eventually he grimaced and shook his head sadly, though lost work seemingly the key to his brotherly compassion. "Aww, you know, I really don't know anything about who was staying there. All I ever did was speak to the owners about it. They called me up all excited, telling me they'd rented it out for a week and I had to turn the water back on immediately. I told them they was nuts. That place ain't got any insulation at all, and if the temperature had went down, then they'd have a real problem. But they asked me to do it, and so I did it. That's all I know."

"Are they the Coopers?" Chris asked, having the name ready to go.

"Yup, that's right," Sam said, nodding, looking twice as troubled. "But I can't give you their number either. If you find it on your own, that's your business—I hope you understand."

"Nah, that's all right," Chris said, making a dismissive motion with his hands. "Listen, thanks anyway." He started to turn away.

"Hey, I'll tell you something," Sam added before Chris could. "Word to the wise. Your employer, Mr. Harper, you probably think he's some nice old guy, right? Well, he's not. He's not what you think he is at all. You know none of them houses are even supposed to be out there. You ever look at a map? That's supposed to be public property: National Seashore, Parks Department, all that. And that's not supposed to change, ever. But somehow it did. And do you know whose was the first house there? His. Mr. Harper's. He was the first one built on that point, and he had that bridge put in, too. I don't know who he paid off to do it, but he did something like that. You can bet your last five dollars on it. So you just watch yourself, you hear me? You don't want to go screwing up on someone like that."

"Right. Thanks. Thanks again." Once again dismissing the information as irrelevant, Chris got in his car and drove away.

21

He was back in the other house that evening, leaving the lights in front dark as Caroline had done, turning on only one lamp in the living room. This time he'd brought along a portable DAT recorder he had for recording shows, a set of headphones, and a microphone. He set up the recorder and the mike on the coffee table, put on the phones, and then tested the setup to make sure it was working—while doing so managing to accidentally play a few snatches of a live X Bomb tune off the old tape and shuddering for a few moments before finding the stop button.

After that, still wearing the headphones, he picked up the phone and held the mike up to the earpiece of the receiver, cupping his hand around them to try to get a little more level. He put the machine into record, then hit the redial button. Musical digits spewed out of the telephone and into the recorder, and he felt a cold triumph as more than the three tones of the 911 he'd dialed that night were repeated. Unless Sam Burnett or someone else had used this phone, she had made a call that morning while he'd gone to get the car. There was a click on the line as the number started to go through, but Chris immediately hung up.

He did the same thing for the phone in the kitchen, standing there holding his breath while he recorded the stored number. After that he went upstairs and found one more phone in the master bedroom. This one's memory was blank, though, the button doing nothing at all when he pressed it, and he stopped the recorder and took off the headphones.

When he got home, he plugged his tape deck into a little phrase sampler he had, played the tape back into it, and took that device and his headphones to the kitchen phone. It took him a little under half an hour to figure out the two numbers, listening back at half speed, going back and forth between the phone and the sampler, having to hang up every time a call tried to go through. Finally, after using up an entire page of the legal pad there, he had two ten-digit, long-distance numbers, which he copied down onto a fresh sheet of paper, writing next to each the room it had come from.

For a long time he just stared at this page. The first one's area code, from the phone in the living room, he recognized instantly. It was 212, for Manhattan in New York. But the other area code also seemed familiar, and when he had the idea of flipping the pad closed and looking at the numbers he had written on the front page, he saw why. It was the same area code as in the very first number written there, the number for Mr. Harper's office.

After that, he almost didn't notice what was right in front of him. When he finally did then, it wasn't so much a shock as just a slow, cold change that came over all his thinking on Caroline, Duncan, and almost everything that had happened to him since he'd moved to this strange, deserted island in the middle of nowhere.

The area codes *were* the same for the number that had come from the phone in the kitchen of that other house and for both Ted Harper's office and home numbers on the pad. But on the receipt that Chris had taken from the upstairs desk—which was still sitting there on the counter, and on which he had written the number that, for whatever reason, Ted had called him from last—not just the area codes matched. *That entire number was exactly the same.*

22

"Dad, how are you doing, it's Chris," he said into the phone, trying to keep his voice calm and neutral. He was sitting on one of the barstools on the other side of the kitchen counter now, still hunched down over the yellow pad, making nervous, random marks in the corner with the ballpoint he'd been using.

"Hey, Chris, how are you? Haven't spoken to you forever. How are you? How's it going?"

"Oh, things are all right, things are all right." Chris tried to picture his father there, with his sunken chest in his big empty house, probably in pajamas or a bathrobe by now. After leaving Chris's mother, he had lived with three other women, married the third one, then got divorced for a second time. So now he was alone again, perhaps the way he liked it in the end.

"How was your Thanksgiving?" his father asked.

"Good, good. Fine. How was yours?"

"Good. Did you go up to your mother's?"

"Nah, I just spent it down here. It seemed like a big trip to make."

"Oh, well, that's too bad. How are things? You're still at Ted Harper's place, I take it?"

"Yeah, I am."

"And how's that going, okay?"

"Yeah, it's fine. It's a little cold and lonely, but basically it's fine."

"Well, good, good. Did you just call to say hi, or . . . ?"

"Yeah, I sort of called to say hi. Also, I wanted to ask you a quick question, though. Ted, uh, Harper; what's he like? How well do you know him?"

"Oh, Ted? Ted's a great guy. You've met him once or twice before, you know, and his wife and kids, although you were probably too young to remember. But I've told you all about Ted, haven't I?"

"No, I mean, you told me a couple of things . . ."

"Well, what can I say. Ted's a one-of-a-kind, a real character. We go way back. We were at Yale together, all those years ago. Why are you asking, is something wrong?"

"No, no. At least I don't think so. I'm just wondering because . . . from what I've heard he seems to be in some kind of a feud with his neighbors, where he doesn't think anyone else had a right to build here or something. Anyway, I was just wondering about that. Wondering whose side I should be on about it."

"Oh, well, listen, Chris, let me tell you something about Ted. He's the type who likes to stir things up just for the fun of it sometimes. Probably he said something he didn't really mean to somebody. You can't always take him seriously."

"Why not? What do you mean?"

"Well, he's a character, that's what I mean. You know the first time I met him he was actually in the drama department at Yale, which, believe it or not, he was very involved with for a while. He was quite a figure while he was there. His big thing back then was plays without the theater, you know, performance piece, encounter-type stuff. He was always trying to get me involved in it. At the time he thought it was going to be the next great art form, and that he was going to be its Samuel Beckett or something."

"Dad? *Ted* Harper? Are you sure we're talking about the same person?" But Chris said it softly, hearing the rumble of blood in his ears.

"Sure I'm sure. You'd never guess it to look at him now, but back then he was even crazier than the rest of us. He actually got thrown in jail once for a couple of days for some kind of civil rights protest piece he did. Ted doesn't ever talk about that now, but I think he actually had a pretty bad time in there, got beat up and all that. Actually, I think that was the last time he ever did one of those. But anyway, that should give you some idea about the kind of guy he is. He's just a real character, and he's always looking for a way to do his number on the world."

"Huh, that's interesting." Chris pressed his fingertips into his closed eyes, trying to convince himself that he had to be wrong about the one insane conclusion he kept coming to over and over.

"Yeah, he was kind of crazy back then," his father said again. "I guess we all were. But listen, you just do your job for him, and he'll treat you right. He means well, believe me, so just don't worry about his neighbors, okay?"

"Okay, thanks, Dad. I won't."

"And everything else is okay with you?"

"Yeah, yeah, fine. I just . . . just more thing, Dad. Did you ever mention to him about my getting arrested, in college?"

There was a long pause on the other end, followed by a sigh. "I had to, Chris. You can understand that, can't you?"

"Oh, yeah, sure, sure. I was just wondering because . . . something else he said. But it's really not a big deal."

"What did he say?"

"Nothing, Dad. It's really not important. I just wanted to know. You take care, Dad, okay?"

"Okay, Chris. You, too."

Eventually, Chris picked up the phone again and took a deep breath as he dialed the first number he'd deciphered, the one with the 212 area code. There were two clicks, one ring, and then the phone was picked up in the dead space before it could ring again.

"Waiting Room Café," a hurried and businesslike, yet ingratiatory woman's voice answered.

"Oh, uh, hi, is Caroline around?" he said as casually as he could.

"Who?"

"Caroline?"

"I'm sorry, is this a customer you're looking for? Do you have a last name?"

But Chris just hung up.

23

He took the legal pad and the pen over to the couch, flipped to a clean piece of paper, threw the pad on the coffee table, and sat down and began printing in big block letters as fast as he could.

MR. HARPER IS OLD ACTOR/DONE THINGS LIKE THIS BEFORE, Chris wrote on the top line. TED'S PHONE NUMBER STORED IN KITCHEN PHONE/UPSTAIRS PHONE HAS NO NUMBER BECAUSE LINE WAS DISCONNECTED AT SOME POINT, SO NUMBER COULDN'T BE LEFT OVER FROM BEFORE, he wrote under that. Then: HOW I FIRST FOUND CAROLINE, and, HE SENT ME OUT LOOKING FOR HER.

He left a little space and then wrote, THE STORY SHE TOLD/HE KNEW ABOUT MY ARREST, which for Chris referred to the fact that, if someone wanted to dissuade a young man with known drug problems in his past from pursuing his dream career in music, what better way was there than to get some beautiful girl to tell him the story she had, throwing in some actual sex and violence for effect. "DUNCAN" REPRESENTS ME was shorthand for how Caroline's ex-boyfriend was even like some evil caricature of Chris, right down to the car he drove—which made Chris wonder for a moment if Ted could somehow have found out anything else about his life: such as the fight he'd had with Kyle, or with his own ex-girlfriend, Cassie. But Chris decided it was immaterial; just knowing what he already knew would have been enough for Ted to concoct his script.

NOT SCARED ENOUGH/KNEW WHAT DUNCAN WOULD AND WOULDN'T DO alluded to Caroline's not wanting to call the police and being perfectly willing to spend the night at that house, when, if you thought about it, some madman chasing her all the way from California should have made her want to flee the first second she could. THE WAY DUNCAN LEFT/CHARLIE was the related idea about how relatively easy it had been to get rid of Duncan, along with an added thought about how Duncan had reacted to Charlie's biting him. Because it occurred to Chris that, had this whole thing actually been set up, they probably weren't supposed to have gone back to Mr. Harper's house that night, and so Charlie wasn't supposed to be there; which was why Caroline hadn't wanted to go at first; and why she'd started to object to his bringing the dog along when he'd walked her home, before realizing it would be too obvious to do that; *and* which was also exactly the way that guy had reacted—when Charlie had bitten Duncan, he hadn't sounded frightened or hurt so much as *wronged,* as if someone should have told him that might happen.

Chris circled AND THEN SHE DUMPS YOU, because, in addition to providing her with a clean getaway, Caroline's final disapproval and dismissal also served to drive the point home. Although, as far as that went, Chris certainly couldn't have played into her hands any better than he had. But their plan, their script, would have had to have been flexible, he thought, and even if he hadn't taken the bait quite as hard as he had, it would still have been plenty effective.

HER SKIN BEING SO WHITE/HER COOKING/THE WINE IN THE HOUSE/HER PUTTING THE FRYING PAN ON THE TABLE/HER BEING AMAZED BY OUTSIDE OF HARPER HOUSE were items that didn't prove or disprove things one way or the other, but that also didn't fit, and so Chris put them down as well.

He left a little more space, then finished with THE WATER TURNED ON/OFF, HOUSE RENTED OUT, which was so obvious he hadn't even thought of it at first. But it was plainly his most solid piece of evidence, proof positive that something was out of whack, and quite possibly a glimpse of the chains and levers behind Ted Harper's stage set—especially since it had been a last-minute job for Sam Burnett; looking back on that talk he'd had with Mr. Harper in his bedroom, Chris could remember what he now thought was the exact moment when Ted had decided to carry out his hoax: right before he'd asked Chris if there would be anyone coming to stay with him.

He sat back and looked over what he had so far, all of the evidence for what he considered to be his main hypothesis: that everything that had happened with him and Caroline and her supposed stalker boyfriend was really just a "play," like one of those his father had described, and which had been scripted, brought about, organized, and paid for by Ted or some agent of Ted's, for the bizarre purpose of teaching his friend's son the error of his ways.

When he was satisfied he'd left out nothing major, he ripped off the page and began a fresh one.

He thought for a moment, then wrote, SHE <u>SLEPT</u> WITH YOU—WHERE WOULD HE FIND SOMEONE LIKE HER WILLING TO DO THAT?! Only Chris thought he knew the answer to that one right off the bat. She was probably some supremely high-class call girl, who worked for thousands of dollars a night and did outlandish and bizarre jobs like this all the time. That he had gone through most of his life not believing such people existed—it would be like believing in the world of James Bond—didn't mean they necessarily didn't. After all, Chris, whose last job was waiting tables, would have no way of knowing about that.

The only other thing he could think of to write down here just said, ?MR. HARPER? which to him signified the concept that, if Ted Harper's whole tough, conservative Southern businessman thing really was an act, as his father had said it was, and as Ted's flamboyant history seemed to indicate it would be, then the man actually shouldn't be the type to care so much about someone like Chris throwing his life away for his music, or at least not enough to stage some crazy, violent, melodramatic interlude to give him instruction.

This idea didn't quite hold water either, though, he decided. Ted Harper *was* something of an actor—Chris had had that very thought during their little man-to-man in the master bedroom—but Chris didn't think that Ted believed in his message, of hard-work ethic and family values, any the less for it. In fact, whatever he had done in his past, and however he felt about it, Ted Harper seemed to believe in his current way of life with a vengeance.

Chris took a moment to consider this page as well, which was supposed to support the antithesis: basically that, in all his time alone here, he had become paranoid and slightly insane, and that this whole thing was one massive, delusional fantasy. Then he began another.

On this one, however, he managed to write only a single word: CAROLINE.

But he thought a lot about her, too, whoever she really was. He thought about her until he had dissected and examined every word and action and nuance of expression that he could remember. He thought about her until in his mind she no longer seemed quite human, but more like some exotic and dangerous weapon that had been loosed upon the world, and that he'd had both the misfortune and the privilege to meet up with.

He thought about her until, when he happened to look up once, it was light outside, the sun beginning its rise over a purple-gray Atlantic. Finally, he tucked his torn-out pages back into the yellow pad and, taking it along in case he wanted to consult it again, went upstairs to bed.

He slept for only about four hours and after that got up and began to pack a knapsack for a one- or two-day trip.

24

The long drive up through Maryland and Delaware to the New Jersey Turnpike and then to the Holland Tunnel passed in disconnected numbness, where Chris often felt as if someone else were driving the car; or that, just as his body was inside the car working the pedals and the wheel, he, the real Chris, were somewhere deep inside his own head, controlling the body that steered that car with the same isolation from its workings. He didn't listen to music and hardly bothered to look at the passing scenery on this clear, cold day, noting only that the trees seemed browner than he remembered from the drive down—of what little he remembered about the drive down. Mostly, he preferred to concentrate on the road and the needle of the speedometer, keeping it right around seventy.

Because he didn't know how long he would be gone or where he would be staying, he'd left Charlie behind, setting out food and water and leaving the sliding back door open for him to walk himself. He had never done anything like that with Charlie before, but he was a smart dog, and Chris supposed he would be okay. Another worry was that if it rained it would do so into the house, but Chris didn't think about that one very much. Mostly, when he did think, he continued to wonder about Caroline: the miracle of her, someone who faked emotions, used her body, her entire being, to manipulate people for money.

He arrived in Manhattan at a little after four and drove east on Canal, getting in line in the snarled crosstown traffic, looking out the window at the funky hardware stores, restaurants, and nightclubs that lined this weird, busy street, glancing to his right every now and then trying to comprehend the absence of those two enormous buildings he'd watched burn, explode, and collapse along with the rest of the country, that event still marking what to him seemed like the begining of the end of the world. As a kid growing up in the suburbs, he'd made many a pilgrimage to this city, to see rock shows at the Garden or just to check out the scene, wandering around the East Village with friends and gawking at the punks and weirdos, taking a thrill from the perceived danger even if it was mostly imaginary. But he'd never once had a gig here. For all of their early success, X Bomb had never made it out of New England, and New York still never failed to make him feel like a rube. He felt that way more than ever now, driving a car with out-of-state plates, having no place to stay.

He'd called up 212 information before he left and gotten the address of the Waiting Room Café, on lower Sixth Avenue it turned out, which he managed to find without having to lean out the window and beg directions off somebody. The place when he drove past wasn't at all what he'd imagined, though, wasn't some small, dark bistro where shady deals were made by an elusive, rich clientele. Instead, it was some huge, gaudy, yuppie, tourist trap with chrome trim and pink and blue neon like some fifties diner. Chris felt his heart sink. He had known that he was going to need a little luck to find Caroline, but only now did he realize just how humiliatingly futile this trip was going to be.

Three blocks away he found a lot to put the car in, for a price that would have seemed like robbery anywhere else in the country, and then he walked back with his hands jammed in his jeans pockets, trying not to stare at the people he passed on the street, feeling like a madman on a secret mission and starting to wonder how, realistically, he was even going to start up a single conversation once he got in there.

The café was even bigger than he'd thought inside, with two rows of blue, upholstered booths by the windows, and then more tables and a big bar toward the back. Facing the door, there was a podium for a maître d', but no one was standing behind it; the establishment was practically empty, with only one or two customers sitting at the bar. There was activity, though. As Chris stood there, he watched a waitress dressed in all black bustle in through swinging doors with a trayful of glasses. It was Saturday, he remembered, and they would be gearing up for a big night.

He took a seat at a table near the bar. *I'm supposed to meet an old girl-friend here,* he told himself, trying to look the part, taking off his jacket and hanging it on the back of his chair. A few minutes passed and no one seemed to notice him, which he supposed was good, until that began to make him feel even more conspicuous. He considered just getting up and leaving, coming back later; he would have a better chance when the place was filled up, he thought. Only now that he was already here, leaving seemed like the worst thing he could do. He decided to at least order a drink. If Caroline had called this place, then it was more than possible that it was to speak to someone who worked here, or was at least a regular, and so maybe all he needed to do was ask the right waiter or waitress.

But as he leaned over to flag the next one passing by him, the world seemed to shift, then seize up altogether. She recognized him only an instant after he'd seen her—wearing the same black uniform as all the other waitstaff, coming right up to him as if she'd been about to ask for his order, only now instead standing there frozen, looking every bit as shocked as he felt.

In that one instant, Chris saw the error in all of his previous thinking about her: not some high-priced call girl, but just some out-of-work actress or model making money waiting tables like in her story; one whose looks, so startling on that deserted strip of sandbar, would barely even stand out in the chic SoHo crowd that was going to start showing up in a couple of hours—it was merely his pathetic loneliness and isolation that had elevated her and made her seem like a goddess. Within that split second it also occurred to him that in all likelihood she had made her phone call to this restaurant for the mundane purpose of seeing if she could get a shift that night.

For some reason, this last thought made him stand up, and then he was moving toward her and didn't know what was going to happen or what he was going to do.

But that was when the pain exploded at the back of his skull, seeming to spread and fill his entire head and braincase, until the level of the pain came up above his eyes and everything went dark.

25

"Oh shit, oh shit, oh shit," someone was uttering frantically, while shaking him not so gently by one shoulder.

"You got to call that guy, Karen, and right now," he heard after that, in a different voice, a male voice.

He opened his eyes then and saw Caroline—or, he guessed, Karen—leaning over him. He was laid out on a leather couch in a dark little office with filing cabinets and a desk and no windows, the hum of the restaurant outside, probably coming from the kitchen. And behind the girl, Chris found it didn't surprise him at all to see "Duncan" here, too. He was in the black pants and black T-shirt uniform of the place as well, his thick bodybuilder's arms exposed in all their glory. Hanging out of Duncan's front pocket was some kind of homemade sap, the kind of thing bartenders and bouncers always kept handy for the quick anesthetizing of drunks and troublemakers.

"Shhh, shut up, shut up," Karen told him quickly, realizing Chris was awake.

When he sat up, it hit full on again, a big, throbbing football of white pain bouncing all around the inside of his skull, ricocheting always off the same spot where he'd been hit. Chris winced as he touched that spot. It was as tender as if all the skin had been scraped away, yet no blood was on his fingers when he checked them. The sap must have been made of something soft on the outside like an inner tube, but that didn't help the pounding, blinding headache he was left with.

"Are you okay?" Karen said.

"Karen . . ." "Duncan" said again.

"Okay," she answered him testily. "Would you just leave us alone now?"

The guy hesitated at first, but finally turned away and headed for the door. "I'll be right outside if you need me," he said on the way.

When they were alone, she sank back in an office chair facing Chris and put a hand on her forehead.

"Are you okay?" she asked him again. "I'm so sorry about that. I guess he saw you when you came in and then got freaked out when you came up to me that way. You were probably going to slap me or something—which I probably deserved."

Chris just sat there. He didn't know what to say because he didn't yet know what the situation was. For some time both of them were silent.

"I guess you probably think I'm crazy to have gotten back together with him," she went on eventually. "But he really needed my help, Chris. And I got us these jobs working here for a while. My real name is Karen, as you've guessed—I was just calling myself Caroline because I thought it would make me harder to find."

Then all at once Chris understood everything and was shaking his throbbing head. "Bullshit," he said.

She looked away from him, took a breath. "How did you know? Did he tell you?"

"Mr. Harper? No, he didn't tell me. The water was on in that house—that didn't make sense if you were supposed to be hiding there and hadn't told anyone. I spoke to the caretaker of the place, and he said it had been rented out. I got the number of this place, plus Ted Harper's number, off the redials of the phones."

Karen closed her eyes, nodded. "So I guess we didn't fool you at all, huh?"

"Oh, no, you did. You know you did."

There was silence between them again, which once more she broke.

"Well, I'm sorry, Chris, I really am. I mean, obviously we never should have done it. I can't—"

"Who came up with the story?" Chris cut her off. "About you as an actress and all that? Was it you or him?"

"It was him. And me. I mean, I guess he sort of told me what he wanted, and then I filled in the rest."

"And then what was supposed to happen? I mean, obviously my dog wasn't supposed to be involved."

"Not that much more. You were supposed to fight a little. No one was supposed to get hurt."

"How did Ted arrange it? How did he first get in touch with you?"

"I got called up by this talent agent who'd given me work before. He said he had a very unusual job, which I didn't have to take if I didn't want. Then, when I first heard what it was, I wasn't going to do it, except I went ahead and met with Ted anyway, and he seemed like such a good person. And you have to believe me that I—that we—only agreed to get involved because it seemed harmless enough. It even seemed like it was going to be a good thing at the time, Chris—"

"Oh, that's a load of shit, you did it for the money. Why don't you just say it?"

"Okay, fine. There was that, too. But it's easy to talk about money like that when you've had plenty of it all your life."

Chris nodded, realizing two things at the same time. The first was that her accent, what little of it there was, was still there, and not something she had faked, maybe suggesting that her personal history wasn't too far from what she'd told him. The second was the real other reason why she'd agreed to do it. It was the way that she thought of him: not as a real person, but just as some spoiled rich kid who'd needed a dose of reality, no matter how manufactured that reality was. And, of course, living in that house, having Ted Harper as his supposed benefactor, it was easy to see how she'd gotten that impression. That it wasn't true—that he had indeed grown up with most of the good things in life, but now had no trust fund or anything like that and was probably more broke than she was—was immaterial.

"So I don't get it, you're a waitress, but you just sleep with men for money on the side, is that it?"

As Chris had wanted, it seemed to hurt her, and she looked down at the industrial, gray carpeting before answering. "Look, Chris, we weren't actually supposed to . . . have sex. That just happened. I got carried away, I'm sorry."

Somehow, Chris could see the truth of that, too, could tell she wasn't lying. But, instead of its making him feel better about her, it did just the opposite; because even if she hadn't screwed him for pay, she hadn't done it because she'd been exceptionally attracted to him, either. She had done it, he saw clearly, because she'd liked, or been excited by, the whole situation: of deceiving him; of being the one in power. For the first time now, Chris thought he could see exactly who this girl Karen was. And while that understanding made him hate her, it was also sort of a relief; he could finally dismiss her from his fantasies.

"Well, I guess I should really be thanking you for the whole thing, then," he said, sitting up a little more, testing his head with his fingertips again. He stood up slowly, but even so he felt as if he were about to black out for a second time. Then the world swam into focus once more, and he was reasonably okay.

"That's about all we need to say to each other, I guess," he went on, still with one hand on the arm of the sofa, pointing himself generally toward the door. "Listen, can I leave now, or is whatever-his-name-is going to finish me off just for the hell of it?"

When he looked over again, gratifyingly Karen had her hands over her eyes and had started to cry.

"Chris, don't hate Ted for doing this, okay? He really cares about you, and he was trying to help. And, I mean, everything I said, apart from the obvious, was true. You really are talented, Chris—"

"Listen, *Karen*, you got me, okay? I was lonely as hell, and you came along, and I fell for you; stupid, I know, but I did it. But now I really don't care what you think of me, or my music, or my life. And I guess I'm not real clear on why I should be taking advice from some dumb bitch waitress, either." He pulled open the door, which "Duncan" had left open a crack, and stopped there, holding on to the metal frame for a moment.

"Oh, and by the way, your cooking sucks," he added over his shoulder.

Outside the room was a short hallway that led to the rest rooms and beyond that to the main area of the restaurant. His two-time assailant was nowhere to be seen, and Chris just walked back to his table to retrieve his jacket and left through the big glass doors.

Out in the cold air again, he breathed deeply and told himself his head was already starting to feel better. In a daze of rage, he walked back to the parking lot and bought his car back. Once he was driving again, he couldn't think of anything better to do than enter the traffic line for the tunnel and start the long trip back.

For that entire return journey, he alternated about equally between periods of cool, even contemplation, and burning, all-consuming rage.

At one calm point he congratulated himself. He had gotten to the bottom of Ted Harper's little mystery drama in just two days' time, with no assistance, using merely common sense and a basic knowledge of telephones—all of his early notions about spies and elite call girls leading him only to one mean bitch of an actress/waitress and some bouncer or bartender that she'd roped into the job with her.

During another interval of composure, he thought that it was funny what he'd said to her about his music, his becoming angry and self-righteous about it, when he'd given up on that anyway. But it was only because he'd felt the need to defend himself that he'd done it, he decided, and didn't go into it more deeply than that.

At those times when he was furious, though, on that much longer drive back, with his head throbbing as if the headrest of his seat had been replaced by a cartoon anvil with the point grinding straight into his skull, and the headlights and the road signs often blurring in his vision so that for seconds at a time he might as well have been driving blind, his thoughts were almost exclusively of Ted Harper.

26

Chris was awakened by the telephone, the sound jangling up from the big room below his bedroom, accompanied and made much worse this morning by a leftover, still-pounding headache.

After hitting heavy traffic on the Turnpike and then missing a turn and getting hopelessly lost in Dover—a place that seemed to exist solely on his road map, since all he ever saw of it were back roads leading to and from nowhere—he hadn't arrived back at the house until well after midnight. He'd pushed Charlie out the door to make sure the dog had walked himself, then gone upstairs and taken three Advils from his supply before going to bed on an empty stomach, where he fell into a sick, uneasy sleep.

The phone was still ringing, but this time Chris thought he would just let it. He had a pretty good idea of who it was on the other end and wasn't so sure he wanted to speak to him. On maybe the ninth or tenth ring, however, his anger got the best of him, and he dragged himself out from under the covers and walked into the master bedroom.

"Hello," he said picking up, still not knowing what he was going to say after that.

"Chris! What's going on out there?"

Ted Harper sounded concerned and mildly ticked off—rather than apologetic and guilty, which Chris realized he'd been expecting. It made him hold off on what he also supposed he'd been planning, which was giving his landlord a piece of his mind.

"What do you mean?" Chris said.

"I tried to call about five times yesterday, I got no answer."

"Oh, sorry about that. I went out once or twice, I must have missed you."

And why are we playing cat and mouse this way? he wondered. *Ted must know by now that he's been found out* . . . only suddenly Chris realized that he wouldn't. Caroline, or Karen, wouldn't have told him, because she'd have thought for certain that Chris would have called Ted himself. Her job was done, she'd been paid, and she was probably dreading *getting* a phone call, worrying about getting blamed for the screwup.

Which meant Chris had an opportunity here. An opportunity to do . . . something.

"Well, I just called because I've been thinking about you all alone out there, Chris," Ted Harper said. "Now listen up, I've got an offer I'm prepared to make you. I actually heard of a job you might be interested in. It's with an old friend of mine up in D.C. It's kind of a start-up company he's trying to get off the ground, some Web advertising thing. It wouldn't be great pay or anything like that. You'd be starting at the bottom, and you'd probably have to do something about your hair. But it would be a start for you. And I think I can find someone else to look after the house, too. So what do you say?"

"Oh, thank you, Ted. Thank you for the offer, but something like that wouldn't interest me."

"No, huh?" Ted seemed genuinely surprised. "Are you sure, Chris? You know the economy's still on the verge of a total collapse out here, and jobs don't grow on trees."

"No. Thanks but no, Mr. Harper."

"All right, Chris, if you say so. Listen, though, you give me a holler if you change your mind, okay?"

"Okay, thanks, Mr. Harper. I will."

There was a long pause on the other end. "Anything else going on out there I should know about?"

"No, not really. Everything's fine."

"Okay, well, you take care, Chris. I'll speak to you soon."

Chris hung up and immediately pounded the desk with his fist. *"Fucker!"* he yelled at the lifeless phone.

After that he stood up and put his hand on the back of his head, trying to calm down, trying to stop the throbbing that had returned to the base of his skull with a vengeance. So everything, all of what he'd gone through, had come down to some job offer, he thought—which, had it been a few days ago, he would probably even have taken. Only Ted had waited too long, and had things gone slightly differently, Chris might not have been around to pick up the phone at all.

Suddenly Chris understood the real reason why he hadn't yelled at Ted Harper, which was also the same reason he'd taken the trouble to figure out the telephone numbers from the other house instead of merely calling them back, and part of the reason he'd lied to his father as well. It was because he'd known all along that he wanted something more than to merely curse out the man who'd played with him like some piece on a board game.

Right at that moment he came up with a possible way. He could never actually go through with it, he thought right afterward. Only soon he knew that he would try; that, in fact, right now, getting revenge was all he cared about.

He was pretty sure that he still remembered a certain middle-aged woman's name.

27

Chris took two more of his Advils before sitting down into the black plastic chair at the haircutting salon he'd found in Ocean City. He told the woman there to try not to touch the back of his head too much because he'd hit it getting out of his car, but still it hurt like hell when she got to that place, unavoidably scraping it with the electric razor. Chris closed his eyes and bore it.

"You've got quite a bump there," the woman told him.

He nodded, wincing.

Soon the vinyl bib cinched around his neck was littered with tiny pieces of two-tone hair, while his head was all dark brown again. The resulting hairstyle was an almost military crewcut, but it was just what Chris wanted, and he nodded and thanked her when she held up a hand mirror to show him the back.

He found the Phyllis Laney Gallery tucked away in a little mini-mall parking lot off Main Street not too far away. It wasn't much, only one step up from the tourist places on the boardwalk that would sell T-shirts and refrigerator magnets and painted seashells during the summer season. Chris could barely see into the dark shop through a lowered grating, but taped to the glass inside the front door was a note written in neat block letters. WINTER HOURS, it said, and then gave them. Basically, the place was only open on Saturdays. Beneath that, in smaller writing, it said, *For enquiries, please call*—and then gave a local number. Chris memorized the seven digits and drove away.

Sitting on one of the kitchen stools that afternoon, hunched over the phone once again, he dialed the number. Then he bent his head over and closed his eyes in concentration.

It was answered on the third ring. "Hello?" A woman's voice.

"Hi, is Donna Laney there?"

"This is Donna."

"Oh, hi," he said slowly, a little tense—although he figured he was supposed to sound nervous. "Listen, I got this number off the front of your art gallery and just took a chance that it would be you."

"Who is this?"

"It's, umm, Chris Nielson. I'm staying at Ted Harper's house. We met that once, when you came by." Chris swallowed once, whether for effect or not, he couldn't say. "Listen, I don't know what your current situation is, and I know that we hardly even know each other, so please just tell me if I'm completely off base here. But could I take you out for dinner or drinks sometime?"

There was a long pause afterward, and Chris was about to speak again, just say anything, when finally she answered.

"That's probably not a good idea. It's not because of you, Chris— although you're right, we do hardly know each other, and I'm actually sort of amazed that you remember me at all. But let's just say there are other reasons in my life why I can't do that right now. But it was sweet of you to call."

"What other reasons?"

"I have my reasons, believe me."

"Something serious."

Another pause. "Serious enough."

"Okay, well, listen, how about this? No date, nothing like that. But why don't you just have a drink with me sometime. It'll just be, you know, friendly. And I have something I need to tell you, too. What do you say? Come on."

She laughed a little, a start. "No, I really don't think so."

"Oh, come on, what harm can it do? Take pity on me and get a free drink at the same time? What could be better than that?"

She laughed some more, a grating, raucous laugh, Chris thought. "Well, okay, I guess so."

The place she suggested was called the Barnacle Grill Restaurant, also in Ocean City, a big seafood place on the water that was probably the upscale, happening scene in summer, but was now like something out of a depressing movie about old townies. On this Sunday night the place was dead, with only about four other souls in attendance. Chris made a point of getting there early and took a table next to the window, well away from the few other customers. There was nothing to see outside beyond the dimly illuminated street but cold blackness and a few distant lights on the water—probably the very same fishing boats he'd spent countless nights contemplating from Mr. Harper's beach. He ordered a Heineken from a dour, overweight waitress while he sat there and soon saw Donna come in. She looked severe and all-business in a white turtleneck with a thick brown sweater under a dark tweed coat, a big brown leather purse tucked under her arm like a weapon.

He smiled and stood up as she came over to the table. She kept her face carefully neutral, but he could tell that she was flattered, that a younger guy chasing after her like this gave her a thrill. If she noticed his changed hair or clothes—he was wearing one of his two white button-down shirts under a light blue wool sweater—she didn't show any sign of it, but just came to the table and sat down across from him.

"Thanks for coming," he told her.

"Okay, I'm here," she announced loudly, ignoring him, shrugging out of her overcoat and leaving it inside out on the chair behind her. Unlike the last time Chris had seen her, she was wearing no makeup, and her skin looked white and chapped from the cold. "So what is it you want to tell me?" she said in the same blunt, rude voice. For a second, just a second, Chris considered throwing his beer in her face.

"Come on, give me a chance," he said instead.

"Give you a *chance*!?"

"A chance to ex*plain*. Come on, have a drink or something. What do you want?" He managed to again catch the attention of the waitress, who came to the table with her pad out.

"Umm, just give me a gin and tonic," Donna told her, barely glancing over. "I think I'm going to need it," she said to him.

Chris managed to smile again at that.

"Okay, you got me here," she said as soon as they were alone again, crossing her arms like a scolding mother. "It's Sunday night on a holiday weekend, and I didn't have anything better to do, so I'm here. Now what is it? What do you want?"

Chris took a deep breath. He didn't know what he'd expected, but it hadn't been this. And now he couldn't see how he was ever going to make this work. At that moment he thought of *why* he was doing it, though, and that made him think of Caroline—or Karen—and what she, and they, had done to him. Just coming up with it on the spot, he said, "Okay, here it is. I've decided to change my life, become a normal person, give up music."

She looked straight at him for a moment, meeting his gaze, then let out a snort of derision through her nose. "You got me to come here so you could tell me *that*?"

Over her laughter, he said, "Well, it's a big deal to me. And I felt like I needed to talk to someone, and I thought of you."

She stopped laughing. "Oh my God. You're really serious, Chris? You're not just kidding around?"

He shrugged and looked down at his beer on the table.

"Oh, well, Chris, I mean, I'm flattered, I really am. I mean I'm flattered, but I sort of don't know what to tell you. I mean, I knew that you used to be in a rock band—I guess Ted probably mentioned it that time I saw you. So what is this? I hope you're not asking me for a job."

"No, come on, Donna. I'm not asking you for a job. That's not why I called you. I don't know what I should do, though. I mean I guess I should probably think about going back to school or something. Maybe business school, or law school. I don't know, though. Right now I just feel so lost. Like I don't have a reason to get up in the morning."

After that he got her talking about her life and her career. She told him about how she'd worked in an art gallery in Miami before she and her sister had decided to strike out on their own. She told Chris what that was like, how they'd found backers, and how they'd chosen Ocean City because there wasn't anything like their gallery there yet.

He kept her talking through another drink, but it didn't seem to him that he made any real headway. He could tell she saw herself as a hip, successful woman and wasn't going to be easily wooed by the advances of a plebeian like himself. And why not? After all, she had had the likes of Ted Harper, a real man with real money, so why would she want to waste her time on him?

When she'd finished her second drink, lifting it up over her head and then clunking it down onto the table almost like some frat guy pounding a shot, she immediately looked at her watch and stood up. "I have to go," she told him. But she sat down again and reached for her purse beside the chair.

"No, that's okay, I got it," Chris said, watching as she pulled out a twenty from a wallet and slapped it on the table.

"It's on me, don't worry about it."

"But I invited you."

"Listen," she said, standing up again, putting on her coat, "it sounds like I can afford it better than you can these days. Anyway, it was nice talking to you—otherwise it would have just been me and my sister tonight, and believe me, I get enough of her."

Chris stood up, too, and grabbed his jacket to follow her out. She waited for a moment, but seemed to correct herself and make a point of walking by herself. At the entrance she couldn't quite bring herself not to hold the inside of the double glass doors for him, however.

"Where did you park, down here?" he asked outside, motioning to the big, practically empty parking lot on the side of the place. She just nodded.

"I'll walk you to your car," he said, and began following close behind again.

Her car, parked off by itself in the vast, cold macadam, was a new-looking American station wagon of a dark, indeterminate color in the dim sodium lighting. She stopped by the door to go through her purse for her keys.

"Well, listen, thanks again for coming," he told her.

"Sure." She was practically ignoring him now, tilting her purse into the light to try to see inside it.

Without thinking about it and giving himself a chance to chicken out, Chris took a step closer and grasped her hand. In the next instant she was looking up at him, and he pulled her close and kissed her square on the lips.

The sensation of the sudden intimacy was shocking, her widening, startled eyes coming right up to his own like some fun-house special effect. Yet for the instant that it lasted, he managed to hold her gently yet firmly, just as he would if he were in love.

Afterward, she looked confused, as if she hadn't yet decided if she should be angry.

"Sorry," he said quickly.

"No, that's . . . I just didn't think you were going to do that."

"Look, can I see you again? Let me take you out to a movie next time, I owe you now."

"Oh, Chris, please try and understand. I might even like to, but with you and me, it just wouldn't be right."

"Please. We'll go see anything you want. Now come on, how many guys would say that?"

She cracked a small smile. "Well, not a lot, I guess."

"I'll call you, okay? I'll call you tomorrow."

He saw her shake her head again, but just turned and walked away.

28

He gave her a day off to keep her wondering, then caught her at home Tuesday evening.

"Look, Chris, I've been thinking about it, and I don't think we should see each other again."

"What? Why not?"

"Because . . . just because, okay?"

"Well, will you at least tell me why?"

"No, I can't do that, either."

"Look, we'll just be friends, okay? I promise. Why don't we go see a movie together or something. I won't attack you or anything."

"Chris, why am I so important to you all of a sudden? This is all just too *weird*."

"Donna, I don't really know the answer to that one. I don't really understand it myself. All I can tell you is that you are. So, won't you please just say that you'll see me again. If you're busy, I'll wait. Just give me a time, tell me when."

"Oh, *okay*. I'm free Thursday night."

"Great, can I pick you up somewhere?"

"No, I'll meet you." She let out a breath of exasperation. "Call me back tomorrow and I'll figure out where."

They went to a mall off Route 50 to see the nine-o'clock showing of the latest indie movie to hit it big, about two gorgeous but down-on-their-luck small-town ex-hippies who meet and fall in love, the kind of movie where everyone lives in beautiful homes and has chic clothes despite the fact that they're supposedly broke—which, in spite of himself, Chris enjoyed more than he thought he would. He hadn't seen a movie or TV in so long, and at times during the show he completely lost himself in the melodrama and forgot all that had happened and was still happening, only to be shocked each time he'd remember whom he was there with and why.

He had arrived first and paid for the tickets this time, and so maybe that was why she said yes when, walking out of the multiplex, he suggested they go get a drink somewhere. Unfortunately, neither of them could suggest anything better than the place they'd been to four nights ago, and so that was where they ended up again, him following her big car in the pitch-black night with barely anyone else on the road.

"Spooky out there, huh?" Chris said, walking inside with her, shaking the cold out of his jacket.

"You get used to it," she said.

They sat at the bar this time, where the same waitress was also bartending, and they ordered the same drinks.

This time, Chris got her talking about her sister, who lived with Donna and who owned more than half of the gallery, and then about the rest of the family: Donna had two younger brothers who were both married, one of them with children. "It's just us sisters who are old maids," she told him. Chris responded reassuringly, telling her to cut it out.

After that, she made him tell about his family, and he dutifully recounted the tale of how his father had left his mother, but then it was his mother who'd ended up happily married in the end. Every time he told this story he was conscious of the spin he was giving it (mother at fault, father at fault, institution of family itself at fault), but tonight he tried to do something new and give it a happy, hopeful ending all around, thinking that would probably appeal to her the most.

After two drinks, she once more stood up to leave, but she didn't rush ahead, and when they got outside, they walked side by side and stopped between their two cars.

Even before they got there, Chris understood clearly that here and now would be the best chance he ever got, and immediately went to kiss her again.

This time, almost unbelievably to him, they began making out right there in the parking lot, her arm coming around to grip his waist, him pushing her back against her car. The instant their bodies were pressed against each other, she was twice as intense, a hungry, sucking animal tugging at him, pushing him back and then pulling him in again—

Chris had the giddy sensation that he'd randomly flicked a light switch somewhere and detonated an atom bomb instead. The blatantly sexual movements excited him, and as his disgust faded, he felt a feeling of triumph. But once again it wasn't really him winning over the girl, he decided. With Donna it was just this place, making her as lonely as he was in these wasteland months between the summer seasons.

Soon his other hand found its way inside her coat, to her sweater, beneath that to reach up to the edge of one soft, surprisingly large breast. Then all at once she stopped and bent away from him.

"Okay, Chris. We can do this," she practically panted. "We can do this, but it has to be a secret, okay? It has to be just between you and me. I can't tell you why, but it does. Can you understand that? Do you agree to that?"

"Yeah, sure. No problem," he said, still leaning against her in his lower regions. In the cold, the saliva on his chin and nose was starting to burn, but he ignored it rather than wipe it off right in front of her. "Why don't you come over."

"I really shouldn't do that. And we can't go to my place because my sister's there."

"Come on, just come over for a little while." Chris leaned into her a little harder. "It's such a big, empty house. And it's nighttime; it's not like anyone's going to see you."

"You're really a persistent little bastard, aren't you?"

"Only sometimes."

"Okay," she said finally. "You get there first and leave the garage door open. I'm not going to follow right behind, so don't wait for me." In order to push away then, she ground up against him one last time.

When she came into the house—where Chris had already turned on lights and put Charlie away in the other upstairs guest bedroom—she looked around avidly, taking the whole place in with a plainly covetous eye. Under normal illumination, her face looked pasty and pale again, and the house also somehow diminished her; her tight, designer jeans and plastic-looking boots all made Chris think of some maid or servant who'd covertly gained admission to the manor while the master was away. He met her in the living room with the garage remote in his hand—which, after he triggered the door with it, he left on the little chest of drawers by the wall there, plainly in view.

"Well, aren't you going to take my coat?" she asked, finally looking over at him.

"It's pretty cold in here," he said. "You might want to keep it."

"Oh yeah, so you're not going to keep me warm, Chris?" Taking a step toward him, she fastened onto his waist again.

For a moment Chris honestly didn't think he would be able to go through with it; yet, once again, the physical contact aroused him just enough so he could play his part. Soon they were kissing again, her savage lunges practically throwing him off his feet, and this time she didn't pull his hand away from under her shirt, letting him feel all of her huge bosom through her bra of thick, rough fabric with a stiff wire running through underneath. Her coat came off and went directly onto the floor, as did his, and then he was pulling at her turtleneck where it was tucked into her jeans.

"Oh yes, baby," she said, making him just about cringe in embarrassment again.

She had a big, womanly torso, and Chris managed to work her bra snap, freeing her voluminous breasts, which had large, hard nipples at their center when he lifted up her shirt.

He went for her belt buckle after that, but she grabbed his hands and held them there. "Where can we do this, which room do you sleep in?"

"Upstairs, in one of the small bedrooms."

"And you have a condom, right?"

"Oh, yeah, sure." He remembered his road kit, which he always left packed for traveling gigs, and which contained such necessities as Alka-Seltzer, his Advil, earplugs, and, even though he'd never actually needed one while traveling with the band, condoms.

It was she who led him up the stairs to his room.

In the middle of it all, it occurred to Chris to compare the physical experience to the one he'd had with Caroline, or Karen. But there could almost be no comparison, and what he came up with instead was a vague analogy: if what had happened with Karen had been like nourishment, this now was gluttony.

At one point, he had a terrible thought: What if he had been wrong about her and Ted? What if they had just been friends, and all her mysterious reasons for not wanting to see Chris and not wanting to be seen coming to this house were just for effect, a part of playing hard to get that she'd do with anyone?

In that case, you just spent a lot of effort picking up and screwing an ugly older woman, he answered himself. Which wouldn't be so bad anyway, he decided. Although in some way he also felt that now, after he had done this, he would always be just a little bit more damned, even if in the end life was meaningless and it was only in his own mind.

When it was all over, and they were lying in the half dark of the light through the open door with her head on his shoulder, she broke the thick silence.

"Chris, there's something I need to tell you. The reason that I didn't want to have anything to do with you at first, and why I didn't want to come over here, and then why I was actually afraid you'd want to go up to the master bedroom, is that for the past three or so years I've had a running affair with Ted Harper. I know that probably sounds strange to you, but the thing about Ted is that he isn't at all the way he seems at first. He's actually a very lonely man, whose wife and kids pretty much don't even speak to him anymore, from what I understand. But that's why Ted can never find out about this, okay, Chris? And I mean never."

Chris hesitated just a moment. "Oh, Donna, I'm afraid he already knows," he said.

She laughed for just a second, then stopped. "What?"

"Look, Donna, I do like you a lot. There was nothing fake about that. It's just . . . this wasn't as simple as you thought."

"Chris! What the hell are you talking about?!" She still sounded more confused than anything.

"It's just, look, you were honest with me, and I want to be honest with you now. Please don't tell Ted about this, but I already knew about you and him, because he . . . well, he told me. And he also . . . kind of told me to do this."

"What!?"

"I'm sorry, Donna. I really am. I don't know why he did it. Maybe it was just that he was feeling threatened by you or something and wanted me to defuse the situation a little. I told him I'd try. I know I shouldn't have done it, but it's like, you know, I'm kind of totally dependent on him these days."

Chris brought both of his hands up to his face, both to feign guilt and to deflect the blow he expected at any moment.

In a sudden flurry of activity she sat up in the bed, but then all movement stopped again. "You're lying. Why the fuck would he do something like that?"

Chris kept his hands over his face. He felt genuinely guilty now, genuinely like a piece of human garbage—which he used and put into his next line. "Oh, I wish I knew," he said. "I mean, then I could at least tell you that much."

After a few more moments of quiet and stillness, her first punch landed. It got him on his left ear, and he quickly flipped over, protecting his private parts and moving his hands to the back of his head. After that her blows fell mostly on his shoulders and back.

"*You fucking bastard!*" she yelled. "*You little fucking bastard!*" She delivered a flurry of punches, one last punch hitting him square on the back of his neck, before she stood up, tangling in the sheets as she tried to get out of the bed. Chris was afraid for a moment that she would start to kick him, but she didn't, and he heard her fumbling for her clothes instead. After that there were just the sounds of her getting dressed, and a throaty gasp from time to time, which he realized was her crying. Eventually he heard the clacking of her boots on the wooden floor.

"Hey, Chris," she said to him in the silence that followed.

Slowly he turned to face her. She was fully dressed now, standing there in the light coming in through the open door, her disarranged hair and the tears running down her face making her look like some recent crime victim. Before he could react, she spit right in his face.

"FUCKING BASTARD!" she cried out again as she went out the door and down the stairs.

Her footsteps crossed the big house, and then he heard a metallic crash as she broke something—something from the kitchen it sounded like. He heard silverware, or maybe it was knives, clatter to the floor, then a smashing like a plate or a platter, then more of those. It all somewhat alarmed him until he realized that he didn't have to care, that he would be leaving soon enough now, and after all, it was Ted Harper's house. In the midst of all the noise, he heard a squealing bark from the next bedroom: Charlie, freaking out about what was going on.

Finally, the sounds of breakage and curses gave way to softer moans and sobbing.

"I hope you rot in hell, Chris, do you hear me!" she shouted up to him, probably standing at the foot of the stairs. "And you better watch your back from now on, too, you fucking asshole!"

After that came one last crash, a big one, which Chris thought he could identify as her tipping over the wooden cabinet by the door to the garage, the one he'd left the remote door opener on. As if to prove him right, he heard the garage door going up a moment later—which gave him a terrible thought: What if she decided to ram his car as she was leaving?

But apparently her appetite for destruction was only so big, because through his bedroom window he saw her car pull out onto the road without incident. The engine revved up loud, the car pulled away, and soon the place had reverted to silence again.

He was still wearing the condom, and he got up and walked into the bathroom to deposit it directly into the toilet. Then he got dressed and went into the other bedroom to check on Charlie, who ducked his head and backed away as if he'd done something wrong.

"It's okay, boy. It's all over now." Chris went in and sat down next to him, patting him on the side and smoothing the fur on the top of his head. "See? Nothing but a sore back and a sore dick. And where were you to protect me this time, huh? Where were you?"

But soon Chris left off talking to the dog and took him by his collar when he went downstairs so he could lead him through whatever wreckage was there without him cutting up his paws. It wasn't that bad, however. She *had* overturned the cabinet by the stairs, an elaborate wooden antique with drawers on the bottom and framed-glass doors on top. By unlucky chance the piece had landed propped up on one open door so that all the little drawers and items inside the top section had spewed out in a heap on the floor. But aside from that it was mostly small stuff: chairs and stools tipped over; a few plates from the kitchen thrown and broken on the floor; the toaster and the espresso machine tumbled onto the tiling. The idea of doing more damage on his own occurred to Chris, but he elected not to. Donna would enact his true revenge against Ted now. Her accusation would explain everything perfectly, and Chris thought it far more . . . elegant to leave things as they were.

Standing there in the middle of the enormous room, holding Charlie by his collar, Chris took one last look around him. This was how he would always remember Ted Harper's wooden palace by the beach now, he thought regretfully for a moment. But then he decided that it was in some way fitting, a lesson about money and power and possessions. Or something like that—he was sure that in time it would all make sense to him. First thing in the morning he would pack up and leave, and probably only decide where he was going once he got on the road.

After a while Chris turned away and went out the back door to take Charlie for his last night walk along the beach.

PART THREE

·//·

Homecoming

29

When Chris came downstairs the next morning, he had already cleared his things out of the upstairs bathroom and laid them on his bed next to an open duffel bag. He was just on his way to the kitchen to pick through the rubble and put on water for coffee, just so he had something to sip on while he packed, when he glanced over and noticed the person sitting there in the chair across from the sofa in the sunken living room. The sight was so unexpected that, even after noticing the middle-aged man in the black overcoat, Chris's feet continued to walk normally. They carried him another full three steps before his body caught up with his mind and came to a full stop.

"Good morning," the man said turning to him, suggesting that he wasn't just some early-morning hallucination. In the hazy sunlight coming in through the big windows, Chris could see that the man had blond, thinning hair, chubby, boyish features, and that beneath the overcoat he had on a dark sport jacket, a black polo shirt, and khaki slacks. Chris couldn't see what kind of shoes he was wearing because blocking that view, sitting there looking contented if confused while the man slowly worked his fingers through the thick hair at the scruff of his neck, was Charlie. "This place is freezing," the man said next, speaking just as mildly as anyone talking about the weather.

"Who are you?" Chris asked him in simple, artless confusion.

"Oh, call me Stanley," the man answered. "Or Stan, if you want to. I already know that you're Chris, and I've also had the pleasure of Charlie here, too." He gave the dog a little shake, jangling the tag on Charlie's collar and causing the dog to lick his lips. "I gave him some burger meat when I came in," Stanley or Stan explained, "just to keep him quiet so I wouldn't wake you up."

With this information, answering a question that Chris hadn't thought of but should have, his mind woke up to a blizzard of hypotheses: *This is the man Donna's hired to come and kill you,* one voice inside him jabbered. *No, it's just some guy who's a little bit weird who's come to fix the burglar alarm system,* another prayed. But, not having any idea more solid than a guess, Chris didn't know what to say or how to act, or even what question he should ask next. So he just stood there, continuing to gaze at the strange man in his living room.

"Chris, before you get all worked up and start asking me a lot of questions I can't answer, let me just tell you what I know about all this, okay?" the man went on, once again a full step ahead of Chris's reactions. "Now, you work for Ted Harper, whose house this is, right?"

Before he could think to stop himself, Chris nodded.

"Well, as I say, I don't know exactly what all this is about, but somehow, in some way, you must have done something that pissed him off pretty badly—and I'm going to take a wild guess and say it has something to do with why this place looks the way it does."

Chris nodded again, and this time Stan made a face and nodded along with him, as if to say, *Well, that was a pretty stupid thing you did, wasn't it, Chris?*

The man looked like a salesman, Chris thought. Or, no, that wasn't quite right. He looked like some guy you'd meet in a bar who would tell you that he worked *in* sales. And yet his act was still slightly different from that. More than anything else, the no-bullshit, just-between-you-and-me solicitousness reminded Chris of some high school counselor or social worker.

"Well, what can I tell you?" Stan said next. "You fucked with the wrong guy at the wrong time, Chris, and all I can do now is what I've been told to do. But let me just make that point again, because sometimes I say that, and people hear it, but they still don't really understand it, they don't really *get* it. You see, I don't know how you were raised, Chris, or what your situation is or any of that, but you have to understand that for *me,* in *my* job, in *my* situation, I do what I've been told to do, and that's all I *can* do. There isn't any arguing or saying 'No, that's not fair, that's not right.' Okay? The orders come down from above and that's the way it is. Are we clear so far?"

Chris didn't nod this time, he just stood there.

"I'll take that as a yes. Now, a quick other point. Right now you probably don't want to believe any of this. You want to think that there isn't anybody else, any other men outside in a car, probably a whole lot warmer than I am right now. What you'd like to believe is that it's just me, and that this whole thing is a big joke, a big prank. Am I right? Well, you'll save both yourself, and me, an awful lot of trouble and pain if you just take my word for it and don't go through the trouble of finding out for yourself. And I mean, if you think about it, you're in a pretty bad situation here anyway, with no one around and only one way off this place with freezing water on every other side, right? So just . . . stay calm, relax, please.

"Anyway, here's the big thing, this is what I'm here to tell you: You can't leave, Chris. I don't even know if you were planning on leaving or what, but you can't now. No leaving, not even for a little while; no going to the store or going to the police or whatever it is that you're thinking of doing. Just hang out here, and it'll be easier for everybody that way. I brought you some food and put it in the refrigerator, so you won't go hungry or anything. Okay? So that's that. Oh, and look, I'll tell you something else, too. Whatever this is about, it couldn't be *that* bad because, quite frankly, if he wanted you dead, you'd be dead by now. Probably this whole thing will be over before you know it. You'll pay back whatever money you owe him or find some arrangement to make up to him whatever it was that you did, and it'll be over. So, once again, just, you know, hang out for a while, stay calm."

With these last words, the man in the black overcoat leaned forward and stood up, but he stayed bent over slightly; and with some remnant of clear thinking, Chris understood that it was to hang on to Charlie's collar with his left hand. *He just doesn't want me to sic the dog on him before he gets out the door,* Chris thought. But slowly, almost casually, after stepping up onto the higher level of floor where it changed from carpeting to wood planking, Stan reached inside both his coat and his sport jacket to pull out a black, snub-nosed revolver. He came to a stop there, not ten feet from where Chris was standing, placed the short barrel of the gun at the back of Charlie's head right behind the thick bone at the top of his skull, and pulled the trigger with a deafening, earth-shattering roar, the echo of which never really died away but only settled down to a medium-pitched ringing in Chris's ears.

At the very end there, right at the last instant, Chris's mouth formed a single word: *"No."* But he never even managed to say it, and all that came out was a single high-pitched squeak before he averted his gaze, looking off to the left and the chair this man had been sitting in. When Chris looked back, Charlie was lying flat on the floor on his stomach, as he normally would have, only with one back leg sticking out an angle that would have hurt him had he still been alive. Chris didn't look for a wound and didn't see one.

Stan was still fumbling inside his coat, trying to put his gun back in its holster. When he finally got it, he rubbed his hands together and looked at them, then put them in the coat's pockets.

"You need to do just two things today, Chris," he said in almost the exact same calm, confiding tone he'd been using before. "Dig a hole somewhere out on the dunes and bury this dog, and then get the house cleaned up."

After that, he turned and, moving at the same measured, composed pace that he'd done everything else in, he walked out the front door.

30

Chris stood there perfectly still for so long that after a while he could almost convince himself that he had been hallucinating, that none of it had happened; and for those moments when the terrible crushing fear and horror would leave him, he would feel so free and happy he would swear that there was an answer, a solution hidden somewhere inside that feeling; and if he could just somehow grasp and isolate that answer, then none of this would have to be real and he could still pack up and drive away; and Charlie could come, too, because in that alternative reality Charlie would still be alive right now, walking around and wagging his tail and waiting for his morning walk . . .

But always Chris fell back to earth. Back to an earth where his dog was lying about ten feet away with his brain scrambled and probably his spinal cord shattered, a small pool of blood forming around his front legs while a somewhat larger one, of urine, had pooled out on the floor around his hindquarters—Charlie, who would gladly have died rather than even let someone punch *him* out, while Chris had merely stood there and watched his murder.

Finally, Chris sank down to his knees in front of the lifeless animal. Barely aware that he was going to do it, not even thinking himself capable of such an act of grieving, he let out a completely involuntary, high-pitched wailing sound. Only just now did he seem to realize what this dog—purchased when he was still a puppy, something like three years ago, back in the good times when Chris had still been living with Cassie, the dog almost like their surrogate child—had come to mean to him. He thought of all the time he'd spent with Charlie, and how much of that time he'd neglected him, giving him skimpy walks and leaving him for hours trapped alone in that little apartment. Not that Charlie had ever complained, not that he wasn't always ecstatic to see Chris when he would get home at five in the morning, and Chris thought that if he could just have another chance . . .

Eventually, however, fear got him moving again. After all, what if Stan, or Stanley, came back and he was still just kneeling here and hadn't even started on either of his two tasks? What then? Would Stan use his gun again, or would he do something worse than that, something worse than Chris could even imagine?

He forced himself to his feet and went into the garage to look for a shovel, half expecting to find another one of Mr. Harper's sweet-talking goons waiting for him in there. But the garage looked just as it always did, and there weren't any shovels either; this wasn't the kind of house that would *have* a shovel. He walked back through the main room to the kitchen, absently crushing shards of broken plates under his boots, and opened the tall cabinet where the broom and the mop were kept. There weren't any shovels in here either, but down at the bottom he saw something he could use. In fact, it resembled a shovel, and although he knew full well that he was slipping into a kind of delusional, POW mind-set, he nevertheless congratulated himself for his ingenuity, thinking himself at least better off than before. He picked up the dustpan, turned around, and only glancing once briefly at his best friend lying dead in the middle of the floor, went outside through the sliding glass doors.

The morning was cold and damp, with the wind blowing straight off the ocean and right through the wool sweater he was wearing. Almost immediately his ears and bare hands were freezing, yet he didn't even think of going back to get his jacket with his hat and gloves stuffed in the pockets. Instead, he walked almost all the way to the beach before finding what seemed to him a suitable place for Charlie's grave, in a flat patch of bare sand in a natural bowl made by the dunes.

He leaned over and started to dig, but on his second scoop the handle of the plastic dustpan snapped off like the branch of a dead tree. After that he was forced to hold what remained of his tool by its corners, his hands twice as frozen as they came in contact with the cold sand. The hole kept caving in and filling up, but soon enough he was lying on his stomach, reaching down almost as far he could with his implement, ignoring the stinging chill on his tearing face and the deeper pain in his back and shoulders. When he hit a wetter, harder layer of sand, he began making faster progress, but he'd only dug down another six or so inches before he stopped. Slowly—like blood filling a wound, was what came to Chris's mind—water began flooding in, calving off the sides of his hole, threatening to collapse the whole thing. Looking out at the ocean, which was almost flat today, Chris saw that it made sense; you couldn't dig down below sea level this close to the shore without salt water flooding in. But it was probably deep enough, he reasoned—and going and trying to find Ted's gunman to tell him why the burying part couldn't be done didn't seem like a good option anyway. So Chris filled in the hole with just enough sand to cover the water, widened it out in a vague approximation of Charlie's size and shape, and started back to the house.

He was chilled to the bone and covered with sand, but he didn't stop and went straight to the kitchen to get a large Hefty garbage bag and then upstairs to take a single white sheet from the linen closet, thinking or hoping this almost meaningless act of decency and therefore defiance might restore a little of his self-respect.

When he came downstairs, however, carrying the two parts of his shroud, it was as if he were encountering Charlie there for the first time.

They killed him . . . they killed him, they killed him, they killed him, his mind kept repeating, telling it over and over as if it might make some sense to him the next time around. *They killed him . . . they murdered in cold blood probably the most innocent, faithful, proud creature he had ever known. They had done it casually, almost as an afterthought. "Oh, and by the way . . ."*

But was that even the right way to think about it? Chris wondered right then. Was it really a *they* who had done it—some organized crime syndicate or whoever, either hired by Ted or somehow connected with him, the way Stan had presented it? Or was it really only two men Chris should be thinking about here: Stan, or whoever he really was, who had pulled the trigger, and Ted Harper, who had hired him to? Because how *did* Chris know this wasn't actually the same as before, where Ted had paid people to put on an act. In this case, that act had included killing an animal—there was no way in the world to fake the carnage lying right in front of him—but was that really such a big deal? Wasn't shooting a dog something that your average thug could be expected to do if you paid him well enough?

For the first time that day, ever since Chris had seen that gun and heard that shot, he didn't feel completely cowed, completely helpless. And daring to feel anger, he vowed that if it was within some kind of reason—if Stanley or Stan wasn't connected to some huge crime organization, and Ted Harper *was* merely a businessman who had hired him—Chris would take, or try to take, his revenge on both of them. He didn't know exactly what type of revenge that would be yet, whether it involved suing them or actually prosecuting them for kidnapping—which was, after all, what they were doing to him right now—but he vowed that, when eventually he got out of here, he would be brave enough to try it.

In this state of mind, Chris found the strength to deal with the matter in front of him, and he did it by first laying the Hefty bag down so that it completely covered Charlie (trying not to breathe in the smells of blood and piss and gunpowder lingering in the air, which he nevertheless did), then rolling the inert dog toward him so that he was on his side, his two upmost legs just stiff enough so they straightened out only slowly to rest on the floor again. After that, Chris unfolded the half of the garbage bag not underneath the dog, extending a bridge over the foul pools of fluid on the floor, then tucked one edge of the sheet directly under Charlie's back, between him and the bag. Unavoidably, when he did this, he touched Charlie's bare fur, which felt exactly the same, just as thick and lush as when he had been alive. He had to touch the dog again after that, grabbing two lifeless legs to roll him onto the sheet, and this time he heard the heartbreaking jangle of his single ASPCA tag, which Chris could remember getting for him and attaching to his collar with a pair of pliers. He took one last look at Charlie's slack face and brownish, lolling tongue, then rolled him over once more and covered him with the sheet.

After that it was somewhat easier. Chris rolled the dog over again and again, until the body was neatly wrapped up, with only the stains that couldn't be avoided coming through the layers of white fabric— those slowly spreading blood spots making the whole thing look like some civil war movie prop to Chris.

He had lifted Charlie many times before, when they were playing together or for one reason or another, but now the dog seemed much heavier, he supposed because of the effect of what people called dead weight. At last, though, he got the miniature corpse up against his chest and went out through the open door.

When he got back to the hole he had dug, he was so out of breath he almost dropped the big dog lowering him in. He picked up his broken dustpan and bent over to start covering the body, but paused. This was the part of the funeral where you were supposed to say something, he thought. Only he didn't have anything to say, and it seemed ridiculous and pathetic to do it under these circumstances. So instead, he silently renewed the vow he had taken earlier: to, if it was at all possible or reasonable, try to eventually seek some justice.

And then, telling himself he would have done something like this with Charlie anyway, Chris began to fill in the grave.

31

While he was in the kitchen filling up a pail with warm water to go clean the blood and piss off the floor in the other room, just feeling numb now, frozen to the core of both body and mind, he looked up and found himself staring at the telephone. Quickly, he looked down into the sink again. He had been so freaked out before, he hadn't even thought of it. *But could it be that simple?* he wondered. *Just pick it up and call 911 and, when the police come, run out to the car and jump in? And was that what they're actually expecting me to do? Is the joke really over now, and I can leave anytime I want—and here I am still cleaning up the house like an idiot?*

Or, was he being watched even now?

But, glancing around the room, Chris didn't see where they could be watching him from. He had just been out on the dunes, so he knew no one was out there, and the three front windows looked out on driveway, road, and then low beach grass beyond, where someone would have to be lying deep down in there, in exactly the right spot, with binoculars.

Suddenly he was almost certain that he had been taken again, that he could walk out of here, or drive out of here, anytime he wanted. Of course he could. The guy coming and threatening him and killing Charlie had just been Ted Harper's parting gift, another play, this time a one-act. Well, he *was* leaving now, Chris thought; he was leaving, but after that he was going to keep a certain promise he'd made to a late friend of his.

Reaching over with the water still running, Chris picked up the receiver of the white wall phone and put it to his ear. Slowly, he set it back in its cradle. It didn't mean anything, he told himself. A dead phone was easy; one snipped cable somewhere; it was probably just supposed to delay him a little more, so that he'd actually have to drive himself to the police station and hopefully think better of it on the way. But, turning off the taps, he went into the kitchen closet again to get the mop.

It was probably pathetic, probably "Stan" was somewhere far away by now, laughing himself silly while he counted out his money on the front seat of his car coasting down the freeway. But Chris couldn't be sure it was a game anymore, and he simply didn't have the courage to take the chance.

He was almost done cleaning up the house, having twice emptied bucketfuls of dark-stained water into the downstairs bathroom toilet, and having used the sandy, broken dustpan the way it was meant to be used to pick up the broken china and glass scattered everywhere, when he found something. He had just righted the overturned chest of drawers by the door to the garage, and while scooping up the various assorted crap—old flashlight batteries, notepads, a book of crosswords, kite string, scissors—he saw it taped to the back of one of the little drawers. Chris snapped off the old, yellowing Scotch tape and looked at it. It was a small key, like for a bank deposit box only with no number on it; it said Kreig, and nothing more. Without a definite reason for doing it, he stuck it in his back pocket.

After he was done with the cabinet—which had one broken pane of glass but was otherwise okay—he went over to the couch and sat down. He was still freezing, his teeth chattering if he let them, and he hunched over and flipped on the heater. The fan inside whirred to life, air began to blow out, and he rubbed his still-sandy hands in the slowly warming flow, eventually getting down on one knee to be closer to the heat. Glancing behind the couch as he did this, he did a double take.

His stuff was gone. All of it: all four of his electrics—his Strat, his SG, his Danelectro, and his Rickenbacker 330—plus his acoustic, plus his amp, plus his entire effects rack, his digital and his DAT recorders, his mikes. He stood up and looked around the room. He must have been in shock not to have noticed it earlier, he thought, and he was still acting irrationally, looking around as if these large items might be hiding behind a chair or in a dark corner where he couldn't see them.

He began to walk across the room. On the way he thought of something else and went and opened the door to the garage and flipped on the lights again. But his car was definitely still there, which seemed strange to him until he happened to notice what was different about it. Looking through the windshield, he saw a red line coming up off the black steering wheel, an object that he could identify even before he'd gotten close enough to read the words "The Club" on the side of the plastic-coated steel bar. It was a device he had never owned, and so driving out of here wasn't an option after all. Or, he supposed that he could drive, as long as it was straight backward into the bay. In a new and rising state of both anger and panic he walked back into the house, went to the front door, opened it, and went outside.

The cold wind was newly painful on his cheeks and hands after his brief time with the heater, but he ignored it and studied the view. He could see no one; the place looked as it always did: road to the right, road to the left, and in front about two acres of beach grass and then smooth, shining water. Before he could lose his nerve, he started walking again, putting his aching hands in his pockets and following the gravel driveway.

He stopped well before the halfway point. To his left, about four football fields down the road, he could now see a car. It was pulled off to the side, sitting with two wheels in the brush facing toward the house—silver and boxy, American, like a Buick or a Cadillac. Chris first kneeled, then sat down on the driveway, wondering if he'd already been seen; wondering conversely if there were even people in the car, or if it, like the phone and his newly theft-proof Mustang, wasn't possibly just another obstacle left behind to slow him down.

The longer he stayed there, the more likely that second scenario seemed to him. After all, why would "Stan" and whoever was supposedly with him want to sit in a car all day when they could just as well be inside. If they were really supposed to be keeping an eye on him, it was a lousy way to do it, and how would they eat and go to the bathroom and all that?

But as if to answer his last question, as he sat there watching over the top of the blowing, undulating beach grass, another car pulled up. This one was black, and it drove up beside the silver one and stopped there for some time, as if its occupants were conversing through open windows. Then it pulled in front of the silver car, and the silver one backed out, did a few K-turns on the narrow road to turn around, and drove away.

Chris felt his stomach sink, his testicles shrink up into his pelvis. So there really was a *they,* and *they* really *were* watching him. And now that Chris thought about it, if all they were trying to do was keep him here, it really wasn't such a bad place for a lookout after all. There was no way he could swim across the bay down at the other end where it was widest, which was the only place they wouldn't see him, and since the spit of land got narrower by the bridge, the beach coming to an end well before the marshy little inlet separating the island from the mainland, his only other conceivable route of escape was cut off as well. He supposed he *might* make it that way, sliding along on his stomach, trying to stay behind dunes and bushes and praying no one happened to notice him, but he wasn't about to try it.

With his heart thudding in fear once more, his missing guitars and equipment all but forgotten, Chris crawled over the sharp gravel to the front door and went back inside. He walked through the house and immediately went out again through the sliding doors on the ocean side.

And then he started running, not toward the beach but directly away from the car he had seen, choosing a course to keep the house between him and however many men were sitting inside of it. He came to a steep dune face and climbed over it rather than go around. He came to a natural hedge of prickly bushes and just blasted right through, keeping his hands up high, ignoring the stinging, scratching pain and the tearing devastation of his sweater. When he judged he'd gone far enough, he found a relatively low pass over the dunes to the beach and cut through, bending over like a soldier in combat. In the soft sand on the other side he struggled to keep up the pace until he came to the turn-in for the house with the spire on top.

Completely out of breath, his heart pounding at a sickeningly fast rate, he stomped up onto the deck. The key was still above the window where he'd last left it, and fumbling it in his numb hands, he let himself in as he'd done before. He ran into the kitchen, spraying sand from his boots and the cuffs of his pants, and grabbed for the phone, clamping it painfully against his ear.

But it was just the same as the other one; he might as well have been listening to a stone. He put the receiver down on the counter and bent over and laid his head down next to it. For a moment he thought of the other two houses. Could it be that this phone had merely been shut off by the phone company, and that they, whoever *they* were, hadn't actually thought about him trying this, and so he might still find one of the other phone lines turned on? But Chris didn't believe it, and suddenly it seemed completely crazy to have risked coming here. Suddenly it seemed more than likely that Stan, or maybe another one this time, would come to check on his progress and see how he was doing, and when he wasn't there . . . But Chris didn't even want to think about that.

Retracing his steps, he quickly locked up the house and headed back.

As far as Chris knew, no one ever did come to check up on him that day, though. He spent the remainder of it either in front of the heater trying to get warm, or walking restlessly from room to room, already missing Charlie, stopping every now and then when he came to the place where he'd died and reliving it all over again, in either extreme grief or the most bitter anger.

At some point he realized he was famished and went and opened the refrigerator. True to Stan's word, it had been stocked. There, still in two plastic shopping bags, were an assortment of basic, no-frills groceries including large tubs of peanut butter and jelly, a loaf of Wonder bread, a six-pack of Miller cans, a dozen eggs, a quart of milk, three slowly thawing frozen pizzas, a box of similarly thawing frozen waffles, and a pack of Marlboro reds with matches.

For whatever reason, these items, or just their being there, freaked Chris out as badly as the cars on the road had, and he shut the door and went to sit on the couch again. Soon his hunger made him stand up and go back, however. He hated doing it, but he'd been planning on leaving for some time now, and practically nothing else was in the house. He pulled open the Wonder bread and made himself a pair of what his mother used to call PB&J sandwiches and ate them standing at the counter. After that, he made a third and even considered cracking one of the beers to go with it. But he decided he should keep his mind sharp and had a glass of tap water instead.

On the couch again, somewhat calmer, Chris thought he figured a few things out: "Stan," and whoever else, were staying out of the house because they didn't want him to be able to identify them at some later date. That first visit had been unavoidable, but now they were content to watch the place from a distance. Which in turn suggested that, whatever this was about, whether it was another "play" like before—albeit a far more serious and dangerous one this time—or the real thing, they at least didn't plan on killing him after it was over. Which Chris found encouraging.

For now, it seemed, they just wanted him here, waiting, without the comfort of either his dog or his guitars, and yet with plenty of food. But what were they all waiting *for*? What was *going* to happen? Obviously it was something, because they weren't just going to keep him here until summer. So, what?

If Chris were to believe "Stan," then even *he* didn't know the answer. *I don't think it's too bad, or else you'd be dead already,* he had said. But *should* Chris believe that? The more he considered it, the less he thought he should. In almost all likelihood, this was just another of Ted's games; and probably, if he really wanted to test that theory, he could walk out of here right now and no one would stop him.

But Chris never did, and when darkness fell, even though it theoretically gave him a better chance of slipping away, he felt less rather than more inclined to try it. In fact, by then he'd even had the idea that he *wanted* to stay, that he *should* stay. Because when it was all over, he was going straight to the police and some lawyer or lawyers, who were all going to prosecute and sue the shit out of Ted Harper, for kidnapping and any other charges that applied. And the longer he remained here and did what he was told now, Chris thought, the more viable those charges would be.

When *that* was all over, he told himself once, he might end up owning this house after all. Although he would just sell it. He never wanted to see the place again.

32

Lying in bed that night, however, Chris's judgment swung back the other way. The exact words that Stan had said, and the way he had said them, kept coming back to him:

You fucked with the wrong guy at the wrong time.

If he wanted you dead, you'd be dead by now.

And what began to bother Chris most was this: He believed that Ted Harper could find some thug willing to come in and threaten him and kill a dog, and certainly others to sit there in a car all day. *And* he believed that Ted Harper could find some actor who could deliver lines like Stan had. But could he find someone to do both—a good actor willing to kill a dog with a gun? That didn't quite add up. And if that didn't add up, didn't *that* mean that Stan, or whatever his name was, *was* basically telling the truth; and that Ted Harper really was a seriously bad man as had been implied, and as Sam Burnett, the disgruntled caretaker, had tried to warn him?

The logic made Chris sit up in bed. If this really was the case, should he then try to escape tonight after all? Or shouldn't he?

Right then he had another idea, though, and reached up and flipped on the lamp on the bedside table. His jeans were on the chair by the dresser, and he felt in the back pocket and pulled out the key he had found. It was about the right size, he judged, and he threw off the covers and began to get dressed again.

Going up to bed that night, still thinking it was to some extent part of the game, he had left all the downstairs lights on in a pretend vigilance, so it didn't worry him too much turning on the desk lamp in Ted Harper's bedroom. The modern lamp had a dimmer in the switch, and Chris turned it down so that it barely put out the light of a candle. Then he put the key in the single keyhole on the front of the desk. It went in on the first try and turned a quarter-turn to the left with an audible click from some internal mechanism. He tried the bottom drawer first and found that it slid open easily.

Inside were file folders, most of them the kind with metal bars running through the tops and hooks on the sides, even though the wooden drawer had no rails for them to hang from. He reached up and slid the lamp to the edge of the desk so he could see better, then ended up sitting cross-legged on the cold floor. Most of the files had handwritten dates on their tabs. *Jan-Feb 89,* said one. *Aug 91,* another. He pulled this one halfway out and looked at the top page.

BILL OF LADING

Chris tried to make some sense of the thin, parchmentlike document, but it was just lists of numbered packages and their weights. There were more behind the first one, along with what looked like amendments to each: last-minute adjustments, perhaps, when they were loading up the ship. Ted ran, or owned, some kind of shipping company, so Chris supposed that this was the kind of records he would keep. Why these files were here in his summerhouse and not in his office didn't seem like an important question. And then he came to a different, more official-looking, sheet of paper.

NOTICE OF IMPOUNDMENT

The title company is hereby informed of the impoundment of the ship Spirit of Galway, *by the United States Coast Guard, for inspection of its cargoes,* he read.

He closed this file and opened the one behind it, *Dec 86.* It was pretty much the same thing: the first pages were more bills of lading for the *Spirit of Galway,* then more attachments behind that. And then, in the middle of this file, too: *The title company is hereby informed of the impoundment of the ship* Spirit of Galway.

So maybe it was just something that happened all the time, Chris thought. And, after all, the ship had still been sailing after this one happened, so they couldn't have found anything. But then in the next file, *Oct 85,* it was the same thing again: another bill of lading for *Spirit of Galway,* followed by the attachment pages, then followed by the impoundment. What did it mean?

But, then again, why *were* these files here, and not back at Ted's office or wherever they belonged? That almost all of them had the metal bars and hooks suggested strongly that they'd been taken from some other filing system, and there certainly weren't enough of them to be his only files, the only business his company had done. It was only this one ship, *Spirit of Galway,* every time she sailed seemed to go straight into impoundment with the U.S. Coast Guard.

Soon Chris noticed something else as well. At the bottom of each notice of impoundment there was a signature that was always the same, and typed below it the name John D. Tomasko, Supervising Lieutenant, U.S. Customs Department.

In between the next two files, jammed down there at the bottom where it looked as if it wasn't supposed to be found, was a yellowing newspaper clipping. Chris carefully tweezed it out and looked at it. It was a small article with the headline:

MAN SHOT IN DISPUTE
OVER PARKING SPACE
Washington, May 21

Police are still trying to understand how a simple dispute over a parking space at the White Flint Mall in Bethesda could have escalated into deadly violence and murder this afternoon, when one of the two men involved apparently drew a gun and shot the other twice in the head. But the one witness to the shooting, whose name is currently being withheld, reportedly states that it was just that simple, the argument starting when the gunman's car attempted to back into the same spot that the other car, the victim's, was driving into going forward.

The victim, 53-year-old Jeffrey Bauer, a Washington lobbyist and businessman and longtime resident of the Chevy Chase area, was dead by the time an ambulance arrived.

Police say they have a good description of both the gunman and the car he was driving, and are currently looking . . .

Slowly, with his hand trembling slightly, Chris reached up and pulled open the wide center drawer of the desk. He took out the framed letter he had read so long ago, before any of this had started, and quickly scanned it again. *I'm writing to you personally today, before lawyers and accountants get involved . . . how my investment capital ended up entirely in I.C.L. stock, when this was clearly . . . I am hereby demanding that the situation be rectified immediately . . . If, however, the situation is not immediately corrected . . .*

The name was the same, Jeffrey Bauer, and although there was no year on the newspaper clipping, Chris had little doubt that the letter, dated May 13, 1976, had been written only a week or so before the article.

For a long time he just sat there, going between the two items. There was still a chance it was some weird coincidence, he told himself. Ted's framing of the letter even suggested it; he wouldn't be so bold as to actually frame a threatening document from someone he'd killed or had killed . . . would he? Or was a fight over a parking space exactly the kind of thing that he might stage.

Chris folded the article up and slipped it back where it had been, then resumed rummaging through the files. He stopped when he came to more newsprint, this time actually crumpled down between the leaves near the back. The whole page was there on this one, and it was much whiter and newer. It had been ripped from a *Miami Herald,* with the very recent date along the top of August 8, 2001. It didn't take Chris long to find what he was looking for.

CUSTOMS AGENT
KILLED IN DROWNING

Quickly, he scanned through this brief article, about a death at sea on a stormy night during some kind of rescue-and-recovery operation. He somehow already knew that the name of the deceased agent would be John Tomasko.

Chris folded the second article and put it back and shut the drawer.

Then he picked up the framed letter, put it back, glass up as before, and shut that drawer, too. Still sitting on the floor, he spun himself around and leaned back against the big desk with his arms crossed over his stomach. His heart was pounding in fear now, and he thought that, if there was still a way, if it was still possible, he would be happy to give up and admit defeat in whatever game they were playing; not go to the police or anything, but just be grateful for his life and his freedom back.

Only now, for the first time in his life, he realized he was in a situation where he had no options, not even running away. Because even if he could get by the guys near the bridge, where would he go? Unless he was prepared to spend the rest of his life on the lam, working for cash and using a fake name, he truly believed that Ted Harper and his men would find him, or maybe even go after his family. And reasonably, in the real world where Arnold Schwarzenegger was just an actor and *Miami Vice* just a dumb old television show, there was nothing he could do, nothing that wasn't crazy and stupid and would get himself killed. That is, if he wasn't sitting here waiting for his execution anyway.

Miserably, Chris turned his head to the side. He was looking at the handle of the other side drawer, the top one. Shaking to the point where it was hard to keep his balance, he got to his knees and slid this one open. But it was empty inside, with no files or anything. He only discovered what *was* there, way down at the bottom, when he bent over to look in—and moaned out loud when he did. With a badly, almost uncontrollably, shaking hand, he reached in and pulled it out and laid it on the desk.

It was the scariest-looking handgun he had ever seen, a sleek, jet-black automatic with beautiful curves etched into its essentially squared-off shape. On the side of the barrel and on the handgrip it read SIG-SAUER P228, and in various other places it said 9MM and MADE IN GERMANY. On the front of the gun was something he had never seen before except in movies: attached to the end of the barrel, about an inch in diameter and elongating the weapon another six or seven inches, was a matte black silencer. Three black magazines for the gun were still in the drawer, and one by one, Chris brought these out and laid them on the desk, too. He wasn't exactly sure why he was doing it, but he was pretty sure that what he was looking at represented the end of his life. Then the image of the gun and the magazines went blurry as he gave in to helpless weeping.

Eventually, Chris put the gun and the magazines back, locked up the desk, slid the light to where it had been, and turned it off. He went to his room again, got back into bed, but didn't turn off his own light and didn't take off his clothes. For a long time he cried, sometimes in self-pity, but mostly just out of fear. He fell asleep for what felt like only a split second, but when he woke up, there was light outside his window. He tried to take courage from that, from making it through the night alive, but in the end he couldn't because, more than anything else, the new day marked the passage of time. And somehow he was positive that, whatever it was they were all waiting for, it would happen today.

He happened to glance at his watch beside the bed, and when he did he saw that the calendar numbers had reset themselves. It was December 1.

33

The big event finally occurred at a little after nine o'clock. Chris was still upstairs in bed, but he heard the crunching of tires on gravel through his window, soon followed by the motor hum of the garage door opening. The sounds were for some reason astonishing, startling, and mind-bending in the silence, even though, when Chris thought about it, it was exactly what he'd been expecting: Ted Harper's black homecoming. Slowly, he threw off the covers and stood up.

So this is really it, he thought. *Now I'll either live or die—right now!*

Yet even after a whole night of sobbing over this idea, he couldn't quite make himself believe it. In all likelihood, he reasoned, the worst he would get was badly beaten up, either by Ted or by someone else while Ted watched. And while Chris dreaded this, too, was terrified and sickened by the very idea of this, he didn't think hiding in his room would help any. If anything, he thought, it would make matters worse. He opened his door and went out.

He stopped in the bathroom first to splash some water on his face and take what he still considered might be his last piss ever, and by the time he came downstairs and into the main room, Ted Harper was already sitting on one of the kitchen stools. He was wearing a white fisherman's sweater over a blue denim shirt this morning, and he must have gone into his liquor cabinet to pour himself a glass of what looked like straight Scotch. In passing, Chris thought that he was never more glad about anything than that he had managed not to plunder that particular inventory in his time here alone.

Everything was pretty much as Chris had expected, until, as he slowly crossed the room, Mr. Harper, instead of turning angrily to face him, turned away, looking down at the bar and his drink. Not knowing what else to do, Chris just kept walking, until he was standing almost right next to him.

"My wife . . . my family. It's all over now," Ted said at last, breaking the weird silence. Shockingly, the man was right on the verge of tears.

"What?" Chris said softly.

"She left me—my wife. This was the last straw for her, Chris. My wife . . . my family. And that was about all I had left for me. That was all."

"Mr. Harper, what are you talking about? Why?"

Ted looked up then, and in one instant his face changed, switched over like some monochrome traffic signal: from red sorrow to red rage. *"Because that dang BITCH that YOU slept with called her up and told about US, that's why!"* he roared.

"What?" Chris barely mouthed.

"Don't you play coy with me, Chris Nielson! Whatever it was you did to her or said to her, she came after me like a mongoose for a snake, boy! And by the time she got through, Ellen was already on the other line calling for a lawyer. Oh, you fucked me but good with this one!"

Amazingly, Chris hadn't ever even considered this aspect of the thing—what Donna would have said or done to Ted to make him send his hit men to kill Charlie and hold his house sitter like a convict awaiting trial. And it turned out it was worse than Chris would have ever imagined: she hadn't even spoken to Ted, *she had spoken to his wife.*

"Mr. Harper, look, you have to believe me," Chris said somewhat unsteadily, standing with one hand on the back of a kitchen stool, trying to gesture with the other while keeping it from shaking. "I didn't know that was going to happen. I just . . . I got upset when Donna told me that she'd had an affair with you, because I—"

"DON'T YOU LIE TO ME!" Ted Harper stood up now, almost knocking over the stool he'd been sitting on. He came right up to Chris, pointing his finger like some Bible illustration of a wrathful God. *"I know what you did, you son of a snake! And I know why you did it, too! I* set out . . . I *reached* out to teach you a lesson and change your life for the better, Chris. I spent my hard-earned money to do it. And for that you saw fit to stab me in the back in the most vile, underhanded way you could come up with. ISN'T THAT RIGHT, CHRIS!"

Chris cowered back from the bigger, taller man, who for a long time continued to stand there, making Chris sure that at any moment the slapping, punching, and kicking would start—which he swore he wouldn't fight back against; which, he told himself now so that he wouldn't forget, fighting back at all against would mean certain death, whether that death was delivered by Ted personally with whatever gun he had on him, or by one of his professional killers outside in a car.

The violence never came, however. Ted Harper finally regained control of himself, took a few meaningless steps while wiping his eyes with his fingertips, and then went back to sit on his stool with his drink again.

"But I'm not going to give in to my anger with you, Chris," he said from there. "I'm not going to because I now recognize that that was partially to blame for what happened with my own son. Because, believe it or not, you're kind of like a son to me. I knew you when you were only yea high"—he didn't bother to show Chris how high—"and I feel that same kind of responsibility toward you. And that's why I now aim to finish the job I started with you myself."

For the first time since Ted had stood up, Chris raised his eyes from the floor. "What . . . what job is that?" he asked as delicately as he could.

"The job of turning you into a man, Chris, growing you up. Your problem, as I see it, is that you never had any real authority or guidance in your upbringing. Now I know your father, and your father is a fine man. But I also know that, due to certain weaknesses in his character, he wasn't always around to take as strong a hand with you as he should have. Now we're going to find out if it's not too late."

"Mr. Harper . . . What do you mean, how?"

"Well, you're going to find out how pretty soon. But first, one more thing. Don't you ever try to pretend like you're not getting off easy with me after what you did, Chris Nielson. Don't you *ever* do that."

"Yes, sir," Chris heard himself saying.

"Now hurry up and get ready. I've got some work for you to do."

"Work? . . . What kind of work?"

"I will show you what kind of work, but first you better go and get ready. Put on a coat, a hat, and some gloves. And if you haven't eaten any breakfast, I guess you better eat something, too."

34

Following Ted Harper's commands in the order he had given them, Chris first went upstairs and pulled on his leather jacket. When he came down again, Ted had moved to the chair in the living room and was looking away from him, staring out through the big window at the half clouded sky and gray ocean. Chris went into the kitchen as quietly as he could. He was so scared that even the idea of eating made him feel like puking. But today he aimed to please, and he opened up the refrigerator and looked inside. Not able to think of anything better and reasoning that it was about the only thing he had a chance of holding down anyway, he made himself another peanut butter and jelly sandwich, a single one this time. He ate it off a plate that was already in the sink, standing out of Ted's line of vision, and washed it down with another cup of water.

He had barely finished when he heard Ted standing up. "Okay, Chris, time to go," was announced.

Chris put his cup and plate in the sink and walked around to meet Mr. Harper by the front door. Ted opened it, and just as they went outside, a car pulled over on the road at the head of the driveway, facing toward the point end of the island. It was the silver sedan that he'd seen down by the bridge yesterday, Chris was pretty sure, and by the time they reached it and Ted got into the passenger seat, Chris recognized the driver, too. It was Stan, the thug who'd shot and killed Charlie. Chris stood there outside the car for a moment, thinking desperately of what this could mean and what he should do or try to do, but finally he gave up and opened the back door and got in with them.

No one said anything as they started to move, and in an instant Chris was certain that he was being driven to his death, that Ted's whole speech about making him a man had been bullshit and just a way to keep him calm before he took him out and shot him. The food he'd eaten began to force its way back up his esophagus, out of which he was about to retch it all over the plush red interior of this Lincoln Town Car, or whatever mob-mobile they were driving. On top of that he felt as if he had a high fever, one of those where everything becomes slightly unreal, or possibly that was his mind buckling rather than face the singular reality it kept deducing again and again.

They drove all the way to the end of the road, stopping where the two lanes dead-ended onto sand and beach grass. Then the engine was killed, and both Ted and Stan got out, slamming their doors behind them. Chris wondered if he just stayed inside, locked the doors, and refused to get out, if they would still kill him. But of course they would. He looked at the steering column, thinking of jumping in the front seat, starting the engine again, and peeling out of here in reverse. But of course Stan also knew about things like that and had taken the keys with him.

Chris opened the door and pulled himself to his feet. Stan had gone around to the trunk and was opening it, reaching down inside for something. What he pulled out was a brand-new shovel, the metal parts shiny and silver and glinting in the sun, the wood of the shaft light and raw, glaring with an orange price sticker. Chris was sure he was going to throw up or pass out or both; he was hanging on to the open car door as if it were a life raft, while also swaying back and forth the way someone would riding a bus or a subway. The two men seemingly took no notice of him. Stan merely clicked the trunk shut, and then he and Ted were walking up the driveway of the last house, the gray box that Chris had been to only that one time before.

Watching them walk away, Stan in his black overcoat, Ted wearing just his white sweater, Chris thought of the thousand and one times he'd seen this scene played out in movies: the repentant, passive victim being taken to the scene of his own murder. And what Chris had never understood until right now was why that guy didn't at least try *something:* running away, attacking, whatever. While perhaps having only a tiny chance of working, it always seemed that you might as well go out with at least that little bit of dignity. But Chris had never factored in the sheer debilitation of horror; the way, knowing you were in all likelihood going to die, your guts had already turned to mush and it was all you could do to take another breath and stay on your feet. It made perfect sense to him now that he should follow his murderers-to-be, and that he should obey all of their orders down to the last one, which would probably be to open his mouth so one of them could put a gun inside and blow his brains out the back of his skull.

Pushing off from the car by dint of sheer willpower, once more feeling something like madness swarming up in his brain, Chris began to stumble after them. He was crying again, which he might not even have noticed for how little he cared, except that once more the tears felt like icicles grafted onto his cheeks.

Halfway down the driveway, they cut off onto the sand, heading toward the ocean dunes, which were much closer than at Ted's place since this house was so much nearer to the water. Still, Chris couldn't keep up, and when they both stopped and turned back to look for him, standing on the last high point before the sand sloped away to the lower level of the beach, he was probably ten yards behind. He finally managed to get within twenty feet of them, but after that he could walk no more. His legs were trembling almost to the point where he was going to collapse, and he couldn't seem to raise his feet high enough to clear the soft sand.

He saw Stan turn away, no doubt in disgust, and then Ted took the shovel and was coming toward him with it. Chris just turned away. He was trembling all over, cowering, and the biggest act of self-defense he could manage was to keep from shitting his pants.

"Okay, Chris, let me explain this to you," Mr. Harper said practically to his back, seemingly oblivious to the hunched-over crying. "Take a look at the beach and the dune line here. You see how, where the greenery ends, how the wind and the water have cut away the sand down flat to the level of the beach. That's because the two kinds of grasses here, what they call marram and woolly hudsonia, hold the sand. They act like a carpet or a big tarp over everything, and as long as they're there erosion can't occur. At least, that's the theory. So what I want from you, Chris, I want you to go around the edges, and I want you to dig up the grass."

Ted demonstrated how where he was standing, driving the shovel into the ground and levering the handle, tearing up a shovelful of sand and grass.

"Okay? I want you to work all along the edge of the point here. Start with, say, two feet, you know, and work your way around. Try not to make it look too obvious, try to keep the same contours it had before, but I want you to make some progress with this. And if you get done with that two-foot stretch today, you can either go back and start on another two feet, or you can keep working your way down the beach in the other direction. Either way, though, you don't have to touch the sand underneath. The storms will take care of that. Yes, sir, the storms will come, Chris. On the old shipping charts, this place was called Point O'Fury, because of the way the big ones would pull through here and the surf would jack up over the bar, and after each one they had to rechart the whole place because nothing was the same as it was before. So just don't worry about that, Chris. Are we clear?"

Chris nodded, barely having heard, and yet having fastened on every word, knowing they might well be the last he would ever hear. And when, out of the corner of his eye, he saw that the shovel was actually being offered to him, and that there was actually a chance—a small chance, he thought, but a chance—that Ted really didn't mean to kill him right now, he practically lunged at it.

He took it and jogged over to where the declivity of the first line of white dunes met the flat of the beach grass, and there, with one foot up on the turf and the other sinking into steep, crumbly sand, he drove in the shovel as he'd been shown to pry up a rough square of plant life. For a moment he almost panicked. Ted had shown him the first half of the process, but he hadn't shown or told him what to do with the stuff he'd dug up. For what felt like forever, Chris stood frozen with his first load balanced on the shovel, positive that if he did the wrong thing, he would immediately get shot for it. Finally, for the purpose of being clandestine, he chose the grass side and threw the chunk of sod deep in where the brush was thicker and it vanished satisfactorily. Immediately he moved over and drove in the shovel again.

Out of the corner of his eye, while working at a frantic pace, Chris saw Ted nod and walk over to Stan. The two of them conversed for a little while—about thirty shovelfuls worth—and then Stan reached into his pants pocket and handed Ted what had to be the car keys. After that, Ted made his way back through the dunes and up the driveway alone. Soon Chris heard the car start, and the next time he glanced up, he caught a glimpse of the silver vehicle heading back toward the bridge and Ted's house.

35

Chris had made it only about twenty feet from where he'd started, chopping away the thin layer of grass down to the white, raw sand beneath in the two-foot-wide swath Ted had asked for, when his shoulder cramped up horribly. He rested for a moment and rubbed at it through the leather of his jacket, but then once he'd stopped, his whole body protested, all of the muscles in his arms and back stitching in sick exhaustion. He'd been working too quickly, he was out of shape, and before he even knew he was going to do it, he bent over and disgorged the entire contents of his stomach, which came up as a yellow, acid-tasting gruel. After he was done with that, he realized he was drenched in sweat, and in a second or two he began to shiver.

Stan, who'd been smoking a cigarette as he watched, came over. "You okay?" he said.

"Yeah." Chris kicked sand over the mess he'd made and didn't look at Stan, didn't want this evil, cruel man to see his fear or worse, his hatred.

"Take it easy, you got all day to do this shit."

"Right," Chris said, trying to breathe normally, picking up the shovel and just concentrating on one move at a time now: dig, pry, lift, throw. Because maybe all he had to do was keep going, he told himself; maybe this was really all they wanted from him, and afterward he could leave.

It turned out Stan was right about one thing, though: he did have all day. Chris worked and worked, making it all the way around to where he could see the smooth water of the bay on the other side of the gray house. By which point his watch, which he'd risked glancing down at, told him it was almost five, and the sun had slid across the sky and started to set, the sand already a dim blue in its waning light. And by which point Chris also thought he had never been in such total pain in his life, from his blistering, freezing-cold hands, to his aching back, to his throat baking in thirst and his stomach throbbing with hunger.

At last Stan came over to him again, this time standing up to do it because he'd been sitting in the sand—just sitting there staring out at the water for hours on end with the collar of his overcoat turned up while Chris grew steadily sicker, colder, and weaker destroying another man's property for Ted Harper's sick amusement—and told him it was time to quit. He patted Chris on the back once while doing it, making Chris seriously consider taking a swing at him with the shovel. Stan, perhaps reading his mind, took it away.

After that, Chris followed him back to the driveway of the gray house, trudging along about ten or twenty feet behind, so utterly spent he thought he might fall down in the soft sand and not be able to get up, and Stan would have to shoot him like a lame horse anyway. Yet still Chris noticed it the instant Stan's right hand, the one not carrying the shovel, disappeared under his overcoat and reached for something on his hip. This time when his hand reappeared, however, it was holding not a snub-nosed revolver but a cell phone. Stan pushed a button, held the small black box to his ear, had a short conversation Chris couldn't hear, and then put the phone away again.

Whatever else Stan might have said, he'd seemed to have called for a lift, because when they reached the road, the other car, the black one, was coming for them. It drove with its lights off despite the impending darkness and U-turned and backed up so that when it stopped, it was already facing the other way.

"Come on," Stan said, opening the back door for Chris, motioning with the blade of the shovel for him to get in.

Chris sat down and the door slammed closed behind him. It was another big American car, an Oldsmobile? Chris didn't care; the heat inside made him feel stuporous, even more exhausted. He heard a knocking sound from behind him, and then the driver leaned over to open the catch for the trunk. Chris had resolved to try not to look at him—to try not to stare too hard at any of them, because if he didn't seem to be memorizing what they looked like, maybe they would be more likely to let him live. But he couldn't help glancing up now, and what he saw surprised him. The driver was just a kid, much younger than he was; some tough kid with a thick neck like the jocks who used to come to their shows and turn the scene ugly and the dancing violent, only this one wearing an expensive-looking if tasteless suede jacket and with a thick head of curly red hair instead of a crew cut. Chris wasn't quite exhausted enough not to care that one of his captors was younger than he was. It somehow made everything twice as humiliating, although he couldn't have said why.

After the trunk slammed shut, Stan got into the passenger seat without the shovel, and with no words spoken whatsoever, the red-haired kid stepped on it and they took off. Chris was just starting to think they might be going somewhere other than Ted Harper's house when the car braked and came to a stop right in front.

"Okay, Chris," Stan said in his familiar just-trust-me voice, and the two of them got out again. The car just sat there as they walked up the driveway.

Stan opened up the front door for him as well, but then stepped back when Chris walked in. He shut it behind him and was gone, leaving Chris in the house alone.

36

Or, not all alone.

Ted Harper, looking very much the same as he had that morning, still with a drink in one hand, now holding a hardcover book in the other with his index finger stuck in the pages marking his place, walked over from the sunken living room.

"Chris, how did it go? Did you make any headway on my little problem out there?" Ted said it both as if Chris had been doing him a favor—as if he'd been slaving all day out in the cold by his own choice—and also as if the work he'd been doing was good, wholesome manual labor, instead of for the most nefarious of purposes.

"Yeah," Chris said. "Yeah, I did a lot. Actually, I'm not sure I didn't do *too* much. I mean I did try to cover it up, you know, make it look as natural as I could, but I think there's just no way people aren't going to notice. I mean, I think it's something you should think about."

"So what you're saying, Chris, is that when my neighbors come back this summer, they're going to observe that there's a little less green on their dunes, a little more beach, and a little less island, is that what you're saying?"

"Yeah, I mean, I can't see how they're not going to. I mean, if I do too much."

"Well, Chris, that's a good point, but it's one that I've already thought about, and I believe there's something you're not considering. *That* something has to do with people's expectations. You see, some people probably *are* going to notice the difference; it's just that, since they're not going to *believe* that I would have actually sent someone out there over the winter with a shovel, they're never going to take the next step in their thinking. When you understand how and why that works, Chris, you'll be ahead of about ninety-nine percent of the population of this planet. The only other thing you have to have is the courage to follow up on that thinking with action—which in your case I have a feeling we're going to have to work on some.

"But now, as far as the other question goes, the real question you wanted to ask but were too afraid and so you had to couch it in this bull-shit about my neighbors, I want to answer that one for you, too. The question, obviously, is, why won't I just let you go? And the answer, Chris, my answer to that is both simple and complex at the same time. The answer is, why should I? And I want you to think about that, Chris. I want you to think about why I would *want* to do that, me being in the position I'm in, and you being in the position you're in. And when you really consider that, Chris, you'll understand that, with what I've *already* done, keeping you here the way I have, there's no reason at this point not to keep you here as long as I feel like it.

"Now, Chris, if you'll just come over here, there's something I want you to see. There's something I have for you."

Chris stood there warily for a moment before following in the general direction of where Ted was motioning with his book (which Chris noticed was some "how to succeed in business" thing), toward the sunken living room side of the house. He saw it when he was halfway there, all brightly lit up by the track lighting. In the area behind the sofa, where some part of him still expected to see his amp and guitars, there was now a very different musical display set up. It consisted of a chair from the dining table, a music stand, and leaning up against the chair, a cello. When Chris got closer, he could see that the bow for the cello was resting on the lip of the music stand, and that the closed book on that stand was called *Beginning Exercises for Classical Cello*.

Chris stopped and stared at the arrangement while a new, different brand of panic began chasing itself in circles in his head, this one more like the kind you'd get receiving a long jail term rather than a death sentence.

"Well, what do you think of it?" Ted asked eventually.

"Umm, I don't know anything about the cello, Mr. Harper," Chris stammered.

"I know that, Chris. I know that. But now I want you to teach yourself. It'll be a good use of your time here."

And how much time is that? Chris's mind shrieked. *How much time before you decide to off me and add my obituary to your collection in the upstairs desk drawer?*

"Oh, Mr. Harper, you know, thanks. Thank you, but I don't think that I could. I mean, I know almost nothing about classical music either."

"Right, well then, it's time you learned. And now I mean that in a serious way, Chris. You're interested in music, right? Well, this is serious music, not that electric rock-and-roll crap. Now I want you to give it a try right now, come on."

For just a moment Chris let himself wonder what had become of his beautiful guitars, not to mention his Mesa/Boogie, his effects, and all the rest of it. But he bit that thought off savagely. The idea of that stuff sitting in some pawnshop somewhere, or in some goon's basement waiting for his kid to get old enough to trash it, made Chris's blood boil, and he needed to stay calm now; he was tired and couldn't see things clearly, and if he lost it right now, it would probably be the last thing he ever did.

He walked over and picked up the cello by its neck. It was true that he knew almost nothing about violins, violas, or cello, but he could tell that this was not a fine instrument. The corners were too neatly squared off, the finish too thick and new, and the pegs were perfectly uniform, machine-made. Probably it was a student model that some music store had recommended. He plucked each of the strings, starting from the highest and going down. They sounded out in dissonance; it was radically out of tune. But how did you even tune a cello? And there were no frets. Looking down at that black, blank expanse of fingerboard, imagining all the notes hidden there, all the scales, all the half steps, flats, sharps, naturals, and trills of classical music, made his already wasted head spin. For a moment, still holding on to the instrument, he closed his eyes and let his head droop.

"Chris, now come on. You get busy with it," he heard Ted say, the man's anger slowly, predictably emerging.

Chris opened his eyes, shook his head, took a deep breath. Then he sat down in the chair, placed the instrument between his legs as he was pretty sure you were supposed to, picked up the bow, and turned to page one of the exercise book.

Two hours later, he was desperate almost to the point of begging. The last of the light had long since faded from the sky, and his exhaustion had darkened with it, regenerating into actual agony. Yet there'd been nothing for him to do but continue his practicing, trying to sound as if he were making an earnest effort. To that end, he had immediately decided to ignore the suggested tuning of fifths in *Beginning Exercises for Classical Cello* and had instead tuned the thing in the fourths that he was familiar with—just like the bottom four strings of a guitar, only calling the lowest string a C instead of a G to keep in somewhat the correct key. Using this method, he could already sort of play and was able to start right in on the scales on the first pages of the book, which he had a feeling Ted Harper expected of him. Obviously, you weren't *supposed* to tune a cello in fourths, and since he'd effectively diminished the range of the instrument, harder pieces would eventually be impossible to play.

But Chris didn't care about eventually. He didn't intend on being here long enough for that to become an issue, and if he was still alive after all this was over, he certainly didn't plan on keeping up with this antiquated instrument, which was maybe good for an effect on one or two songs on an album, but was otherwise pretty worthless. All he wanted was to keep Ted Harper happy for as long as this strange punishment lasted, and it was hard enough making a cello sound halfway decent without knowing how to use the bow, and without knowing where the notes were without the frets, and without having seen staff notation since taking band class for a few semesters in high school—and also while struggling to keep his eyes open even as his back and shoulders cramped up viciously from sitting up straight and stiff after all that digging and throwing.

Yet what he was most desperate for now, and what he was coming to realize he wouldn't be able to stop himself from crying and pleading for, was the food. At some point Ted had started to cook, the most intense smells of onions and spices and some kind of frying meat wafting over from behind him in the kitchen where he didn't dare to turn around to look. Chris told himself that he could hold it together, that he could wait, until at some point he had a terrible thought. What if Ted didn't intend to feed him? What if this was some kind of Nazi-concentration-camp-meets-*Cool-Hand-Luke* torture, where Chris would be slowly worked to death, shoveling sand all day and playing the cello all night while Ted ate sumptuous dinners in front of him but didn't feed him at all? Chris told himself it couldn't possibly be true; after all, he'd been encouraged to eat something this morning before starting out. On the other hand, though, he hadn't even been allowed a drink of water since then.

Finally, after fifteen or twenty minutes of catching over his horrendous playing the maddening sounds of plates and silverware being moved around, Chris couldn't stop himself anymore and turned around. He tried to keep a casual, questioning look on his face, but when he saw Ted already sitting at the dining room table, and that table set with plates and glasses and silverware and food in the middle, he knew he couldn't hide his desperation.

Ted looked away in distaste as soon as their eyes met. "Yes, come on, Chris, I suppose you can eat, too," he said.

Chris was so tired and spacey after all his concentration and work that he didn't even notice Stan sitting there at the table as well until he was halfway across the room—Stan who, like Chris, was wearing his coat in the chilly house, while Ted seemed mysteriously oblivious in his sweater. Three places were set, with Ted at the head of the table and Stan sitting on Ted's left. Chris took the other, sitting across from the kitchen and the bar.

Immediately, Chris reached for the pitcher of water on the table, barely able to keep his hands from shaking and spilling the liquid all over. One of them had actually taken the trouble to put ice in it, and when he finally got his glass to his mouth, he thought cold water had never tasted so good, like some foreign substance he'd never tried before.

"Well, come on now, guys. Don't make me look bad, dig in," Ted said, and passed on to Chris a steaming plate of corn. After that there was steak and mashed potatoes, as well as some kind of bean dish. The bread on the table was just the Wonder bread from the refrigerator, sitting there on a plate without its colorful plastic wrapping, but all of the food tasted incredible, and Chris ate it with an appreciation he thought he hadn't known since he was a child (which, he also noted, was probably the last time he'd had so little control over what, and when, he was able to eat). A bottle of red wine was on the table as well, and both Ted and Stan had a full glass in front of him. There was no wineglass at Chris's place, which was just fine with him. He felt too sick and weak to even think about alcohol.

"Ho, Chris, don't eat so fast, you'll bite off a finger there," Ted said, laughing. "You hungry, huh? Yup, working outside all day'll do that for you. By the way, how'd he do there, Stan, did he get anything done, or did he just stand there shivering?"

Stan, Chris noticed, left a polite, distancing pause before he answered. "No, he did good. He got a lot done."

"Really," Ted said. "I wouldn't have thought so. I wouldn't have thought Chris here could do anything like a good, honest day's work."

Equating what he'd been doing all day to goodness and honesty was an irony that Chris decided to let pass, and he just continued eating, a little more slowly now.

"That's okay, Chris. I understand if you're tired out," Ted went on. "I just want to let you know that today was the first day of the coming change. In the weeks and months to come, me and Stan here are going to change you, are going to turn you into a new man, free of charge you might say. From here on in, you can just think of this as a kind of boot camp, preparing you for the rest of your life. What do you think about that?"

Chris stopped eating for a moment, but once more he decided not to answer. It was just more bluffing, more trying to scare him; Ted was merely trying to get some kind of rise out of him when he would probably be allowed to leave as early as tomorrow morning. He wondered what he would do then, if he would go to the police, get a lawyer, as he'd promised himself. He knew he wouldn't, though. Ted Harper and his thugs had turned out to be the real thing after all, and Chris just wanted to get as far away from them as possible.

"Okay, Chris. That's all right. You're all right," Ted said finally, then turned to Stan again. "You know that I knew this guy when he didn't know he wasn't supposed to piss in his pants?"

"Oh, yeah?" Stan barely muttered.

"Oh, hell yes. Knew him when he was just a little nipple sucker. Cutest little tyke you ever seen, so cute his mom completely forgot about his big brother. That guy was lucky if he even got a bath once Chris here was born. Chris, what was your brother's name again?"

"Seth."

"And how did he turn out? What ever happened with him?"

"He's a lawyer. He lives up in New York near Albany. He's married and has a daughter."

"Is that right? So he's a big lawyer, huh? Got a family and everything. So what the hell happened to you?"

Chris shrugged, rapidly losing his appetite. He considered not answering again, but then slowly set down his silverware and put his hands on his pounding forehead. "Look, Mr. Harper," he said. "I told you I was sorry for what happened with Donna, and . . . and your wife, and I truly am sorry. I was angry at you, because what you did to me really got under my skin. But you must know that I never intended for anything like that to happen. And, look, it might not seem like you've paid me back for what I did to you, but really you already have. Charlie, that was the dog that . . . Stan shot, was about the only friend I had left in the world, and so it seems to me we're even now. I don't know what it is exactly that you're trying to prove here, but if it's about revenge, you've already gotten your revenge."

Ted Harper was regarding him steadily, all the jollity and coyness drained out of his expression.

"Well, but you see, Chris, that's just the thing, though, it's *not* about revenge, or at least not completely. Now, you see, now you're like a project that I've taken on, and I don't like to fail at anything I take a hand to. Like I already told you, I'm going to change you, Chris. I'm going to take you out of your little imaginary world and bring you into the real one. I'm going to make you a man, and it's going to be the best thing that ever happened to you, even if you don't like it one bit. Now, if you're done eating, why don't you take your plate and bring it to the sink and then get on up and hit the hay. You look like you need some rest, and tomorrow's going to be an early day for you."

Chris stood up from the table, picking up his plate, gathering his utensils, glass, and napkin onto it. Getting some sleep actually sounded pretty good to him. He had eaten about all he could hold down, and the food was just now bringing on a second wave of exhaustion that was almost like nausea. He still didn't really believe that Ted Harper would keep him here, forcing him to work the land like some sharecropper during the day, enduring self-inflicted cello lessons in the evening, plus whatever other beneficient tortures were involved. But he believed that pretending he believed it, and seeming resigned to it, was the best way to satisfy Ted Harper now.

So he went into the kitchen and scraped his plate into the garbage before placing it in the sink. And then, without a word, like the obedient slave/convict/music student he was supposed to be, he crossed the room again and went upstairs to go to bed.

37

He was awakened from his sleep by a crescendo of string instruments that seemed to emanate directly from the walls and floor of his bedroom. It was so loud and so shocking, and he was still so tired, that at first it seemed like some other phenomenon altogether—a malevolent spirit haunting the house, or maybe a bomb going off. Finally he realized it was only the downstairs stereo blasting classical music. Outside, it was barely light, and when he checked the clock it said five fifty-five. He pulled the pillow over his head to blot out most of the sound and was just starting to slumber again when there was a banging on his door. A moment later Ted himself poked his head in, his face unshaven, his hair still in corkscrews from bed, but otherwise dressed, wearing the same fisherman's sweater as yesterday.

"Up and at 'em there, Chris," he said. "I'm making breakfast downstairs, and I don't think you want to miss it."

For just a moment their eyes met, and Chris knew he couldn't keep the loathing out of his expression.

Either Ted didn't notice or it was so unimportant to him that he ignored it without thinking. "Let's go" was all he added before he went downstairs again, leaving Chris's door standing open, admitting the soft early light of presunrise coming through the windows facing the ocean, the music even louder now.

Alone again, Chris tried to remind himself that this was all, within limits, a practical joke, and probably almost over. But it was notably harder to believe in the cold, dark early morning with what felt like every muscle in his body plus his head aching to the point of stinging pain. He thought about just staying in bed, only he had a feeling he knew what would happen if he did that. Already he could smell the pungent aroma of frying bacon downstairs, so probably if he took too long, he wouldn't get any; he would be sent out to work with no food at all this time. Remembering how hungry he'd become yesterday, he threw off his covers and dragged himself up, pulling on his dirty jeans over his long underwear, finding a clean pair of wool socks to wear. In the bathroom, he found and swallowed three Advils and then, realizing how thirsty and dehydrated he was, drank three full glasses of water from the green, toothpaste-smelling plastic cup there.

Downstairs, the music was twice as loud—still not *truly* loud, as Chris, who knew loud music, could gauge—but once he was in the direct throw of the speakers, the sound level nevertheless passed into *his* threshold of pain. The table was set for only two this morning, with silverware and napkins and glasses of orange juice and coffee, along with a big plastic bottle of syrup on a plate in the middle.

Ted was at the stove, cooking again, using the pointed index and middle finger of his left hand as a baton to conduct with the music while he worked with a spatula in his right—the conceit of a complete asshole, Chris thought. He forgot about that as he came into the kitchen, though, and the mingled aroma of bacon and pancakes cut through his fatigue to awaken the desperate, needy animal his stomach had become since yesterday.

"Do you know this piece, Chris?" Ted said without turning to face him, almost shouting over the din.

"No, maybe I've heard it before, I don't know," Chris shouted back.

"Really? It's hard to believe you don't know it."

Chris shrugged—an expression Ted couldn't see. "I know almost nothing about classical music, Mr. Harper, I told you," he yelled again, glad to further clarify his ignorance in the matter, if it made this asshole happy.

But when Ted turned to him, Chris still found his expression infuriating. He had a disdainful, superior look on his face, as if what Chris had just admitted to meant more than he knew. Chris once again dismissed it, however, when Ted produced a plate of four big pancakes with strips of bacon on the side.

"Why don't you just get started on those there, Chris," Ted boomed over the violins, handing the food over to Chris.

The places were set the same way they had been last night, minus the one for Stan, so Chris sat down in the same chair as before. The pancakes were thick and doughy, the bacon barely cooked, still red and greasy on the inside. Chris poured syrup over everything and dug in mightily, almost happily. When Ted came and sat down next to him with his own plate, Chris was even glad for the music. It meant it was harder for them to talk.

"This is called 'Ave Maria,' Chris," Ted said in spite of it, effortlessly speaking over the volume. "It's by Franz Schubert, who lived his life in poverty after being kicked out of his music school when his voice changed, and only ever gave one performance and then died of typhoid fever right after he'd finally saved up enough to buy his first piano. What do you think about that? And just listen to his music. Isn't that about the most beautiful thing you've ever heard?"

Chris thought all classical music sounded pretty much the same: complex, meaningless melodies all woven together into a tapestry of boredom. And so what if Schubert had died poor, didn't all the famous composers have stories like that? Was he supposed to feel guilty about it? For just a moment, Chris thought of telling Ted about Kurt Cobain, who'd practically been homeless while he was still in high school. But he knew it was pointless.

"Just you listen to that music there while you eat that food, Chris, all right?"

He thought he would be glad to, if only Ted would shut up.

Chris only got about halfway through the pancakes and three-quarters through the bacon, however, before his stomach did the same thing it had last night, clamping up on him, deciding it had had enough. Yet if he was going to work straight through an even longer day outside, he knew he had to eat more; and so he continued to force the thick, syrup-covered compound down his throat, deliberately chewing and swallowing, getting an image of himself as a dog with stolen food that will soon be taken away—and then unavoidably thinking of poor Charlie.

Sure enough, before he'd even finished, the front door opened, letting in a gust of cold wind, and then Stan was looking in at the two of them sitting at the table. Ted glanced up and, using almost the same casual hand motion that he'd been conducting with, pointed at Chris and then the door. Feeling furious all over again, Chris stood up to leave. But Ted stopped him, placing a hand on his arm. He pointed to Chris's plate this time, for him to take it to the sink.

38

Outside, it felt even colder than it had yesterday, with a frosty wind blowing off the bay, the air crisp with a winterlike chill. The silver car was parked in the road this time, empty, and Stan got in the driver's seat without a word, leaving Chris to decide whether he should get in the front or the back. He chose the back, since that was what he'd done yesterday, and then once again Stan drove him off toward the point.

When they got out, Chris had just a moment of hope. Yesterday, they'd left the shovel in the trunk of the black car, and if they hadn't remembered to transfer it, he would at least have some time to relax and digest his food while that was sorted out. But Stan, putting on a black watch cap and a pair of ski gloves he hadn't had yesterday, popped the trunk and got out without delay; and when Chris reluctantly opened the door, Stan was already standing there with the same shovel, which this time he presented to Chris immediately. He then held out his hand for Chris to lead the way down to the dunes and the edge of the beach, probably so as not to turn his back on him.

The first few shovelfuls were the worst. The muscles in his back and shoulders felt as if someone had injected tiny splines of glass into them, and the blisters under his leather gloves screamed and probably popped. Plus there was the cold wind, which every time he bent over seemed to maliciously delight in getting underneath his jacket and giving him a fresh chill. This morning Stan sat down almost immediately, flipping the collar of his coat up and turning his back to the wind.

Chris worked for what he judged to be about two hours—he didn't want to look at his watch because he couldn't bear to know how much longer he had to go—before he started to feel that new brand of fear encircling his intestines again: the kind he got when he thought that Ted really meant to go through with whatever this was and really keep him here for . . . Chris didn't know how long. But suddenly, perhaps for the first time, he realized there actually *was* no reason why Ted couldn't keep him here for months if he wanted to.

He stopped working and just stood there, leaning on the shovel, looking down at the sand in front of him with his face turned away from Stan.

After about a minute, he heard a voice directly behind him.

"Come on, Chris." Stan was more pleading than threatening—although Chris remembered he'd sounded that way right before he'd blasted Charlie off the face of the earth, too.

"Stan, why is he making me do this?" Chris said, his panic seeping into his words.

"Who cares, you're still alive, right? Just do it."

"But he's not going to keep me here that much longer, right? I mean, how much longer can this go on for?"

"Chris, you're not listening to me. You're not hearing me. You're very lucky to be alive right now. Now come on."

Chris turned to face his guard and foreman, not caring about the tears that were running freely down the sides of his face yet again. "Stan, I don't think I can do it, really. I'm going to freeze to death out here. I'm going to pass out or something."

"Oh, come on, don't be a pussy, Chris. You can do it. And look, you're probably going to get out of here before any of us."

Chris blinked once or twice and wiped his face before he registered what Stan had said. "Why, what do you mean?" he asked after he had.

But now Stan gave him a dark, forbidding look that Chris didn't like at all. "You keep working, Chris. And don't make me come over here again, you got it?"

"Yeah, okay, okay." Once again Chris picked up the shovel and started in on another line of beach-grass annihilation.

The next time Stan came over to him, Chris thought he was about to faint. It was sometime near midday, and for the past two or so hours he had been running on empty, his muscles not really working anymore but just twitching, the splines of glass having multiplied until, in certain places in his shoulders and lower back, they had replaced the muscle itself. His work had become slower and slower, and twice, while tossing his load of greenery into the brush, he'd stumbled and fallen in the infuriatingly soft sand.

"Take a break, Chris," Stan told him now.

Immediately he fell into a sitting position, tossing the shovel aside and hiding his face in his hands.

"I'll tell you what, I can trust you to stay here, right? You're not going to try something stupid, are you?"

"I think I'm too tired to try and run away, if that's what you mean," Chris moaned.

"Good, then you just stay here, I'll be right back."

Chris watched Stan walk inland, back toward the car, where he heard the trunk open and then slam closed. When Stan returned, he had a little red cooler under one arm.

"Over here, Chris." He stopped short of the beach and Chris's work area, planting the cooler down in a little valley made by two dunes. "Less windy over here," Stan explained as Chris dragged himself over and took a seat against a steep scarp of sand.

Stan sat down across from him and took out of the cooler a big silver thermos and then an orange and yellow McDonald's bag. Immediately, Chris's stomach went into its vicious-animal mode again, seeming to roar inside him with a power that defied his utter exhaustion. Stan poured him a lukewarm coffee into a styrofoam cup, which Chris took gratefully and drank from, even though he knew it was probably bad for him, that he was dehydrated and coffee would only make it worse. But he was down to moment-to-moment survival, he felt, and abstract health theories were as irrelevant as whether what he was wearing would get him in the door at a chic nightclub or restaurant. As far as that went, nothing he had ever eaten, at any restaurant anywhere, had ever tasted better than the cold, limp Big Mac, or double cheeseburger, or whatever it was that Stan handed him next. This time his stomach didn't protest at all, and he wolfed down the whole thing, perfectly oblivious to how it looked.

"Don't hurt yourself there," Stan said to him once. Chris barely even heard.

When he was done, though, when he'd finished the fries that came next and downed the last of his coffee, Chris realized he had a problem.

There was simply no way in the world that he was going to be able to stand up again when this break was over; and therefore, at that point, Chris reasoned, when Stan was done and decided it was time to get back to work, there would be nothing for Chris to do except beg and plead not to be shot, and the rest would be out of his hands.

And by the time that Stan, eating at a normal human rate, had finished, put the scraps of garbage and the thermos back in the cooler, then sat there for a while and finally stood up and taken the cooler back to the car, this seemed more, rather than less, inevitable. Chris felt as if his arms were made of wet, poured concrete, while his legs had all the drive and power of overcooked pasta.

An odd thing made Chris move again, however. It was the idea that Stan might very well have arranged for this little meal on his own, without Ted Harper's knowledge or approval; that Stan was actually looking out for him independently, and perhaps in direct contradiction of his boss. Because if that really was the case, Chris's weakened, almost drunken thought process went, then it seemed a lousy way for Chris to repay him, by just refusing to get up afterward and making him look bad for doing it.

In fact, part of Chris's mind knew this logic made no sense, knew that Stan had shot Charlie, knew that the ally he was imagining was the same man he was in fear of being shot by. But since this sense of loyalty was enough to get him moving again and would keep him alive for as long as he could then last with the shovel, Chris didn't question it. There seemed to be no doubt in his mind that he wanted to keep on living now, and if this illusion of gratitude would buy him even another minute, he would take it.

He wound up being amazed at how much more he got done that day. He worked until the light had started to fade and his watch told him it was after four. Since he'd started, he estimated he had cleared perhaps the equivalent of half a city block of beach grass, spread out over maybe a quarter mile of dune line. Then he fell over again, and when he tried to get up, fell over yet again and had to just lie there.

When Stan came over this time, though, he wasn't angry or threatening; he was laughing. And Chris, even through his utter despondency, humiliation, and exhaustion, had to agree with him. It was sort of funny. He had worked himself until he literally couldn't stand up anymore.

"I think that's all for today, Chris," Stan told him, once he'd finally got control of himself enough to speak.

39

There was nothing at all funny about that evening, however, when Stan took him back to the house. It was the exact same thing as yesterday: he was walked to the door and left there, and Ted greeted him on the other side in the same bizarre manner, giving his hearty thanks for the work he was doing, and then suggesting, as if it were something Chris wanted to do, or as if it were a privilege, that he should now practice *his* cello. This time, Chris asked and was allowed to use the downstairs bathroom, where he spent most of his brief time alone drinking water directly from the tap. When he came out, though, Ted was right there, waiting to usher him to the same chair with the cello and the music stand and everything else just as he'd left that nightmare yesterday.

Where, from almost the moment he sat down, he was struggling desperately, fighting to keep his eyes open and his fingers working, his arms feeling as if someone had strapped cinder blocks to them so that even just holding them up, just keeping them so they didn't drape straight down at his sides, seemed like excruciatingly hard work.

At one point, to see what would happen, he stopped playing, leaving off in the middle of an A-major scale he was running—something that would have been so easy for him on the guitar, but with the bow and the strange fingerboard it was like trying to write cursive left-handed—and just closed his eyes and fell almost instantly asleep.

"Chris!"

He jerked his head up to find Ted standing two feet away, holding in an oven mitt a steaming pot of something with a wooden spoon sticking out the top.

"Sorry," Chris said quickly, immediately starting to play again, just putting the bow to the strings to make sound and then correcting, finding his place in the scale once he'd started.

Ted seemed mollified, and out of the corner of his eye Chris saw him wander back toward the kitchen, where he was once again cooking dinner. Only after he left did Chris's heart begin to pound, as he wondered if that boiling pot had been brought along as a threat.

He was summoned for dinner that night by more classical music from the stereo—a lighter piece that Ted put on at a softer volume than this morning's wailing reveille. The food this time was a good-looking glazed and marinated chicken dish with yellow rice and peas and corn bread. When Chris sat down to it, however, with Stan also there to join them again, the switch that controlled his hunger lately seemed to be jammed in the off position, and he was barely able to swallow three forkfuls of the rice and mostly sucked on the one or two pieces of chicken he cut for himself.

Even Ted seemed to sense Chris's utter depletion and took pity on him. He merely announced that they were listening to Mozart—as if Chris would take careful note of the fact—and then ignored him, making small talk with Stan instead.

"So, how are the boys doing out there today?" Ted asked at one point.

"They're fine. They're doing fine."

"They takin' care of business, same as always?"

"Right."

"Well, I just hate to think about them, sitting out there in their cars all day and all night. I hope you at least rotate them and give them time off for good behavior and all that."

"Don't worry, I take good care of them."

"Well, okay. I guess you know what you're doing."

"You don't need to worry about that."

Chris knew that he should be paying careful attention here, that the means of his escape or survival might possibly be hidden in a conversation such as this one. Yet all his weary mind could deduce was a thing he'd already noted: that Stan was overly subservient in his answers to Ted, almost as if he were humoring him, or as if they shared some inside joke. It was, Chris thought, probably a worthless, meaningless observation, but he could do no better.

Soon after that, Ted sent Chris up to bed anyway, saying that if he wasn't hungry, he could take his plate to the sink and "go off and get your beauty sleep." It wasn't even nine yet, but once more Chris did as he was told, trudging up the stairs like a terminally sick old man. He lay down in bed in all his clothes, then started to cry again when he caught a whiff of the air coming out from under his jacket—the smell reminded him of the New York City bums who can clear a subway car by merely walking in. That made him think about the future again. He only had one more pair of thermal pants (already dirty, but spring fresh compared to the ones he was wearing), and two more tops. So what would happen when he ran out of clean clothes? Would doing laundry soon become a part of his routine here as well? And then how long *really* could that routine go on? And what would happen when it was over?

At some point Chris couldn't have identified, his crying gave way to a fitful sleep, broken frequently by muscle spasms that always seemed to correspond in some way to the nightmare he was having.

40

The classical music woke him again the next day, wailing up from downstairs as if some plaintive, melancholy version of hell itself had broken through, Chris thought. He was sore all over, cramped, exhausted, and definitely sick, with his glands swollen and his throat raw and scratchy. The clock said three minutes after six today, but Ted didn't come to his door, and so for another ten minutes Chris lay there in bed, wondering whether this meant it was okay to go back to sleep, or if today would be the same deal as yesterday, with his only chance for survival resting literally on his getting downstairs and eating some breakfast before Stan came to take him out onto the dunes again.

In the end, though, he decided that, however much he felt as if he couldn't even move, it was foolish to be taking the chance, and he crawled out from under the covers and hobbled into the bathroom.

When he finally came down then, stumbling on the last step and almost falling, the music blaring around him possibly even louder than the day before, he found Ted already at the table. The moment he saw Chris, he made a show of looking at his Rolex and shaking his head.

Chris had a pretty good idea what that meant and hurried over and sat down in front of the plate already waiting for him. It was French toast this morning, which he immediately began eating, scooping in huge mouthfuls of the eggy bread, not bothering with the syrup until he had a big mouthful going and could pour while he chewed. Even despite what felt like a fever, his stomach obligingly switched over to all-out-starving mode, and once more without thinking about it he abandoned manners and pride in favor of sustenance and survival.

Only having eaten about three mouthfuls, however, the front door opened, and there was Stan, wearing his black watch cap with the lapels of his overcoat already turned up. Ted briefly turned to look, then stood and reached for Chris's plate.

"Okay, Chris, time to go," he said over the music.

Chris watched his barely dented breakfast moving away from him, like a missed ship leaving harbor. At the very last second, however, thinking he truthfully wouldn't make it through to midday when Stan might or might not give him another lunch, he reached out and snatched the four pieces of French toast, quickly folding the syrupy mess and sticking it in his jacket pocket.

"Chris, that's disgusting, put it back!" Ted yelled, but still holding the empty plate, somewhat immobilized by the game of keep-away he had just lost.

Already Chris had a cup of orange juice and was guzzling it down as fast as he could, his hunger making him not care, his hunger making it worth it, even when Ted swung the plate he'd been holding, and Chris just barely pulled back in time and the cup was smashed away and the remaining liquid, plus more syrup, splattered all over his face and the front of his jacket. The breaking glass against the hardwood floor after that was barely audible over the stereo.

"OKAY, YOU GET OUT!" Ted roared, knocking over his own chair as he backed up, slamming what was left of Chris's plate down on the table hard enough to shatter that as well.

Chris quickly stood up and moved away, not sure what was going to happen now. The same as last time, though, Ted didn't come after him. Instead, he was leaning over, closing his eyes as if making a great effort to control himself. Chris decided not to stick around and see if Ted would change his mind. He went directly out the door, passing by Stan—who was looking away, as anyone would witnessing domestic trauma at his boss's house—and didn't stop until he was sitting in the backseat of the silver car.

He ate his stolen fare in small, quick bites on the walk from the car to the dunes, too shook up over what had happened to take any pleasure in it, keeping the food hidden as much as possible so as not to seem disrespectful to Stan. The plate hitting his hand and arm hadn't hurt so much as the shock, the fear, the degradation of the thing, mostly the fear. It was just like what everyone always said about battered wives and children, where the real damage didn't come from the blows but from the general situation they were forced to live and breathe in. Chris had now entered that tormented state where, no matter what he thought or tried to tell himself, the foremost thing on his mind was what Ted would eventually do to get back at him—or when, for any reason at all, he did finally lose control of his temper.

From the moment Chris started digging, he could barely even stand up, and he had to pause for as long as thirty seconds sometimes between shovelfuls of the weedy grass, which he was learning to hate just for its existence. (He had already decided he hated the people who owned the gray house on the point, just because it made his task that little bit easier.) Today Stan didn't object to the rest intervals, and somehow Chris made it through to lunch again, which once more Stan provided. This time it was cold heros wrapped in cellophane that he'd brought for them in the trunk. And this time, along with the coffee, there was a bottle of Deer Park water, which Stan threw to him, and which Chris stowed in his pocket for later.

"What's the matter with him, anyway? Did something happen to him or something?" Chris asked at one point during the meal, not thinking about it beforehand but just saying it.

Stan at first didn't answer. Then he shrugged and shook his head. "I don't know. Maybe it's just that some people are more intense than others, you know? Like everything's turned up a notch."

Perhaps because of the water, Chris had to stop to piss twice that day, which he also did without asking, tossing down the shovel and opening up on a sand wall of dunes. Stan didn't object to this either, and during these breaks Chris closed his eyes and very nearly slept, dreaming of all the things in life he had once taken for granted.

41

Coming in that evening, Chris immediately looked over at the table and the floor, which the last time he'd seen had been splattered all over with orange juice and syrup and stippled with shards of glass. But everything had already been cleaned up, the place looking exactly as it had before his and Ted Harper's morning showdown over the French toast. And then Ted, too, either because things like that happened with him all the time and he'd honestly forgotten, or because for whatever insane reason he'd decided to pretend to have, greeted Chris in the same manner as both times before. Chris was even allowed another bathroom break before he sat down to play.

Perhaps since he hadn't actually thrown up or collapsed that day, he managed to start in on the first "Key of D" melody pieces in *Beginning Exercises for Classical Cello*. They were boring little tunes, quarter notes mostly with a half or whole note thrown in seemingly at random to break the monotony. But, as with all musical instruments, there was something satisfying in doing it right, in nailing it, which he could appreciate even on top of everything else going on. In only three days of intensely fatigued practice the bow was already becoming more natural to his hand, so that he wasn't constantly slipping onto the wrong string every time he tried to hold a note.

Just a half hour or so after he'd started, however, he was interrupted when Ted called his name from somewhere behind him.

He left off in the middle of a phrase and waited, wondering if Ted merely wanted to correct his playing somehow, or if he was now finally going to receive his retribution for that morning.

"Chris, would you come over here for a moment please," Ted said then.

Bracing himself for the worst, Chris hung the bow on the music stand and stood up—yet still he felt a shock as if live electrical cables had been hooked to his temples when he turned around to look.

"Chris, you remember Donna. I believe you have something you want to tell her, don't you?"

Chris felt his throat catch as he tried to swallow. Donna Laney was sitting there at the head of the table—wearing no makeup again today, Chris noticed, her white face looking parched and wounded. Ted was standing behind her with a comforting hand on her shoulder. She was still wearing her coat buttoned up to her neck, as though she didn't plan on staying.

"Chris, please, come over here," Ted said again. "Donna's come over to hear what you wanted to tell her."

Chris managed to shuffle his feet and move closer to them, coming up to the other end of the table and stopping there. He opened his mouth to speak, but then froze, too tired to think the situation through, bewildered as to how he was supposed to respond, and horrified imagining the ways that this could possibly end.

In another moment, however, what he supposed was his will to live kicked in and he heard himself saying, "Yes, umm, I do. I'm, umm, sorry . . . very sorry for what I did, umm . . . did to you. I was just angry . . . I was very angry at Ted because I just . . . I've been going through a hard time lately, and I just got angry at Ted, you know, jealous of him, because he was rich, and I was working for him, and somehow, I don't know, I just decided to take it out on you . . . and him. And I really, I can't explain it any better than that, but once again, I'm just, I'm very, very sorry."

Afterward he looked down at the floor and kept his eyes locked there.

"So why is he still here?" he heard Donna ask.

"Well, I'm not completely sure myself," Ted answered easily. "His father was a good friend of mine, though, and so I thought I'd give him a chance to redeem himself. So far he's doing all right, aren't you, Chris?"

Chris just nodded, still looking down.

"Well, come on, Donna, I'll walk you out," he heard after that.

"You want my advice, you should fire the son of a bitch."

"Well, maybe I still will, I don't know."

And then Chris heard the door and they both went out into the night, and he was left standing there, relieved, but also feeling cowardly and ashamed. Ted hadn't brought her by for her benefit, Chris was sure, but for his own, just to prove to Chris that he could. He had brought her here in complete confidence to see his prisoner, who he knew would be too terrified to do anything but beg and plead for forgiveness.

It was strange that Ted apparently harbored no ill will toward her, Chris thought for a moment, since she had been the one to actually make whatever phone call she had made. On further reflection, though, he didn't find it either surprising or reassuring; Ted had clearly decided only one person was to blame.

Eventually, thinking that he didn't want to have to be told to, Chris returned to his chair, took up the bow, and began to play again.

If bringing Donna by had been special punishment for what he'd done that morning, that seemed to be the end of it, because the drill for dinner afterward was exactly the same, too, with Ted putting on soft music to announce the meal, Chris turning around to find the table already set, the food already cooked and laid out, and Stan also already sitting at his place. Tonight the music was Johann Strauss, Ted informed Chris when he sat down. The food, which he was far more interested in, was salmon with white rice and a spinach dish that tasted wonderfully buttery. Chris found that he could actually eat normally this time, without either gobbling like a starving man or his stomach clamping up immediately into the meal.

Perhaps because of that, or possibly because the stunt he'd just pulled having Donna over had left Ted in an unusually good mood, he started in on his guest of honor almost immediately.

"So, let me ask you something there, Chris," he drawled. "Now, I know that you'd be perfectly happy to sit out the rest of your life in one of your father's friends' summerhouses, but what if—and I guess you're just going to have to imagine this part—what if you *were* married, and, you know, all settled down, and then you found out someone else was sleeping with your wife. What would you do about it?"

Chris assumed Ted meant to compare the situation with what had happened with Donna. "Probably not much," he answered.

"No? So some guy's diddling your wife, but you'd be okay with that?"

"Well, I wouldn't go and murder the guy."

"No? But so what would you do?"

"I guess I'd want to talk to her about it."

"So you'd want to *talk* to her about it, huh?"

"Yeah, I'd find out what was really going on, hear it from her, then decide what to do."

"But what if, like, you caught the two of them together? You know, while they were actually doing it?"

Chris shrugged. "I don't see how that would change things."

"It would change things because when you walk in the door, his pants are down around his ankles and his dick is deep-sixed between her legs, that's how it would change things."

"Okay, right. You're right. I'd definitely be angry. I'd be very angry. But if you're trying to get me to say I'd kill the guy, I still wouldn't do that. And why is it any more his fault than it is hers? I mean, if he's not raping her, then it's something they both wanted to do. So am I supposed to kill both of them?"

Even as he was saying this, Chris was aware that he was arguing with a man who could decide if he lived or died, and so he couldn't possibly win. But he also had the idea that Ted wanted him to be defending himself like this, and so in a way it was the same as before, where he was playing a role in the hopes of eventually assuaging Ted Harper's wrath.

"I'm not telling you what you're *supposed* to do, Chris. I'm just telling you the situation, trying to find out *about* you by what you *would* do."

"Well, I'm sorry if I don't measure up."

There was a long pause after that, during which Chris wondered if his last comment had gone too far. Yet when Ted spoke again, it was still in the same calm, mocking voice, just more serious now.

"It's not that you don't measure up. It's just that the way you live, the kind of values you have, you'll never know if you measure up or not. Do you see?"

Chris was going to just hold his tongue and knew he probably should. But then he spoke anyway. "So, stop me if I'm wrong here, but so I would know if I 'measured up' or not by how well I could beat this guy up, or kill him?"

"Well . . . yes. I suppose that's one way to put it, in this instance at least. You see, the way I see it, life is like one of those horse races where the horses all have to jump over those crazy obstacles, like the two walls that are ten feet apart with the pool of water in the middle, or the one where there's just a little wall but then right behind it is a taller wall and then the ground is much lower on the other side where the horse can't ever see it. You see, we're all put through this thing called life whether we like it or not, Chris, and even though it looks pleasant enough at first, with all the greenery and the flowers and whatnot, it ends up being a deadly serious business.

"But you, Chris, your problem isn't that you can't jump high enough or far enough. You, you're like one of those horses that comes up to the first jump seeming like he's going to go, but then at the last minute steps on the brakes so hard he practically throws his rider ass over teacups. You're like the horse that you can't make jump, not even with the whip and the spurs. There's only one small difference, though. When that horse stops short, there's no doubt in anyone's mind, and also in the horse's mind, I imagine, that he went and stopped short because he was scared shitless. But you, you wouldn't even admit to that, would you, Chris? You'd say, if you was a talking horse, 'I didn't go over the jump because I don't believe in going over jumps,' or some nonsense. Well, it's all fine by me, it really is. But if you're going to stand there and shake the hand of the man who's screwing your wife, probably with his hard-on still half inside of her, you should at least have the guts to admit that you're a coward. I mean you should at least have that much self-respect."

After Chris finished that night, when he was standing up to clear his plate and leave Ted and Stan at the table as he had for his past two dinners with them, Ted said, "Chris, you look like you've still got some energy left in you, why don't you take care of clearing and washing tonight. Stan and I have some things we need to discuss in private anyway."

So after that, accepting his change of course blandly enough—just so long as he could still get away—Chris began to clear the dishes and plates, bringing them into a kitchen that, with dirty pots and pans on the stove and a slimy cutting board by the sink, looked fully operational for the first time since Chris had moved in.

While he worked, Ted joined him to use the cappuccino machine, making one for Stan and one for himself, and it made Chris stop to think for a moment of what a truly unusual man Ted Harper had turned out to be. He was a good cook, who kept a well-stocked kitchen and a neat house, and liked classical music and used to be interested in acting and performance art, but who also, as nearly as Chris could tell, killed people, smuggled drugs or something like that in his ships, had a bunch of goon hit men working for him, and seemed to relish talking trash in just as foul a manner as he could—with a Southern accent that was sometimes thick like a hillbilly's, and at other times almost entirely absent.

And who had also taken on the full-time hobby of torturing his house sitter, Chris added to his list. Yet even that wasn't so simple, he amended. Ted wasn't cruel to him all the time. He had him sit down to dinner as an almost equal and cooked him breakfast before sending him out to work all day, even if Chris didn't always get a chance to eat it. Plus, for instance, Ted hadn't asked him to make the coffee just now and bring it to them like some servant. So what exactly *was* Ted treating him like? What *was* he to Ted Harper?

But then Chris remembered what Ted himself had already told him and wished he'd never stopped to wonder.

On a trip to the stove to get another pot, Chris glanced out quickly, looking under the counters and over the bar, but Ted and Stan were gone, having left while he was at the sink, probably upstairs now having their private conversation in Ted's room. Very much the way the son of a strict and vindictive father might, Chris found himself praying that they weren't talking about him.

PART FOUR

·/·

Dinner Parties

42

"So, Chris, by now you've probably wondered what it is that could possibly have turned good old Ted Harper, your pop's old buddy from college, into the cruel, dangerous old bastard I've become," Ted said from the head of the table. "Am I right, Chris?"

But Chris just stayed quiet as he served himself, even though he had thought about that question quite a bit. He didn't actually expect to get an honest answer, and he also had a feeling he was going to hear what Ted wanted him to hear no matter if he begged not to.

That morning, after waking up reasonably lucid for the first time, he'd managed to splash some water over himself and change into his other pair of long underwear before making it down to a breakfast of ham-and-cheese omelettes. And then he'd worked another day through, first doing his beach-erosion thing, then teaching himself the cello. His interminable practice session had just been ended by a full orchestra piece that Ted had put on (Mozart, he'd been told), and all Chris wanted to do was sit and eat tonight's dinner of rare steak, home fries, and string beans—and be left alone.

"Well, I think you have a right to know," Ted went on. "And now that you aren't sleeping through dinnertime anymore, I even want to tell you. Because I think it would be instructive for you and might bring you a few steps along in your own thinking also."

Ted poured himself an almost brimming glass of red wine, which he took a large swallow of before continuing. Tonight, Chris even envied Ted's alcohol, although not enough to risk asking for any.

"Something you probably don't realize, however, Chris, is just how large a transition it was that I went through, and that I'm about to tell you about. Because, believe it or not, there was a day when I was a lot like yourself, thinking I was going to win the world over with my raw talent, thinking I just *had* to be special somehow. I don't like to talk about it much now, since, quite frankly, I find it embarrassing, but, like your father, I used to want to be an actor. Oh, yes, and you knew that about your father, didn't you, Chris? That when he was younger he was just mad for the theater? A Shakespeare man to the end he was, loved all that highfalutin, dress-up-and-prance-around-like-a-fairy crap. Never did care for Shakespeare myself. But your father was strictly a summer actor: summer stock, summer festivals. During the school semesters he was all business, although he used to come down to the campus theater sometimes and hang around like a lovesick pup. Got to know all of us in the drama program that way. Just never could quite bring himself to pull the trigger, never could get off the A-student career path. Too smart for his own good, you ask me, which isn't quite your problem, is it, Chris? But that's a different story.

"Anyway, for me it wasn't just Shakespeare and that kind of theater. I and a few friends of mine back then at Yale drama had become interested in something altogether different. We'd all studied Bakhtin, and Strindberg, Antonin Artaud and his theater of cruelty. And after many late nights of heated discussion and argument, we came up with our own theory, leading us to what we called our theater of fear. Our thinking was that the public had become too used to the garden variety of drama, overloaded so to speak, so that no matter how good your movie or your play was, it couldn't possibly have a lasting effect anymore. Only when truly afraid, or truly angry, did people open up to new possibilities and changes in their thinking. So our little skits, designed for performance in public spaces, were aimed principally at achieving those states. They involved no stage, and only realistic costumes. There was no script, exactly, only an act of violence, or implied violence, and then a direction we wanted to go in, a direction we wanted to take people in—which may all sound very strange to you now, but you have to understand that this was a different time, the sixties, when doing things out of the ordinary kind of was the ordinary.

"Now, you've obviously already had a taste of this, Chris . . . which I understand you didn't like very much, and I can't say I blame you for that. But the kind of things we were doing back then were much bigger. We once shut down a bank for a full three hours while I pretended someone had stolen my wallet, which was quite a scene since I basically went around accusing innocent strangers of robbery. Or we used to go onto crowded buses and trains and talk about a crime we'd just committed. It was almost like research, to see what people would and wouldn't do. The thing that was too bad, and why it wasn't ever going anywhere, was that there was no way to record what we did and what happened, so while it might have been a great experience for us and the people who happened to be there, all we were left with in the end was a story. Nowadays they've got these tiny little video cameras all over the place. Well, back then I would have cut off my right arm for something like that. But I'm getting off the track here. The only reason that I'm telling you all this is so you can understand the kind of person I was and then what happened to me."

Oh, but I already know what kind of person you are, Chris thought. Except for eating steadily, though, he kept his mouth shut.

"Now what happened first," Ted continued, "was that we got caught. The 'act' that finally got us into trouble was this thing that I had come up with about racism. It was a real PC kind of number, where we dressed up the one woman in our small troupe as a blind old lady, and I would go up and try to rob her, and this black guy we had would stop me, and then we'd get into this big fight about it. It always worked out beautifully, because there would be just a few people who actually saw what had happened, and whether they liked it or not—which they most often didn't, by the way—they would have to take this black guy's side. But of course just about everyone else would immediately assume it was the darkie, even though we made a point of never dressing him up any worse than I was. And so then what you'd end up with was this situation where you had strangers lecturing each other on prejudice and racism, getting a real dialogue going for probably the first time in their lives. We would end it by Felicia—that was our female player—suddenly declaring that she didn't care and felt sick and wanted to go home. And then we would all hightail it out of there, usually straight back to campus to party right through the night.

"Well, what we did wrong was that we did it too many times in the same city. Apparently, a lot of the people who saw us went on to file police reports and they pieced together what was happening, because the next time we tried it, in a supermarket, we hadn't even got to the part where Tully, our black guy, tells his life story, before they showed up. And, man, the three of us were arrested and in the squad cars before we even knew what happened. We were taken down and booked on the charge of conspiring to incite a riot—which, believe it or not, is a pretty serious crime—and thrown in the slammer with our bail set at three thousand dollars apiece—which also may seem like a paltry sum now, but back then was a lot of money.

"Well, there was no way I was coming up with it. I was in school on a grant and a scholarship *and* taking out loans, and my father, who didn't approve of what I was doing, would have laughed if I'd called him. As it turned out, though, the money wasn't necessarily a problem. That afternoon we found something out about Fearless Felicia, as we used to call her. It turned out that she was the granddaughter and sole heir of Dewey Cole, the magazine publisher tycoon of the twenties and thirties. We found that out after she used her one phone call, and not one but three lawyers came down to the courthouse, all of them looking like walking mannequins from a men's clothing store. The first thing they did was post her bail in cash, bringing out these wads of bills that looked like they'd been minted just that morning. Right after that they started screaming about suing for unnecessary physical abuse. And after that, almost as an afterthought, they offered to pay our bail, too. Ah, beautiful Felicia, all that time hiding her big secret from us, what a woman she was. It was a shame when, later that same year, she took a whole bottle of sleeping pills. Not so fearless after all, it turned out. Well, it's hard to understand some people.

"Anyway, there were just the two of us besides her—there had actually been more, but we three were the only ones the cops had identified and caught—and Tully immediately, wisely, accepted the money, posted bail, and bought his freedom back. Why I didn't, why I couldn't, is something that's hard for me to understand now, but I can still recount my reasoning well enough. First of all, I was sort of the leader of our group, and so I felt responsible for what had happened and wanted to take on the most blame myself. That was one reason. Then there was my sense of outrage. I felt like what had been done to us, breaking up our masque that way, was a crime, a crime just as bad as turning water hoses and dogs on peaceful protesters. I imagined an upcoming trial in which I and all of my troupe would be vindicated and honored as the heroes that we were, and I somehow thought my actually having gone to jail would be significant in that. And then there was one more reason I can remember. It was that I wanted to know what being in jail was like—for the experience, you know, something that I might be able to use later in my career.

"Well, I got my experience all right. What happened, or what I'm sure happened, was that our story made it around that county courthouse building like fire through a shantytown—Felicia's three lawyers hadn't helped that any, as you can imagine—and so the guys there, the bailiffs and the guards, prepared things for me the best they could. Maybe favors were exchanged, maybe money even changed hands, but however it was worked out, I ended up in this little cell that was down at the end of this long, dark hallway, off somewhere in the middle of nowhere in that old building. And my cellmates, doubtless handpicked for me, were three of the biggest, meanest niggers I'd ever seen.

"Now, we're all eating dinner right now, and I don't want to ruin any appetites. But let me just say that what happened to me in that jail cell that night was every bit as bad as you can imagine, Chris, and probably a little bit worse than that. Whatever it is that you're thinking, yes, I'm not proud to admit it, but it happened. And whatever it is that you're sort of thinking, not quite thinking but almost, yes, that happened, too.

"And sometime in the middle of it, the beatings and all the rest, I remember having this revelation—which at the time seemed like the single most significant, honest, and *true* thought I'd ever had. It was that we *are all perfectly equal,* Chris, *everyone*. Because, you see, before then, before that night in that jail cell, I'd never really believed that at all. I'd gotten involved in the civil rights movement just out of some vague feeling that I should, never stopping to really think about what it meant. I guess, if I thought anything at all, it was just that we were going to be nicer to each other in the street or something, not that it would ever change the true *order* of society. Since you were brought up in a different time, Chris, you probably do believe that blacks and whites are equal, and that's good, that's smart. But me, I always thought that no matter what happened, we would always just sort of find our respective places, just out of the natural order of things. Until that night when I learned, in the hardest way you could possibly imagine, that that wasn't necessarily going to be the case.

"And then, right on the heels of that revelation, another one quickly followed. It was that I didn't *want* us to be equal. It was like, what I found out that night was that my place in society, among what I'm going to call the dominant class, wasn't necessarily guaranteed at all, and in fact it was all pretty random that we were on top and they were on the bottom. From that point on I decided that I was going to do whatever I could to preserve my advantage in this world, instead of so foolishly working to diminish it. And that one decision, once I'd made it, and once I'd really seen what it meant, changed my whole life."

While Ted had been talking, he'd completely neglected his food, but now, in silence, he took a swig from his wineglass as if he'd just made a wholesome, hearty toast and picked up his knife and fork and dug in.

Chris swallowed one last piece of meat and put his knife and fork down. Once more, he found he'd lost his appetite, although this time not due to overtiredness but because of the weird story with the sickening, racist ending he'd been forced to sit through. Was any of it really true? he wondered. He wouldn't think so, except that his father had already verified some of it. So was it merely exaggeration? But if Ted was going to lie, why not start from scratch? Or, had the phones possibly been bugged all along, so that Ted knew what Chris's father had told him? But, no, that didn't make sense, because then Ted would also have known he'd been found out in time to warn Karen in New York, or Donna for that matter.

"The way that it changed my life and what happened after that isn't as simple as you think, Chris," Ted added through a mouthful of food. "But I'll tell you the rest of it tomorrow or the next night. For now you can clear your plate and excuse yourself if you're done, although I'd appreciate it if you came back and did the rest of the dishes after we've finished."

As Chris stood up, he decided he wouldn't even care whether the story was true, except that in its truth or falsehood might theoretically lie an important indicator of his chances for survival. Those odds were definitely better if Ted Harper *had* been lying, he decided, and so that was what he prayed for tonight: that the dinner story had just been another part of the whole thing, the running monologue of this new lesson, or whatever it was. And that both of them were almost over.

43

Chris went upstairs and opened the door to his bedroom—but then closed it again right in front of him, still standing outside on the balcony.

Something else occurred to him right then, and he whipped his head around to check the reflection in the big windows. If he could see them, it meant they could see him, still standing out in the open, blatantly trying to eavesdrop on their conversation. He thought he might just be okay; he *could* see them, Ted and Stan, still sitting there at the big table, but when he tried to see himself, he was in darkness. Just to make sure, though, he dropped down to his knees, and then finally to all fours, lowering himself until the lip of the overhang blocked out their images.

From there he tried to listen, attempting to tune out the music and somehow focus his hearing on the table below. He couldn't get anything, however, only the occasional clink of silverware or glass. The problem was that his bedroom was nearest to the stairs, which meant that right now he was closer to the stereo than the table. He thought about it for a moment, then slowly turned and began to crawl along the smooth, cold floor, keeping his boots in the air so as to be perfectly quiet. If Ted called for him, Chris was pretty sure he could still make it back to his bedroom door and open it, then pretend to be coming out of that room. If on the other hand one of them for some reason watched carefully when he did this or came running up the stairs, he was in big trouble. But he told himself the risk was worth it; he might find out they were planning on killing him tomorrow, in which case he could at least try an escape tonight.

He stopped when he reached the last bedroom door, reckoning from the back of the cabinets above the Formica bar that he was roughly even with the dining table. He didn't dare raise his head up to look at them in the window now, because from here his reflection would be facing Ted almost directly.

Ted said something, but Chris still couldn't hear it clearly. *You've got to call* . . . someone, it had sounded like.

And then Stan mumbled something back.

It was the music, echoing all around this big open space—and for a moment Chris wondered if that was one of the reasons it was on, if Ted knew he would try something like this. But that was being paranoid, he decided. Ted's stereo, Chris had already noted, had a CD-changer, so it wasn't likely that the album would run out. There was still the chance that he might hear something between pieces, though, or during a quiet passage, and he decided to stay put for a while.

Soon being on his hands and knees became uncomfortable, and he gradually brought himself to a sitting position, crouched over to keep his head down. That eventually made his neck start to hurt, and so he twisted his head around the other way to relieve the muscles a little.

He found himself staring at Ted's family triptych. There was mom, daughter-whatever-her-name-was, and closest to Chris since he was lowest on the wall, son. Chris couldn't remember his name either, but he studied the smiling face, trying to discern in that expression some indication that he'd grown up with a madman for a father. He didn't get anything, though; Jock Boy was a handsome blond without a care in the world.

Still, what was it Ted had said, on the very first day he'd come back to the house: *I was partially to blame for what happened with my own son.*

Chris's eye slid slowly off the picture, then came to rest on the object almost right next to it: the doorknob to that son's bedroom. He never had gone into either of the kids' rooms since he'd been here, and he now also remembered how Ted had barely shown him this one.

He stared at the door for a long time, but finally looked away. He had pushed his luck far enough, he thought—and for nothing; he obviously wasn't going to hear squat.

For some reason he was twice as afraid the moment he started to crawl back, as if the enormity of what he was doing was hitting him for the first time; literally anything might happen to him if Ted discovered this type of disobedience. By the time he finally reached his own door it seemed to loom above him like some ancient, hexed portal that he was cursed to be on the wrong side of. But he *needed* to be brave now for just a little longer, he told himself.

And then he did it: in one motion he turned the knob and opened, even while spinning around and standing up (like some old dance move, Chris's tired, frightened mind babbled—*do the Doorway Faker!*). After that, making a point of not looking down at the table, he walked straight into the bathroom, where he stayed until his heart had stopped pounding and he was reasonably certain that he was going to be able to keep down his dinner.

He did possibly learn one thing that night, however, lying awake in bed after going down and doing the dishes without waiting to be told to: He heard Stan go out the front door, start up a car, and drive away. The clock said 11:23.

44

"All right, so where was I in my little story I was telling you, Chris?" Ted said as soon as they sat down the next night, to a garlicky pasta with olives and sun-dried tomatoes and a lot of bacon. Chris had by then mostly forgotten about the unlikely account the previous evening of his warder's violent fall from grace, but when he realized it was going to continue, he immediately got a leaden feeling in his stomach. Tonight, however, he promised himself he wouldn't even pay attention, much less be taken in by whatever bizarre tales he was forced to hear.

The day outside had been windy and, for the first time since he'd started this, completely overcast. Without any sun to warm him, his sweat never seemed to dry, and every time he'd stopped shoveling to move to a different location or just take a break for a few moments, his exposed skin felt like little patches of ice. He'd been angry at himself for still not having done the laundry (not asking Ted and just throwing in a load after dinner was his best option there, he figured). He had changed back to his other pair of long underwear because he judged the others to be even worse now, but he'd felt damp and uncomfortable all day, not to mention that he was getting used to smelling like something dead and decaying.

"Oh, right, I remember," Ted went on, although he'd obviously known all along; he spoke with the scripted relish of some folk story-teller, Chris thought. "Well, for the next phase, if you want to call it that, we have to have a change of location, Chris. You see, soon after my little experience in that jail cell I dropped out of school. That whole thing ended as pointlessly as it started, by the way. Overnight, somehow, Felicia's lawyers managed to get the charges dropped, and in the morning I, or what was left of me, was a free man. But I was also a changed man, and one who quickly decided that acting was a profession without any real power or influence, and therefore not one that much interested me. Oh, yes, I know what you're thinking, and I considered the possible back door into politics; at the time Ronald Reagan had just stunned the nation by being elected governor of California. But I wasn't cut out to be a politician, and anyway, that seemed like a very, very long shot for me to keep going the way I was going.

"Now, if you were interested in power, and the application of power, there was only one place to be in 1967 as far as I was concerned, and that was Vietnam. I hadn't really thought about the war too much before then, except how to avoid the draft, which wasn't too hard for me since I was in a good school and anyway was a couple of years too old. They drafted mostly teenagers for that war, Chris, did you know that? They were interested in the less fortunate kids whose parents and families didn't have any connections or pull in society, and who weren't educated or smart, and so could be turned into killing machines quickly and efficiently. It was a good policy—maybe the only good one they ever came up with in that whole fiasco. Take some eighteen-year-old just out of high school and teach him how to shoot an M16 or fly a Huey, then tell him it's okay to kill gooks and send him over there and just kind of let nature take its course.

"Well, the way *I* went to Vietnam was on a Pan Am flight that stopped in San Francisco and then Tokyo, with plenty of time for sight-seeing in both places, before finally transferring to Air Vietnam and touching down in Saigon. I'd gotten a visa through a buddy of mine at school, a poli sci guy, who put my name on a list of students okayed to go over there on a fact-finding mission or something—even though I wasn't officially a student anymore—which, by the way, was where my money was coming from; I was living off my student loans. At the time I didn't have any idea what my future held for me, but I also didn't much care. The world as I'd always thought I'd known it had fallen away beneath me, and what I was left looking at were the real facts, what really made the world go round. I still didn't much like what I was seeing, but I thought at least I finally understood it. It turned out I wasn't quite there yet, but I'll get to that."

And I still won't be listening when you do, Chris said to himself. Although in truth it was almost impossible not to.

"When I first got into Saigon, I just took my two suitcases and went and wandered the streets, and, man, that place practically blew my mind clean off. The heat, the smell. There were people being cycled around by these skinny old men that looked like they couldn't climb a flight of stairs; there were girls selling themselves on the streets—these beautiful thirteen- and fourteen-year-olds whose fathers or brothers were their pimps. There were drugs everywhere you looked: opium and hash for sale at every bar you went to, like tobacco, regular and menthol. I ended up finding this place for seven dollars a night, a nice little room with a sagging bed and an old woman who sat outside my door all night just in case I wanted anything. It overlooked the Tu Do, which was kind of the main drag there. And after that I just started hanging around, seeing what there was to see. And let me tell you, I saw a lot.

"Mostly what I saw was something everyone over there knew like daylight, but which never quite made it into the papers back home: that the REMFs—rear-echelon motherfuckers, that would be, basically anyone who wasn't on the front line—were living like kings off the slavery of the Vietnamese, and making a fortune off the black market, to boot. And then there were the soldiers on R and R, boys straight off the farm or from the inner city, most of whom were already so hooked on dope they were more ready for rehab than being shipped back to the front. The stories they told would have stood your hair on end, too, about all the tortures, maimings, and rapes they'd either seen or participated in.

"But pretty soon I got bored of passing the time with the soldiers and the hookers and the bar girls. The interesting ones were only around for a few days at a time; the soldiers either headed out to Tokyo or back to the front, and the girls usually found some high-ranking American to move in with, set up house like a steady job, you know? So what I started doing, I started pretending I was a reporter, or more like a correspondent on assignment. That was what my visa said anyway, and so I started throwing on a sport jacket every night and going over to the Hotel Caravelle—that was where all the press hung out, at this rooftop bar. And, little by little, I got to know people, no one you would have heard of, but important press people, writers for the big papers. Everyone just assumed I was some kind of writer or reporter, and of course I didn't do anything to set them straight. And it was kind of fun, you know, because after a day of wandering the city, I'd go over to the bar there and listen to the latest inside scoops, the latest scandals. I quickly learned another truth over there, which was that the government we were fighting to support was every bit as corrupt as the one we were fighting against. Not that I am or ever was a communist, and not that what the South Vietnamese ended up getting wasn't far worse than what we would have done for them. But you have to understand that in the scene over there at the time, everything was already so far off the mark it was hard to know what was right.

"Well, anyway, one night, at what had become my regular haunt at the bar of the Hotel Caravelle, a man walks up and introduces himself simply as Jack. And now, how can I describe Jack and the way that guy stood out? There wasn't anything different about his clothes—he was wearing a sport jacket and a white shirt like the rest of us. His hair was maybe shorter than your average reporter's, but I guess really it was his body, and not just that he stood about six foot and another foot. It was like he was made of a thicker material than the rest of us. The guy looked like if a bus hit him, the outcome would be in question. He had this entire system of muscles just for his forearms, and sometimes when he'd turn his head, the strings of his neck would stand out just like high-tension cables.

"I don't remember quite how our conversation went in the beginning, but I do remember that I didn't fool him for a second. He took one look at me and said, 'So, you over here for laughs, huh?' But, as many have in my life—and in this way I'm quite fortunate—Jack took a liking to me. He introduced himself as an adviser to the Saigon Ministry of the Interior, which essentially meant that you didn't know what he did, and he wasn't going to tell you, and that was good because you probably didn't want to know anyway. And then he pulled his drink up to mine and started telling me stories.

"Well, I'd obviously already heard a lot of them by now, but Jack's were different. They were different mostly because they were on a larger scale: firefights in the rain where entire companies are pinned down for days and by the end the blood is thicker than the water and the wounded are begging their buddies to shoot them just to get it over with; rapes and massacres of whole towns and villages, where the peasants are lucky to die early so they don't have to see what happens to their friends and family. But also, they were different because with Jack you really believed them, you really got the feeling they were true. I often thought the soldiers told you things just to shock you, just because they knew you wanted a thrill. With Jack, it was all matter-of-fact. He seemed to be one of those men who'd found a way to distance himself from things, so that even his own death one day would be only another matter for cold, calm consideration.

"Anyway, I guess at some point we started talking about airpower, about how so much of the war was being fought from the skies with helicopters and jets dropping bombs. And right then, it was probably about midnight, he looks at his watch and asks me if I want to see some action right now.

"Well, you know, at first I was sure he was kidding, that I'd gotten Jack all wrong, and he was just trying to see how scared he could get this dumb civilian, you know? So I said, sure, let's go.

"Well, it was probably the stupidest single thing I ever said in my life, because before I know it I'm downstairs and in an army jeep headed out to Tonsonhut Airport. I still didn't really think it was real, though, until we stepped out on the tarmac. But there, waiting for us with its rotors already wound up and screaming, already kicking up a storm right in front of us, is one of those mean, black gunship Hueys. Jack, you know, he doesn't even pause. He's out of that jeep before I can sneeze, and then I'm following him and we're climbing in and that big side door is sliding closed. Inside is four more guys, all got up in bulletproof vests and flak jackets, all looking like they're ready to kill or get killed. I barely get a seat on one of the benches, there in the middle, before that bird is dusting off, gaining altitude like crazy even while it's spiraling around to head off in the other direction.

"Now, I'm so scared by this point all I can do is sit there and try not to sick up my dinner, but soon I stop and think how strange it is that these guys hardly even notice me; they're all in uniform, after all—everyone except Jack, that is—and here I am just sitting here in my chinos and shirt. Well, it turns out, once I figure out how to use the intercom doohickey in this helmet they give me, that these guys are used to it—because in the beginning, before the press turned against the war, they took riders all the time. In a little while, I also realize these guys are as relaxed as can be. I mean they're pumped, they're ready, you know, but it's like they're completely used to it, and soon they're either falling asleep, or these two next to me start up a card game.

"We flew up North high over the Mekong River, which, as the sky started to get light with the rising sun, and the way the black water from irrigation canals made snakes and patterns through the brown and green, was just about the most beautiful sight you've ever seen, like something out of a fairy tale.

"And then all of a sudden I realize two things at once. The first is that we're not alone; there are about eight or nine other choppers right behind us, which have obviously been there all along. And the second is that we're starting to dive down, like this pilot means to plant this unholy thing right into the turf. In another second the doors on both sides are sliding open, and that's when all hell breaks loose. Out of nowhere, tracers are being fired up at us, arcing all around like fireworks. And then our guns and rockets start firing, these two guys in the doors blasting away at whatever they can see down there. Man, the noise, the concussion of these things, I can't even tell you, but I was certain that I was going to buy it right then and there. Only I keep looking around, you know, because I want to at least see it. I figure, if I'm going to die, I want to see the one that gets me, right?

"Well, this pilot, he just keeps taking us lower, right into the maelstrom, and soon I can actually see these little guys on the ground there, all of them running around like a Chinese fire drill with their AK-47s and their black pajamas. The main target is some kind of big thatch hut down there with no windows, and all of us are diving in on it, blasting away with everything we've got, the place turning into nothing but fireball for what looks like about four square acres. And these stupid little motherfuckers who are too stupid to run are just getting mowed down and blown to pieces by the dozens. I mean, as far as I can tell, it's not a war, it's a slaughter. You've never seen anything like it, Chris, the kind of carnage we inflicted that morning. We must have killed about, I don't know, two or three hundred of them it seemed like.

"And then, with one last massive fuckin' explosion, as someone nails this hut and sends it to the moon, it's all over and we're all climbing up again just as fast as we can. The guys shut the side doors, clap each other on the shoulders, and settle back for the long ride home. That was it, that was what they'd come to do and it was all over.

"Chris, I tell you, after I saw that, I would have bet everything I had that that war would be over in about a week."

Once again, with an unnatural abruptness after how animatedly he had been speaking, Ted broke off and took a big drink from his wine-glass, pausing afterward to swirl the liquid around before he took another. It seemed as if he would go on then, but, the same as last night, story time was over, and he picked up his silverware and began to eat.

Chris looked down at his own meal, which tonight he mostly hadn't touched yet either. In spite of himself, he'd become even more involved in Ted Harper's continuing saga.

Which, also once again, he couldn't quite dismiss as ridiculous. The man wasn't portraying himself as some war hero, after all. Or was it crazy that a young Ted Harper, fresh from dropping out of graduate school, would be offered a ride on an attack helicopter in Saigon early in the Vietnam War? Chris, whose only ideas and images from that time and place came from movies and TV, plus maybe a single chapter from a history book, had no way to judge. Nowadays, in Afghanistan or any other American conflict he could imagine, something like that would almost certainly be out of the question. But he knew that things had changed quite a bit since back then, and he had no concept of what may or may not have been possible in that distant war, which had ended before his first memories.

Looking for some kind of clue, he glanced up at Stan, sitting across from him. But, as always, Chris could read no indication on his face whatsoever about what he did or didn't know.

Thus the punishment continued, Chris thought, still with no end in sight. If you counted the day Stan had first shown up, they were now on day six.

45

Waking from a shallow daze, Chris got out of bed and opened his door. He was just heading for the bathroom, he told himself. Out on the balcony, though, he stopped and looked around. For a second night in a row now he'd been awake to listen to Stan starting up a car and driving away. Tonight, however, he'd forced himself to stay up even later and heard something else as well: Ted turning off lights, climbing the stairs to his room, his footsteps going right past Chris's door. That happened at 12:42.

This time, getting up, the clock had read 3:07, which Chris supposed was as good a time as there would ever be for this. Instead of turning right, he turned to his left.

A little moonlight was coming into the house through the big windows, making a pattern of deep shadows in the open space below. Hardly any light made it upstairs, however, and straight ahead of him, where the balcony ended and turned into a hallway, there was only a black hole—where, for all he knew, Ted Harper might at this very moment be sitting on the steps that led to the door of his room, watching. But Chris managed to keep that appalling possibility at the back of his mind. He walked as quietly as he could, nearly sliding his socks along on the smooth floor. He passed by one bedroom door, then a second, the daughter's room. And then he came to it.

Probably this was just another insane, pointless gamble he was taking, Chris thought, where he would once again risk everything and learn nothing. But it had seemed worthwhile before when he hadn't been scared out of his wits, he reminded himself, and put his hand on the chrome doorknob. Ever so slowly, he turned it, opened the door, and stepped inside.

There was no light at all once the door was closed behind him, and he reached for the one item he'd brought along, a plastic Bic lighter he'd fished out of his jeans pocket and tucked into the waistband of his long underwear. He finally got it to catch on his third try, the hissing flame casting a dim, flickering glow, eaten up mostly by the blue walls, which appeared nearly black. He put up a hand to try to shield the light from the window, thinking of the men he'd once seen outside in the car. It was probably more of his paranoia to imagine they were watching the house right at this instant, making careful note of which window lit up, but Chris wasn't going to chance it.

He held his sputtering torch in front of him and began to walk slowly forward. He saw something on his right and brought the flame closer. It was a poster of a big ship on the ocean, like a container ship or a tanker, crashing though a heavy sea and throwing spray off its bow, which glinted in bright sunlight. Chris raised the light a little more and read the words *Phillips Petroleum* in big yellow letters across the top. It was an advertisement, like one of those shots a corporation would put on the cover of its monthly prospectus. Remotely, he wondered why it was here—if Ted now owned the ship or something.

When he took another step, though, he thought he at least knew the answer to that one question. Another picture was right next to it, this one smaller, and on yellowing paper that was curling up at the corners. Chris brought the flame close again, to see a child's drawing done in both Magic Marker and pencil. It was a copy of the photo next to it, with great big gashes of blue to represent the water, the ship all sharp angles and corners, rendered with the pencil to make it look even more ungainly. The two pictures were hanging side by side in a kind of collective presentation: *Look what I copied*. Yet both had to be ancient; the paper that the drawing was on was nearly petrified, crumbling away with age; and even in the yellow light of the Bic, the photo looked faded, sun-bleached with time. Smoothing out the lower right-hand corner of the illustration, Chris found what he expected to: a child's signature, in block scrawl. The name was legible, though: David Harper.

He moved on to see more drawings, all done by the same child's hand. Chris judged that hand to be about eight or nine, although he admitted he might be off by as many as three or four years. They were all on the same yellowing, parchmentlike paper, and all curling up off the wall since none of them had been framed but were merely tacked at their upper corners.

Chris thought that he had gotten the idea—even before he crossed to the other side of the room and noticed that the sheets on the one small bed were a spaceships-and-planets pattern, or that a half-completed model of a racing motorcycle was on the dresser next to it, the dust covering the various plastic pieces like a coating of fur. Unlike the girl's bedroom, which was merely filled with the artifacts of childhood, this one was frozen in time.

But why?

Chris stood there staring into the middle distance, trying to figure it out, and while doing so almost missed what was right in front of him. At the back of the dresser, about two inches behind the biggest piece of the model, were two orange vials with white tops like the kind that came from pharmacies. They were coated in a roughly equivalent layer of dust, but when he brought the flame close, he had no trouble reading the nearer, yellowing label.

ONE TABLET TWICE A DAY
60 LOPRESSOR TAB 25MG
REFILL 5 TIMES

Chris had to crane his head around to see the other one, something called Dilantin, which was to be taken once a day. Both drugs were from a place called Donnay Pharmaceutical in Charlotte, North Carolina, and both had been prescribed by a Dr. Raymond Varger. The dates agreed as well: 06/05/81. So these, too, had been left over from the past, like the rest of the tableau. Although, Chris thought, they looked like pretty serious drugs, and who would ever leave drugs in a child's room with him, even in spite of the childproof caps? But then Chris glanced at the bed again. You would, he surmised, if you knew that child was too sick to even reach over and try to get at them. So had David been very sick once? But if so, he had certainly gotten better.

It was another mystery, Chris decided, and it would probably stay that way until Ted finally got tired of having a hostage and decided to off him.

Chris started to look around again, but right at that moment jerked his thumb off the lighter and shook out that hand; the whole top of the Bic had become too hot to touch. He was left standing in darkness.

Whatever, he thought; he had seen enough and it was time to get the hell out of here. Moving slowly in the direction he had come, he found the door without crashing into anything and opened it and stepped back out into the hallway. He shut it behind him, but then stopped once more.

Now, to his right, there were the family pictures again. Also in that direction, however, was the black cave leading to Ted Harper's bedroom.

Managing to hold off his fear a little longer, though, he knelt down beside the picture of the son for a second time. The lighter was still hot and burned his thumb when he flicked it, but the flame lit on the first try. Chris brought it right up to that smiling, contented face. Still, there was nothing out of the ordinary—

And then he noticed it, up underneath the top of the frame where no one was ever supposed to see. He leaned in for a closer look, for a moment forgetting he was holding fire and almost singeing his eyebrows off. He found he could just make out the words that way, though, half-concealed by the metallic silver frame.

They read: *Sweater, p. 22.*

Chris felt a layer of thick blackness descend from above and cover him entirely, adding to the layers that were already there, draped over his shoulders, settled heavily in his stomach somehow—only all at once he realized he had an even bigger problem, because he was falling . . .

He managed to catch himself, just barely, but his hands made a loud thumping noise on the floor, and the plastic lighter went skidding across the slick boards toward the edge of the balcony, where he watched it come to a stop not less than an inch from the perfectly smooth lip.

After taking a moment to thank God it hadn't fallen, Chris just held perfectly still, listening to his breathing and his heart pounding—which together sounded loud enough to wake up Ted Harper by themselves.

The shot had been clipped from some clothing catalog! his mind was jabbering at him again and again in the meantime, as if he would definitely come up with some simple explanation for that fact the next time he repeated it. From where he was, he looked up at the other pictures, but even in the dark mom and daughter looked real in a way that son didn't, probably because they weren't paid models, sitting carefully posed behind a bank of lights, or whatever.

So something *had* happened, but what? And how could Ted possibly be keeping it a secret?

Unless the medications *had* been unrelated, and his son just used to do modeling work and Ted had merely liked the shot; and also merely liked his son's room just *exactly* the way it had once been when he was around eight.

But all that, Chris thought, had the feel of some very wishful thinking.

"So what do you think, Stan? After this is all over, Mr. Harper just let's me drive out of here?" They were eating lunch under another cloudy, cold sky, Chris exhausted all over again from having stayed up most of the night.

"Yeah, he'll let you go. Don't worry about it," Stan replied absently.

"So you don't think it's going to be like what happened with his son?"

That got Stan's full attention, and he slowly lowered the French fry he'd been about to eat. "That wasn't his fault, Chris. His kid had some kind of heart problem, congenital thing. And it practically killed Ted when he died."

"Really, so then why did he tell me his son has a job on Wall Street? And why does he have a picture of some model on his wall, posing as his happy, healthy college-age kid?"

"You noticed that, huh? Don't worry, it's nothing. He just doesn't like people asking questions. I mean you can understand why he wouldn't want to talk about it."

Chris just dropped it. He knew Stan wasn't going to tell him any more anyway, and he thought he should save the begging and pleading for when he really needed it. But he got the feeling there was a lot he wasn't being told: like whether the boy had died in this very house; or what, exactly, Ted *had* done that would make Stan feel the need to say it wasn't his fault; or, whether Chris was actually here to replace that lost son, and also, possibly, die an analogous death.

230

Whatever it was, it was becoming pretty clear that this was about something more than Ted's merely getting revenge, or wanting to change Chris into a better man, or any of that other crap. What that something was, though, Chris didn't know.

But the scariest part of all, he thought, was that Ted Harper might not know either.

46

"Well, of course, as you know, Chris, that war in Vietnam never did end up finishing anything like the way we all thought it would," Ted started out that night, Chris changing his mind on the spot and actually feeling thankful for this installment of *The Ted Harper Story;* it was better than just sitting here wondering what hideous family secret the man was hiding from the world, and possibly himself as well. Chris fully realized that yet again the tale was being picked up exactly where it had been left off, but didn't know what, if anything, he should make of that.

"Long before it did, though, I started spending more time with Jack, the man who'd taken me on my little chopper ride," Ted continued. "Because after that night, he began inviting me to these parties. Unbeknownst to me before then, there was this whole circuit of cocktail and dinner parties for the rich and well-connected in Saigon, usually given at these old French villas, which were like palaces, with everyone either in uniform or dressed to the nines, and all these servants running around. The French villas were left over from when the French had colonized Vietnam. Basically the same thing had happened to them as happened to us, by the way, and when we first started getting involved in the fifties, the Vietnamese had already been at war with the French for over a decade—and before that had fought the Japanese, the Dutch, the British, and even before then held off the Chinese for literally thousands of years. Did you know *that,* Chris?

"Anyway, I'll tell you, I can't even remember half the important people I met going to these things. I was introduced to Ellsworth Bunker once. He was the new American ambassador then, who, by the way, had also gone to Yale, and so we had that to talk about. I indirectly spoke to Tran Van Huong, the ex–prime minister of South Vietnam. And I was once in the same room with General Westmoreland. You know who he was? He was basically the guy in charge of it all, the one who conceived and engineered the entire first half of that war. When I saw him, things were still going well. The kill ratio was astronomical, you know, and he was struttin' his stuff, probably already imagining how the history books would remember him. There was a man with real power, you could practically see it burning out from behind his eyes.

"Well, needless to say, there weren't only men at these parties. There were a lot of women, too; some Americans, but mostly they were Vietnamese women. And not just prostitutes and consorts, either, though there were certainly plenty of those. But most of them weren't like that at all; most were well-educated, wealthy women who'd one way or another, usually through their husbands, taken an interest and gotten involved in the war and the international political scene that went along with it. And one of these, introduced to me by Jack maybe two or three weeks after I'd first met him, was a woman named Lei Ling.

"Now, Chris, you're probably not going to believe me when I tell you that Lei Ling was the most beautiful woman that you or I have ever seen. She was Vietnamese, you're thinking, and they all look about the same. Well, that's what I thought, too, before I went over there. But really, you know, it's just your ignorance, your mind's being unused to what you're seeing, that makes it seem that way at first. The Vietnamese are actually an incredibly handsome people. They're smaller than we are, sure, but they're not less proud. And what they give away in strength and height they more than make up for in grace and agility. Anyway, Lei Ling: The first time I saw her she was wearing this thin, silky, cream-colored dress, with just the thinnest straps you ever saw holding this thing up. Her black hair was cut short, like a boy's page cut, and the only jewelry she wore, besides the wedding band on her finger, were two tiny diamond studs in her ears. But you have to understand, any trumpery or accessories on Lei Ling would have been overkill; her face was so perfect just the way it was that you wanted to scrub off even the little bit of makeup she was wearing. I tell you, both men's and women's heads snapped around to look at her wherever she went, like she had everyone's eyes on a string or something.

"Now of course, I knew right off I didn't have a chance with her. Probably, she was married to some general or high-ranking official. But when Jack brings her over, I do my best to talk it up anyway. I figure, when else will I get a chance to speak face-to-face with a living angel.

"So, anyway, we fall to talking, and it turns out that she speaks perfect English and actually studied in the United States for a while, at UCLA. I tell her that I'm still in graduate school because I think she might like to hear it, and she asks what I'm studying. So I tell her—I lie to her—about that, too. But now it turns out that she's very interested in experimental theater also, which at this point I thought I'd given up entirely, only the light pouring out of this girl's eyes is enough to make me rethink the whole thing over again.

"Well, we must have talked for nearly an hour, to the point where everyone else has left us alone together, and the people passing us by are starting to give us strange looks. Because, after all, she is married and probably shouldn't be seen having some soul-searching one-on-one with a single, young, American guy. I guess we realize this at about the same time, and then there's nothing for it but that she has to say, 'Well, nice to meet you,' and I have to say the same while gently shaking her beautiful, little hand.

"And do you know what that's like, Chris? Have you ever met a girl, when you're traveling or something, and so help you God it seems to you like, to both of you, that you're just perfect for each other, only there isn't time, or one of you is with someone else? It just makes you want to cry out loud, doesn't it? Well, that was how I felt right then.

"But, I pull myself together the best I can and take myself to the bar, tell myself it's time to drown my sorrows and be a man about it, tell myself that later, after a reasonable amount of time has passed so I can excuse myself without it seeming like I did it just because she walked away from me, I'm going to hire myself one of those pedicabs and drive all over the city and see if I *can't* find some little prostitute who doesn't at least remind me of her.

"Only for whatever reason I never do leave. I guess probably I got in some kind of conversation—about the war, since that was almost all anyone ever talked about—and had a few drinks, and the time passed. And then it seems like all at once I look up, and I see her again. She's leaving now, standing on the other side of the room saying her good-byes to a few people, wearing this demure black wrap over that knockout dress. But our eyes meet, and suddenly I just know that she's been standing there for a long time, drawing the thing out so she can get my attention again. Well, I probably would have noticed it sooner if I wasn't three sheets to the wind by that point, but once I finally do, I immediately put my drink down, straighten up, and try not to knock anyone down on my way over there.

"Now, since for this whole time I'd been there at the bar, all I'd really been doing was thinking about this girl, you'd think that she couldn't possibly look as beautiful to me anymore, that by that point I would have built her up in my imagination so that seeing her again could only be a comedown. But it wasn't. If anything, she looked even more beautiful, and it wasn't just the drinks. In fact, by the time I'm standing next to her again, I'm literally speechless. I actually feel faint, like my knees are going to buckle up underneath me.

"She says these words to me exactly: 'It was very nice to meet you. I hope that we can see each other again to talk about our mutual interests.' And then, taking it from underneath this wrap she's got on, she pulls out a small origami bird that she'd made—folded from a piece of green paper that I recognize as having come from the napkins they're using at the bar. 'Welcome to Saigon, Mr. Harper,' she says as she hands it to me. And then she turns around, and before I can even think of anything to say, she's gone, out the door and into the night. And I'm left standing there, half-stunned, staring at this long-necked bird like it's some rare gem she's handed me.

"Well, I almost went after her, but I didn't. Even more than half-drunk, I still knew I couldn't just up and give chase like a coon dog, not with everyone in the room watching us, or watching her at least. And so I end up turning right around and going back to my place at the bar and my drink. After those few moments of hope, I'm twice as despondent now, and I really start throwing them back, drinking like there's no tomorrow. I guess I did that a lot when I was over there. I was pretty lonely for the most part, and still very confused, as most young men are, whether they admit it or not.

"Anyway, the next morning I wake up with such a hangover, I'm sure you know what *that's* like, Chris. I'm in my own room and in my own bed, okay—by now, I've moved into this incredible little château that Jack found for me, for only a couple more dollars a day—but I'm still dressed, and I can't hardly remember anything that happened to me, least of all how I got back there. Only when I roll over, the first thing I see is that little origami bird that Lei Ling had made for me, crushed now because I must have gone to sleep holding it and rolled over on top of it. Well, I almost cry when I see that I've ruined it. But then when I pick it up to try to stick it back together, I notice something deep in the main fold of the body where I couldn't see it before. So I open it up the rest of the way, and penciled in there, in just the tiniest, most precise letters you can imagine, it says: *24 Rue Catinat. Come at one.*

"I'll tell you, I must have stared at that little piece of paper for twenty minutes straight, going from disbelief to rage and the worst kind of cursing yourself and God and everything else you can think of. 'Come at one' meant even more than you think it might, since there was a curfew on and unless you wanted to take your chances with the MPs, where you were at one was where you'd be spending the night. And in all, I was doubly mortified. Now, having been granted the chance of a lifetime, not only do I blow it for myself, but now *she* thinks I'm not interested in *her.*

"And then, without hardly even thinking about what I'm doing or what I'm going to do, I start moving. I get up off the bed, and as far as I can remember, I walk straight out the door.

"In a kind of a daze, my feet carried me straight to the address she'd written out, to another château not too far away, much larger, with French doors looking out on a garden so that you had to go through a gate and then down a path in order to get to the door. I don't even hesitate, but just keep walking, right up to this front door, which is thick and solid, carved out of some dark, exotic wood. There was a polished gold doorbell to one side, and like a complete idiot, I reached my hand out and pushed it. It was still the early morning, I remember, and it was quiet, and I could hear this bell jangling away inside somewhere. And then I just stood there. I can't imagine what I must have looked like, having slept in my suit, my hair probably a big rat's nest.

"Well, when the door opens up in front of me, I come out of whatever sleepwalking stupor I've been in right quick. Because standing behind it isn't Lei Ling—Lei Ling, still wearing the cream gown she was wearing last night, as I'd somehow imagined it would be—but a young Vietnamese boy, a teenager dressed in servant's whites. And standing right behind him is an older man, a small man but with a clever and alert face, wearing the uniform of an officer of the South Vietnamese army.

"Now, I'm so horrified at that moment, that I can't think of one blessed, goddamned thing to say, not even 'Hello,' much less 'Sorry, I must have the wrong address,' which probably wouldn't have even helped anyway since the truth of why I'm there is written all over my face. Well, this guy immediately sizes up the situation and then barks something at this servant boy in Vietnamese to send him away. After that it's just him and me, and he steps out of the doorway to look me over a little closer. When he does, I notice that not only is he wearing his uniform, he's also got a sidearm, this beautiful silver-plated revolver, which doesn't do anything to cheer me up, let me tell you.

"He walks straight up to me, all the time looking me in the eyes, freezing me where I am so I don't even realize what he's going to do until he does it and it's too late. You see, all that time, ever since I woke up and opened up Lei Ling's note, I'd been carrying that dang thing around with me, and now, before I hardly knew it, he'd snatched it away. It hardly even resembled an origami bird anymore, and it only took him a moment to read what was written there—and even if he couldn't read English, I knew he'd at least recognize his own address. Once he had, you know, he looks me up and down, looks me in the eyes again, and I was just about sure my goose was cooked right then and there and that I was about to die with a bad hangover in a wrinkled suit.

"Instead of shooting me right off, though, this guy, he looks back over his shoulder and he hollers out something I *can* understand: 'Lei Ling.' So great, I think. Now I'm going to get to watch this guy beat up his beautiful wife before he gets around to killing me.

"In a few moments, from behind him in the dark hallway, I see her. This morning she's wearing jeans and a white pullover top, walking with a little trowel in her hand like she's just come in from working on the garden. She's every bit as beautiful as the night before, and right then I decide that, if it comes down to it, if this guy goes to hit her, I'm going to try and stop him, even it means my own ass. At least that's what I tell myself, standing there with my heart pounding like I'm about to have a seizure or something. She comes right up to us, barely even looking at me, and this guy hands her the note, says something else to her in Chink. She looks down at it, then looks away like she's trying to hide tears or something. I want to jump in right then and say something, do something, but I know I can't do anything that won't just make everything worse.

"So this guy turns back to me, and now for the first time he speaks English. He says, 'So, you are young man I have been hearing about. You better come inside.'

"As you can imagine, I'm practically in shock. Now I'm trying to think what she could have told him, even while I'm trying to guess how long I have left to live. I almost just turn and run at this point—I'm still hungover as hell, remember, my head's pounding up a storm, and I feel like I'm going to throw up all at the same time. But, like some prisoner, I lower my head and follow the two of them into this house.

"Well, we get in and the door closes behind me, and it's so bizarre what happens next it takes me almost forever to figure it out, but when this guy turns around to face me again, he's got this big smile on his face. He comes right up to me and offers me his hand to shake, and he says, 'So, tell me, Mr. Harper, do you always show up seven hours late for your appointments?'

"As I said, it was all so strange, I couldn't figure out what in blazes was going on. So I look over to Lei Ling, and now I see that all along she hadn't been crying; that really she'd been laughing, trying to hold back her laughter.

"Well, once I got over my embarrassment, we all had a pretty good laugh over it. It turned out that the guy wasn't her husband at all, but just a friend of hers. His name was Kai Tieng, a total fairy boy, but also a nice guy, and later we became friends.

"Finally, I got to talk to Lei Ling alone. I apologized for my appearance, explaining to her that I hadn't found her note in time, and that after she'd left the party I'd been so depressed that I had to get drunk. To my surprise, she told me she understood completely. She said that if she wasn't allergic to the stuff, she would have done the same, and instead, when I hadn't shown up, had called Kai Tieng to come over and keep her company. So you see, Chris, it wasn't just me. We'd both had the same effect on each other.

"That morning, the three of us ate breakfast together in her garden back behind the house, and after that I took a nap in this screened-in gazebo they had. When I woke up, I bathed myself and shaved using her husband's razor, and we made love for the first time that afternoon, also out back in that gazebo, which she said was her favorite place on earth. Chris, I'm telling you, that was an experience unlike any I'd ever had, or will have again in my life. For those first hours that we were together, we had the very best of everything: We were young. We were madly in love and trusted each other completely even at the same time that we were practically strangers. And also, needless to say, we were both horny as hell.

"And that was how I met and started my love affair with Lei Ling, a married woman living in a country that was tearing itself apart even as we diddled away the afternoon in her little garden sanctuary, where only a few tens of miles away men were dying in firefights and from land mines and in close-up knife fights, and on most days and nights you could hear the shelling on the outskirts of the city—outgoing most of the time, but a few times a week they would land one on us, and then the explosion would echo through the streets like some omen of great catastrophe.

"And I guess I really should have seen what was coming even then. But, as I already said, I was young, and I still had a lot to learn."

Ted looked down at the table meaningfully and shook his head. Then, as he always did when he'd finished his nightly chapter, he went for his wine.

"So what happened, was she killed or something?" Chris asked before he could think to stop himself.

But Ted merely raised his eyebrows before picking up his knife and fork, and all the question accomplished was to let Ted know that his story had piqued the interest of his captive audience.

47

And the next day, working under an even darker gray haze, with an even brisker wind blowing, and in his even dirtier, smellier long underwear, Chris found himself again thinking about the tale he was being forced to hear. He cursed himself for it; last night he'd been too tired to do anything but sleep, and so it seemed to him that he was losing ground, that Ted Harper's agenda was once more consuming him entirely. For a while he tested out the idea of somehow consolidating the Vietnam story with what he'd possibly learned about the man's son, trying to make some kind of sense of the thing that way. But there was nothing there, beyond the fact that Ted didn't talk much about his family. Other than that, they were separate and seemingly unrelated incidents from entirely different parts of Ted Harper's life; even if everything that Chris suspected and everything he'd been told were perfectly true, the most he could say was that they were both just more of the unique and unlucky circumstances that had allowed this whole crazy thing to happen to him.

And yet still something was missing, Chris felt, or at least he hadn't yet discovered what he was hoping to, which he supposed was a fact or an angle he could use to help him get the hell out of here.

At one point soon after that, he found himself suddenly furious. He'd let himself think about what Ted had said at the end, about the men fighting and dying in the jungle nearby while he'd been having his romantic Asian encounter, and it came back to Chris with a power and tangibility it hadn't had the first time. After all, he thought, even if the rest was complete bullshit, that much had to be true: that at the exact moments the rich and powerful in Saigon had been going to their cocktail parties, and having affairs, and taking hookers, other men, other Americans, were over there living in the jungle and getting shot at and dying, or in POW camps getting tortured daily. Which was nothing that Chris hadn't already known or thought about, only now, in his current situation, it seemed indisputable and terrible in a way it never had before and made him absolutely livid.

In his rage, he imagined himself as some grunt digging a foxhole on the front line, in terror and waiting to die—even as he acted out in his mind a pornographic version of Ted's encounter, after his morning nap, with Lei Ling in the gazebo. The concept ended up getting him aroused, however, his hard-on making shoveling uncomfortable. Which in turn depressed him; he was no different from Ted. And life was infinitely unfair, and even that was understating the matter somehow.

Sometime roughly in the middle of the illicit fantasy, Stan stood up and began talking into his cell phone. And then he came jogging over.

"I got to go do something," he said quickly. "Don't do anything stupid, okay?"

Chris didn't say anything, but just watched in amazement as his guard began to run again, taking a wide turn to head back to the gray house and the car. He ran all the way, got in, and drove away.

Chris was left standing there, all alone and unobserved as far as he knew. Or was this some kind of test? But even if it wasn't, what was he going to do about it? There was the bay to try to swim across, but could he make it before freezing to death, or before being discovered and whatever would follow that? He'd never tried either of the two other houses for phones, but he still considered the odds of finding a working one too slim to risk it. So there was really no advantage at all; Stan's absence merely meant a break from shoveling, and not even that much of one since Chris still had to stand up in order not to get caught gold-bricking when the car came back.

But now, for the first time since the true severity of his situation had become known to him, he began to think seriously about escape. It could very probably be done, he thought; maybe not during the day, when Stan was usually close by, but at night when he was alone in the house with Ted. He knew for sure now that he could get out of his room and move about unnoticed, and if they even had a guard on then, he would probably be asleep in a car down by the bridge, where Chris had seen them that first time—although he hadn't noticed anything since and would almost be willing to bet that they didn't bother anymore. But even assuming someone was there, maybe that redheaded kid whose job was the night shift, there was a better than good chance that he could slip by on the beach side. And then, instead of going across the bridge, he could go underneath, wading or swimming across the calm water there. It would be cold, but he wouldn't have to be in it for long, and he would survive. And after that he would be home free. He had never checked the distance on the odometer, but it could only be one or two miles before the first occupied houses in Whistler's Cove. Now all he needed was the bravery to try it.

In only a matter of minutes Chris saw the silver car returning and bent into his strange work again. When Stan came back, he offered no explanation for the aberration, and Chris didn't ask for one.

48

"If you're going to understand the rest of my story, Chris, you have to first of all understand just how deeply involved I became with Lei Ling," Ted started out that evening.

"For well over a month, we saw each other almost every single day and night, and by the end I'd practically moved in with her in her mansion villa. She had three servants: the teenage boy I saw when I first came to her door, and two women who worked mostly in the kitchen— all of whom, after about the first two days, we stopped bothering to try and hide things from. We mostly stopped bothering going out to the sort of party where we'd first met, too, preferring to just hang around the house. I would read, usually, and she would do her gardening. Sometimes her friend Kai Tieng would stop by. Often, when she had to go out to make one of her social appearances—her husband wasn't a general, it turned out, but he was some kind of high-ranking adviser to the SVA, and the importance of her keeping up the appearances of a dedicated wife was the same—I would just stay behind, like a faithful dog, to wait for her return. I'm telling you all this so you'll understand the way things had progressed between us, and so what happens next won't seem so strange or outrageous to you.

"Now, Chris, to my mind, for a man, there are basically three ways of falling in love with a woman. The first isn't really falling in love at all. That's where you think you're in love, you know, you've convinced yourself that you must be, but really you're just lonely or horny or what have you, and you've found someone to fixate on. The second kind is simple, where you think you're in love, and sure enough, you are in love. But this kind is more rare than you might think, since men generally tend to be confused about the subject.

"And then there's the third kind, how most guys do it, where you do, you have, in fact, fallen in love, but you just don't know it yet because for one reason or another you won't admit it to yourself. This way is the most dangerous and powerful of all, because, when something finally happens to make you see the truth of the matter, well, now, since you've been in denial for so long, it's like it's twice as strong, and very often, it's too late to do anything about it.

"For me with Lei Ling, it was that third kind, no question. I had actually been madly in love with her for quite some time, but I wouldn't admit it to myself because I well knew all the problems it would cause. My realization only came to me—and came to me full bore, like a point-blank shotgun blast—the night she informed me that she was pregnant.

"Now, Chris, I don't know if you've ever had the experience of getting a woman that you loved pregnant, but it's like . . . it changes things, it does. It's like suddenly you realize that what you thought you were doing just for the hell of it, just for the fun of it, had this magnificent purpose all along; like suddenly, for a moment, even if you lose it later on and never get it back again, you can see the whole scope of your life and life itself perfectly; almost as if, as a kind of payback for procreation, God has temporarily granted you a view of your true place in the universe. Well, as I already said, the moment that Lei Ling told me on that one long-ago night, also out back in her little garden gazebo, was the moment I realized that I loved her and wanted to spend the rest of my life by her side, along with any children that she would bring to me. Now, as you can probably imagine, it took quite a bit of talking to convince her of this. But after I finally did, she told me that she felt the same way, and so then there was nothing to do except try and work out a plan as to how we could make that happen.

"What we came up with went like this: Since she knew her husband would never agree to a divorce, she would change her identity. It wasn't too difficult in Saigon to get a new set of ID papers; there was a black market for just about everything. And then after that we'd somehow manage to get her out of the country and back to the U.S. Once over there, I would marry her under her new name, and now she would be a U.S. citizen with *my* last name, and the chances of her being traced back to her old identity would be next to nil. She would leave a letter for her husband telling him that she had gone away, needed some time alone, that sort of thing, but since she wouldn't ever mention leaving the country, he wouldn't immediately think of it, and it would probably give us the jump we needed.

"There was just one problem, though. Her husband was coming back for the New Year holidays, which started within the week, and if we were going to make a clean break, leaving right then wouldn't give us enough time to make our arrangements. Well now, you can imagine—or maybe you can't even imagine—how I felt right at that moment. Of course I'd known for some time, in the back of my head, that he was coming back, but after learning what I'd just learned, I practically broke down and wept in front of her. Then I screamed, and then I put my fist through one of the slats of lattice in the gazebo. This made her start to cry, of course, and so then the two of us were sitting there, crying in each other's arms. It was quite a scene, let me tell you.

"In the end, she was the strong one. She soothed me by telling me there was nothing between them anymore—which I thought was a lie, but which, in my desperation, I tried hard to believe and hold on to—and finally she ended it by sending me away. We had already been seen together too much, she said. She could fix it with her servants, but there were others who she thought suspected things. She told me to go and spend time with Jack—our mutual friend, remember, who had introduced us—and just try and act normal, like before. She said she would get in touch with me when she had everything in order—in other words, I thought, when he had finally left again. He was just coming home for Tet, the Vietnamese New Year, and so I figured he'd be home for about ten days. That left me with a little more than two weeks to kill. At the time, I honestly wasn't sure whether I could make it.

"Well, for the first few days, I didn't do anything except sit around my own place and drink. My idea was, if I could just knock myself out, anesthetize myself for the duration, then when I finally woke up, it would all be over, like a bad dream, you know? Problem was, alcohol isn't really a very good drug for doing that. You pass out from it finally, yeah, but first it fills your head with all sorts of crazy ideas. I imagined all kinds of things: that she was going to tell her husband about us, confess everything; that he was going to make her have an abortion; that he was going to come and find me and kill me. At one point I thought about switching from alcohol to something a little stronger, opium or hash maybe, but I wasn't the type to smoke that stuff, and anyway, I had a feeling the side effects might be even worse. But I was desperate, Chris, you understand? More desperate than I'd ever been in my life.

"Anyway, one of those days, I wake up with this hangover that makes that first one I told you about seem like a little headache, and suddenly, for whatever reason, I'm remembering what she told me about Jack, how she'd said I should spend time with Jack. Suddenly I'm just sure there was some reason for it—like this is how she plans on contacting me if she needs something or if there's a change of plans. Well, now I'm in a panic. I'm thinking, what if she's already tried to tell me something and I missed it? The only way I know how to get in touch with Jack is the one phone number I have for him at his apartment where he stays when he's in Saigon. But I haven't seen him for weeks at this point, and I'm almost sure he's away somewhere, on one of his mysterious assignments. But I call him up, and I actually get him on the line. 'Jack, what have you been up to?' I say. 'Hey, I haven't seen you for a while, we should get together,' trying to be casual about it, you know?

"Only Jack is all business with me. Tells me he's got a lot of projects going at once and doesn't have the time, he'll call me in a few days. Well, of course, for me at that point a few days might as well be all eternity. So suddenly I'm almost begging, breaking down right there on the phone. 'Jack,' I say, 'you have to come and just speak with me for a little while. It's about Lei Ling. She and I, we've been having this affair—'

"Well, Jack stops me right there. 'Where are you?' he says. And then: 'Stay there, I'll come and get you.'

"So he comes over to this little house he got me what seems like years ago, and of course finds me looking more like an animal than a human being. I'd spent the better part of the last three or so days in this bamboo chair next to my bed, but he grabs me and stands me up—you remember how big I told you Jack was? Well, he takes me and walks me straight into the shower, turns on the water with what clothes I'm wearing still on me, and then just holds me there until I'm screaming and begging to get out.

"After that I was a little better, and he stood by while I shaved and dried myself off and got some new clothes on. Then he took me out to this dark little restaurant, where he made me eat rice and drink tea and soda. He said he wanted to hear all about what had happened with Lei Ling, like he was real concerned about me. Well, so help me, I told him almost all of it. I told him everything except her being pregnant and that we planned to run away to the States together and change her name. Which I guess was leaving out a lot. But what I couldn't hide was how upset I was about her husband's being there, living with a woman I now considered to be my own.

"Jack just keeps asking me these questions: When was the last time I'd seen her? How did she seem? Was she anxious about something?

"I thought he was just trying to help, and so I couldn't get too angry with him. 'Hell, yes, she was anxious about something, you jackass,' I finally told him, though.

"After that, Jack just sits there for a while, thinking, and finally he says, 'I think you should try and see her. At a time like this, it'll let her know you still care.'

"Well, that didn't really make any sense to me. If Lei Ling didn't know I cared about her after our last little scene in her gazebo, she was a pretty stupid girl. But I was like a drowning man right then, grasping at straws, you know, and I thought that he must be right and I must be wrong.

"So that afternoon I try and call her, and the boy she called Dinh answered the phone. After hearing my voice on the line, he says the rehearsed phrase: 'She not home no more to you,' and hangs up. I didn't bother calling back. But now, not being able to think of anything else, I just did the same exact stupid thing I'd done when I'd first unfolded that origami bird she'd made me: I started walking toward her house.

"When I got there, it was around seven. The sky was dark and it was raining, and I guess I was soaked through to the skin, although I hardly even noticed it. I had intended to just wait outside, wait across the street somewhere and see if I could catch her coming or going, but now that I was so close and could see all the lights on and imagine her there inside somewhere, it began driving me crazy. And so, what I did, there was a fence in front of her villa, but it only went so far in either direction, and I walked to where it ended and started to force my way through the bushes toward the back. I had to kind of loop around at one point where the brush got too thick, but suddenly I was right there, out in the open, staring at that white gazebo.

"I almost went into shock. Not only was I looking right at her; I was looking at them! Somehow, I guess in my narcosis, I must have miscounted the days, because I hadn't expected him to have arrived yet.

"She was dressed in a pink sundress I hadn't ever seen before, and he was in that same dark green uniform of the SVA, a far bigger man than Kai Tieng, though, and older, with a darker complexion and a more severe expression. They were standing together, leaning back against the railing side by side, holding hands . . . well, the emotions that started tearing through me were almost more than I could handle. For a few moments it almost seemed better that I should walk forward and try to kill this guy and probably get shot for it than to have to stand still and watch what I was watching. In my experience, Lei Ling wasn't a woman to withhold favors, and if they were holding hands, it meant they were going to do more or had already done more.

"Frankly, I don't know what would have happened if she hadn't looked up right then and seen me. I guess I probably wouldn't be alive right now to tell you this story. But she did, and immediately she put her hand on this guy's shoulder, and whatever it was she said to him got him up and moving inside, leaving her there alone. She waited about five seconds, then came rushing over to me.

"'What are you doing, Teddy?' she says—she always called me Teddy. 'Are you crazy? If he sees you here, he'll kill you!'

"'I don't care. I don't care about any of that,' I say. 'Look, I can't stand it. You have to come away with me right now.' And then I go to grab her arm.

"Only the moment I even touch her, she leans back and slaps me across the face just as hard as she can—a real whack I mean, *pow*, you know? And she says to me, 'You have no idea how much I'd like to do that Teddy Harper. You have no idea because your life has always been so easy for you. You've always been able to have anything you ever wanted. But my life is different. So much different that we might as well be two different kinds of animals. Now I told you what you had to do if you ever wanted a chance to be with me, and so you can either start doing it right now, or I swear I'll scream as loud as I can and that will be one of the last things you ever hear.'

"Well, I had never heard her talk this way before, never even knew she *could* talk this way. I'm so stunned that I just put up both my hands and start backing away, all the while looking into her eyes, searching for some kind of forgiveness there. But she never gives it to me, just keeps staring me down until I round the corner of this big tree and can't see her anymore."

Ted took an unusual break from his narration here, closing his eyes while taking a deep, unsteady breath. Then he went on.

"As you can imagine, I made a vow to stay away from Lei Ling after that. I figured, no matter how horrible I felt, nothing would be worse than her treating me that way. So I went back to my routine in the bamboo chair, crying a lot, trying not to drink so much because it only made things worse.

"I guess it was the next day or the day after that when Jack gives me a call. He wants to see me, he says. Well, after all the great advice he gave me last time, I tell him no thanks. But after that he starts getting really strange with me, asking me whether I'd seen her; what, exactly, she said to me; what I thought she'd meant by it. Finally I just tell him to go to hell and hang up—thinking I should be a little more careful about how I choose my friends from now on.

"Anyway, I never did try to call or visit Lei Ling again, and the next time I saw her, all of Saigon was under attack, and my whole view of life was changed around completely yet again."

He stopped and picked up his wine, making Chris almost groan out loud at the letdown. This time, though, as soon as Ted had taken one sip, he looked at his watch and put the glass down again.

49

"I'll tell you what, I may as well just finish and get it over with," Ted said—Chris just managing not to feel grateful for it.

"The Tet Offensive, as it came to be called, began on January thirty-first, 1968, in the morning of the New Year holiday they call Tet over there. If you don't know, and you probably don't, it was a coordinated, countrywide surprise attack by the Vietcong and the North Vietnamese army, an all-out play to win the war where for the first time they invaded cities and went after crucial American installations. One of these was the U.S. embassy in Saigon, not more than two miles from where I lived, and in the early darkness I woke from a thin sleep to the sounds of sirens and machine guns and explosives going off.

"I didn't know what to do, and I was frankly terrified. The war had always been this distant, safe thing up until now—even in that helicopter, it hadn't really seemed real. I tried picking up the phone, but instead of the low-pitched hum it usually made for a dial tone, it was beeping out some kind of distress signal. There was a transistor radio beside the bed, and I turned it on and started flipping around to try and find out what the hell was going on, but all it played was music—the Vietcong had taken over the radio station, it turned out, and to keep them from broadcasting someone had cut the cable to the transmitter and switched over to a prerecorded program.

"I thought of Lei right off, of course, wondering if she was safe, where she was. But what could I do? It was after curfew, and even if I did make it to her house without getting shot or arrested, what then? Break in and get shot that way? I figured she was probably safer than I was anyway, being after all married to some bigwig in the army. So I forced myself to lie down again.

"Well, the noise outside finally died down somewhat, and I guess eventually I must have dozed off, because the next thing I knew I woke up to banging on the front door. Someone was really laying into it, scaring the bejesus out of me all over again. I decided to just lay still and not open it. But then, almost like in a dream, I heard the sound of her voice.

I really thought it was a dream at first, and I lay there for maybe another thirty seconds or a full minute before I finally came to my senses and got out of bed.

"When I opened the door, then, she was standing there, wearing her jeans and a black top this time. Her face was distorted in crying, and she was gasping for air in between her sobbing.

"'Teddy, help me,' she kept saying, holding a hand out to me but keeping the other one on her hip in a way that was odd enough for me to notice it.

"Well, at first, like an idiot, I thought she was here because she missed me, and so I take a step forward, you know, to take her in my arms. But when she sees what I'm about to do, she pulls away, sidestepping around me into the room. Now she's in the light, and I can see what the problem really is: she's been shot. I arrive at this conclusion in two ways: one, because that whole side of her jeans and top is soaked with blood; and two, because in the hand which she has pressed to her hip she's holding a small black revolver, also covered in blood.

"'Lei, what happened?' I ask, rushing up to her, grabbing her high up on her shoulders, not wanting to touch her where she's injured.

"'Help me, Teddy,' she says. 'Help me, take me away with you.'

"After all the energy she spent banging on the door, now it's like she can barely speak, and I can feel that she's getting heavier, too, starting to collapse. I need to get to the phone, I think, and find out if it's working again, only I don't want to let go of Lei because I'm afraid she'll fall down and hurt herself even worse. But while I'm standing there, holding her up like that, trying to solve this grand little predicament I'm in, I hear the front door swing open again.

"'Step away from her, Ted, she's VC,' I hear from behind me.

"So I turn my head around, to see my old friend Jack walk into my living room. He's dressed in green army fatigues now, and holding a much bigger gun, what I now know to be a Colt .45 automatic. He's got his out in front of him like he's ready to use it, too.

"Still, the very first thing I feel when I see him is intense relief, thinking that he must be here to help us. It was, in retrospect, my one last split second of believing that everything in my life could still turn out okay.

"And then he says it again: 'Step away from her, Ted, she's VC.'

"But I *still* don't really get it. 'Jack,' I say, 'she's been shot, she needs a doctor,' or something like that.

"What happened afterward I'm still to this day not quite sure about. Someone else came through the doorway right then, a soldier holding a rifle, and his appearance seemed to trigger it. All I know is that I see Jack's hand with the gun going up, and then there are four shots fired, three of them coming from Jack's gun, bang, bang, bang, just as fast as he can squeeze them off. I'm not looking at Lei when this is happening, but when I turn back to her, she's already falling away from me, her chest covered in blood now, her eyes wide open, staring up at the ceiling.

"I fall to the ground beside her. From somewhere far away I'm aware that I've been shot myself, in the left shoulder. But I'm not even feeling that. Instead, I'm watching myself die. I'm seeing myself dead right in front of me. Everything I had, everything I cared about was right there, and now it was as gone as gone could be.

"Eventually Jack comes and pulls me off her, but by then I barely even knew what was happening; I barely even heard him when he told me it was her who shot me, and that she was going to kill me."

Ted stopped and took a breath, looked away, and drummed his fingers on the table—purely for effect, Chris was sure. He himself was nearly stunned, but it was only because he was so tired and couldn't think clearly; it was obvious to him now that this was all just more of his ring-master's drama acrobatics.

"Well, then I guess there's a lot that happened after that," Ted went on in a quieter, choked-up tone. "There were about five or six debriefings that I went through with some U.S. army shrink, or spook—or both—who called himself Steve and wore a bow tie. The whole story, or as near as I ever got to know it, was that they'd been onto Lei and Kai Tieng for some time, who were both communist spies for the North Vietnamese and the Vietcong. Steve wouldn't tell me what it was they'd done that night once they were called into action, so to speak, but he did say that Lei Ling shot and killed her husband—who apparently wasn't a commie and didn't know about her. So I guess what happened was, once her husband was found, and once that first wave of attacks on the city had been turned back, Jack had known who she would run to and where to find her.

"It actually turned out that American intelligence had come close to blowing the whistle on the whole operation, which was why Jack had been so frantic the week before, and also why he'd been pumping me for any information I could give him about Lei Ling. If only they had, it would have almost certainly leaked back to the communists, and then the whole thing would have been called off and she might still be alive today. But, of course, that wasn't the way it happened.

"Would it even matter, though? you're probably wondering. After all, did I ever really know Lei Ling at all? Well, I wondered about that for a long time, too, but finally I decided that, yeah, in the most important ways, I did. That last angry speech she'd given when I'd been spying on her and her husband had been the truth, I think. She *had* wanted, and *planned,* to run away with me and be my wife. The aim of the Tet Offensive was to rally the people into revolution and win the war in one fell stroke, which, had it been accomplished, and had she still been alive, I believe she would have kept up her side of the bargain—because then, as she saw it, her job would be done. She really had loved me; if in the beginning she'd thought there was any kind of political or strategic advantage to seeing me, she'd quickly figured out the truth about that; which is also how I know she wasn't lying about her pregnancy.

"But so, had she tried to kill me at the end there? You're probably thinking now that she hadn't. But I was the one who was there, and who knew her, and eventually I came to understand that, yes, in fact, she had. Why? Well, because I think at that point, having made her decision and stuck to it and lost everything, she wanted to take that one final step and make it irrevocable even while she was still alive—just so she'd know for certain that she hadn't been weak, and that she'd done all she possibly could. Strange, psychotic behavior? Well, yes, it seems that way to us. But, I mean, think about this woman and what she'd already done: living among her enemies for years, being married to a man she probably detested. And even with me, so much of her had stayed hidden; of course she'd never gone to UCLA or been interested in the theater. She'd just come up with those lies to make her familiar to me in the same way a phony fortune-teller can tell you all about yourself. She was smart, you see, Chris. Whipcrack smart. And they had trained her. Someone had trained her.

"But the main thing about her, the main thing about Lei Ling that was different from you and me, was that her *priorities* were wholly opposite from what we're accustomed to, so much so that it's hard for us to even imagine."

Ted paused again, this time shaking his head to express something between awe and sadness. Chris was sure that now he would stop, but once again he went on.

"Now you also probably think I left Vietnam after that, Chris. But I didn't. I stayed. Of course my shoulder was badly wounded"—he touched his left shoulder lightly, as if it still bothered him—"and so I couldn't immediately travel. But even after that I stayed. And I guess what I did after that was start to put it all together, all I'd learned. And soon I began to see that what had happened to me, first in that jail cell and then with Lei Ling, was really the same as what was happening to us as a whole in Vietnam: people thrown into an arena where they can't win because their very conceptions of winning and losing are grossly out of sync with their opponent's.

"And then, continuing on with that theory, I started to see how it was happening *worldwide:* how the USA itself was like a soldier out in a jungle he can't understand and can't even see to fight in. As a country we had become wealthy, and our wealth had made us powerful, but it had also made us weak. And now it was just a matter of time before our own walls came tumbling down and we had to confront the reality outside our borders.

"But I'm not even talking about an invasion of soldiers or wacko terrorists now. No, I'm talking about an *economic* invasion, Chris. It was happening then and it's still going on today. I don't care what kind of bullshit you think you know or that you've read in the papers: the real problem with the U.S. economy is that in industry after industry, we were and still are losing to the third world countries because the people are always hungrier and willing to work harder for less. It's that simple. Think about it. It happened in the auto industry, where they moved all the factories to Mexico, then it happened in electronics, with everything going to Taiwan and China. It happened in agriculture, where we still literally pay our farmers not to grow their crops. We were losing the trade war with the Japanese in just about everything, until their economy became even more top-heavy than ours. It's going to happen with computers; already I see those things are being made in Taiwan. As the world continues to open up to free trade, we're just going to meet the same enemy again and again, and each time, just like in Vietnam, we're going to lose badly.

"Well, it was way back then in 1968 when I saw that life as we'd always known it was coming to an end in this country. And only just now you're finally starting to see it: in the way they're cracking down on the welfare rolls; in the skyrocketing prices of real estate and education; and basically in everything that's happening to separate the classes into a new world order which will have little to do with what country you're from, and a whole lot more with whether you're a have or a have-not. Don't you see that that *has* to happen, Chris?

"Well, I decided to do something about it, decided that I wasn't going to be one of those people left out in the cold when a new kind of war was declared back home, a war of rich against poor. I decided that somehow, at all costs, I was going to put myself ahead in the game.

"And, as it turned out, I was in the right place to do that, because once I started looking around, there were all sorts of business opportunities in Saigon. There was money laundering on the black market, where the U.S. was trying to support the local currency by artificially holding down the value of military scrip and the dollar against the piaster, which was the Vietnamese money, and so all you had to do was open a phantom corporation to take in the MPC, the military money, and the piaster, then get a better exchange rate on your dollars and work it both ways. And of course there were the drugs. You couldn't make nearly as much on them then as you can now, but we made it. Me and Jack. He didn't turn out to be nearly so straitlaced as I thought, and he had all kinds of access to planes and ships heading back to the States. Now, of course, I have my own ships, and every now and then one of them makes a detour to Colombia or Venezuela, then inevitably gets impounded in Florida for a while—you just have to know people, which I do. Otherwise, Intercontinental operates at a loss; it's all just a cover. Hell, I got my job in finance as a cover, too, when I first got home."

Ted finally reached for his wine again, and this time Chris was relieved. The narrative had gone on way too long tonight and had also taken a turn he didn't care for at all.

But as Ted picked up his fork for the first time that night, to start in on another steak dish that had to be as cold as the frigid air by now, he began speaking once more. "That world that I predicted way back when is almost here, Chris. Pretty soon now, it's going to be like Victorian England, with two distinct classes of people, only this time the walls around the rich communities are going to be more like something out of medieval times. You wait and see. It's already really happened, you just can't tell yet because right now it only exists on paper, on balance sheets and in bank accounts. But it might as well be as real as stone.

"And that's the world that I'm trying to prepare you for, Chris. Can't you see that? Can't you see that all I'm doing—all I'm doing in all of this—is trying to help you?"

After their protracted dinner, Chris got to bed later than usual, and then on top of that he couldn't sleep thinking about Ted's biography-turned-economic-*Apocalypse-Now* discourse that night. None of it was true anyway, he kept telling himself, furious at his own mind for wasting precious sleep time worrying about it.

The trouble was, once again, he couldn't dismiss all of it. Ted Harper had gotten where he is somehow; not everyone had a house like his and a handful of full-time goons following him around. So was it outlandish, or even unlikely, that his empire could have been started in Vietnam during the war, getting a head start on drug dealing and whatever else? And the stuff about the coming class war actually made a certain amount of sense, too, although Chris admitted that he wouldn't know enough to say one way or the other, and didn't really care so much either since it was a foregone conclusion which side of the walls he would be living on.

The rest of it, though, the part about the woman, Lei Ling, didn't ring true, and Chris refused to believe it. That story line, he remembered, was even essentially similar to the tale "Caroline" had told him (after Ted had told it to her, Chris was sure), with in both cases a pregnant woman deserting a man who desperately needed her. So maybe that was some kind of weird theme with Ted. Chris could see exactly the intended lesson of this latest version, though: that the world was far worse than even his own cynical outlook could imagine, a place where he couldn't trust anyone or anything. Ted was trying to scare him straight, whatever Ted Harper's idea of straight was.

But he wasn't buying it. Despite his exhaustion and fear, his mind was still stronger than that, and he wasn't throwing his entire life view out the window just because of one deranged psychopath who could tell a reasonably spooky story at dinnertime.

Chris had one last thought before he finally let go and drifted off: The story was over now, or at least it seemed as if it had ended. So how was that significant? What should that mean to him?

The next day, however, he would not remember having wondered.

PART FIVE

·/·

Departure

50

Chris knew something was different even before he opened his eyes the next morning, before his waking mind could do anything but register and identify the strains of classical music coming from downstairs. Then he sat up and saw what he'd somehow already discerned: that just as Ted had promised, another storm had come. Once again it was pouring rain outside, the drops spattering on the windowpane, the sky almost pitch-black. Even over the music, he could hear the low drumming on the roof.

An instant after verification came the certain knowledge of what this particular rainstorm would mean to him in his present circumstances, and Chris leaned over and put his head in his hands. It was December 8, his ninth day since first becoming a prison laborer here (he knew this without having to think or count), and now, already exhausted, he was going to have to go out on the dunes in this freezing downpour and shovel wet sand and weeds all day. Rage welled up inside him like an enormous tidal wave, threatening to break and explode—a familiar feeling, but dangerous now, even deadly. He would control it, he thought; he had to. But something had to give. Something.

Coming downstairs, however, everything was the same as it had been every morning. Ted, already seated at the table, was quite probably even wearing the exact same clothes as he had on that first day, his sweater a few shades closer to gray now than the white it had started out as. Ted might still have looked almost exactly the same if he hadn't stopped shaving, his beard coming in salt-and-pepper grizzly like Ernest Hemingway's. Breakfast this morning was omelettes with buttered toast and bacon, but when Chris sat down, he barely glanced at it.

"Mr. Harper, you're not really going to send me out in this stuff, are you?" he said, trying to sound firm yet calm, and managing neither.

Ted was busy cutting his toast diagonally in half with his knife and finished the task before he answered. "Why not?"

"Because it's pouring, look outside!"

Ted waited a moment, then barely glanced up at the enormous windows he sat facing. "So?"

"So, it's going to be freezing!"

"Won't be so bad. There are rain parkas hanging in the garage. Take one of those."

"Mr. Harper, come on, listen, be reasonable. I'm not going to get anything done anyway. It's hard work when the sand is dry. When it's wet, it's going to be twice as hard, or three times."

"Just do what you can, Chris."

"Look, can't I at least stay in until it clears up a little? I'll use the time, I'll practice. Listen, you're right, okay. About everything. I understand why you're doing this. And you're right, I do have to change. I do *need* to change. And I will, I will change, really. But my getting pneumonia right now's not going to help anything, is it?"

Ted looked up, squinting a little as if just realizing Chris was sitting there. "What do you mean by that?" he said, his accent coming on strong suddenly. "What do you mean you *understand* why I'm doing this?"

Chris noticed the change and moderated his own tone somewhat. "I just mean I get it. Like that story last night, I . . . I understand why you told it to me."

"Well, Chris, that's okay, that's all right," Ted answered, still looking right at him. "But just one thing. That there wasn't a *story.* That there was my *life.*"

"Okay, fine, I just—"

"No, it's not fine, Chris," Ted interrupted. "I wouldn't waste my breath telling you some story. Not at this point, I wouldn't. Now everything I've told you—everything I've told you since I've come here—has been God's honest truth. You got that?"

Chris closed his eyes for a moment. Even overriding his fear at this point, he for some reason wanted to argue this ridiculous point with this murderer. Finally, though, he let it go. "Okay, well, I understand what you meant by what you said *before* that, about me . . . about me not being a man, about the way I've lived my life."

Ted seemed appeased and went back to his toast, spreading out melted butter in quick back-and-forth motions. "No, Chris, I don't think you do understand, though. I don't think you understand at all. Not yet."

For a moment Chris almost couldn't control himself and came precariously close to flipping the food on his plate into Ted Harper's beard-stubbled, insane face. "This is nuts! This is all just so nuts!" he said instead, daring to raise his voice. "Why are you doing this?!"

Ted seemed to hardly notice. "Well, you just told me you knew why I'm doing it," he said with a chuckle. And then he motioned to Chris's plate. "You'd better eat that up."

Chris looked down at his food and took a deep breath. This was senseless, he told himself again, and it was stupid to be getting Ted pissed off this way. Yet still he was too angry to eat. In fact, suddenly his anger seemed to encompass everything, not just this megalomaniac sitting beside him, but the entire corrupt, diseased, unfair world.

"You don't want your food, that's fine, you don't have to eat it," Ted said right then, standing up and taking both of their plates away, even though he'd barely touched his, either.

Chris didn't try to grab anything this time and watched the spongy-looking eggs and two pieces of toast along with the ubiquitous strips of bacon going away. He had just done something very dumb, he thought, even forgetting the missed food. But in terms of his emotional state, he was still somewhere out there in deep, cold space, orbiting the containing atmosphere of normal, rational feelings, and couldn't make himself care. He hoped he died out there in the freezing rain anyway. He hoped he got pneumonia and somehow died instantly from it.

Stan arrived soon after that, with a giant black umbrella, which he closed and shook out before bringing it inside. When the door opened, Chris could feel the cold wind and hear the pounding rain. He stood up and was about to just walk out into that deluge when he thought that that might actually be suicide and detoured into the garage. He had discovered the parkas long ago, had worn one once or twice walking the late Charlie when it was wet out. Now he chose the biggest of them and pulled it over his head, the sleeves of his leather jacket making a tight, uncomfortable fit inside the rubbery garment.

He went out in front of Stan, so angry the world seemed to collapse into a tunnel of dark fury he could barely see through. The moment he cleared the doorway, the rain pelted furiously on his vinyl hood, the wind yanking it back like a hand trying to uncover him, trying to get at him. He got into the back of the silver car and slammed the door as hard as he could, although that particular disobedience most likely went unnoticed over the noise of the storm.

When the car stopped, he immediately got out to wait for the ritual Handing Over of the Shovel. This time, though, after Stan brought it to him—trying to keep his umbrella from blowing away while he worked one-handed—he stepped back around to the driver's side.

"You're on your own today, Chris!" He practically shouted to be heard. "I'm going to come and check on you, though, so don't be sleeping!"

Chris just kept his face a mask until Stan got back in the car. And then he turned and started down the path toward the beach.

Even with a total lack of supervision that morning, Chris nevertheless went to work, tearing up soaking-wet clumps of sand and grass and heaving them as far as he could while the wind and rain lashed him in rhythmic bursts, like getting whipped in uneven, random strokes. Within minutes, the lower half of his jeans and long underwear were soaking, and he could feel the icy water making inroads in other places, too: coming down his collar below his chin, into his boots. His soft leather gloves, already worn thin by all the industrial use they'd been getting, practically dissolved, and he took them off and made them into a ball and threw them away. It was pointless to be working like this, he told himself again and again—even while he dug with all his strength, taking his aggression out in the familiar drudgery. His whole life was pointless anyway, he reasoned, so he might as well.

Or maybe it did all have some higher purpose, he thought at some point. Maybe it was *all* a punishment, and not just Ted's punishment. Maybe Ted *was* the punishment, inflicted by an angry God for all of Chris's arrogance and pride; or for his temper, his rage, his envy; or for all the drugs he'd taken in his life—what better punishment for a user like himself than to suffer at the hands of the men who brought the stuff into the country? Or perhaps it was for more specific crimes: pushing Kyle off that stage in Boston. Or what he'd done to Donna. Or Cassie.

Chris stopped working for a moment. That was a topic he'd pretty much managed to avoid thinking about in all the time he'd been here, either alone or with his jailers: what had happened with his old girl-friend. Or, actually, she'd been more than that. She was the woman he'd lived with for over five years, lived with happily for five years, and then one day kaput, over just like that when he'd had his big breakdown.

But Chris put it out of his mind once more. He turned slowly around in a full circle, looking at his surroundings in disbelief.

The rain had switched over to slow-falling snow.

By the time Stan called for him Chris was sitting down with his parka over him like a tent, looking out at the windswept ocean, the snow by then having settled into a cheery, slow sprinkling, which wasn't quite sticking yet but which seemed as if it might go on for the rest of the year. He got up casually, listlessly; he'd decided he honestly didn't care if Stan saw him like that.

As it turned out, he didn't have to worry. Stan was all the way back at the gray house, standing under an overhang of the roof on the back deck. He didn't mention the weather, but merely handed over a McDonald's bag, which Chris accepted equally listlessly, taking the food and sliding down with his back against the wall under the slim shelter. The way he was sitting, his feet and lower legs stuck out into the snowfall, but he didn't care about that either since they were already soaked through. Stan hadn't brought any food for himself, but it seemed as though he was going to stay with Chris while he ate. Until about five minutes later, he abruptly reached inside his coat and once more pulled out his cell phone. This time when he got it into the open air, Chris could hear it vibrating.

"Yeah," Stan said into it.

And then he left; turned away and was gone without even saying good-bye. Chris wondered what it was about again, but didn't won-der very much because by then he was preoccupied with a savage depression—sitting there on someone's soaking-wet deck like a homeless person, a reject from the human race, his sandy shovel his dunce cap, the proof of his worthlessness in case anyone was confused, in case anyone wondered.

Stan never did return to tell Chris lunch was over and it was time to get back to work. But eventually Chris went on his own, not even wanting to know why he was doing it anymore, whether it was out of anger, fear, self-hatred, or merely habit. He just got up, picked up his trusty shovel, and headed out into the snow again, tossing his fast-food garbage under the deck as he went.

51

Stan came back that evening to drive him home, where, instead of walking Chris to the front door as he normally did, he used the remote control to open the garage and pulled halfway inside. Chris understood why and got out and sat down on the concrete floor to wrench off his soaking, icy, sandy boots and peel off his socks, which had turned black from his nonwaterproof footwear. He went into the house afterward and didn't ask for permission to go upstairs and take a shower. Ted, who was seated in the white chair in the living room, didn't try to stop him.

When he came down again, perhaps because of the storm Stan was still there, sitting on the couch facing Ted—right where, it felt like years and years ago, Chris had once sat begging and pleading for the job that had led to all this. He went to his chair with the cello and the music stand, picked up the bow, and started to play.

"You took your time, Chris," Ted said over the very first notes he made.

Chris stopped playing. "I'm sorry. It's snowing out there if you haven't noticed, and my hands were freezing. I was just trying to thaw them out." He didn't quite manage to keep the anger out of his voice.

Ted didn't answer, and Chris started up again. But in a minute or two Ted interrupted once more.

"Hey, aren't you ever going to be done playing scales? I mean, is that all you're ever going to do with that thing?"

In fact, Chris had mostly left scales behind by that point. He had worked out and was able to play, with varying degrees of proficiency, the first five "pieces" in his book. Today he'd backslid merely out of mindlessness.

"I was just warming up," he said.

"Yeah, well, you're done warming up now, all right. You've been playing for an awful long time now, you should be done warming up."

Chris told himself to let it go and knew that he should, *knew* that. Yet somehow he couldn't. "I just meant for right now, Mr. Harper. Before,

I was trying to learn where the notes were. This time, just sitting down to play now, I was warming up."

"Oh, really, Chris, really?" Ted drawled. "Because from over here it sounded a whole lot like you were jackin' off. Which is what I assumed you were doing upstairs before."

Chris was furious all over again, but this time understood that he really needed to keep his mouth shut. His book was still opened to the last exercise piece he'd been working on—in A major, with three ugly sharps written on the left of every stave—and he studied the first few notes, trying to remember how it started. In the interim, however, out of the corner of his eye, he saw Ted stand up.

"I'll tell you what, Chris," he said, coming around the couch to stand in front of him. "Being as Stan's with us today, why don't you give us a little recital. You know, like real music students do."

Chris shrugged, still trying desperately to bite back his anger. "All I can play is the last exercise I did in this book. Do you really want to hear that again?"

"Yeah, *that's* fine, but here's the thing, Chris. I don't want you to just play it for me, I want you to *perform* it this time. Do you know the difference?"

Chris, who a few hours ago was convinced that he'd hit absolute rock bottom in terms of his self-image, realized he had further yet to fall, because this question didn't just rankle him, it *outraged* him.

"Yes, I know the difference, but that doesn't mean—"

"Well, okay, Chris, so why don't you show me that instead of telling me."

Chris looked away and took a breath. A part of him was able to realize just how insane and meaningless all this was—the end of his worthless career and possibly his life marked by one last performance of a child's instruction piece on an instrument he could barely play. But another part of him, a part he couldn't seem to control, still wanted to nail it and put Ted Harper in his place.

"Fine," Chris said, trying to sound nonchalant about it, even as his heart was hammering and he was actually getting the same kinds of butterflies in his stomach he used to get before a show. He flipped the page back to the last piece he'd learned—a dull little ditty in C that had nevertheless probably introduced legions of nerdy kids to eighth notes—took another deep breath, set the bow to the bottom string, and began.

At first he was concentrating too hard and knew he had to relax a little, had to make it sound more majestic than merely perfect. Yet the instant he had this thought it reminded him of the last time he'd had it, or one just like it. It was in almost this exact same spot, performing his two songs for Caroline, or Karen. That spooked him, and he was so distracted that he bobbled it badly, bowing two strings at once and then correcting in the wrong direction.

When he finished, he just lowered the bow and sat there. Do-overs would not be allowed in Ted Harper's household, Chris surmised. Once again, though, he wondered why he even cared.

Ted stood there for some time, nodding and considering. Then he turned his back on Chris to look out the wall of windows. "What did you think of it, Stan?"

Stan, who was sitting on the couch facing the other way and hadn't even turned around, said, "Sounded fine to me."

"Right. I would say it sounded fine, too, Chris," Ted said, slowly circling around to face him again. "For what it was it sounded fine, except for that one mistake there. But now, see, here's my problem with that: while fine would be okay for most people, you, Chris, well, you're supposed to be a musician, aren't you? And, I mean, a real musician's just supposed to be able to pick up any instrument, aren't they?"

"I don't know, Ted, are they?" Chris said, half-mocking, half-bitter, calling Ted by his given name for the first time ever.

If Ted caught that, he ignored it. He looked up at the ceiling instead, like a man trying to articulate something he can't quite grasp himself. "Do you know why I wanted you to take up the cello, Chris?"

"No, why?"

"It's because the cello, and classical music, are things that *I* myself understand, and that *I* myself feel able to judge. There's no noise from an amplifier, none of that racket to distort the true music, do you see?"

Chris just shrugged.

"And what I just heard . . . Chris, let me ask you a question. If I was a farmer and you were my boy, would you say that I should let you out of your chores to practice your music because you had this great talent, this great aptitude? Would it be worth it to us, as a family, say, to risk losing your work in the field so that you could stay in and practice, and maybe make good that way someday?"

Chris remembered what Ted had told him that very first day he'd come to the house, about growing up on a farm, and right on the spot came up with a brand-new theory about what it was they'd really been doing all this time: it was some weird reenactment of *Ted's* childhood, where *Ted's father* had forced him to work on the farm instead of act in after-school plays, and at some point maybe even given this same speech, about how Ted just didn't have the talent to make it worthwhile.

"Now, I'm also betting you cut all kinds of corners learning that music, too, didn't you?" Ted went on. "Stuff that you didn't think I'd notice, and so you said, what the hell? Am I right about that?"

Chris was so alarmed about what he thought he'd just figured out that for a moment he couldn't keep things straight in his head and actually found himself feeling guilty about the guitar tuning he'd been using. He immediately tried to erase whatever expression it was he had on his face, but of course that only made it worse.

"I'm right, aren't I, Chris?" Ted said immediately. "Now don't try and hide things from me, I can tell. I can read you like a book."

Chris just looked away, ashamed, and perhaps more angry than he'd ever before been in his life.

"Well, Chris, let me tell you something now," Ted continued. "This isn't going to be easy for you to accept, but this whole music thing was never about you having any real talent. It was just about you, period. You acting like a child, you wanting to be famous, wanting to be the center of attention. And probably you would have come to terms with that by now if someone had taken the time to make you understand it."

The words felt like yet another blow, heaped upon all the many blows Chris had received in the last few weeks of his life. Yet in the next moment, in some remote corner of his mind where he could still think, he realized that—besides everything else going on—this was really just another lecture, only a little more severe than all the other lectures he'd heard throughout the years. Suddenly he felt a flash of his old self, the hopeful one, the one who still thought he had a chance at achieving some small part of something in his life. Inside of that instant he had an inspiration and didn't think long enough before giving in to it.

"Here, just give me one more chance," he said. And then, hanging the bow on the music stand, he placed his bare fingers on the strings. He played the first thing that came to mind, which for some reason was "Wipeout," that old surf classic, possibly one of the first picking songs he'd ever learned on the guitar. The way he knew it, it was all low strings, so the fingering was no problem, and playing this way, plucking with his fingers, it was just like playing the bass. And God it felt good to really play again.

"*Chris, you stop that right now!*" Ted bellowed at him over the opening notes.

But Chris kept on playing just as loud as he could. At the end of the first refrain he did a slide up the fingerboard, then hit the string on the way down again, the effect sounding like a whistle at a pretty girl.

"*Chris, I said stop!*" Ted shouted even louder, but right at that moment Chris went into the drum solo, beating out the quick roll on the hollow body of the instrument. Chris wasn't even thinking about what Ted would do to him, and when the older man turned away after that, he felt as if he'd won.

He was still going at it when he saw Ted lean over to say something to Stan, then looked away when Ted stood up again. He was just going to get all the way through this one song, he decided, and after that Ted could do whatever he wanted—not feed him for a week or make him work at his shoveling all night long.

He had just a moment's warning of what was about to happen when he felt the cold touch of metal against his earlobe. But before he could even think to react, Ted shot him, the roar of the gun exploding in his head, *imploding* his skull as the bullet went directly into his ear through his eardrum.

Chris collapsed, threw himself onto the floor, putting a hand over the bloody hole where the side of his head used to be. He was in so much pain he couldn't see or think, and in that moment he had the weird sensation that he was hanging from the floor, that his body was working against gravity and starting to pull free of the planet, which had to be the first sign of dying. Only something was wrong. He wasn't dead yet, and there was no blood. He was still here, still writhing on the floor of this rich man's summer beach house in winter.

In his spastic paroxysms he felt a foot, a leg, another leg, and only realized what had happened and what Ted had done and was about to do again when the second shot rang out. At the very last instant, Chris jerked his head away from the gun, so the second blast didn't get him quite as badly as the first one had. But still, it was almost the same. Once again his head exploded in pain as if a brad nail had been driven straight into his ear canal—this time his left—and then his head had turned into a huge, high-pitched bell, which instead of merely ringing someone had set off a grenade inside.

After that, Ted's beet-red face was right in front of him, yelling at him—at least, Chris could tell he was yelling and not merely speaking from the way his lips were working and the spit was flying from his mouth. It was like watching a movie where the projector is malfunctioning wildly, and instead of a sound track there's only a shrieking, wailing ringing.

Somehow, though, Chris was able to make out the words.

"FOR YOUR OWN GOOD!" Ted Harper was hollering at him soundlessly. "IT'S FOR YOUR OWN GOOD!"

52

At some point Chris became aware that he was being carried, and then that it was Stan who was carrying him. He was taken upstairs and laid down on his own unmade bed, then brought four of his Advil tablets from the medicine chest along with the plastic cup filled with cold water. Stan made sure that Chris took the pills, and afterward left him lying there alone with the light off and the room almost dark with the quickly dimming sky outside the window.

Chris resolved to just stay there forever. Yet almost immediately he was up again, stumbling and half crawling to the bathroom, where he retched what was mostly stomach acid and the water he'd drunk into the toilet. He was nauseated and the world was spinning, but unlike being drunk or high it didn't seem as if it would ever stop. He curled up into a ball and wrapped his arms around his head, clamping his eyes shut and pushing his forehead into the bath mat, which was still damp from the shower he'd taken. It was better that way, he found; if his head was pressed to the floor, it seemed to lessen the terrible seasick feeling his destroyed inner ears were giving him.

At the very worst of it, he was positive that he was going to die anyway, that Ted Harper might as well have fired those two bullets into his brain instead of the floor, because the end effect would be the same: something breaking, hemorrhaging in there, some final seizure ripping him out of this world forever. Which Chris thought would be fine, which, in fact, he thought would be just fine and dandy.

Instead, however, little by little it faded, both the maddening ringing and the horrible, sickening gyro effect. Eventually, he was able to open his eyes, and he found himself staring down at the miniature Martian landscape of the red bath mat, lit on a slant from the light over the mirror, which Stan must have left on. Chris had been in here for what felt like days, and his neck was starting to cramp from the position he was holding his head in. But he was terrified to move. Now, when he moved or made any kind of noise at all, he would know and it would all be real.

Only soon something occurred to him: What *else* wasn't he hearing? If Ted and Stan were still here, or if it was still snowing and windy outside, he should be getting something besides the steady ring, which for whatever reason seemed to him to be emanating from a point about an inch behind his left ear. But he wasn't. As far as he could tell, both the house and whole world had gone completely silent. In a dawning state of panic, he couldn't help testing himself. He was mostly on his left side, so he brought his right hand around and reached out to the base of the fiberglass shower. He knocked against the side of it with his knuckles.

His panic flared into terror. There was nothing. He sensed the shock of the impacts through his hand and arm, but as far as his ears were concerned, it was another silent film. He knocked again and finally pounded harder and harder, until it felt as if he were about to break his knuckles against the enamel finish. But still there was no report whatsoever from ears to brain.

He couldn't help speaking then, just making an *A* vowel, and the effect was even more bizarre, even more horrendous. He could feel the vibration in his throat, but that was the only way he knew he was making any sound at all. He did this louder and louder, until he supposed he was screaming at the top of his lungs, and that if anyone was listening to his meaningless, random cries, it would sound as if they were coming from a deaf person, because they were.

53

He came awake in his bed in the middle of the night after finally passing out—at that time hoping he was actually slipping into a coma, or that he had a concussion and would at last succumb in his sleep. Only once again he hadn't died, and he woke up remembering what, under the circumstances, he thought was a pretty twisted dream. It had been about, of all things, earplugs, the precaution he'd so often taken playing live, all for nothing it turned out now.

He had been back playing at The Cat's Paw again, the club where he'd played his infamous last gig with X Bomb, and it had been, he recalled, one particular night when he'd tried an experiment, wearing a single earplug in his left ear in order not to go deaf from the stacks on that side of him, while still being able to hear his stage monitor to his right. Both in the dream and at the time it hadn't worked at all, because the sensation of being muted in one ear and having the other one open was excruciating, as if a single volume knob in his brain controlled the level of both ears, and so they'd both become more sensitive. The dream had gotten one thing wrong, though. For some reason in the dream he'd been wearing the earplug on his right side.

Chris sat up in bed. His headache came bursting back, exploding like fireworks behind his eyes, but he winced and ignored it. Slowly, with a feeling too dim to be called hope yet, he brought his right hand out from under the covers and raised it to his right ear. Using his middle finger, he flicked above the earlobe, right over the hole that led to the ear canal. Besides more pain, though, there was nothing at all. Whatever systems and mechanisms had once been in place were destroyed now, down for the count, and he might as well have applied the fillip to his elbow.

He brought his left hand up after that, took a breath, and thought a thought that was closer to a real prayer than anything else he'd ever thought or said before.

Then he tried his left ear.

He almost broke down sobbing and thanking God. There was still something there. It wasn't right, it wasn't as loud or as clear as it should be, but it was *there*. And didn't that mean that it might heal even more? Didn't that mean that, if he went and talked to a doctor or some specialist and got advice, he might be able to nurture it back to somewhere near normal again? No, he would probably never be able to play loud again, or if he ever did get another gig with a band, he would always have to wear that one earplug. But someday, just possibly, he might play again, and right now that one, simple idea filled him with more joy than he thought he'd ever before felt in his life.

Ever so slowly, he stood up. He stepped on his leather jacket on the floor from when he'd at some point wriggled out of it and picked it up and put it on. By the clock it was three minutes after four. He still felt weak and tired and sick, but his equilibrium seemed to have returned to the point where he could at least stand up straight.

In the hallway it was dark except for a small amount of light coming in through the windows. He turned right and moved as silently as he could, taking the stairs as slowly as he could endure, transferring his weight from one tread to the next like a cat burglar trying not to set off weight sensors. Downstairs, he thought about the sliding doors, but decided the front would be quieter and moved swiftly across the big, nearly pitch-black space, which he'd come to know well enough to navigate blindly.

He put his hand on the doorknob, then stopped and stood there, wondering if there was something he hadn't ever thought of, some obvious trap or alarm that he was about to trip. Finally he decided he was just being a coward again and twisted the knob. It wouldn't budge, which terrified him, until he realized that Ted, like most people, was merely in the habit of locking up at night. After that he unlocked the door, and it pulled open smoothly, revealing a cloudy, windy night, with no more rain or snow, and even brighter moonlight than he would have liked for this. He barely hesitated, though, and stepped outside and pulled the door shut behind him, keeping the knob turned until it was all the way shut so the bolt wouldn't click.

The moment he got clear of the house, the cold wind hit him and he bent into it, hunching over like a man with a wound in his side, his hands shoved deep into his tattered pockets. He was still wearing only socks, and the gravel of the driveway poked through to his feet, stabbing at them painfully—until he reached the side of the house, where they were almost instantly soaked through from the freezing, wet sand. Now for the scary part, he thought: directly beneath Ted's bedroom window. But Chris didn't stop and didn't look back, passing by the house and continuing along the path to the beach. He supposed he was finally about to find out just how much of a guard they actually put out at night.

Soon he began thinking about the future, after he escaped—if he did escape. What would he do then? Change his name and go into hiding after all? Go to the police? Once again the idea of Ted going after his family occurred to Chris, but he decided that would never happen. Though definitely deranged, Ted's mind just didn't work that way; in his other persona the man was still supposedly friends with his father. He should have done this days ago, Chris thought, when he still had his hearing in both ears.

But so many things seemed crystal clear to him now that had been muddled and confused before. Like his playing: now he knew that he would never quit, and it didn't matter if he never got rich or famous or made any money at all—which he also now knew that he wouldn't; that, in every likelihood, he would go on living like a pauper and eventually become one of those old music guys who play in ski lodges and at weddings and give lessons and try to write jingles; who never went anywhere but stuck it out anyway because for them there simply wasn't anything else.

He also knew why he had pushed Kyle off that stage. It wasn't out of anger or even jealousy. It was out of fear: the fear that he was becoming a person he'd always dreaded being, a person he himself would have regarded as a pathetic failure before all this, which was also the same fear that had driven him to try to kill himself with pills, or to come down here to the ends of the earth to escape from humanity. Or, why he'd done what he'd done to Cassie.

Chris halted in his tracks for a moment. He was almost to the last line of dunes before the beach started, not quite out of theoretical danger of being seen from the house. But he had smelled something, a sharp smell, dark and dirty and yeasty. Then it was gone with the next random gust of air. Chris thought of Charlie again, buried somewhere nearby, but he put it out of his mind and resumed walking.

By the time he reached the little inlet where the ocean met the bay, his socks were as wet as if he'd stuck his feet in a bucket, and so caked with sand that they were starting to work their way off, flapping back and forth from his toes with every step he took. His actual feet felt like two blocks of ice, and the cold was spreading up his legs and into the rest of his body, the sensation like death itself overtaking him from below.

The island was so much thinner here that in places he was able to make out the dark shape of the road not a hundred feet away through the dunes. But he still hadn't seen any cars or people, and he now decided to modify his longtime plan and just go over the little bridge.

Putting that strategy into action before his fear could get the best of him, he leaned forward and began to jog. These dunes were smaller, more like the steep bank of a river, and he scrambled up the side and ran almost full out, his flapping socks long enough to threaten to trip him up. He didn't stop until he had crossed over both the bridge and the junction of the main road on the other side, then fell to his hands and knees in the trees on the far side to catch his breath.

Slowly, he turned and looked around him. But there was nothing, no movement at all. There was the wind billowing the trees—which he couldn't actually hear over the maddening, one-sided whistle in his head—but aside from that the world was static, empty. He stood up and began to jog along the verge, heading toward the highway and the town where the closest houses were. He still didn't really know what he'd do once he reached one, but he was so close to being free it seemed like the last thing he needed to worry about.

He was debilitated and exhausted, and soon his jog had turned into a walk. By that point his footwear had become nearly ridiculous, with at least six inches of wet toe dragging from each foot. He considered pulling off the socks completely, but thought that might be even colder and settled for reaching down to pull them up again.

It was as he was standing up that he felt the hand on his left shoulder.

He was so startled that he jumped up even as he began to twist around—and in doing so managed to finally trip himself. He fell to the wet pavement with a thud, then just stayed there, breathing hard, waiting for his life to end.

He looked up slowly to see Stan standing over him, a car with its lights off behind him. He, or they, could have been following from the moment he had crossed the bridge, for all he'd heard.

"You shouldn't be out here, Chris," Stan said—which Chris *could* hear, even though he could barely make out the words, like a conversation in a nightclub where you're yelling over the music. Unfortunately, there was no music, and Chris had also unconsciously twisted his head to the right to listen like some deaf old man.

"Are you okay? Can you hear at all?"

"Yeah," Chris said, gauging it to try not to speak too loud and sound like an idiot—although why that would matter to Stan, who'd been watching him jog up the road in the middle of the night with wet, sandy socks hanging off his toes like a court jester's shoes, Chris couldn't say.

Stan shook his head. "You shouldn't have fucked with him like that, Chris. You got to just let him have his say."

"Now you tell me."

Stan shook his head again, then he put out his hand, which Chris looked at but didn't take. "Come on," Stan said.

"What are you going to do to me?"

"I gotta take you back, Chris."

"That's all?"

"My friend, I keep telling you, you don't even know how lucky you are to be alive. Now let's go."

Chris considered the hand for a moment longer. He so badly didn't want to take it, if only to stand up on his own for just that tiny bit of dignity. But giving Stan any reason to be angry at him right now was a seriously dumb idea, and he honestly didn't think he had the energy to get up anyway. So he reached out for Stan's thick, hot hand, and Stan helped him up and walked him back to what turned out to be the black car. He opened the back door for him, and Chris got in to find someone he hadn't yet seen behind the wheel, an older man with thick, black glasses and a balding head, who once again Chris couldn't quite stop himself from looking at. The three of them drove back in silence, until Stan told the driver to stop about halfway from the bridge to the house.

"I hope you didn't lock yourself out," Stan said—or something like that—when Chris was getting out. Then the car did a U-turn and drove away, and afterward there was nothing to do but walk back to the front door. In order not to leave a wet, sandy trail inside, he finally bent over to peel off his ruined socks from his freezing-cold feet in the driveway. By then he was crying again and had to make an effort to keep it quiet on his way back upstairs.

54

Chris woke up on his own accord the next morning and immediately, almost instinctively, looked over at the clock. His first thought was just that he was late; it was past six, and if he didn't get downstairs, he wouldn't get any breakfast, which this morning he couldn't afford since for some reason he felt even weaker than usual. Then he noticed the silence.

And a moment later everything came back: the rain, his little recital, the gunshots fired point-blank to his ears, his failed escape attempt. Now that Chris recognized it, the ringing was still there in his left ear, though noticeably softer. There was nothing at all from his right ear; he was permanently in mono now, which he guessed he would have to get used to.

He brought his left hand up and tapped lightly his one remaining ear, hitting it with about the same force he would use to see if a microphone was live. It seemed better still, and he snapped his fingers about a foot away. He could definitely hear that, so it wasn't just that he couldn't hear the music that Ted had woken him with every day since this had started; this morning, Ted wasn't playing it.

Which meant what? That the game was over? Or had at least moved on to some new phase where Chris didn't have to get up every morning and go out and try to single-handedly defoliate the other side of the island? Or, had Ted found out about the escape attempt and was even now downstairs with Stan working out some horrible new punishment? Yet, the same as every morning, Chris could smell the friendly, if unwelcome, aromas of food and coffee wafting up to him from the kitchen.

Then all at once Chris thought he knew what it was and immediately tried to stand up. When he did, he almost blacked out, but he grabbed on to the doorknob and rode it out with his head lowered and his eyes clamped shut. After that he looked around for his jeans and began frantically pulling them on.

Ted wasn't playing the stereo this morning, Chris surmised, because by his thinking he had completely deafened his surrogate son yesterday, and thus it would no longer do any good either at waking him or at educating him musically. But things *were* still going on as "normal," and it wouldn't be long now before Ted came barging in here the same as he had that very first morning—which terrified Chris because if he did, and Chris was to somehow let on that he wasn't completely deaf by responding to something when he shouldn't have, he thought that Ted Harper was the type of man who would try again.

For a moment Chris had a wretched idea, about Stan. Chris was almost sure he wouldn't tell Ted about the failed breakout (although ultimately faithful to Ted, Stan seemed generally interested in getting Chris through this with as little harm as possible). But would he unwittingly let on about Chris's hearing? Being there to prevent that if he could when Stan came in was another good reason to get downstairs as fast as he could, and Chris almost panicked when he couldn't find his boots. Then he remembered they were still in the garage, probably still soaking wet from yesterday. Chris skipped the bathroom entirely on his way down; he would just take a piss on the dunes he was killing.

When he got to the base of the stairs, he stopped. Ted was cooking at the big range with his back to him. From here, Chris could see that the cello, the music stand, and the exercise book were now gone, vanished sometime in the night just like his own musical equipment had. He took a few more moments to compose himself, thinking about how he should act. He should be angry; he should be surly; he should be scared. No problem on all counts, Chris thought, and went and took his place at the table.

Only a single glass of orange juice was waiting for him; besides that, no place mats or silverware were set out—which was not, however, entirely unprecedented. Lately, the meals Ted was cooking, in their presentation at least, seemed to be moving from fine dining to greasy spoon. Ted was almost starting to look the part of some overworked, underpaid short-order cook—with his thick beard and his white hair, which was completely unkempt this morning, plus his eyes, which were often red and puffy at breakfast, as if he didn't sleep well at night. Out of some weakness for normalcy, Chris would have liked to attribute the change in Ted to his recent depraved activities. But more likely it was just this place that was taking its toll on Ted Harper, and not nearly enough for Chris to take any satisfaction in.

Ted banged his spatula twice on his frying pan—a sound Chris wasn't supposed to be able to hear—and then came to the table with two plates of food, simple eggs over easy and toast today. He went back to the kitchen and returned with a handful of silverware and the butter dish.

Should he be too angry to eat? Chris wondered. But that seemed pointlessly combative, not the way he intended to ride out the rest of his stay at Chez Harper. He picked up his knife and fork and started listlessly into his eggs, skipping the pewter salt and pepper shakers in the middle of the table as well. It was a mistake he should have seen.

"Chris, just hand me the salt there," he heard in his good ear, which Ted was facing—and heard it plain as day, his acute terror probably making up for any actual hearing loss.

He prayed he hadn't reacted, hadn't moved in some manner that would give him away. Out of the corner of his eye he could see that Ted was staring at him, and he glanced over once because he didn't want to give it away the other way, by acting too out of touch—thinking for a moment that his future and possibly his very survival had come down to an acting contest with a man who had once studied acting at Yale, and whose whole life was now essentially an act.

After what seemed like a very long time, Ted looked away and leaned over the table to pick up the metal saltcellar himself. The eggs had begun to taste like glue and the toast like wood, but Chris forced himself to keep eating, to keep his eyes trained on a spot about two feet in front of his plate. Ted didn't say anything else after that, and little by little Chris decided that his ploy had actually worked. But he also wondered how long he would be able to keep it going, how long before he eventually slipped up.

As the silence stretched out between them, the absence of the blaring stereo making this meal for the first time uncomfortable as well as merely torturous, Chris began to wonder—if he was really right about all this—what specific event this was supposed to correspond to in Ted's life: a morning very similar to this one, after his father had beat him up and made him quit the school play? But Ted had gone back to acting after that, in college where he had met Chris's father. So did that mean that Ted had backslid after his own father's life lesson? Or was this silent, instrument-free morning supposed to represent a general, more universal truth about life?

Either way, Ted's reenactment, or whatever it was, still wasn't working. If Chris was supposed to feel shame at not having been good enough at the cello, or not having worked hard enough at it, he didn't. And if he was supposed to miss it—his last connection with music—he didn't feel that, either. If he were truly deaf now, he would be very, very upset about that, but no more or less so than if he hadn't gone through his almost two weeks of Ted's faux farm life. All Ted had done was make Chris hate him, more than he had ever hated anyone or anything in his life.

After allowing Chris enough time to drink about a half cup of the black coffee he'd brought out from the kitchen, Ted stood up from the table and motioned to follow. Only right then did it dawn on Chris that his head guard was way late showing up this morning, and suddenly he was close to terrified again. He was so trained now, he realized, that each new departure from his routine brought him close to panic. But Ted merely led him into the garage where, as well as his damp, sandy boots and the first pair of socks he'd ruined yesterday, the shovel Chris had come to think of as his own was now leaning against the wall. Then Ted was yelling at him.

"STAN CAN'T MAKE IT TODAY, BUT I WANT YOU TO WORK ANYWAY!"

Chris turned to face Ted slowly, wondering if that had been a test, and if so, if he'd already failed it.

But Ted only seemed annoyed. "Oh, Christ," he muttered. "STAN CAN'T MAKE IT TODAY, BUT I WANT YOU TO WORK ANYWAY! YOU CAN JUST WALK TO THE POINT BY YOURSELF. DO YOU UNDERSTAND!?"

Slowly, appropriately gloomy, Chris nodded his head.

"GOOD, SO COME ON, GET MOVING!"

After that a part of Chris's mind acted out the following scene: *turn-*

ing, picking up the shovel; turning back, lifting up said shovel and bringing said shovel down squarely upon Ted Harper's face; watching Ted crumpling to the ground even while raising said shovel to hit Ted again; continuing to beat Ted with said shovel until his head was collapsed in like a broken coconut and there was blood spattered all over everything, including his pretty blue Mercedes-Benz.

But in reality, Chris didn't even take the risk of raising his eyes. He just went over to his boots, which couldn't have been more sandy if someone had dipped them in Elmer's glue and dragged them across a desert, picked them up by hooking two fingers behind their laces, then grabbed the shaft of the shovel with his other hand. Ted worked the button for the garage door, raising it on a sunny, blustery cold day, and as soon as Chris ducked outside, the motor reversed and the door shut again.

55

Chris's rage stayed with him all the way on the long walk to the gray house and the point. But inevitably, with the slow, methodical task he began, it ebbed again, cycling back to the cool, smooth hatred he felt for Mr. Ted Harper all the time now.

And why was he working today, he wondered, when Stan was probably asleep in some motel somewhere, and there wasn't anyone within three-quarters of a mile to see what he was doing?

But this morning, Chris knew why he was doing it. He was doing it on the tiny chance that Ted himself might walk down the beach to spy on him, or that Stan might be watching in a way Chris hadn't thought of. He was doing it because he wanted to be good; because, having almost lost it all yesterday, he now more than ever wanted out of here in one piece. He imagined just getting in his Mustang and driving away, that simple thing, but it seemed so wondrous now, the very concept of freedom a miracle. He could go anywhere.

Yet Chris knew where he would go now, too. Straight back to Boston. To Cassie. He wondered if she would even speak to him, wondered if what they'd had for so long would count for anything over what had happened.

He decided to let himself think about when they'd first met. It was in that very same Boston club, The Cat's Paw, just around the time when X Bomb was starting to happen. He'd actually been playing the very first moment he ever set eyes on her.

She was standing near the back, off to the side, just another pretty blonde college girl surrounded by a pack of friends, as ultimately untouchable and unhavable as the next, he'd thought. He always scouted the house when he played, squinting through the lights for anything of interest out there. But Cassie had truly been a find: a small, thin girl with straight, long hair and a little pug nose. All through that show he'd kept looking for her, every time sure, positive, she would be gone. It was always that way with girls when you were up on the stage. They might even flirt with you and make eyes at you, but you'd look up again and catch them leaving with some other guy on the next song.

Cassie hadn't left, though, and then on the break, walking through from the back room to the bar to pour himself a glass of soda water from the spigot, he'd found her standing there all by herself.

God, you really play the crap out of that thing, don't you? She'd said those words to him exactly.

He remembered stopping, just gazing into her eyes and her hopeful, lovely face. And right at that moment it seemed to him that he was destined for something great, so destined that he didn't even have to worry about it because he had all the time in the world to make it happen. The house music they had on was Alice in Chains' "No Excuses," and Chris would forever remember that song together with the way he'd felt right then: totally alive, at peace, safe.

Thank you was all he finally said. *Thank you so much. I'm Chris.* And then he put out his hand, and she took it.

And, according to her at least, everything that happened between them after that—she practically moved in with him while still taking her sophomore classes at UMass—was inevitable, even from the time they'd first seen each other during that show; while he'd been up on the stage playing, still the lead guitarist for an all-but-unknown out-of-college rock band trying to hit it big in Boston.

Thinking of all the time they'd spent together, leaving her the way he had (in reality, she had moved out nearly a month before he'd finally departed, but that didn't change anything) seemed like utter madness, an act of insanity that was all the more insane for the way he'd barely even acknowledged it to himself until today.

He still wasn't willing to actually let his mind go *there*—only this time there seemed to be no stopping it, and he stood up straight and let the shovel fall to the ground, bending his head down and closing his eyes like a man in shackles hearing his crimes.

Those last weeks had been ugly, the peak of his self-loathing, when he'd taken to doing absolutely nothing but sitting there on the couch in front of the television, drinking beer after beer and using the empties as ashtrays for his chain-smoking, keeping himself just dosed up enough so that he tingled a little, his hatred sharp and keen like a knife while the rest of him didn't really exist. In a progression of events that somehow made perfect sense at the time, his life meltdown had taken place only a week or so before the terrorist atacks in New York City and Washington, and in his wretched state he had watched the news nonstop, escaping from darkness into more darkness, he supposed. He would go outside only for more supplies, walking to the deli on the corner by day or night, stopping sometimes at the cash machine, feeling giddy each time he saw his checking account get closer to that magic, somehow infinite, number zero.

And then there was that last night when Cassie had come home—she worked as a paralegal at a law firm—to find him in his familiar perch on the couch, the whole apartment reeking of cigarette smoke, and it had finally finished itself.

Chris, are you still doing this? she'd said to him, or something like that. As he had taken to doing lately, he'd merely ignored her.

At first, the disaster had actually been a relief to him, like a shield he could hide behind. It made the past seem unimportant, his old problems frivolous. For a while, it had even somewhat reunited him and Cassie in their mutual grief. Yet after only a week or so that changed, around the time when it became clear that for everyone else life would go on again. That made him twice as angry. He would be walking down the street and see someone laughing and feel like killing them.

Chris couldn't we just talk about it, please? she might have said after that.

She knew exactly what the deeper problem was. He hadn't told her but she knew everyone in the band; she was an outgoing person who kept in touch with people, writing up countless cards every Christmas, staying up-to-date with old friends, making sure that Chris's friends were her friends. It was a trait of hers he never imagined he would come to detest.

Chris, why won't you just fucking talk to me!? she shouted suddenly. *I mean, if you had a fight with Kyle, so what? Get over it already! The guy's a stuck-up prick and it's no reason to go loony and take it out on me!*

This was new, and Chris could remember wondering if it wasn't something her friends had put her up to, confrontation generally not being her thing. He looked over to where she was standing on the other side of the room. Tears were streaming down her face now, but it only made him think how her pain couldn't possibly touch his own pain; how she was over there in the land of the living, in a world where people chatted and said *Hello* and *Have a nice day* to each other. She was in *that* world, while he was deep in hell, and so how dare she even *presume* to cry in front of him and equate their two pains?

He'd thought of saying something to her, just giving her something at that point. But still he hadn't. And that was when something he would never have predicted had happened.

In the next moment she was right in front of him, blocking his view of the TV set. She put her small hands on his shoulders and squeezed, probably as hard as she could. It hurt like hell, and then she was shaking him, throwing him back and forth, her face contorted and ugly.

Goddammit, Chris, you're going to talk to me! she'd hollered at him. *You're going to fucking say something or I'm going to kill you!*

If he could have done anything else at that point, it might still have been okay. If he could have grabbed her hands or spun away and laid down, or maybe just hugged her—Christ, if he could just have done that, then none of this would ever have had to have happened; she would have saved him from this; it now seemed perfectly clear and rational to him that this was what she'd been trying to save him from all along.

But instead, maybe partly because he'd been flying a little higher than he thought, he'd done what he had never done to any woman ever before. He had pushed out with both hands, connecting with her small shoulders to shove her as hard as he could, the blow coming back down through his palms and then his arms to rock him into some even blacker world than he'd ever before known existed.

Cassie had staggered backward into the TV, falling against it and taking it and its rolling stand down to the hardwood floor with her, all three of them coming down with a tremendous, unbelievable crash, the screen breaking with a popping sound, coughing out shards of dark green glass.

Afterward, for maybe a full minute, she just sat there, cross-legged on the floor in the perfect silence, Chris too stunned to even think of asking if she was all right or helping her up. Then, moving in what seemed like slow motion to Chris's pumped-up, suffering mind, she stood up and, sniffling once or twice on the way, picked up her purse off the kitchen counter and walked out.

And that was the last time he had seen or talked to her. Her friend Lillian called the next day and left an icy message on the machine saying she would be accompanying her that night when she came over to get her stuff, but Chris made a point of being out of the house. He tried to go to a bar, but by then he was too sick to drink anymore and ended up just walking the streets, winding up in Boston Common most of the night watching the skateboarders and roller skaters go by. He'd thought about killing himself, but of course he hadn't. And it was only a day or so later when he'd gotten the phone call from his father, who had heard from Chris's mother about their son's dire straits.

How bad had he actually hurt Cassie? Chris wondered now. Bad enough to leave bruises? Bad enough to sprain a wrist or twist an ankle? He thought he would give anything just to know that, or to know if she hated him, and how much. If he could just apologize, he thought. If he could just live through this thing to apologize for doing that, and for treating her like that.

The way things were going, though, it was a lot to ask for.

56

All the wet weather had left a thick crust of sand almost like a topsoil, which crumbled into big, satisfying chunks on the shovel, and Chris thought that he made better than average progress in spite of his woozy state. He worked until well past two o'clock, when finally he stopped and looked around. Not only had Stan not shown up to take him out to the point this morning, he was late bringing the customary lunch, too.

For a long time Chris stood there, wondering what he should do. His stomach was grumbling in objection, but he still felt light-headed and nauseated, and in terms of relative discomforts, it wasn't terrible (and complaining to the management wasn't exactly an option). He was still supposed to get a break, though, he figured, so he slung his shovel over his shoulder and began to walk back toward the road. When he got there, he looked all the way up past the house to the bridge, but there was no sign of either the silver or the black car.

He ended up in the same place he had yesterday, on the deck of the gray house. In the bright sun today, he leaned up against the railing facing west, with the ocean to his left and the light and heat beating down on him. He closed his burning, tired eyes. Instead of eating he would just nap for a little, he told himself, justifying it in his mind ahead of time so that if someone did show up and catch him, he would be ready. He was even more tired than he thought, and in a moment he dropped into deep slumber.

"What the hell are you doing here!?" the words wrenched him awake in a cold instant.

He opened his eyes, and was at first too stunned to speak. He *had* been caught—only the person who had caught him was someone entirely different from anyone he'd expected to see, someone whose meaning and significance in being here seemed to hit him over and over again, like an elaborate logic problem with seemingly endless permutations. It was Sam Burnett, the caretaker he'd visited, whose advice about Ted Harper he'd completely ignored. The man was standing over him, blocking the sun, but Chris might still have thought he was hallucinating if it weren't for the details: the black baseball cap, the beige Carhartt overalls, the Amish beard.

There were suddenly a million things to consider: *They* had to know that Sam Burnett was here, but would they now let him leave unmolested? Obviously, if he could leave, he could be given a message—but what message? How could he be made to see and believe what a dangerous position he was in so that whatever action he took wouldn't immediately get him, or both of them, killed.

Chris glanced over at his shovel. He made up his mind about what to do even as he was thinking up a good lie. "Umm, it's actually kind of embarrassing," he said, making a show of clearing his throat and rubbing his eyes to stall for time.

"What's embarrassing?" Sam said.

"What I was doing, it's kind of embarrassing."

"And what the hell were you doing?"

"Burying something. Burying a cat."

Chris thought that it was close for a second, but then Sam looked as if he bought it; maybe just because any other explanation would be outlandish, and Sam Burnett wasn't the type of guy to go in for outlandish explanations. Although, all the man would have to do at this point would be to turn his head to the right to see something pretty outlandish indeed: the dunes, where, in nine days of hard labor, Chris had completely changed the landscape here at the tip of the island, pushing back the grass line a good thirty or forty feet from where it had been, defoliating probably acres of beach grass down to bare sand.

"Oh, yeah, your cat died?" Sam said matter-of-factly.

"Yeah, she was old. It happened just last night, and so I thought I'd bring her out here to the point, you know?"

Sam was nodding to this, but still looking at Chris intently. "You okay? You don't look so good."

"I'm okay."

"You been spending a lot of time outdoors lately, in the sun?"

Chris guessed at what Sam was referring to. On top of everything else, and mostly ignored by him since they were so far down in his pecking order of hardships, his lips had been chapped, cracked, and bleeding ever since that first day Ted Harper had taken him out here to the dunes, and he'd also gotten a wicked sun- and windburn on the rest of his face, at least on the parts not now covered by his own beard, which was longer than it had ever before been in his life.

"Yeah, I guess so," Chris said, not sure how to duck that one.

Sam Burnett nodded for a while longer, still staring. "Hey, you haven't seen any strange guys hanging around here, have you?" he asked finally.

"What do you mean?"

"Someone over in the Cove told me they'd seen some guys hanging around the road over here, like they were staking the place out or something. So I thought I'd drive over and check out the houses."

"Huh. No, I haven't seen anyone. As far as I know, all the houses are fine."

More staring and nodding from Sam Burnett, but at the end of it he just turned away. "Well, have a good one," he said, raising a hand and walking off, disappearing behind the house as if he had been a hallucination after all.

Chris let out a breath that was half relief and half sick regret. He had quite possibly just sent away his last chance of getting out of this place alive—for a moment seeing an image of himself hiding under a tarp in the back of that rusty pickup, slipping away to freedom that way. But, on the other hand, if he was caught with someone else there as a witness, he had a feeling things would get very complicated and very ugly very quickly. In which case he would never be able to deliver his apology to Cassie after all.

He was listening for it with his one good ear, and he heard Sam Burnett's truck start up, then watched it drive out from beside the house and make its way down the road until it disappeared from his view behind dunes and greenery. After that Chris was alone again, feeling foolish and cowardly, like an insane old man in a long-abandoned asylum, so cowed by his years of captivity that he was too frightened to stand up and walk out the open door.

57

Whatever new regimen he was on, no one came to pick him up that evening either, the usually magic hour of five o'clock coming and going with nothing to herald it but a slowly darkening sky. Chris decided to call it a day on his own at ten after, starting the long walk back to the house with his shovel like a convict coming off a chain gang, the dread sinking into his bones like a disease, getting worse with every step he took. Now he had two things to worry about, he thought, or two things foremost: continuing to hide his hearing from Ted, and his little talk with Sam Burnett that day.

Chris wondered again if they had seen the pickup truck; what Ted would do if he knew about the brief meeting; and then if that might, in turn, make him realize Chris could still hear—but finally he stopped thinking about it. The possibilities and combinations were almost endless there, too, and he needed to keep it simple and concentrate on his evening performance of The Deaf Guy.

When he reached the driveway, however, he saw something surprising. Not only the silver car, but his own Mustang, with The Club still on its steering wheel, was parked outside. Either they had found the keys on his dresser or pushed it.

Chris couldn't imagine what it meant, and he went in the front door with his head down and his expression carefully blank. At first the house looked empty, with only the overhead track lights on and the sky almost black through the big windows. Then his eye was drawn to the door to the garage, which was standing wide open and brightly lit from behind. A moment later, Ted Harper leaned out from behind it.

"Chris, would you come in here, please," he said, also motioning with his hand before disappearing again.

Chris hadn't had a chance to show his confusion, and he considered just standing there, waiting and making Ted say it again. But then he figured that, in any case, Ted's gesture had been clear enough, and he needed to put his shovel away anyway. As he crossed the room, he surmised that he was about to receive his new duties for the afternoon now that Ted wasn't humoring his musical fantasies anymore. Chris had no idea what those would be, but once again the suspense made him want to throw up whatever little he had in his empty stomach.

As he came through the door, however, the first person Chris saw wasn't Ted, but Stan, leaning back with his arms crossed as if he were very tired. He was leaning against a large, primer-gray pickup truck, and when Chris recognized it, his legs almost gave way beneath him.

He quickly turned away, ostensibly to return the shovel to where it had been that morning.

"You know why we had to do this, don't you, Chris?" Ted said while Chris's back was turned.

He didn't answer, not knowing what he would say anyway, trying through his terror to remember that he was supposed to be stone-deaf. He turned back with his face a mask of nothingness, he hoped.

"That's okay, Chris, it wasn't all your fault," Ted continued regardlessly, giving the words a breezy, carefree tone, as if he were God himself. "Anyway, now that you're here, you can help us. Jump up."

And then Ted motioned for Chris to climb into the back of the truck, the tailgate of which was already open, the edge of it clearing the closed garage door by only inches.

Chris hesitated, both out of horror and because he wasn't supposed to be able to hear Ted's commands. To play it safe, however, he decided to hedge his bet a little, looking confused but also doing as he'd been shown. It was, after all, a simple request. He walked to the back of the pickup and hoisted himself in.

He saw the body even before he had. Sam Burnett was on his back, wrapped in clear, thick plastic, like the kind you would buy as a drop cloth for painting. The plastic was bound up with twine in three places, and spreading out from the dead man's chest was a huge, steamed-up, brown and red bloodstain. Chris looked away just as soon as he could get control of himself enough to do that.

"Pick him up and bring him, Chris. Bring him!" Ted shouted.

He hadn't really yelled as loud as Chris had made him yell that morning, but once again, under the present circumstances, he decided not to push his luck. He turned back to the corpse in the truck and bent over, turning his head away while getting his arms under the crinkly plastic. He could barely support the weight of the victim and ended up half sliding Sam Burnett to the tailgate. After that he jumped down again and just managed to hoist the body up in a clumsy fireman's carry.

"Come on," Ted said, and walked across the garage to pick up the shovel himself. He went into the house then, and Chris followed, balancing his heavy load on his shoulder, trying to keep his face away from it, trying not to think about what was inside that plastic or look down at the old, worn-out work boots sticking out and dangling in front of him. Ted crossed through the sunken living room, unlocked and slid open one of the glass doors, then left it open for Chris. On his way through, Chris turned back to shut it with his free hand, but saw that Stan was following, too, empty-handed, and left it for him.

They started out on the familiar path to the beach, Chris trying to keep up with all the weight he was carrying in the soft, uneven sand, breathing heavily, his back already protesting with quick jabs of pain. Unavoidably, he was reminded of what he'd done with Charlie; now, here was another murder he'd indirectly caused, this one of a human being, a man with a family no less. He wondered what would happen. Would they get away with it? Would it be as simple as that? Briefly, Chris indulged the fantasy that they wouldn't, that tomorrow, while he was down at the point, the police would storm the place and shoot and kill all of them, including Ted. But Chris knew it was more wishful thinking. They obviously did things like this all the time, and if he was wishing ill for Ted, he might as well hope for him to slip on the soap in the shower; that had at least a theoretical chance of happening. No, the world was the way the world was, Chris had learned, and he was through deluding himself that he would ever be able to change it one iota.

Depression struck him deeply again, and right then for some reason he realized that Ted's Vietnam story had been true after all. Chris had sworn at the time that it wasn't, but now he couldn't remember why he'd thought that anymore. He suspected it was something to do with an idealism he'd once had, and also in order to keep pretending Ted was something he could understand so that he wouldn't have to fear him so much—and could hang on to another of his favorite fantasies: the one about getting out of here alive. He tried to conjure some of the strength he'd been feeling earlier, thinking about his new and revised future—if he had one—as a better and saner man, possibly with Cassie. But it was no good. Right now he was cold and tired and hungry, and all that just seemed like another fantasy. He had been dreaming his entire life, he thought, up until right now.

They stopped sooner than Chris would have guessed, and Ted pointed to a grassy spot behind a low wall of scrub.

"There, Chris, put him there. There!" Ted repeated himself, also pointing for Chris's benefit.

Chris looked confused, but once again complied, bending over to set down Sam Burnett, who crashed into the thick brush where in the dimming light you could barely see his body. Chris just stayed there, waiting for what he was sure was coming next: the shovel being handed to him to dig another grave in the dunes.

But that didn't happen. "Come on," Ted said, "we'll move him later." And then, bizarrely, they continued on toward the beach.

58

They had only gone another two hundred feet or so, however, when Ted turned around again, this time holding out the shovel.

"Okay, Chris. While we're out here, I want you to dig up that damn dog wherever it is you buried it. Otherwise that thing'll just be stinking up my beach for months."

Chris stopped and stared at Ted Harper, so shocked and enraged that for a moment he completely forgot he was supposed to be deaf.

"Yup, you heard that just fine, didn't you, Chris?" Ted said immediately. "Well, that's all right, you don't have to worry about that. You're a lousy actor and I already knew it. So, I'll tell you what, you dig up that dog and get rid of it somewhere where I won't have to smell it, maybe put it somewhere for one of my neighbors to find, and we'll call it even for your little joke on me. How about that?"

Chris thought it was a lousy deal indeed. His throat closed up in old shame while his head boiled with hatred. But Ted had said that he wanted it done, and so there was nothing else but to do it, and why should he make things worse for himself by arguing or pleading?

"Okay," Chris said, almost under his breath, barely able to get the word out. He went over and took the shovel by its handle and veered off the path toward where he'd once dug Charlie's grave with a broken plastic dustpan. On the way, he prayed for Ted and Stan to at least go back to the house so he'd be left alone with this chore of ultimate disgrace. But when he looked back, they were following right behind.

They wouldn't miss this for the world, Chris thought, then quickly looked away because he was sure the hatred was etched into his face.

He smelled it even as he was coming over the second line of dunes this time, that same repulsive reek he'd only gotten just a whiff of last night. Today it was much stronger; there was less wind, and maybe the drying wetness had brought it up to the surface more. When he'd gone another fifty feet, he honestly didn't think he would be able to do it. He considered a ploy. It was getting dark fast now, the sunset just about gone and the hills of cold sand starting to lose definition to the eye, so would it be unbelievable if he couldn't find the place, if he just kept digging and coming up with nothing? Yet, even as he thought of it, Chris knew that it wouldn't work. He was far too angry to successfully pull it off, and he'd only just got caught trying to fool Ted Harper. Soon he came to the end of his walk and stood on the spot, the sand perfectly smooth and flat again except for the new footprints he'd made. He turned around.

"Mr. Harper, it's getting dark. I'll do this first thing tomorrow, okay?" he said, trying to keep the emotion out of his voice and failing.

"Nope, you're doing it right now, Chris. And I do mean *now.*" Ted came to stand about fifteen feet away, crossing his arms like a man who's come to see some great injustice put right.

Chris looked down, took a breath, and planted the shovel. With the first sand he turned over, the smell was immediately twice as bad, the stench reminding him of the dead birds he used to find sometimes by the lake near their house when he was growing up—only on a whole different scale, of course. When he'd buried Charlie, it had never occurred to him that *this* would happen, that the reason you couldn't bury a body in shallow sand where it was wet was because it would start to stink to high heaven. But how was he supposed to know that? Unlike the two men facing him, he'd never had any experience with dead bodies weighing more than a couple of ounces.

There must have been flies crawling in the sand, because suddenly they were all over the place. He had to stop to slap at a viciously smarting bite at the back of his neck, and then another one under his chin. They were swarming all over him and trying to wave them away had no effect at all.

Dreading what he was going to find, Chris dug his hole wide and flat, keeping his head turned away and timing his breaths when the wind would blow so that he didn't have to smell it full on. He tried breathing through his mouth, but found that even worse, as if he were tasting it, as if it left a residue on his tongue.

By the time he'd reached about the two-foot mark, his nose was running and his eyes were watering like crazy. He could barely see what he was doing anymore, could barely even think with the flies buzzing everywhere. Then suddenly, shallower than he would have thought, it felt like hitting slippery rubber, and he glanced down and saw an exposed patch of dark brown bedsheet. He could stand it no longer and had to turn away and take a step back.

"The faster you do things you don't like doing, the less time you'll have to be doing them, Chris," Ted drawled from somewhere behind him. "But I guess you haven't learned that one yet, either, have you?"

In his terrible, impotent rage, Chris shut his eyes on fresh tears. "I'm going as fast as I can," he all but moaned. "I'm just trying not to stick a shovel into him, is that okay!?"

"Whatever you say, but you're only making it harder on yourself."

Chris couldn't help it and spun around to face his torturer. *"You're* making this harder on *me!"* he whined and yelled at the same time. "Why can't I just do it tomorrow? And you know if I don't get a plastic bag, all my clothes are going to end up smelling like this. I don't have another jacket, so do you want *me* smelling like this for the next month, or two months, or however long you plan on keeping me here?!"

"Yeah, well, it's pretty hard to imagine you smelling any worse than you already do, but I guess that's a good point. You better take off your jacket," Ted answered perfectly, infuriatingly at ease.

Chris just let his head drop to look at the ground again, feeling a fresh river of tears pouring from his irritated eyes. As he did so, though, he heard a strange sound in his one ear, which he nevertheless recognized from somewhere. He realized what it was a moment later when Stan reached inside his coat and took out his cell phone.

"Yeah," Stan answered it, exactly as he had before. He listened for only a second or two. "Okay," he said to whoever was on the other end. "I don't know," he said quickly to Ted. And then, the cell phone still in one hand, he turned and started to jog back toward the house.

Ted watched all this happen nonchalantly, then afterward turned back to Chris. "Dig," he told him, pointing to the grave.

With only Ted watching, logically the task should have seemed at least somewhat less humiliating. But the exact opposite was true. With just him and Ted it felt more personal suddenly, more like a rape; and even as Chris stood there and told himself that he *would* start digging again, that it wasn't worth it not to, he couldn't seem to actually translate that thought into an action anymore.

"I told you to dig, goddammit!" Ted said. "Dig up that smelly mutt. If I have to be stuck out here all winter, I'm not going to spend every single day catching whiffs of your rotting pet!"

The next charge of rage that went through Chris's body, from the tips of his toes to the cap of his skull, seemed to annihilate all rational thought from his head. And yet, when it had passed, when he had withstood it, he had an instant of perfect understanding as if he *had* been struck by a kind of lightning.

"Why *stuck* out here, Mr. Harper?" Chris said slowly. "Why are you *stuck* here?"

He watched Ted's face after that and saw it happen: the eyes flashing, getting bigger for a split second as Ted realized he'd finally been caught at his lie. "Well, you know, because of you," he faltered. "To be taking care of you. Trying to teach you something."

"Bullshit," Chris told him.

And, of course, it was bullshit. Finally now, Chris understood what he should have figured out a long time ago, and probably would have if he hadn't been so self-centered as to actually believe all this could really be about him. He should have known from a thousand things, from *everything:* from the guard car being parked on the other side of the bridge last night, where you would park if you were trying to keep someone from coming *onto* the island, not from leaving it; from Stan being called away those times, for false alarms probably; or from the things Stan had told him, like, *You're getting out of here before any of us* or *You fucked with the wrong guy at the wrong time;* or from the way Ted never left the house; or how he hadn't been at all angry at Donna— Chris should have known.

He should have known that Mr. Ted Harper, former drama student turned gangster and killer, had finally fucked with the wrong person or persons and was currently out here in hiding on his little island with Stan and the rest of his goons as his bodyguards, even more of a prisoner than Chris was.

Chris could have almost laughed out loud at the simple, brilliant joke of it: Ted Harper's best charade yet, taking advantage of a bad situation to skew reality in a way that was subtle, and yet, for Chris, as substantial as life itself. And Sam Burnett hadn't been killed because of what they thought Chris had told him; they'd murdered him because he'd figured out something was going on, probably demanded to know what they were doing here, maybe surprised or threatened one of them.

For just a moment Chris doubted himself. The timing was too perfect, too lucky—until he remembered that the last time he'd called Ted he hadn't been at his office, either. Ted had given him some new number, even though he'd already told him about fifty telephone numbers beforehand. So it had started for Ted sometime before then; sometime between then and when Chris had first come to the house.

"I know why you're really here, Ted," Chris went on, feeling almost out of breath from the way his heart was thundering in his chest. "It's because someone wants you dead, right? That's why you have all your guys here guarding the place; not for me. It's because you killed, or had killed, one too many people, and now someone's coming after you. So you're hiding out here where you can lay a trap for them. But then you figured, while you're at it, while you're here, why not mess with my head, too. And your wife didn't leave you because of me; she probably left you a long time ago, because you're a psycho—or because you killed your son." Chris added that last part without having really thinking it out beforehand, although realizing full well that he was crossing a line, he knew not to where.

Ted came right up to him, already taller than he was and standing on slightly higher ground, towering over Chris with his face deformed in rage. *"How dare you say that to me?"* he spat out. *"My son was sick. He was born sick."*

"Yeah, but you did something." Chris raised his face to meet Ted's, the two of them only inches apart.

"I exercised him," Ted said with the self-righteousness only the truly insane can muster. *"He needed exercise!"*

"How? Like this? Digging?" Chris shouted, raising up the shovel to refer to it, the motion becoming more like brandishing at the end.

Once again, Ted looked startled enough to let Chris know he was right, or at least close enough. And then it was clear that the man had had enough.

"I GAVE YOU A JOB TO DO!" he railed. "NOW GET RID OF THAT DEAD CUR BEFORE I TAKE IT OUT ON YOUR HIDE, YOU LITTLE RUNT!"

Chris had to step back to swing the shovel, putting his right leg behind him to get purchase while he swung it like a baseball bat. He swung it as hard as he could, but wasn't quite brave enough to do what he should have done and go for the head. Instead, the blade of the shovel made contact with Mr. Harper's arm below his shoulder, where it probably hurt a lot but did no real damage.

It was still enough to throw the older man off balance, however, and while he was stumbling and recovering, Chris raised his weapon again. Unfortunately, in the heat of the moment, he somehow managed to forget about the hole he'd just dug. Suddenly, as he followed Mr. Harper's slow trajectory, his left leg was plunging downward, scraping the sandy side of the grave until his foot actually came down on the soft, bloated body that was Charlie. Chris came down with a crash on his side, twisting his leg, just barely managing to keep a grip on to the shovel.

In an instant Ted Harper was above him and had ahold of that shovel, trying to pull it away, both of them gasping in all-out exertion as Chris was dragged through the sand. The next thing he knew, however, the direction of effort changed, and suddenly the shovel was being forced down on top of him. In a moment he was pinned on his back, while Mr. Harper used all of his greater weight and leverage to force the shaft of the tool ever lower.

At the last moment, when it became clear that he was going to lose the battle, Chris used the remainder of his strength to at least lower it down a little, so that it came down high on his chest, where it immediately constricted his breathing anyway.

"You want to fuck with me, Chris?" Ted Harper said in almost intimate voice, between coughing, spitting breaths only inches above him. "You still think this is a game? You still think things will turn out okay for you because the world is really just here to take care of you? Is that what you think?"

But Chris couldn't even answer by that point, even if he'd had something worthwhile to say. As his strength ebbed further, Ted was able to move the wooden bar higher and higher, until it felt as if a line of fire were crossing his shoulder blades, beginning to crush his windpipe and cut off his breathing altogether. He was starting to see dark, smeary spots at the edge of his vision and understood fully that he was about to die. Randomly, he wondered why Ted didn't just save himself the trouble at this point and pull out a gun and shoot him.

Yet suddenly the fire was removed, and Chris felt himself being dragged. Before he realized what was happening, the world had flipped over in a dizzying one-eighty, and his head and shoulders were being forced down into the damp sand. He felt a foot stomp down on his back, his neck forced to bend. And then his face was driven directly against the bottom of the hole he'd just dug, where only a thin, meaningless layer of sand and linen separated his nose and mouth from the fur of Charlie's decomposing body.

Chris told himself not to breathe, not to smell it, but his lungs were already hitching, crying out for air. And then the foul, fetid stench came into him in a great rush, poisoning him with its sickly-sweet richness, tasting every bit as bad in his mouth as it smelled to his nose.

"There's your childhood, Chris!" Ted said from somewhere above him—somewhere where there was light and sky and the air wasn't tainted to the point of being poisonous. "That's what's left of it, okay! So do you think you can let go of that? Do you think you can finally accept it and move on?"

The idea that Ted might still not kill him entered Chris's mind. After all, he'd had the chance and hadn't taken it. So if Chris just got through this, if he was just good from now on . . .

But right then, as his mind and body returned to full, excruciating consciousness, he felt something against his right arm, which he knew was Ted's other foot. Summoning all of his strength, he brought that arm forward, practically wrenching his own shoulder out of its socket. It worked, though. The pressure on his back grew momentarily greater, to the point where he was sure his neck would snap, but after that it was gone and he felt the great weight of Ted's body come down on his legs.

He scrambled to get his head out of the foul grave, rolling away from it and Ted as fast as he could. When finally he got to his hands and knees, fresh air had never smelled so sweet to him; he didn't even notice what had seemed like such a terrible stench before.

It was all over for him now, of course. Ted Harper was already standing up and coming over to him, the man never having lost possession of the shovel. But still it seemed completely worth it.

Ted stood there above Chris for some time. He had some sand on him, and his white hair was tousled and his face was bright red, but aside from that he looked just the same as he always did, oblivious to the cold in that one sweater. Chris wondered if, after Ted killed him, he would temporarily throw him into the same hole with Charlie. That seemed fitting in some way, and Chris supposed he wouldn't mind it so much when he was dead.

"Well, I guess in the end you're just a disappointment to all of us, Chris," Ted drawled out, back to the unflappable-Southern-gentleman act.

"Fuck you, at least I'm not mentally ill," Chris told him softly, sitting back and looking up defiantly.

"I tried with you, Chris. I tried so very hard with you."

"You . . . you tried to suck my dick," Chris answered, just saying the first thing that popped into his head, a slow, tired smile spreading across his face.

Ted's expression grew more solemn after that, and perhaps for the very first time since they'd met, Chris felt that he was seeing the real Ted Harper; that, in Chris's last moments on this earth, Ted was finally not acting with him. "Well, I guess you've pretty much decided how you want this thing to end then, haven't you?" he said.

But Chris didn't even answer; just gave Ted the finger from his sitting position. Then he turned his head to the side to wait for the first blow, which he was sure would this time mark the beginning of the end of his life.

Out of the corner of his eye, he saw Ted start to do something with the shovel, raising it up a little while readjusting his hold.

59

The moment was broken by a loud, ringing car horn that sounded and just kept on going, cutting the peaceful silence of the place in half, seeming to freeze time itself. Whatever Ted had been about to do, he appeared to reconsider now, eventually lowering the shovel to his side. The horn just blared on and on, eating into the night with its one insistent note.

"Come on. Get up," Ted said, kicking Chris in the leg. So Chris stood, and Ted poked him in the back with the blade of the shovel. "Move."

And so Chris began walking toward the house, clearly the general locus of the sound. Ted kept him marching at a fast pace, giving him little jabs in the small of his back. When they got within a few hundred yards, he started talking again.

"Well, you might as well know you were right about one thing, Chris. I am in hiding out here. And I did kill someone, or, actually, have him killed. He was Jack Tomasko, the man who started working for me in Vietnam. When the war was over, he got a position in U.S. Customs, to further assist me in my dealings, you might say. That worked for years and years, until this summer it came to my attention that he was offering his services elsewhere. So of course I couldn't have that. What never occurred to me was that this other group didn't know about our previous arrangement and would eventually discover my act and see it as an attempt to take over their business. Funny how things work out sometimes, but, really, it's all just another battle in an ongoing war."

At the steps up to the deck, Ted used the shovel to pat Chris on the left shoulder. "No, go around the side."

So Chris turned and followed the sand path he'd taken so many times, which led out to the gravel next to the front door.

"Anyway, now it looks like we're going to find out who's got the bigger *cójones,* Chris. And if they think I'm going to turn and run, they've got another think coming."

When Chris got to the front of the house, he stopped. The silver car looked as if it had started to back out of the driveway, but then just kept on going, ending up facing toward them in the sand and bushes on the far side of the road.

"Go look," Ted said, giving him one last jab in his lower back.

So Chris stepped out into the open in front of the house. He looked back at Ted once, who wasn't following, but decided the prospect of going forward was still better than going back and continued on.

About halfway there he saw a figure in the front seat: someone was slumped forward on the wheel, which was why there was all that racket that was keeping him from thinking clearly. He crossed the road and then stepped off it again to go up to the passenger-side window. The engine was running, and even in the almost-darkness, he could identify Stan by his light, curly hair. The man's face was turned away as if he were napping, but Chris still wasn't really thinking when he opened the door and reached in to pat him on the shoulder. The horn stopped instantly, but to Chris's horror, Stan fell over toward him, lying down sideways on the seat with his shirt and his hands covered in blood, his throat plainly cut open, the gash looking just like something in a fish market under the illumination of the dome light: one big, bloody gill, the skin around it white as paper.

Chris was completely paralyzed, too dumbfounded to use the information in determining what he should do next, and so he just stayed there, bent over, hanging on the open door, until suddenly the glass in that door exploded in his face. He heard the shot only after that, zinging past him, and then the next bullet went right by his left ear, whirring like some insect, probably only missing him by inches.

After that he was running, just instinctively heading for the house and the front door, stopping to yank it open even while another bullet buried itself in the wood, sending little splinters into his open mouth.

Without really thinking this part out either, Chris ran for the stairs, flying up them two at a time. He still had the key to the desk in his back pocket, and he reached under his jacket to get it even as he started down the upstairs hallway. The door to the master bedroom was standing open, and he rounded the corner so fast he barely stayed on his feet.

He came to a lurching, skidding halt on the other side. The top desk drawer was already open, a ring of keys hanging from the keyhole above. Standing on the other side of the room, up against the wall so as to stay away from the big windows looking out at the ocean, Ted Harper now had possession of the big black gun. As a meaningless observation, Chris realized he hadn't been armed all this time—even now remembered him bending over the couch to get Stan's gun the one time he'd needed one.

"No, hiding won't help, Chris," Ted said calmly, assuming he hadn't known about the handgun, of course. "I'm afraid it's hopeless. They've already seen you, and they'll tear this place apart if they have to."

Ted was holding the gun in his right hand while cradling it with his left, and Chris observed that he was in the process of unscrewing the long silencer. Right at that moment he came to some decision and reversed the direction, tightening it again.

"I'm going to do you a favor now, Chris," he went on while he did. "You see, these other people, they aren't as civilized as I am, and if they found you still alive, well . . . you'll have to trust me that it's better for you this way. And, anyway, maybe I'll finally be paying your father back for what he did to me."

"What? What did he do to you, Ted?" Chris said, for the moment just trying to keep him talking.

"You know what he did to me, Chris. I told you what he did to me."

"No, no. You never did, Ted. You left that part out, I swear you did."

"I did, huh? Well, it's obvious anyway, isn't it? He was the one who talked me out of it. All those years ago, when I got out of jail that first time, I was sitting in a bar near campus, just trying to put things straight, just trying to get drunk and nurse my cuts and bruises. And he walks in with his fine, expensive clothes, and some beautiful girl on his arm. And he invites me to join them, and we all have a drink together; and he starts telling me how foolish I'd been, and how the whole profession is for the birds, and about all the money he's going to make, and about all the things he's going to have. And it was right then when I made my deci-sion. So it was all his fault, do you see? I mean, if it weren't for him, I could have been . . . I could have been great, Chris . . . I could have been right up there with the best of them: Brando, Hoffman, Curtis . . ."

Once more that evening, Chris came perilously close to laughing, this time hysterically; all of this in the end, everything that had happened, perhaps even the course of Ted's entire life, came down to a lecture, a single instance of one-upmanship dealt out so long ago by Chris's father, who at the time was probably as unsure of himself as Ted had been; and who just a few weeks ago Chris had been cursing for having the very opposite attitude of the young man Ted Harper remembered. Chris would probably even have laughed, but sometime during the confession Ted had screwed the silencer tight, and now he just stood there with his eyes looking up somewhere above Chris's head, either imagining that conversation he had picked over so many times, or perhaps still lost in the phantom career he had also invented over the years. That lasted for maybe as long as ten seconds, until abruptly he came out of it, racked the slide and leveled the gun at Chris's chest.

"Anyway, that's all in the past now, Chris," he said. "And so are you."

Then, before Chris could think of anything else to ask or say, Ted Harper pulled the trigger, and Chris felt a spasm of pure terror before the hammer snapped closed with a metallic click, and nothing else.

There were a few moments of perfect silence.

"Wow, that's a good silencer," Chris heard himself say afterward, shocked and terrified by his audacity even as he uttered the words.

Ted racked the slide again and looked in the chamber of the hand-gun—which *hadn't* been reloaded, and the ammunition for which, as far as Chris knew, was still hidden in a sock between his mattress and the wall in his bedroom. Ted immediately went over to the desk, slammed the top drawer all the way open, and pulled out one of the other magazines. He looked at it and threw it to the floor.

"Where are the bullets!?" he yelled.

Chris put up both his hands. "How would I know?"

"Because you took them, somehow you took them, *you little bastard!*"

As Ted started toward him, Chris backed up into the hallway and slammed the door shut behind him. And then, getting a running start, he did something he would have thought absolutely insane when he first arrived here: he launched himself up and over the side of the balcony, pulling his legs up as far as he could, just barely clearing the metal handrail and hearing one of his heels ding against the top of it as he did. For a moment he thought he'd misjudged it and would hit the far wall on his way down. But he didn't, and he came down with a crash, his knees coming all the way up to his chest, feeling the wooden floorboards give a little and take some of the shock.

He stood up and looked around him. He could hear Ted, already out of his room and halfway to the stairs, and so he had perhaps a total of three seconds to decide what to do. Yet there was really no choice to make, he realized; he could see clearly that he was about to die one way or the other, only for some reason the fear had left him, and he merely backed up to the wall. He listened for it, and when Ted was about to emerge from the stairwell, he raised his leg.

It sent him sprawling almost halfway to the big dinner table. Chris had been holding on to the wall to brace himself, and he pushed off it now to get up speed quickly, crossing over to the older man in four big steps. Perhaps still thinking of getting bullets for it, Ted rolled over to protect the gun, and when he did, Chris wound up and kicked the back of his head as hard as he could, not holding back at all this time, connecting the toe of his boot to Ted Harper's skull with such force that it hurt his whole foot.

Chris heard Ted's teeth clack together, just as loud as if someone had made a single percussive snap of a pair of castanets in the room. Afterward Ted groaned, seemed to shake himself awake, and started to lean forward and roll over. This time Chris nailed him in his back, right at the base of his spine, and he convulsed and hollered out, changing directions to lie down flat looking at the ceiling. The next one went into his ear, and the one following that as well; Chris following through on his kicks, remembering the feeling in his leg muscles from all those afternoons of soccer in high school, the simple joy of punting that ball solidly, bulleting it down the field. Now, in whatever parallel universe he'd arrived in, he watched Ted's head snap to the side again and again with no more feeling for it than he'd had for that leather ball.

The sound of the gun clattering to the floor stopped him for some reason. He'd been about to kick Ted right in his face, right in his already bloody mouth, when suddenly he thought, *I'm kicking the shit out of some old man.*

He halted his leg in midstroke and instead leaned over and picked up the heavy gun by its long silencer. And then he stood straddling Ted Harper over his slowly heaving chest.

"DON'T YOU *EVER* TRY TO *TELL* ME OR *TEACH* ME ANY-THING EVER *AGAIN,* YOU *SICK, INSANE* OLD *FUCK*!" Chris screamed at him, punctuating his words by whacking the man across his blinking face with his own weapon.

After that he just leaned down and placed the slightly bloody stock of the empty gun in Ted Harper's outstretched hand. "You go get 'em, cowboy," Chris said quietly, patting Ted's confused, gripping fingers.

From somewhere there came the quick stuttering sound of rapid-fire bullets, and the front windows exploded inward, followed by a large sec-tion of the back windows, which came crashing down to the floor and deck outside like an avalanche of ice. Chris hadn't even stood up before he was diving across the room, landing on his stomach, sliding into and knocking over one of the dining-table chairs, which came down right on top of his head before toppling to the side.

There was a kind of lull after that, and he sat up and looked around. To his horror, *all* of the perfect white walls were riddled with black bul-let holes. They *were* surrounded, and it *was* hopeless, he thought—until he remembered who had told him that.

He began to crawl as quickly as he could, but at the little step where the wooden floor turned to the white tiling of the kitchen, another vol-ley of machine-gunfire tore through the house, the bullets hitting all the china and pots and pans and appliances; and it was as he was bringing his hand up to shield his face from all the glass and whatever else flying around that he felt it smacked away again.

It didn't feel like anything at first. It happened with about the same force that his brother would have used when they used to get into slap-ping fights as kids. Yet when he opened his eyes again, two of his fin-gers, both his pointer and middle finger, had been shot clean off.

For just a moment, on the tiny parallel stubs that remained, Chris could see his own white bone and gristle inside the pink flesh. It wasn't real somehow; it couldn't be, he thought. A moment later, however, blood began to ooze, and then to flow, and then his hand, or what remained of it, was covered in blood, the red fluid pooling at his wrist, soaking into his clothes and running down his arm to his elbow. The real pain hit a second after that, and Chris moaned and shuddered and shoved his wound inside his jacket, wrapping it in the loose folds of his sweater. It was all he could do for now, and he started across the floor again, hobble-crawling, using only one elbow. He might have passed one of them on the way then, an inch-and-a-half-long tube of red and white flesh, but he forced himself to look away. When he reached the sink, he even had the presence of mind to turn over and sit up and make sure he wasn't leaving a trail of blood, which, thankfully, he wasn't yet.

And then Chris played his last card, possibly the very last one he would ever play, pulling open the cabinet door underneath. If he couldn't actually fit inside, then it was game over, no question. But, knocking over all kinds of cleansers and scrubbing brushes and other assorted crap, he found there was just enough room for him, holding on to the U-joint in the pipe, to pull himself in. His disfigured hand and whole arm screamed in pain when he did, but after that it came back to within limits he could stand—although it was definitely close, and he had to slam his head back and push out with his legs with all his might to keep from thrashing around when the throbbing started. With the doors closed it was perfectly dark, and he closed his eyes to wait out his fate.

There was gunfire, more gunfire, and then following that there came a crescendo of gunfire that seemed to encompass the entire world outside of his black cabinet, shaking the house as if to take it right off its foundations. When finally it subsided, there was a quick scurry of feet, which Chris assumed was Mr. Harper finally taking flight to wherever he would go. And then for a while there was silence.

At one point, Chris almost panicked, when he noticed that his jeans were soaking with blood and became sure that he was bleeding to death. He tried to tourniquet himself, grabbing on to his wrist and squeezing as hard as he could with his other hand, but found he was so weakened he could only keep it up for short periods.

Soon after that the screaming started, Ted Harper's deep voice moaning and coughing in between all the hollering, Chris hearing just snatches of the other people in the house —terse commands, the clumping of feet, some furniture being moved.

He passed out sometime in the middle of it, and when he came awake again, he smelled smoke and reasoned they were burning the house down. After a while the smell was no worse, however, and so he just waited. He could hear nothing at all now, but still he waited, keeping his eyes closed, feeling his heart pounding in his chest, trying to contain the world of pain emanating from his severed fingers, and knowing nothing anymore except that he was still alive.

60

He had passed out again at some point, and so he couldn't have said how much time had gone by when he finally crawled out of there. He could have checked his watch, but it seemed unimportant and so he didn't bother. His hand was stuck to his clothes with drying blood now—which he didn't try to remove, but merely unzipped his jacket the rest of the way and then pulled up the bottom of his blood-soaked sweater, forming a kind of sling, packaging up the whole mess so he wouldn't have to deal with it. When he got to his feet, he was practically delirious, hanging on to consciousness only moment to moment. But he braced himself against the countertop until he could walk again, then started off across the debris-covered tiles toward the front of the house.

Someone had turned off the lights, and the place was almost perfectly dark, a cold wind blowing through all the broken windows, making it feel as if he were outdoors. At the front door, he leaned up against the molding and transferred the end of his makeshift sling to his mouth so that he could work the light switch. When he did, and when the lights came on again, he thought he came the closest he had to dying so far, of a simple heart attack.

They had tied Ted Harper to a chair at the foot of the big dining table with what looked like black lamp cord. He was sitting up straight, with his head lolled only a little to one side and his arms neatly beside him, almost the way he'd sat at breakfast or dinner sometimes. Other than that, however, things were very wrong. His dirty white sweater was soaked, caked with blood, and above and behind his face, where once there had been a full head of white hair, now there was nothing. Chris stared at him for the longest time before he realized what it was; and even after he had, he still couldn't quite make himself believe and comprehend it. It was just that he had never seen anyone scalped before, and so the image his mind kept on trying to feed him was Ted wearing a red shower cap. The other problem, and what Chris realized he must have smelled before, was the eyes, both of which had been replaced with smoking, charred black holes, as if someone had taken a hot soldering iron or perhaps a torch directly to them.

Chris didn't want to get close to him, didn't even want to look at him. But the left arm of his fisherman's sweater was already torn somewhat, and he knew he wouldn't get another chance; so, after a moment of indecision, he stumbled over. Being careful not to overturn the body, he reached his bloody fingers inside both the unraveling sweater and the shirt beneath it to widen the rip into a gaping mouth, then raised up the sizable hole he'd made until he could see most of Ted Harper's hairy, white left shoulder. But of course there was nothing—a small, puckered, pink scar, but that could have been from anything.

Chris turned away and, without knowing he was going to, buckled over and fell to his knees, the shock of the impact sending a white-hot spike of agony from his wrecked hand so that he cried out through the piece of sweater he held in his teeth.

My God, have I completely lost it? he thought; he'd been standing there playing with a mutilated corpse in a major crime scene while bleeding to death, all in order to answer some stupid, imaginary question about an insane man's past.

Which anyway didn't even matter to him anymore, he told himself; after all, his life, too, was basically over. Or no, he supposed that in all probability he would survive and go on living after this, but things would never be the same; just turning off the lights and getting to sleep at night would be a noteworthy accomplishment, and holding down a job as a waiter would be a minor miracle. Although of course it went much deeper than that.

Even now, though, Chris wondered if it were really true. He couldn't help thinking that he still had one good ear, and he had lost the two fingers off his right hand, where he could still hold a pick between his thumb and ring finger.

When he stood up again, the world went gray, then began to fade off into black until he jerked his head up and forced cold air into his lungs. He started toward the door again and on the way caught the low wail of police sirens off in the distance, either because another of Ted's goons had been found dead out on the road somewhere, or because someone had heard the little war from across the bay and finally decided to call the cops about it. Either way, he would go out and find them, pull Stan out of the driver's seat and drive that car if he had to. He would be taken to a hospital, where it would be quite a scene for him once they saw this place. But he had nothing to hide. He would tell them the whole story from beginning to end, if they wanted to listen that long.

Someday, Chris thought, he might even write a song about it.

Acknowledgments

I had so much excellent help writing this novel, it's actually a little embarrassing. The author would like to thank, roughly in the order in which they provided their invaluable assistance: Gail Greiner, who was kind enough to read a manuscript and point me in an entirely new direction; Jennifer Rudolph Walsh, who made this happen and who gives incisive, eerily accurate advice like a magician; Susanne Kirk and Susan Moldow from Scribner, who were brave enough to take me on as a project and who showed me the next level and challenged me to get there; and Michael Stern, M.D., for some of the medical stuff as well as so much more.